HERO DAWNING

Hero Academy Series Book 1

P.E. PADILLA

PARTIAL MAP OF DIZHELIM

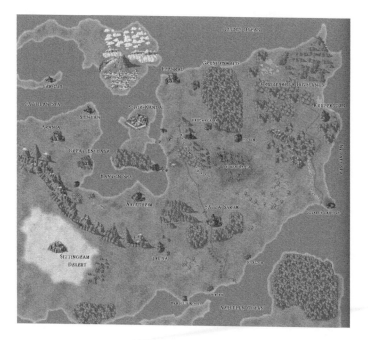

"What is that you say? Minor prophecy isn't worth studying? Perhaps you should return to your basic lessons. All things are connected. Ignore supposedly 'minor' prophecies at your peril."

Record of a scholar's interview of the Great Prophet, Tsosin Ruus, from two years before his death. Year 1, AOD

PROLOGUE

"**A**re you sure?" Denore Felas asked.

Tsosin Ruus, archmage of the Souveni Empire, hero of a number of the most stunning victories in the War of Magic, rubbed his tired eyes and turned from the view out of his tower window. "I am."

"Tsosin, you must be sure. This isn't a second-rate vision of the death of some noble we're talking about. It's the—"

"—end of the world, perhaps more than one world," the archmage finished. "Yes, Denore, I am well aware of the magnitude of what I have seen."

"I...it's the most significant prophecy ever recorded," Denore said. "If it's true—"

"It is. I would stake my life on it. In fact, I will do so. Once I have properly recorded my glimpse of the future, I will publish it to the world. More importantly, I will begin immediately to take steps to prepare for its fulfillment. Some will not be happy about it."

Denore scoffed. "From what you explain, it is perhaps thousands of years in the future. Long after you and I, and everyone we will ever know, are dead."

"Does that make it less valuable?" Tsosin said. "Do the lives of everyone living in Dizhelim mean less than our own, even if they won't be born for centuries yet?"

"That's not what I meant. It's just—"

"Leave off, Denore," Iowyn said. The master mage shook out her long, sand-colored hair—how did she remain so beautiful after so many decades?—and turned away from the window on the other side of the tower room from Tsosin. "You know Tso." A small curve of her lips made Tsosin want to run his tongue over his own. "He does not cling to anything this fiercely unless he is sure. Do you suddenly doubt his ability?"

"No, of course not," Denore said.

Iowyn glided toward the two men. She trailed a finger down Tsosin's cheek. Goose bumps ran up his spine. How she still had such power over him, he didn't know. At his age?

"You are sure?" she asked.

He swung his amber eyes to meet hers. "As anything I have ever been sure about. If I'm to be honest, it scares me to my core. I saw what could be the end of all humans. All life."

"And there is no magic that can prevent it?" she pressed.

"Magic is waning. We have spoken about it. Can you not sense the qozhel growing weaker as time passes?"

"The war," Denore said. "Both sides are using incredible amounts of magic. We are depleting the pool. It will replenish, in time."

"No, my friend. It will not. The weakening of the magical structure in Dizhelim is not due to overuse, though that is a convenient way for the emperor to prevent people from panicking. We are near the end of the age. The next will be... less illuminated than our own from the start, but nothing compared to the end of that era, the time for which the Age of Darkness is named."

"Is it so bleak?" Iowyn asked, sighing.

"It is, *emora*."

She stood tall, lifting her chin and locking eyes with him. "Then what must we do to save the descendants of our current world?"

"We have to prepare for our only hope; the chosen, the Malatirsay. We must ensure that what little magic we can preserve and what skills we can impart will be available. We must create an academy, one whose sole purpose is to prepare for the end, hoping it will aid the Malatirsay to *prevent* the end. To safehold the information needed for the prophecy to be fulfilled."

"That is a big project," Denore said.

"It is.

"Where?" Iowyn asked. "How?"

Tsosin Ruus deflated. "I don't know that yet. But I will. I vow to spend every moment, every resource, even every grain of my life force and magic, to this cause. It deserves nothing less. With aid from others or without, I will do it. I will build a Hero Academy."

The man groaned as Marla Shrike stepped over him. Stepped *on* him, actually. She wasn't about to waste the effort to avoid him. If he wanted compassion, he shouldn't have attacked her in the first place.

The other four assailants were in various states of unwellness. She didn't break many bones, and she hadn't killed any of them despite the fact that two of them—the last two—drew their weapons and attacked her with them. Not very chivalrous, that, seeing as she hadn't drawn her own.

Marla tossed her full head of red hair. She was in a tavern and people crowded all around her. Well, there were people around her in a circle they had cleared when the men attacked. Their faces showed everything from shock and fear to anger and even a few looks of pride or satisfaction. Those last were worn by women who seemed to take particular delight in her beating up the men.

Drawing on the training she had received in the School of Communication—specifically the classes on nonverbal language—she put on a completely neutral face, as if she was strolling down a street and not stepping around—or on—men she had knocked to the ground. She let the hint of challenge leak through, as if to dare any others. *Is there anyone else who wants to try me?* the look said, very subtly. She wished she knew how to put out the dangerous feeling, the "bad vibes" that people and animals picked up subconsciously. She hadn't had those classes at the Academy yet. No worries, the look she could conjure would do. For now.

"Thanks for not busting the place up," Josef, the tavern's owner said.

"You know me, Jo," she said, "always trying to be compassionate to others. She glanced down at one of the men who was groaning and trying to get up on his hands and knees. She kicked him hard in the ribs, and he rolled over with a grunt and didn't try to get up again. When he weakly reached for a knife on the floor nearby, she stomped on his hand, breaking several of his fingers.

"Yep."

She didn't understand why this always happened to her. Actually, that was not correct. She did know. Looking like she did, men typically had one of two reactions. They would primp and show off, trying to impress her and catch her interest, or they would try to dominate her. The first was irritating; the second just pissed her off.

Marla didn't think she was a great beauty, though people —both men and women—had argued with her about that. She thought it was that her fire-red hair and green eyes were so uncommon that it made her mysterious, even alluring.

At five feet and nine inches, she wasn't too short nor too tall, though some men didn't like that she could look them in the eye. That was their problem, not hers. Her oval face was pleasant enough, she thought, but she didn't like her thin lips. She was a woman, and that was enough for most men to act like fools.

Then again, the attack may not have anything to do with her appearance.

She looked over at Josef, whose appearance fit that of the typical tavern owner. Plump, receding hairline, a face that switched between smiling subservience to customers and harsh taskmaster for his workers in the blink of an eye. He was a good man, though. He glared with the best of them, but he was kindly and treated his employees well, from head cook down to the lowest scullion.

Even now, he was directing his "boys"—the men he kept on hand as bouncers to prevent precisely the type of thing that just happened—to gather up the five men on the ground and unceremoniously throw them out of his tavern. Yarl, a man who could only be described as large, and Benny, the smaller of the two but still plenty big enough to break up most fights, grabbed the clothing of a man in each hand and dragged them to the door, where they would toss them into the street.

Josef didn't tolerate troublemakers in his establishment, and with how small the town of Dartford was, most stepped carefully around him lest they need to ride more than twenty miles to get a taste of ale somewhere else. The altercation never would have happened but that the five men had apparently planned it out beforehand and acted so quickly the boys couldn't stop it in time. It hadn't been a problem. Marla had taken care of it before the boys had taken two steps.

She had come in for a drink, to relax for a little while and ask some questions. Josef chatted with her for a few minutes at her table in the corner of the room. When he left, she sat there finishing her drink and thinking.

She noticed the men's awkward behavior right away.

Marla, at only nineteen years old, was experienced in the ways of the world. Not in actually *being* in the world, but her training and the things she had been put through had honed her danger sense to a fine edge. Not only that, but she routinely engaged in practices that protected her from potential dangers. Things like positioning herself so her table was near enough to the door for an escape and against the wall so she couldn't be surrounded. Sure, she could also be penned in, but with her back toward the wall, she could literally see any danger that might come for her without being obvious about scanning the room. That was how she noticed something was amiss.

The men, originally mixed in with the crowd in different parts of the main room, moved in with obvious synchronization. They did their best to make it look like random movement—one man going near the fire to warm his hands, another walking toward the window to look outside—but she saw it for what it was: they were spiraling in closer to her.

All of them looked similar. They were big, much larger than her, with calloused hands and eyes that indicated they had seen—and done—dangerous things. Their clothes were dirty, but not filthy, and middle class in their cut and quality. In other words, these were typical thugs for hire, but ones who were hired out more often than not. Their employer must be important, but not too important. But she would figure that out later.

She, for her part, sat and waited. They would come to her and do what they were planning. She had only to wait patiently for it.

She didn't have to wait long.

All five closed in at once. There was no conversation, no interaction with her at all before three of them reached out to grab her, the other two close behind.

It was a simple thing to evade the grasping hands. She upended the table in their faces, making them stumble and curse. Then she took the opportunity to move around to engage them in a more personal manner.

Master Shanaera's words echoed in Marla's head. "Normally you should do everything you can to avoid combat, but once committed, end the confrontation quickly. Do not waste time or effort in fancy movements. Move in, strike to disable or kill, and move out of danger. That is the way." She did just that. The Master of Unarmed Combat would have approved.

Coming around the table to her right, she shuffle-stepped into range and struck the eyes of one of the men with her fingers—which she had toughened through striking practice over the course of several years—blinding him. Before he had even brought his hands to his eyes, a sharp strike to the throat took him from the action. The man next to him received an elbow to the jaw, a savage kick to the groin, and a knee to the midsection, which doubled him up, wheezing and trying to get his breath back.

The third assailant was surprised when Marla stomped on the instep of his foot, brought her knee up into his groin, and struck his face five times in quick succession. The last punch—an uppercut—lifted him off his feet to land on a table behind him. Master Tufa, the Master of Body Mechanics, often stressed the importance of generating power through hip rotation and body positioning. She had said Marla was one of the best students the she'd ever had in that regard.

The last two men apparently decided they needed help, so one drew a dagger and the other pulled a club from somewhere. Marla didn't like it when people brandished weapons at her.

A quick step toward the two assailants brought Marla into range. She kicked one of the men—a low strike that damaged the knee, a mid-height kick that pulled all the breath from the man, and a high kick to the head that was so powerful it threw the attacker into a trio of patrons sitting at the next table, the knife in his hand flying free before he'd had a chance to use it.

Without pausing in her motion, Marla continued the rotation from the kick to blast through a hasty block from the last man, staggering him despite the brunt of the force being absorbed by the club he held aloft. She continued to turn, throwing a left hook—which connected to the man's jaw—a spinning backfist to his temple, and another kick with the full power of her rotation behind it, this one striking at the side of his neck. Marla had actually held back on that kick to prevent breaking the assailant's neck. She could be ruthless, but there wasn't a need to kill these men. Yet.

Marla halted her rotation, ending in a stance that was both casual and also ready for any further attack. She didn't need it. All of the men were down and showed no sign of being able to further inconvenience her. She had ended the altercation so quickly no one else had really been able to move. The boys gaped that she had already taken care of things and they were only a step or two closer to where the action had occurred.

The quick resolution was good, because if she'd had to use magic, *that* would really have stood out. The bystanders would have easily connected her with the Academy and she'd have more explaining to do once the tale reached the ears of the masters.

"Any idea what that was about?" Josef asked, bringing her mind back to the present.

"Nope, not really," Marla said, not being entirely truthful. "I figure someone wants me to stop asking questions. It's obvious it was planned."

"You want me to have the boys get information out of them?"

"Sure," she said. "If they can get a name, that would be nice."

"I'll tell them and let you know what they find out." Josef tilted his head quizzically. "You don't seem all that concerned about it or about who hired them."

"Yeah. When you get attacked as much as I do, it all sort of runs together." She hoped he would leave it alone. She didn't want to have to lie to the man. He was about as close to a friend as she had outside the Academy.

"I getcha. All right, I'll stop prying. You need anything?"

She smiled at him, showing all her teeth. "I could use another drink. It seems that mine was somehow spilled."

He chuckled and nodded to one of the serving girls to get her one as he righted the table and then went to talk to Yarl and Benny before they threw the men into the street.

The others in the room weren't so nonchalant. They whispered to each other, pointing toward one area of the room or another or simply watching the men being carried out of the room. Whenever Marla looked at any of them, their gaze skittered away from her like she was some sort of feral animal that would attack upon eye contact. Great, this was going to create more stories. Who knew what the tale would be by the time it got around the tavern, let alone the rest of the town. It might even make its way back to the Academy. Well, there was nothing she could do about it now.

She settled back and sipped on the drink the serving girl brought her. This mission was going to be a dirty one, she thought. Two days in and she had already been attacked twice. She needed to remain alert. It would get worse as time went on, she had no doubt.

2

I t had all started three days before. She was in the
School of Combat at the Hero Academy, training. Her
opponent was Sewell Glannis, a hulking man with a
reach one and a half times the length of hers.

Of course, arm reach didn't matter much at the moment.
They were training with long weapons; him a halberd with a
wide, flat blade on the end and her with a simple spear less
than half the diameter of his weapon. Whereas his halberd
was stiff and strong, her spear was flexible and graceful. Especially the way she wielded it.

Sewell rushed in, twirling his weapon and bringing the
blade toward her in a sweeping motion. She smiled. Always
the direct, aggressive attack. She had been sparring with him
for years and though he was skilled, she knew his favorite
techniques and his little quirks.

The weapons were not sharp, though the metal tops of
both of their chosen polearms could still do damage. If they
made contact.

Which his didn't.

Marla flicked her spear upward, the shaft flexing and

whipping out to contact the shaft of Sewell's weapon just below the metal with a crack. The momentum of his strike was redirected and she moved in as it whizzed over her head.

A quick movement of her arms guided the spear downward, slapping her opponent's leg with a thwak. He grunted and pivoted, bringing his injured leg back and swinging the butt of his polearm toward Marla. She angled her spear to catch and deflect the strike to the side while snapping a front kick and connecting with his abdomen.

He made a whoofing sound as the air left him and he stumbled back a few steps, only to take up his stance again quickly. He was well-trained and persistent, something she had always appreciated about him.

Marla smiled and brought her spear around to a ready position, steel head facing Sewell.

He relaxed, at least as much as he could while he tried to regain his breath. Marla followed his eyes to the person she had sensed behind her. It was a non-threatening presence. If she didn't miss her guess, it was...

"Lucas Stewart," she said, turning so she could keep her opponent and the newcomer both in her field of vision. Just because they were only sparring didn't mean she should relax her guard.

The young man gave a little hop, seeming to be surprised she knew he was there before she turned. He was a good lad, one of the younger students. He'd only been at the Academy for two years, but he worked hard—even at the many menial tasks he was given, like being a messenger—and Marla had been keeping an eye on him. She planned on helping him in his studies however she could. He had promise.

For now, though, the thin boy with the mop of sand-colored hair seemed to have a task. He stepped forward two steps, but then backed up one when he realized he was within range of the spear. As if a step or two would save him if she decided to attack.

Marla grinned inwardly and snapped the spear to her shoulder. She brought her left arm up across her chest and the vertical weapon in a salute and bowed slightly toward Sewell.

"Marla," Lucas said. "I have a message for you from Master Aeid."

The Master of Prophecy. Interesting. "Yes?"

"He requests that you see him at your earliest convenience."

"That's it?" she asked.

"Yes. Oh, he says he wants to speak to you about an important matter."

Marla looked up and noted the position of the sun. "I have formal classes with Master Yxna in a few minutes and Master Vaeril right after that. Please tell him I'll go to his office straightaway after those appointments."

"I'll tell him." The boy started off.

"Lucas," Marla said. He turned back toward her. "Thank you. Good work."

He smiled, his thin face opening nearly in half to show all his teeth.

Master Jusha always said that recognition and valid praise cost the speaker nothing but could mean the world to the receiver. Again, as so many other times every day, Marla appreciated the things the masters had taught her—and continued to teach her.

She turned back to Sewell and bowed slightly again. "Sorry to cut this short, but I better get going. You know how Master Yxna hates for anyone to be late."

"I do. Thanks for the...uh...beating," he said, rubbing his midsection. "Until next time." He swept his halberd out and then shouldered it in his own salute.

Marla nodded to him, jogged to the practice weapon rack to return her spear, and trotted toward Master Yxna's office. Luckily, it was close, since she was already in the Mundane Combat area.

Marla attended her classes. She got caught up in the learning, as she always did, and didn't think of her summons for the next four hours.

It was remarkable to her that after twelve years—much more than half the time she'd been alive—she still thirsted after any and all knowledge she could get her hands on. Not only that; she also had a burning love for new skills to learn and practice. It was one of the things that made her such a good student, she thought.

Some might call it arrogant for her to recognize it, but she was the undisputed star of the Academy. No one had mastered as many schools at her young age. In fact, no one in history had mastered more schools than her, period. And she was only nineteen. She thought she had a better than fair chance of actually mastering *all* forty-nine schools, something unheard of and thought to be impossible.

But she didn't need to think about that right now. Surus knew, she thought about it far too often. Some of the masters had privately counseled her not to dwell on it. That way lay hubris, they would say. Didn't she know it.

The forty-nine different schools, or colleges, of the Academy were grouped together in ten lycads, which were compounds or sections of the whole campus at Sitor-Kanda. Each lycad had its own library, though each was dwarfed by the main library in approximately the middle of the Academy grounds. The schools shared resources inside each lycad, things such as training fields, equipment, and sometimes buildings.

The offices of the Master of Prophecy lay in the main education building in the Lycad of Magic, within sight of the massive main library. Marla smiled as she passed the front doors to the repository of books, scrolls, etchings, and even carvings. It was the largest accumulation of recorded knowledge in all of Dizhelim. She had spent much of her life in this building and planned to spend much more of it there. She had a special fondness for the place, even more so than the smaller libraries maintained in other parts of the Academy, those specialized toward knowledge for the particular lycad in which they resided.

She wondered how the original library had looked. That had been destroyed in a fire two centuries into the Academy's operation, a sad byproduct of thieves trying to steal treasures from the school. Nearly all the books and scrolls were lost in the fire, most of them irreplaceable. How much more would they know if they had those original works?

It was no exaggeration to refer to Sitor-Kanda as a large city unto itself. With three hundred seventeen students and fifty masters, along with an army of servants and workers, Marla sometimes felt spoiled at the space she was afforded. She'd read about cities smaller than the physical area of the Academy that held tens of thousands of people.

As she rounded the corner toward the School of Prophecy —the full name was actually the School of Prophecy, Scrying, and Clairvoyance—she noticed more people about than was normal for this time in the evening. What was going on? Had there been a special lecture she hadn't heard about?

Her mind shifted from pure curiosity to worry when she spied three masters near Master Aeid's office. Masters Yxna, Isegrith, and even Headmaster Qydus were present. A lump formed in her throat. Had something happened?

"What—" she started to say as she stepped up to the masters.

"No one is allowed in," Master Isegrith said.

Marla snuck a look past the three masters and saw

through the half open door a figure on the floor of Master Aeid's office, a cloak over the top of it. The edge of a puddle of red liquid peeked out from under the cloth.

She gasped, putting a hand to her mouth.

"Come, child," Master Qydus said, taking Marla's other hand and pulling her toward the office next to Master Aeid's.

Even as Marla was pulled away, Master Nasir arrived with several of his students who acted as the security forces for the Academy. They immediately made a human wall in front of Master Aeid's office and began setting up a perimeter, nudging or shoving the onlookers away.

Marla allowed herself to be shuttled into the other office, Headmaster Qydus Okvius tugging on her arm. His narrow face was pinched into what looked to be a scowl underneath his bushy mustache and well-manicured beard. That was his normal expression, white eyebrows drawn down and forehead crinkled. His bald head, strangely pointed, and his sharp ears completed the picture, making him look like a bird of prey on the hunt. She thought his face must be very similar to the last thing a rabbit saw before being scooped up from the ground to be eaten for lunch.

"What happened?" she asked, ignoring how furious the headmaster looked. Although he seemed fierce, his expression rarely described how he actually felt or thought.

"Master Aeid is dead," Master Qydus said plainly.

Marla gasped.

A firm hand on her shoulder distracted her. Master Yxna Hagenai, Master of Edged Weapons, stood at her side, her grey hair framing the too-young face with lips in the typically pursed expression. Like Master Qydus, her expressions—or lack thereof—were not indicative of her mood. Her light hazel eyes, too old for the face they were set in, were large and liquid, radiating compassion.

If forced to choose, Marla would have to name Master

Yxna as her favorite master in the school. She had grown to love the woman not only for her exquisite skill with anything bladed, but also because they connected on some deeper level. Marla thought of the master as a mother, or possibly a close older sister.

"How?" Marla asked. "Why?"

"That is the question, isn't it?" said a deep voice she recognized. Master Nasir Kelqen, master of the School of Research and Investigation was not a tall man, standing lower than both Marla and Master Yxna, let alone the headmaster. He wore his customary cloth cap, its bill shading his deep-set dark eyes. It was uncomfortable for Marla to look too closely at his face, at the furrows and wrinkles that didn't diminish the tattooed designs etched there so many decades ago. "It is something that will need to be investigated. That goes without saying."

"Yes, yes," Master Qydus said. "All in good time, Nasir." He turned to Marla. "Young Lucas told us Master Aeid requested for you to attend him. Is this true?"

Marla blinked. Did they think *she* murdered the master?

"Yes. I received the message several hours ago. I—"

"How many, exactly?" Master Nasir asked.

"I...uh...I'm not sure. Perhaps four or five." Marla shook her head. "It was before my class with Master Yxna"—she nodded toward her favorite instructor—"so it must be just over four hours."

Master Nasir hmmed.

"Nasir," the headmaster said. "Please restrain yourself. We are not investigating the poor girl."

"Of course, Headmaster."

Master Qydus cleared his throat. "Very well. Now, Marla, we understand—from what Lucas told us—that you had previous engagements with the other masters and that you would be attending Master Aeid at approximately this time. Do you know what he wanted to speak with you about?"

"No, Headmaster. Lucas only said it was something of importance."

"Important enough to merit his death?" Master Nasir asked.

Marla didn't know how to answer the question. She looked to the other two masters and realized that Master Isegrith had not entered the office with them. Master Yxna and the headmaster were glaring at Master Nasir.

He readjusted his cloth cap, then put his hands up. "I mean no offense. I am merely trying to piece information together in my mind."

"Perhaps you should inspect the master's office, Nasir," the headmaster said. "Begin your investigation with that."

Master Nasir bowed his head. "Of course, Headmaster." He turned to go but stopped to train his eyes on Marla. "I meant no offense or accusation, Marla. You are accomplished enough in the teaching of my school to understand this, yes?"

Marla forced a smile. "Yes, Master Nasir. Thank you for clarifying."

His mouth twitched up into a semblance of a smile, crushing the wrinkles on his cheeks and around his eyes, making interesting—if a bit disturbing—designs of his tattoos. He stepped out of the room and walked quickly to the office next door to begin his investigation.

As the master said, Marla was accomplished in research, though not quite as much in the techniques of investigation. She wished she had spent more time learning that part of the information available in the school. It was one of the many schools she had not yet mastered.

Master Yxna let out a breath, almost a sigh. "That man. Sometimes..."

"It is no matter, Yxna," the headmaster said. "He means

well and is doing as his training dictates. We will be glad of his services in this matter, I believe."

Master Yxna nodded.

"Headmaster, Master Yxna," Marla said. "Why would someone kill the Master of Prophecy?"

"It is something we must determine, Marla," he said. "You have no idea what he wanted to speak with you about?"

"No, Headmaster. I can only assume it had to do with prophecy."

"Ah, yes. That would be a logical assumption, considering that he was the Master of *Prophecy*."

Marla blushed and looked toward her feet.

"I'm sorry, child," the headmaster said. "I should not have spoken in such a way. I am...out of sorts due to this matter."

Out of sorts? The headmaster looked as he always did: in complete control and as comfortable in the situation as anyone else would look relaxing in their favorite chair. She, on the other hand, wasn't sure she would be able to keep standing upright or to keep her belly from emptying. A *master* had been murdered! Only a few minutes before she had arrived, it seemed.

"Marla," Master Yxna said. "You may go. If you think of anything that may be useful in figuring out what happened, please come and see me, the headmaster, or Master Nasir."

"Yes, Master," Marla said, glancing at the headmaster. He looked thoughtful, but only nodded to her.

"And please don't speak to anyone else about this," Master Yxna added. "Not until the official announcement."

"I won't."

"Off with you, then," the headmaster said, already leaving the room, no doubt to go to the room next door.

The room where one of the forty-nine masters of the school at Sitor-Kanda lay dead by someone else's hand.

3

N *ineteen years ago*

PEDRAS SHRIKE PUT THE LAST OF HIS TOOLS IN THEIR assigned place in his maintenance shed. He had inspected them meticulously for damage and wear and found them to be in suitable condition. If he had found something in need of fixing, he would have set the implement aside to be worked on.

He sighed. Who was he kidding? If he found something wrong, he would spend the time to fix it now. He was never one to put off something as important as maintaining his equipment.

Thankfully, he found nothing and so, after placing his spade in its assigned slot, he closed his shed and headed for home. Senna would have made dinner hours ago, expecting him home at his usual time. He did hate to disappoint her, but last night's storm had blown a tree down and he'd spent much of the day cutting it into pieces he could move and clearing the damage so no one would be injured.

No, that wasn't completely true. All who may have passed by were masters and students of the Academy. Nothing as simple as a fallen tree would harm them. The fact was, he couldn't bear to see the grounds in disarray. He was the groundskeeper for the Administration lycad and that meant he had to keep the grounds in acceptable condition. His pride would not allow his area to be messy.

So, he had worked late. Very late. Senna would understand. She was a kind and intelligent woman. All the more reason he felt bad. After nearly twenty years, though, she knew him better than he did himself. She'd have expected him to be late on account of the storm's damage. Just not quite *so* late, he thought. Well, he was on his way to their small home at the edge of the grounds now. Best to get on with it.

He whistled as he walked, limping slightly. That left knee was bothering him again. He wasn't getting any younger and he had worked hard all day. Still, he was satisfied with what he had accomplished. The headmaster had stopped him around midday, chatting with him briefly about how wonderful the small part of the Academy around the Administration and Preparation areas looked. Pedras smiled at the memory.

Headmaster Qydus Okvius was a good man. Folks thought his stern face was indicative of his personality, but it wasn't so. He always had a kind word to say and was as understanding a headmaster as Pedras had ever met. He'd even insisted the groundskeeper take a break and had food brought for him out where he was working on the downed tree. Why, he'd even helped to hoist a large branch Pedras was trying to position so he could saw it more effectively. Yep, a gem of a man, his boss was.

As Pedras made his way slowly back toward home, he

scanned the area around him. He slipped between spaces lighted by those wondrous lamps, which didn't need oil or other fuel, and darker patches in between. One never could know if he'd find something out of place. Pedras wouldn't stand for that. Nope, the headmaster had complimented the condition of the grounds and Pedras wouldn't stand to let the man down.

He passed the huge doors at the front of the Academy. They were closed at night, but not guarded. Who would try to break into the great Sitor-Kanda? That would be a foolish thing indeed. Still, there was no reason to keep the gates open and allow anyone or any animal to wander in. Pedras inspected the two steel-banded doors as he passed, not noting anything amiss.

He stopped in his tracks as something on the wind reached his ears. A noise. It almost sounded like the screech of a gate with unoiled hinges. Pedras breathed out, plunging himself completely into the silence, keeping still and listening for it.

Nothing.

The groundskeeper lifted his foot to begin moving when it reached his ears again. A screeching, or crying. It sounded far away, reverberating strangely.

As if on the other side of a solid surface.

Pedras stared at the gates. The noise seemed to be coming from the other side of them. He still couldn't place the sound, but he didn't think it was dangerous. It sounded like something was injured. Maybe an animal had been hurt and needed his aid.

He stepped up to the gates and drew back the latch. The great crossbar was not set, both overlapping halves still resting in their notches on each door. It took little effort to pull the gate inward and peek outside. The gate made no sound. He had just oiled it the day before.

On the stone threshold was a basket filled with blankets. A shrill cry emerged from it.

Pedras's mouth dropped open in wonder.

Wrapped in soft cloth, a baby cried its discomfort, though it wasn't the whiny cry Pedras had heard from some infants. It almost sounded angry, spitting. The baby equivalent of cursing.

The groundskeeper searched the darkened landscape. The lamps affixed to the walls on either side of the gates cast a globe far enough for him to see maybe twenty feet, but nothing stirred.

Nothing except the caterwauling baby in front of him.

It wasn't unheard of for people to leave their babies or children at the Academy. Poor families wanting a better life for their offspring or some such nonsense. No, not unheard of, but it had only happened one other time that Pedras could remember in his more than twenty years there.

The baby fussed, its cry changing to one that almost sounded questioning. He looked over to see its tiny head turned toward him, its eyes considering the man before it. As his eyes met the baby's, it stopped crying altogether and gurgled at him.

Pedras chuckled. Smart little thing.

"Come on, then," he said, scanning the area in front of the gates one more time. "Senna will skin me alive for delaying and causing you to get a chill."

The infant gurgled at him again, making him wonder if it was actually saying something in its own mind. Babies were mysterious things. Though they'd tried, he and Senna had never had any children, so to him the denizen of the basket in front of him was like some strange magical creature.

He picked the basket up, marveling that it was so light, and brought it inside the gate, only to set it down while he closed the doors and set the latch again. That done, he picked up the baby, which was now making soft noises to itself—as if it was discussing something—and headed home.

"I knew you'd be out late," Senna said as he came through the door of their little cabin. "Supper's almost..." She stopped speaking mid-thought as she caught sight of him. "What are you carrying, Ped?"

He gave her a lopsided smile. "Just something I found out in the yard." He held the newly quiet basket up to her. It seemed that the baby had fallen asleep.

Senna's eyes went wide. Her mouth worked, but no sound came out. She wiped her hands on her apron as she stepped closer and cocked her head at him, but he said nothing. He was content to see what she'd do.

Pedras's wife reached in and extracted the bundle of blankets with the baby inside. Its little head moved and its eyes flicked open slowly. They locked on Senna's and she made the sound—as far as he could tell—all women made when they saw babies.

"Awww. So tiny. So sweet." She moved some of the blankets out of the way, then ruffled the cloth bound around the baby's lower half. "A girl. A beautiful, perfect little girl."

The baby squirmed at the air hitting her skin and Senna covered her up again.

"She wasn't there long, I don't think," Pedras said. "She stopped crying when she saw me. Trusting little thing."

"Her swaddling clothes are dry, so she doesn't need changing," Senna said, eyes still locked with the tiny one. "So, yes, she wasn't there long. Did you see anyone?"

"No. I looked, but it's obvious they wouldn't want to be seen."

"Yeah." She was still looking into the baby's eyes. For a wonder, the infant was still fixed on Senna's eyes as well. Weren't babies supposed to have trouble focusing on one thing? "Get yourself washed up, Ped. Dinner'll be done in a moment. I'm going to warm up some milk and see if she's hungry."

Pedras stepped over to the basin and did as she told him.

"Don't get too attached," he said. "I'll present her to the headmaster tomorrow. He'll decide what should be done with her."

He wasn't sure Senna heard him. She was still staring at the baby.

"Senna?"

She blinked and shook her head. "What? Oh, yes. Of course. Be a dear and go to the Medica first thing in the morning to get a proper bottle to feed her. One of those nipples they use to feed the young animals they use as test subjects will do nicely."

"I'll go now," he said, but his wife was too absorbed in studying the baby's eyes.

Pedras smiled, but turned his head to hide it from her. She was already smitten. It was too bad they had no say in what happened to the little one. In any case, he knew she would be well cared for, regardless of the headmaster's decision.

As directed, he went to the Medica—the lycad of the healing arts—and got some supplies useful in caring for the baby for the night.

When he returned not too long after, he found that the baby seemed to be taking her new situation in stride. She made noises to herself or to Senna—even to Pedras. He watched her move her tiny hands around, trying to gain better control of them, he thought. It was fascinating. He could almost see things moving in her little brain, trying to figure out the world. What would that be like?

"Now, you make sure to keep her face covered with the blankets," Senna told him the next morning. "I'll not have her get ill because you couldn't take care enough to keep her warm. And you tell the headmaster that she just ate but that she'll need feeding again soon after you make your way over there. I put some extra cloth in the basket so you can change her, and—"

"Hold on, woman," he said with a smirk. "I won't remember everything you tell me. You're coming with me."

"I...I can't, Ped. I have to be at work soon. I've already spent too much..." Her eyes went liquid and he took her hand.

"Come on," he said. "The headmaster will excuse you from work for an hour or two. I need you to come with me."

She nodded and sniffled. He patted her hand and reached for the basket, only to have her nudge him out of the way and pick it up herself.

Half an hour later, they were in the headmaster's office. Luckily, his assistant had let them in without an appointment. One look at the baby and Aletris Meslar wouldn't take no for an answer from Master Qydus, though she was decades younger, he was her boss, and she was fairly new in her position.

"What is it, Pedras?" Master Qydus stepped toward them from where he had been standing by one of his bookshelves. He always did go right to the point of things. He was very busy, after all.

Pedras ducked his head, hat in his hand. "I'm truly sorry to bother you, Headmaster. It's just, well, I found something last night as I was making my way home after working."

"Something?" he said, pointedly looking at Senna and what she was holding.

"Someone?" Pedras said weakly. "That is, sir, I heard something at the gate and I...well, it was a baby. This baby. Someone left it there."

"I see. It is not unheard of, of course." He was still watching Senna as she was offering her finger to the baby.

The girl snatched it and squeezed, bringing a smile to Senna's face. She hadn't noticed the master was watching.

"Yessir. It's been a while, though, so far as I know. I don't rightly know what should be done, so I came straightaway to you."

The master still wasn't meeting Pedras's eyes. He continued to watch the interaction between Senna and the child.

"Typically," the headmaster said, "the procedure is to give the baby over to the Medica until such a time that a home could be found for it—"

"Her," Pedras said before thinking. "Uh, I mean...that is, the baby is a girl, Master Qydus." Heat rushed up his neck and face. Interrupting a master! What was wrong with him?

Master Qydus shifted his gaze to Pedras, his face softening and the sides of his mouth twitching briefly as if threatening to smile.

"My apologies," the master said. "The baby would normally be given over to the Medica until such a time that a home could be found for *her*. However, the Medica is understaffed at the moment and, I am afraid, overworked. It would be a burden I hesitate to give them.

"Now, if it were possible to find the girl a home quickly, perhaps that would be best. Would you have any thoughts on how we could do that, Pedras?"

"I...uh, I'm not an educated man, Master Qydus. I would never presume to give you any of my ideas..."

"Pedras, how long have you worked here at the Academy? How long have we known each other?"

"Twenty-two years, three months, and nine days now, sir. Uh...thereabouts."

The master's left eyebrow hitched briefly. "And in that time, have you not come to know me?"

"Yes, Master, as much as anyone such as I can, I reckon."

"Do I seem to be a man who would ask for a suggestion and then disregard it out of hand?"

"No, sir. I meant no offense."

Master Qydus put his hand up. "Stop, Pedras. I took no offense and I do want your ideas. If given your choice of any option in the world, what would you choose, if you were in my place? How would you deal with this child who had been unexpectedly dropped into our lives?"

Pedras twisted the hat in his hands. "Well, Master, I would want to make sure she was well taken care of. That she could grow without fear of harm, in a place where she was happy. Where she was loved."

"Ah. See there, how you expertly found the root of the issue?" He tapped his bearded jaw. "Now, if only we could find such a place. Perhaps a caring family with room for another member they could love. Such a thing would be a blessing and would ease our minds that we have acted wisely and in the interest of the girl."

"Yessir. I...you are correct. Of course."

Master Qydus Okvius did smile this time, his mustache slanting upward as he showed his teeth to Pedras. "Let us end the games, Pedras. I do have work to do. I would like you to keep the girl, if you are so inclined."

A gasp from Pedras's left caused him to snap his head in that direction. Senna stood there, baby in her arms, mouth wide and eyes wider.

"I expect Senna here would agree with me that it would make us both very happy, Master Qydus." Senna nodded wordlessly.

"Good," the master said. "So be it. Adopt the girl. Any help you need from the Medica—or from the Academy in general—just ask and we will do what we can. I think it will be a fine arrangement."

Pedras was still in shock, but he couldn't keep the smile

from his face. He had hoped, but...well, the master had decided. "Thank you, Master. Thank you."

"Thank *you*, Pedras. She will make a fine addition to your family. Perhaps we can enlarge your house or find another place, a bigger one, for you and your family to live."

"It's not necessary. We have enough room."

"We'll speak about it later. For now, take your new daughter and get settled in. I will speak with the Mistress of Housekeeping and let her know Senna will not need to work for the rest of this week. I would say the same of you, but I know you would sneak behind my back and do your tasks anyway. Please, though, do take some time to settle in.

"Oh, and make sure you let Aletris play with the girl for a few minutes. She would not forgive us otherwise."

"Yessir. Thank you, Master."

"Not at all." He walked behind his desk, but before he sat down, he cocked his head at them. "Incidentally, what will you name her?"

Pedras hadn't even thought about that. It was audacious enough for him to wish to be able to adopt her. He opened his mouth to say so, but Senna beat him to it.

"Marla," she said, kissing the baby's forehead. "We'll call her Marla."

❦ 4 ❦

"Is it true?" Skril Tossin asked as he followed Marla and Evon Desconse to the main auditorium in the Academy's administration building.

Marla glanced at her friend. Even under the current circumstances, he was a bouncy pile of energy. He was very nearly skipping as they crossed the grounds to the mandatory gathering. Of course, part of that could be that he was not as tall as his two friends and had to shuffle-step to keep up with them.

"The masters told me not to say anything, Skril," she said. "You'll find out what it's about soon enough. Be patient. Like Master Jusha always tells you."

He frowned at her, but it only lasted a moment before his normal expression—a smile—broke through and replaced it. How could he be so insufferably happy all the time?

"This is going to be big, isn't it?" Evon asked. "I mean, this will be one of those times we'll look back on years from now and say, 'I was doing this before and everything changed afterward.'"

"Could be," Marla said.

She didn't like keeping secrets from her friends, even if it was because the masters gave her a direct command not to tell them about it. A master, killed at the Academy, in his own office. Evon was right. This was big.

They joined a stream of students entering the auditorium. More than two-thirds of the entire student body was already there, it looked like. Well, it *was* a mandatory meeting. More, most of the rumors got it right: there had been a murder. It had only been a day, but news traveled fast, so everyone knew basically what to expect.

She wasn't concerned with the news itself. What was on her mind was what the masters would do about it. Had they found the murderer?

"Please take your seats and wait patiently," Master Isegrith's voice boomed out. She was using magic to amplify her normally calm and quiet voice. It was to be expected of the Master of the School of Fundamental Magic. "We will start in a few minutes."

The room immediately quieted. Not completely, not with so many, but it was remarkable to Marla, even after all this time, that so many different people had immediate obedience so embedded into them. Within a minute, there was only a low buzz of whispers.

She and her two friends found seats at the very front row. Of course. Some things were constant with humans, and the fact that the front rows typically filled last was one of them. As they waited, she turned in her seat and scanned the crowd. Was the murderer here? Would he or she strike again, or was it a one-off thing? Her back itched, right between the shoulder blades. She wasn't fond of having so many people behind her.

"Relax," Evon said, hand on her arm. "You're tense like you expect combat."

She took in a breath and then let it out slowly. "I'm careful. You know that."

"Paranoid," Evon corrected.

"We do," Skril said, still smiling. "Ever since those games a few years ago where we tried to attack each other randomly for Master Shanaera's class. You never quite did get over expecting someone to jump you at any inconvenient time."

"She was paranoid before that," Evon said, "but yes, that made it worse."

"It's a hazard of all the stuff I've learned," she said. "Better to be paranoid and not surprised than to be ambushed." She gave Evon a side-eye. "I won that little contest, if I remember correctly."

Evon rubbed his jaw, exactly where she had hit him when he jumped out at her from the darkness during that time. "You remember correctly."

The room suddenly went completely silent. Marla knew what that meant before she turned her attention from Evon to the front of the room. Headmaster Qydus Okvius stepped up to the podium on the small stage.

"Good afternoon," he said, his deep, rich voice needing no magic to project what he was saying to everyone in attendance. "I know of the rumors, so I will get right to the heart of things. It is true that Master Aeid Hesson was murdered yesterday while in his offices."

Whispers mingled with gasps from all around the auditorium. There was likely no one in the room who had not heard, but it was still a shock. To hear it stated so plainly was a jolt even to Marla, and she had seen the master's body the day before.

The headmaster raised one hand and all sound cut off once more.

"We are unsure as yet who the perpetrator is, but Master Nasir has the investigation well in hand. When the mystery is solved, we will inform you. Until then, please direct any useful information you may have to Master Nasir. Anything out of the ordinary you may have witnessed should be reported. Every bit of information could be helpful. We are sorry, but we will not be answering any questions you have at this time. Whatever answers we could provide would likely be hearsay or conjecture. We hope you understand.

"We would ask that those of adept status remain. The rest of you are dismissed. Please continue with your normal schedules unless you have information for Master Nasir. Thank you."

Marla looked at her friends. A student was granted the status of *acolyte* when they had mastered at least one school. If they had mastered three or more schools, yet remained at the Academy, they were named *adepts*. Those who mastered three or more schools and left the Academy were named *viri*. At times, the general term *graduate* was used for a student who had mastered three or more schools, whether still at the Academy or gone.

The headmaster stepped down from the stage and Master Isegrith took his place. Using her magical amplification once more, she said, "Adepts, please remain seated. When the non-adepts have departed, please come to the front of the room." She left the stage and sat down in one of the chairs lined up next to the stage.

"Adepts only," Skril said. "I wonder what it's about."

"We'll find out in a moment, I suppose," Marla said.

They looked at Evon, who was frowning. "Adepts only," he repeated as he stood.

"Sorry, Evon," Marla said. "Maybe they'd make an exception for you. You're so close."

"No. It's okay. The headmaster said adepts only. I only have two schools mastered."

"Yeah," Skril said, "but in a week or two, you'll be officially recognized as mastering your third. It's not like you haven't mastered the School of Mundane Energy. It's just a formality that the final pronouncement hasn't been officially made."

Evon shook his head. "Rules are rules. Tell me what you can later on, okay?"

"We will," Marla said. She felt bad for Evon. He was better than many of those who had four or more schools mastered. She suddenly hated that stupid designation. *Adept.* Who bloody cared if someone had been *officially* recognized as having mastered a school?

As Evon headed for the door, Marla's eyes met the cool, grey eyes of Master Yxna Hagenai, Master of the School of Edged Weapons. She willed her thoughts to reach the master and, for a wonder, the older woman looked to Evon, then tilted her head to the side and whispered something to the headmaster.

"Evon Desconse." The headmaster's voice cut through the din of the other students. Evon gave a little jump, obviously startled. "Please remain. You lack but the formal ceremony naming you an adept."

Evon smiled and nodded at the masters, then retook his seat.

Marla smiled at Master Yxna, mouthing *thank you.* Master Yxna nodded. Had she really conveyed her thoughts to the master? Shaking her head with a little chuckle, she realized she must have been giving the master a sad look, nothing more. It had worked, though, which was the important thing.

"That's great," Skril said. "See, I told you."

It didn't take long for the non-adept students to exit the auditorium and those remaining to gather at the front of the room. When the masters closed the doors, there were only around three dozen people left in the room: six masters and the rest adepts.

"We have a dilemma at hand that you may help us with,"

the headmaster said. "Per protocol, the masters must sequester themselves for at least seven days in consideration of appointing a new master. While this isn't a complete isolation—we may sleep in our own chambers, for instance—it does not allow us to carry on any meaningful work other than the selection process.

"That presents a bit of a problem when there is a murder to investigate."

Master Nasir's wrinkled face scrunched into a frown at that, but Marla didn't need to see his expression to know that he would be disappointed with the shackles that had been put on him.

"Seven days is a long time," the headmaster continued, "when one is referring to an investigation such as this. As such, there must be a way to perform this critical task without breaking protocol.

"So, we are asking your help. We would appreciate volunteers to investigate the murder of Master Aeid while the masters are indisposed. Preferably, we would like those who are proficient in the discipline of research and investigation." The headmaster looked at Marla as he said that last part. She was possibly the most experienced student in that school who was present. There were few still at the Academy who had mastered that school and even fewer that had mastered at least two others.

"I'll volunteer," she said without hesitation. The headmaster's eyes glimmered, though his expression remained his normal, stern visage.

"Me, too," Skril said, smiling at the headmaster, then Marla, then everyone else in front of him.

"I would like to—" Evon started, but was interrupted.

"You may not, Evon Desconse," the headmaster said. "I'm sorry, but you are the *assector pruma*, First Student, in the

School of Prophecy, and we must ask your assistance in choosing the new master."

"*First Ass*," Marla whispered, repeating the old joke about the position.

Evon ignored her and nodded to the masters, eyes showing his disappointment. If he had formally mastered three schools, he would have been eligible for the post of master himself. Marla thought he probably would have gotten it, too. Master Aeid had relied on Evon as his assistant, even utilizing him to teach classes at times.

Skril patted Evon's arm and whispered to him. "After you help them, you can join us, and maybe you can do something in between what work they require of you."

Their friend nodded again.

The headmaster, eyes focused on Skril as if he was reading the student's lips, continued. "You may take part in the investigation after we are finished with you. We will not need you for the entire sequestering period."

In all, four other students besides Skril and Marla volunteered. Ailuin Lufina, a pinch-faced woman who looked as if she was constantly irritated but who had the most delightful personality of anyone Marla knew, had mastered three schools. Erlan Brymis, a square-jawed boulder of a man who always had his feet planted as if readying to withstand a cavalry charge alone, was also a master of three schools. Calarel Kelhorn, a curvy woman barely over five feet tall who usually had her long hair in a single tight braid, was one of the most beautiful women Marla had ever seen. She had mastered four schools. Taron Gennelis appeared unexceptional in every way, with his blond hair and blue eyes and average height and physique. He had also mastered four schools and had a keen mind, from what Marla had heard. Of the four, she only knew Ailuin well.

The six nodded in acknowledgement to each other, standing among the other students who had not volunteered.

"Very well," the headmaster said. "You six, remain. The rest of you may leave. Thank you for your time. Evon, please attend us in one hour. We will be in the large meeting room in the administration building."

The others shuffled out, whispering softly with each other. Several of them cast looks back at the six, seeming to regret not volunteering. It was too late for them to change their minds, though. If there was one thing common in all schools of the Academy, it was the admonition to make decisive choices in any situation, even if that decision was that you didn't have enough information to make an educated choice.

Evon whispered to Marla, "I'll wait for you outside." She nodded her acknowledgement.

"As for you," Master Qydus said as the last of the others left the room, "I thank you for volunteering. We have a few instructions for you, though we cannot spend much time, I'm afraid. Much of this investigation will, by necessity, be self-directed.

"Master Nasir will speak to you for a moment, and then all the masters must sequester ourselves."

Master Nasir got up from his chair and stood before them. He dipped his head to Marla and she returned the gesture. She was well along in his school and so they were familiar with each other. Even so, she had to focus on his blue eyes or she would get caught up in how the tattoos and wrinkles on his face seemed to merge and complete some kind of pattern that she had never quite deciphered.

"Because of certain...ah, necessary rules, I cannot spend my time or energies solving the murder of Master Aeid. I therefore must allow you children to attempt the task." He shook his head sadly, as if to bemoan the state of the world in general. "I have written what I have found so far in this book." He held up a packet of papers that had been crudely bound into the semblance of a book. "Produce copies if you wish and distribute them. For those of you who have learned in my school, use sound investigation tactics and record all your information meticulously. For those of you who have not trained in the College of Research and Investigation, well, stay out of the way of those who know more than you do. I suggest you draw lots and investigate the master's room one at a time. It has been left essentially how it was found, other than the master's body being removed. That is all."

He handed the book to Marla, turned, and sat back in his chair, appearing to have washed his hands of the entire thing.

Master Qydus stepped up and addressed them again. "I must say one more thing before we leave you to your task. You are being given freedom that is rarely given to students of the Academy. You may face danger, and you will definitely experience things you have not had to confront before. Be careful, remember your training, and under no circumstances are you to go into areas that have been classified as danger level three or above. Good fortune to you, happy hunting, and thank you for aiding us in this most extraordinary of circumstances. I will have writs produced for each of you giving you permission to conduct your investigations. See Aletris to obtain yours."

The other masters rose and followed the headmaster out of the auditorium. Before she left the room, Master Yxna bowed her head to Marla, their eyes meeting. A glimmer of a smile graced her too-young face, and then she was gone.

Marla sighed. She was a bit disappointed that Master Qydus had thrown in the part about not going to dangerous areas. Danger level was something the Academy used to rank different parts of Dizhelim. There were only six specific places with a danger ranking of three or four, so it probably

39

didn't matter, but she didn't like the thought of rules tying her hands in this matter. She was finally going to be able to travel freely, at least until the investigation was complete. Her heart beat more quickly at the thought.

This was the type of thing she had been training for.

❧ 5 ❧

Outside the auditorium, the other investigators eyed the book in Marla's hand hungrily. She hefted it and cocked her head. Master Nasir had given it to her, either because she had more schools mastered than any of the others or because she was simply more familiar to him.

"We're all reasonable," she said. "How about we agree to hand this over to the scribes and allow them to make copies? If we do that, by the time we're finished investigating the scene of the murder, they should have several copies complete. With the number of pages of notes there are, they should be able to finish copying it by later this evening, if they have several scribes copying it at once."

"I think that's a good idea," Skril said. Evon bobbed his head in agreement, but didn't say anything. He was not officially able to take part in the investigation anyway. Not yet.

"Sure," Erlan said. "Why not?"

"Okay," Taron said.

Calarel nodded, making her appear as if someone was pulling on that long braid and making her head bounce.

Ailuin's pinched face considered Marla for a moment and Marla thought she'd disagree. Then it broke into a smile.

"Very efficient," she said. "Yes, that's a fine idea. May I suggest we draw straws, as Master Nasir said, to determine the order each of us will examine Master Aeid's office?"

All agreed to that as well. Marla was relieved things were going so smoothly. Some at the Academy could be difficult to interact with. Egos were not in short supply at the famed facility.

Evon was chosen to create the straws they would use. He ran out of the room, returning a few minutes later with a handful of small sticks he had gotten from somewhere. They looked like the pieces of wood used to poke around in a dissected animal in the medica, less than a quarter of the diameter of her little finger and the longest of them about seven inches long. Evon explained that he had already broken them to different sizes, though he held them so they looked to be the same size.

"I can't think of a fairer way of doing this than to let the eldest go first and work our way down to the youngest," he said.

Marla frowned at him, but couldn't really argue. There had to be some kind of arbitrary way of letting them select their pieces. She wasn't about to seem like an egomaniac and suggest going in order of how many schools each had mastered.

Taron Gennelis went first. He was more than twice Marla's age. Next were Erlan Brymis, then Calarel Kelhorn, Ailuin Lufina, and Skril. Marla took the sixth stick, leaving six unused in Evon's hand.

The investigators compared sticks and Marla was happy to see she had drawn the longest. That meant she would get first crack at the room. Ailuin got the second spot, Skril the third, Taron fourth, Calarel fifth, and Erlan resigned himself to being last with a frown that could have soured milk.

Marla handed the book to Evon.

"I'll run this over to the scribes," he said, "with instructions that it's top priority, per the masters. I'm sure Jhanda will have some of his scribes get right on it."

"Thanks, Evon," Marla said. Jhanda Dalavi was the Head Scrivener at the Academy, and he was as diligent as he was protective of his works. Like Evon said, he'd get the job done. "We might as well get started. The sooner we all get a look at the room and get our copies of Master Nasir's notes, the sooner we can solve this mystery and bring the killer to justice."

They traveled together to the College of Prophecy. The others entered the room Marla had been in the day before, the one next to Master Aeid's office, while she stepped up to the guard at the office door. She knew him; the Academy wasn't *that* big a place. His name was Ramsay and he always seemed to be a reasonable fellow.

"We're investigating the murder," she told the tall man standing with his hand on the pommel of his sword. "The masters told us—"

"It's fine, Marla," he said. "They already spoke to us. Please don't take anything. I've been instructed to allow each of you fifteen minutes. Master Nasir told us you'd be examining the room one at a time."

Marla smiled, which made him smile back. He seemed to think the expression was for him, but the real reason was that Master Nasir had already known they would take his suggestion as a command.

"Thanks, Ramsay. I'll try not to disturb the room."

She stepped into the office and got to work.

Master Aeid's office was large, perhaps twelve paces by fourteen, but it seemed much smaller because of all the clutter. If she'd never been in the room before, Marla probably would have thought that whoever murdered the master rummaged through the place to find something, turning over and upsetting a neat, organized office of a master, but the truth was that Master Aeid was not the tidiest of people.

Bookshelves lined the walls. They were great beasts of hardwood, sturdy enough to have survived several small fires and minor mishaps over the decades upon decades they had been in place. The books were arranged haphazardly, some standing upright but a shocking number that were stacked or simply stuffed into available space, no matter their orientation.

Objects, too, populated the shelves, mixed in with the books, scrolls, and carvings. A skull of some small animal, bones of another, items in jars that Marla had never wanted to inspect carefully. So many things.

But all those had always been there and they did not seem to have been disturbed. She had little time to do her investigation. It was best to scan the room as a whole and then focus on what might be out of place.

In the center of the office, in front of the master's massive desk—which was cluttered with papers, half-used candles, several inkwells and pens, and the remains of his last meal—was the place the body had fallen for the last time. The blood had not been cleaned up, though the body had been removed.

Marla knelt and reached out to the puddled blood, which had turned a dark brown color and gave off the foul odor of death and decay. Master Nasir, or someone else, must have cast a preservation spell to keep the stench from becoming overwhelming and to prevent insects from doing their grisly work. The decomposition process and the order of appearance of the different scavengers after a death were fascinating to Marla, though she didn't know a great deal about it, not having mastered the forensics part of Master Nasir's classes yet. Another thing to learn about. Eventually.

Her mind was wandering again. She snapped her focus back to the blood. There was surprisingly little of it. Did that indicate the assassin was skilled and had chosen a target that would not splash too much blood on him or her, or was it simply chance? One thing was certain: the master was dead before he struck the floor. There were no streaks, no disturbances in the blood that would indicate he had moved after coming to rest. Skill, then, not chance. She would need to inspect the body to be certain, but she was confident they were dealing with more than a random occurrence or a flash of anger.

Marla eyed the food on the master's desk. He often ate in his office, too wrapped up in his research to be bothered with going to the dining hall. What had he been working on?

She looked over the papers scattered on his desk, but her eyes kept coming back to the food and the cup of wine sitting there. *I wonder*, she thought. It was not unusual for her to keep more things in her belt pouch than was probably necessary, but for at least this moment, she was glad she did. She produced two small vials and quickly filled one with the wine and the other with scraps of the roast chicken the master had picked over but had not finished. The containers went back into her belt pouch. She'd use some of the skills she had learned in the College of Alchemy later to analyze them.

One spot on the desk looked conspicuously empty. A closer look revealed a thin layer of dust with an outline of something that had been lying there and was removed. Something with roughly the shape of Master Aeid's self-produced notebooks.

The master had often created little books of scrap paper and bound them crudely—often with just a few stitches of thread—so he could jot down ideas without worrying about ink spills, splotches, and smears. Then, when he went back over his notes later, he would rewrite them in a legitimate book made for him by the Academy's binders, taking great care in his penmanship and neat overall organization. He produced some of the most beautifully written research reports that Marla had ever seen.

Someone had taken one of the notebooks. Had it been the master himself, or the killer? Marla searched the rest of the large desk's surface, and she didn't find the missing notebook. There were others, but the dust on them was undisturbed and consistent with the other items on the desk. None of them had been moved.

Marla wasn't sure if she'd ever find what had been taken. If the murderer was smart, he would take in the information and then destroy the evidence. But there were more ways than one to determine what the master's project was. She went through the items on the desk again, this time to figure out what they were about. What had the master been working on? She kept coming back to that question, and one more: did it have anything to do with what he wanted to see her about?

As the Master of Prophecy, it was not a surprise his desk mostly contained works of prophecy. There were thousands of bits of predictions and visions scattered throughout his own collection and the books in the main Academy library. Most were relatively unimportant flashes of talent from people over the ages, though some were from those who could be called legitimate prophets. Not *the* Prophet, by any means, but people with a minor skill in seeing a short distance into the future.

Master Aeid was one of those. Several books on his shelves contained his own prophecies. Marla had read many of them.

None of those books were on his desk, or piled on the

chairs next to and in front of his workspace. By far, most of the notes, reference works, scrolls, and drawings had to do with only one subject.

They were about the Bhavisyaganant, the Song of Prophecy. It was the reason for the existence of the Academy itself, a masterwork of prophecy so powerful it moved Tsosin Ruus, the Great Prophet who wrote the Song, to build the Academy at Sitor-Kanda to prepare for the prophesied ending of the age.

Of course, interpreting the Bhagant—as it was called at times—was one of the main purposes of the Academy, but what specifically had Master Aeid been looking for? How many years could one man devote to the same subject?

Marla shook her head. She was going to miss the master. He was a brilliant scholar, a talented scryer, and a good teacher. But he was also a good man, one who'd always been kind to an orphan girl trying to find her way in the most prestigious learning institution in the world.

Marla shook herself out of her reverie. She had a job to do and could think about these other things later. Her time was almost up.

She turned in a circle, scanning the room one last time, trying to decide if she had forgotten anything. No, she had done what she needed. Well, all but one thing.

Closing her eyes briefly, Marla cast a minor divination spell. When she opened them again, she could see the glowing aura of magic representing spells that had been cast in the room recently. The age of the aura a caster could see was dependent upon their skill and their magical power. Marla's spells typically would let her see the residual magic for spells cast in the last week.

She examined the glowing remnants of power, recognizing the casters. Master Aeid had cast spells, of course. Her simple divination spell didn't tell her what kind of magic it was, only that it had been used. The only other residue was from Master Nasir, no doubt something he had cast during his investigation, like the preservation spell for the blood. There was no other trace of magic. She could deduce that the master had been killed by mundane means, then, not attacked with spells.

The door creaked open and Ramsay poked his head in.

"Your time is up, Marla. I'm sorry."

"No problem. I'm done." She followed him out into the hall. "Thank you."

Marla nodded at Ailuin as Ramsay was telling her the same thing he had told Marla about not disturbing the room. As she passed the others who were waiting for their turn, she said to Skril, "I'll see you later. How about sixth bell in Evon's room?"

❦ 6 ❧

Marla headed to the Medica. She had enough education in that lycad to be familiar with corpses, but didn't look forward to seeing her master and friend lying cold on an examination table. Such were the things one had to do as an Academy graduate, though. She didn't have to enjoy it to do her job. If it meant finding the person who killed the master, it would be worth it.

Marla made her way to the morgue. One of the students, Tan, was there working. She was originally from Shinyan but —like most of the students—had spent the majority of her life to that point at the Academy so she had no discernible accent. The woman was more than ten years Marla's senior, but she had always been friendly.

"Hi, Marla," she said. "You're the first one to inspect the body. The masters left word some would come."

"Really? Interesting. I thought they'd come while they were waiting their turn to look over the master's office. I can understand, though. It's not too pleasant a task, is it?"

"No," Tan said. "I'll leave you to it, then. If you have any questions, let me know. I'll be right outside."

"Great. Thanks."

Tan stepped from the room and closed the door, leaving Marla alone with a man-sized shape covered by a sheet on the table in the center of the room.

I might as well get right to it, she thought. *The sooner I'm done, the better*. She wasn't particularly bothered by inspecting corpses, but this was the first one she had known when it was alive. It made the entire process even less palatable.

She lifted the sheet and pulled it back off the body slowly. The master's body was the pale, ashy color she recognized from other dead people she had studied. She winced to see the wounds on the chest. They were cleaned of the blood and other fluids that were no doubt on them when the body was found, and the punctures in the skin were plainly visible.

Marla traced the two slits with her finger, an inch from touching the skin itself. One was wide of the heart, and by the size and damage, it appeared this one was thrust in more forcefully, and more deeply. She posited that the knife's blade was wider than the other, as well.

The other cut was thinner, without the bruising and tissue damage of the larger. This knife was smaller and sharper than the first. The cut was also angled diagonally to miss the sternum and ribs so it went directly to the heart. It was obvious that was the cause of death, but why the other wound? Did the assassin miss his mark the first time and had to thrust again? Obviously not, seeing as the cuts were made with two different blades. Why would a killer change knives in between attacks?

No, they had to be made at the same time, or close to it. Didn't they? There were no other cuts or bruises on the chest or abdomen, and the attacks were not slices but punctures made by the knives plunging into the master's chest.

She lifted the master's arms and inspected the hands and the forearms. There were no injuries to those parts. She turned the body over and looked for other telltale signs on his back and shoulders. Nothing. A scan of his legs and feet also showed no apparent injuries. Not even bruises.

Marla rolled the body back to its original position, lying face-up. Using the small sticks provided, she pulled back the master's lips and inspected the teeth, gums, tongue, nose, and eyes. None of them showed any of the evidence of the most common poisons that would be present if he had died in that manner.

No, wait. There was a slight orange tinge around the outside of the master's tongue. She had to bring close one of the small lanterns with mirrors used to focus light to see it, but it was definitely there. Shu root?

Tan spoke to someone out in the hallway. Marla didn't have much time left. She quickly used one of the flat sticks to scrape some of the skin cells from the master's tongue into a vial and put it in her belt pouch just as the door opened.

Tan poked her head in. "Doing all right in here?"

"Yes." Marla put the sheet back over the master. "Have you done your investigation yet?"

"I've done a preliminary examination, but nothing else. The masters wanted him to be in essentially the same condition he was in when they found him, other than cleaned up a little. We'll do an autopsy after you all have a chance to examine him."

"Any ideas or observations you can share?" Marla asked.

A flicker of suspicion flashed in Tan's eyes, but then disappeared. "The assassin was skilled. The second thrust, the one that killed the master, was expertly placed to puncture the heart. Either that, or it was pure luck that it glanced off a rib or the sternum and made its way to its target. I'll know more when we autopsy him and I can inspect the path of the damage."

Marla nodded, though she didn't agree. She'd already decided it was two different knives.

"There were also no other wounds from prolonged combat, no bruises or damage to the arms or hands from the master trying to block or deflect the knife, so the assassin was stealthy and was able to surprise Master Aeid. That's about all I have so far."

"Thanks, Tan," Marla said. "That's helpful."

"Ailuin is waiting outside," Tan said. "Are you finished?"

"Yes, I think so. Thank you for your help."

"Uh, Marla?"

"Yeah?"

"Did you notice anything else?" Tan asked. "I've studied in the Medica, but I haven't studied with Master Nasir, so I'm not sure about the investigation part of it. What I told you before, they're just guesses, based solely on my medical knowledge."

"You did great," Marla told her. "Master Nasir left us his notes. They'll probably tell us more once we can go over them. I'll bring mine by so you can look at them if you want."

"That would be great. Thank you. You know how it is: so many schools to study in and only so much time in the day. But then, I guess you're not the one I should be talking to about this. You seem to be able to find time for it all."

Marla laughed. "Nope. I'm with you, Tan. I'm wishing I had spent more time in some of my studies and studied in some of the other schools. I don't think we'll ever feel like we're totally prepared, no matter who we are."

Tan nodded. "Thank you. Coming from you, that makes me feel a *lot* better."

"I'm glad. Speaking of the notes, I better go and see if the scribes have copied them yet. I'll come see you in the next day or two and we can look at them together."

"That would be wonderful."

Marla left, nodding at Ailuin as she passed. She went around the corner, found a chair, sat, and pulled out her little book for notes. She jotted down her thoughts while they were fresh, then continued on her way. Yes, she had to check on the scribes, but the Mathematics and Science lycad was on the way and she had some samples to test in the alchemy laboratory.

Marla had about an hour until she was set to meet up with Skril and Evon. She sat in one of her favorite places, off the main pathway from the administration area to the lycad for mundane combat, also affectionately called the Grinder.

She sat back within the trees, all but hidden to any who might pass by, but her position gave her a full view of both the practice grounds and the park-like expanse of grass and trees bordering the different learning areas.

A smile came unbidden to her face. She always felt a warm fondness for this particular viewpoint. Ever since she was a young girl. Marla closed her eyes and pictured it back then. It had looked nearly the same, only some of the trees weren't quite as big, though it was hard to judge size because she herself had been smaller.

Just a skinny girl, barely seven years old. No, not skinny. She had been wiry. No amount of eating—and she had made a contest of stuffing as much food in her mouth as possible— could add an ounce of weight to her.

It was a day like today when her life had changed completely.

Seven-year-old Marla had heard the discussions. Her adopted father had done his best to make a better life for her, but he was constantly frustrated in his efforts.

"Pedras," her adopted mother, Senna said, "all we can do is to keep trying. Eventually, Master Qydus, or one of the other masters, will realize Marla's place is with the other students."

Little Marla was supposed to be sleeping, but there were many things in her life she was *supposed* to do or be. She rarely let those interfere with what she wanted.

"I know, Senna, but I keep trying and I keep running into walls. She's already older than many who are accepted. I'm afraid she'll be at a disadvantage."

"Ped, you shouldn't blame yourself for it. Would it be so bad if she followed in our footsteps? There's nothing wrong with doing good honest work. We're happy. She could be, too."

"I want more for her," Pedras Shrike said. "I want the world to be open to her. She should be able to make a choice as to who or what she should be. I want to do the best we can for her. If she chooses a life like ours, then I will be happy, but I want her to have the choice. The Academy will give that to her."

Marla waited for a response, but her parents started speaking softly, no doubt huddling close together. She wouldn't get any more information this night. She didn't fully understand what they were talking about, but she knew it made her father unhappy.

She wished she could help him as she helped with his work around the Academy. He had taught her many things as she followed him in his everyday chores. In the last year, he had let her do some of the actual work, even going so far as to allow her to perform simple tasks on her own, without his presence. It made him happy, which in turn made her happy. Very early on, she learned to equate working hard with pleasing both her parents, so she did everything to the fullest extent possible. It was a rule her parents applied to their own lives, and she had grown assuming it was just the way things should be.

Two days later, she was proudly trimming a messy growth of bushes near the edge of the administration area's grounds, very near the combat training grounds at the Magic Lycad. She whistled as she raked and cleared away some of the branches she had trimmed, happy her father had allowed her to do the task herself.

Her hair was pulled back into a tail, but some stray strands had escaped, giving her a feral look. With the rugged work clothes she wore, and the smudges and even a few scratches from some of the hawthorn trees, she appeared more a beggar than someone who would be on the grounds at the famed Hero Academy.

"Oi," a voice said from behind her. "What're you doing here, street urchin?"

She assumed whoever was talking spoke to someone else. She continued her work.

"You can't ignore me, waif," the voice said again. "Turn around when I talk to you."

Marla wondered who was arguing—though she'd only heard one voice—so she turned to see what was happening. A boy, larger than her and probably two or three years older, was looking right at her. Three other boys and two girls were scattered around him. Their gazes were fixed on her as well.

She looked from face to face, trying to figure out what was happening.

"Are you talking to me?" she asked, setting her rake aside and looking the one who had spoken in the eyes. Her father and mother had always told her it was polite to face those you spoke to.

"That's right," the boy said. "What are you doing here? They don't allow beggars in the Academy."

"I'm not a beggar," she said. "I'm clearing up these bushes. My father keeps the grounds for the administration area."

He laughed, a chittering, silly kind of laugh that didn't fit his attitude or his form. She would have expected it to be the laugh of a girl. Maybe a fat girl. With warts.

"Your father is one of the servants here? What does that make you? Maybe you're lower than a beggar."

"I'm not," she said, turning to pull a weed from the ground at her feet. She had been polite, but this boy was saying mean things about her father. She didn't want to talk to him anymore.

"Don't you turn your back on me," he bellowed. "Do you know who I am? My father is Lord Sirusel, of Rhaltzheim. I could have you flogged."

Marla calmly turned back to him. "No you couldn't. Your father isn't in charge here. The masters are. Go away or I'll tell them you are trying to start fights."

"That's it," he said. "No one talks to me like that. You won't go to the masters if I beat you until you can't remember anything."

Marla looked him up and down, then smiled. "You can't. You're too fat and slow."

The boy didn't say another word. He charged her, his hands balling into fists. When he was close enough, he swung one of them at her. Slowly.

Marla ducked out from under the blow, balled her own fist up, and lashed out at him, striking him square in the jaw. She followed up with another strike with her left fist, throwing the boy off balance. She ended with a kick straight in front of her, connecting with his belly. The air rushed out of the boy in a whoosh and he fell back onto the ground, whimpering.

Marla stood over him, fist raised threateningly. The boy curled up into a ball.

"No, stop," he said. "Please, no more. Stop."

Marla scoffed, but didn't press her attack. She turned back to her gardening, putting the boy from her mind.

"I'll get you back," he said from behind her. He hadn't moved closer, judging by the sound of his voice. "You can't—"

He cut off abruptly. Marla wondered why until a strong hand grabbed her shoulder.

She spun, looping her arm around as she'd seen some of the students do while practicing applying joint locks. Her attacker bent his bigger and stronger arm, rendering her attack useless. When she had completed her movement, she was staring into the face of a full-grown man.

One with a master's sash tied around his military-looking uniform.

Marla gulped and dropped her hands to her sides.

"Come with me," he said in a deep voice. "Both of you."

The other children scattered, running off toward the practice grounds. The master glared in their direction, but let them go. He turned the scowl to Marla and the boy who had attacked her.

"I can explain," the boy said.

"Save it for the headmaster," the master told him, grabbing a handful of the boy's pants and lifting him off the ground with one hand as he started walking toward the main administration office. He raised an eyebrow to Marla.

She followed him, not wanting to be dragged like some wild game that had been hunted down.

They were soon in the office of the headmaster of the entire Academy. Qydus Okvius was her father's boss, the one who had hired him and who let him take Marla when she had been found at the front gate.

The air turned thick and hard to breathe. She gulped. Would her father get in trouble for this? She hung her head as the master who had brought them here talked softly with the headmaster's assistant. Marla wished she could talk to the assistant instead. Aletris Meslar was always kind to her and not scary at all. Not like the headmaster.

He had to be about fifteen feet tall and his pointed beard, pointed mustache, and pointed head seemed like weapons. He also scowled. All the time. She had never seen any expression on his face except that frown. It appeared even deeper now that he was sitting silently and aiming it toward the two children in front of him.

The master who had brought them closed the door and sat down in one of the chairs at the side of the headmaster's desk. Marla and the boy were sitting directly in front of the huge slab of wood filled with papers. Directly in the line of sight of the headmaster.

"Thank you for bringing this to my attention, Master Goren," the headmaster said. "It is a very serious thing, fighting within the Academy."

That didn't make sense to Marla. Weren't the students here trained to fight? They practiced it all the time. She had watched them.

The headmaster must have noticed her confusion. "You would not know this, Marla, but combat training here is controlled carefully." He knew her name? She hadn't expected that. "Fighting outside the training rings is strictly prohibited."

"She attacked me," the boy said. "Her and five of her friends. I was walking on the path and they jumped out of the bushes. I fought off some of them, but—"

"Close your mouth, Barda Sirusel," Master Goren said. "If

59

you lie in my presence again, I will paddle your behind until you can't sit for a week."

The boy opened his mouth to speak again, but the head-master cut him off. "I suggest you do as he says, Barda. Master Goren is fair, but he always acts according to his word. Do not make things worse for yourself."

Barda closed his mouth, looking like he had eaten rotten fish.

"Now," the headmaster said, "what is this all about?"

"This one," Master Goren said, gesturing toward Marla, "was clearing up brush when Barda and his friends came upon her. He hurled insults at her, to which she replied politely at first, but then grew offended. She then turned back to her work, ignoring further taunts. This seemed to enrage Barda, who attacked her without notice or justifiable provocation."

Barda opened his mouth again, but closed it when Master Goren swung his eyes in that direction and raised his hand a few inches.

"Yes," Goren continued. "I saw the whole thing. No lies will avail you in this, boy."

The headmaster drilled his eyes into the boy's. Barda didn't meet them for even a second. He began studying his feet, hanging over the edge of the chair he was sitting in.

"Well, then," Master Qydus said. "It is clear that Mister Sirusel deserves punishment for instigating combat, and with a non-student, at that. Go out in the waiting area. I will discuss the specific punishment with you shortly. Marla, stay where you are."

Barda shuffled out of the office, kicking at the floor as he did it. Marla looked to the headmaster and found him studying her. She locked eyes with him for several seconds, but then became too uncomfortable to continue, so she shifted her gaze to the window.

A noise from the doorway drew her attention and her

breathing stopped abruptly as her father stepped in and closed the door behind himself. He had his hat in his hands, as he normally did when speaking with the headmaster.

"Ah, Pedras," the headmaster said. His voice seemed not quite so deep and threatening. It was almost pleasant. "Thank you for coming promptly. We have something of a situation here."

The door opened and then closed again quickly, revealing Marla's mother as well. The girl could feel tears welling up in her eyes. What had she done?

"Senna," the headmaster said. "I'm glad you could come as well. Please, both of you, sit."

Master Goren bowed his head to Marla's mother and stood, offering his chair to her. Her father sat in the chair vacated by Barda.

"Did Marla do something wrong, headmaster?" her father asked. "I've been letting her work on her own because she has shown she is responsible. If she caused any harm, it's my fault."

Mother glared at Marla, until her eyes met the girl's and saw her distress. Her face softened to more of a curious look.

"No, no, it isn't like that. As far as we can tell, Marla acted correctly. She had an...interaction with some of the students, one in particular. I say interaction, but perhaps a better word is altercation."

"She...what?" Pedras stammered.

"The gist of it is that she was doing the task you had given her and some students began to insult her. She wisely ignored it, but the boy out in the hall assaulted her."

Marla was still looking at her mother, whose face had fallen to a sympathetic look.

"Assaulted her, Master?" Father said. "But he is older than her and twice her size."

"Yes," the headmaster said.

"Are...are you all right, Marla?" Father asked.

"Oh, she's fine, just fine," Master Goren said. "In fact, he was never able to lay a finger on her."

Father breathed out in relief. Mother's shoulders slumped.

"In fact, she very effectively evaded his attacks and laid him out on the ground with a combination of her own," the master continued. "Interestingly, she used the exact movements of Turquoise Sequence Number Two. And when I say exactly, I mean a point-perfect execution that students five years older than her would have trouble matching. I saw the entire thing."

"She...sequence number two?" Father said. "I'm sorry, Master Goren. I don't know what that means."

"What it means," the headmaster said, "is that she has somehow learned what is taught in the College of Unarmed Combat. How did that come to be?"

"I don't know, Master," Father said. He seemed to be getting more and more nervous.

"I'm sorry," Marla said. "I like to watch the students on the training grounds. I practice sometimes. I like how it feels to act out the fighting."

"Is that so?" the headmaster asked. Was that a small smile under all those white whiskers?

"It's impressive, headmaster," Master Goren said. "She obviously has a natural talent."

The headmaster stared at the girl, his eyes drilling into her. His brows drew down slightly and Marla felt something. It was like a small tingling going through her body, as if she had banged her elbow on that spot that made it feel like ants were running up and down her arm and biting her. Master Qydus's eyes went back to normal, not so intense, and the feeling went away.

"Do you know, Marla, that the training, those techniques,

are meant only for students of the Academy? Some might consider learning them without permission stealing."

"No, Master," she said. "I didn't know that."

"It's really very serious."

"Headmaster." It was the first time her mother had spoken since she arrived. "Ped here has been asking for Marla to be enrolled, but the answer has always been no. Can you blame a girl for imitating things she's seen? She meant no harm. She's just a child trying to occupy herself."

"I understand that, Senna, but the fact remains that Academy knowledge is jealously guarded. What are we to do about one who has observed classes without permission and taken that knowledge for her own?"

"Let her become a student," Mother said without a pause, chin up.

Master Goren chuckled at that, but the headmaster simply stared at Mother. She met his eyes and didn't look away.

The headmaster sighed. "You are correct. That is the most logical solution I can see. Very well. Marla, would you like to become a student?"

Marla's heart jumped, and then she did. "Yes, headmaster. More than anything."

"You may begin with the next class. I am stretching the rules a bit to allow this, so you must work hard and prove to everyone that you belong here. We don't accept everyone, you know. I tested you a moment ago, and it seems that you have the ability to use magic as well. Can you work hard, Marla?"

"Yes, Master. I will work hard and will make you proud. You'll see. I'll be the best student ever."

The headmaster turned to Marla's mother. "Fine. Please speak with Aletris and ask her to begin an admissions packet for Marla. Master Goren and I have to deal with the other half of this situation. Pedras, please have Aletris send in the boy before she beings the paperwork."

"Yes, Master Qydus. Thank you, sir."

"Of course, of course. I am sorry to take your best helper from you. I'm afraid it will mean more work for you, in the end."

"That's perfectly fine, Master. Perfectly fine."

Marla looked from the headmaster to her parents to Master Goren as they all stood up. She wasn't sure what she was supposed to do.

"Go on, Marla," the headmaster said. "You have paperwork to fill out and preparations to make. Congratulations and welcome to the Academy. We will no doubt be speaking to each other soon."

Marla followed her parents out of the room. It didn't sink in until she had already started in on the papers Aletris Meslar gave her. She was going to be a student at the Hero Academy. Just like she had always dreamed.

❧ 8 ☙

On her way to her prearranged meeting with Skril and Evon, Marla dropped by the scriptorium to see if the scribes had finished copying Master Nasir's notes. She was pleasantly surprised that they had finished all seven copies. Evon must have asked them to make an extra for him. She took three of them, as well as the original, telling the scribes the other investigators would be coming to get their own copies.

Her two friends were already waiting when she arrived at Evon's room.

"Sorry I'm a bit late," she said as she swept through the door without knocking. "I stopped to get the copies of Master Nasir's notes." She handed them each a book, which the scribes had kindly bound in a flexible leather cover.

"No problem," Skril said. "Thanks for grabbing copies for us."

"You even figured out there was an extra one for me," Evon said. "Master Nasir allowed me to examine the office, too. I just finished not too long ago."

Marla nodded as she flipped through her copy. The duplicates were thicker than the original, for some reason.

"Oh," Evon said. "The scribes included some blank pages in the copies. They must have predicted we'd want to take our own notes."

"Very clever," Marla agreed. "I'll have to do something nice for Jhanda. So, do you want to talk about the notes or do you want to compare what we discovered from the investigation of the master's room and the body?"

"Um, the body?" Skril asked.

"Yeah. You know, Master Aeid's corpse?"

"We didn't go and look at the body," Evon said. "We're allowed to do that?"

Marla shook her head. "Of course. It's part of any good investigation."

The boys looked at each other, then both dropped their gazes to the books in their hands.

"Okay," she said. "Well, let's talk about what we learned, then. I'd like some time to look over the notes before we talk about those."

"Master Aeid isn't very organized," Skril said. "I mean, *wasn't* very organized."

"Not so," Marla said. "He had his own way of organizing things. He could find anything in an instant, though I never figured out his system."

"It's kind of complex," Evon said. He would know. He spent more time with the master than either of the other two had. "I'd explain it to you, but there doesn't seem to be a reason. Did you notice the missing notebook?"

"I did," Marla said. "The pattern of the dust clearly indicated something was taken. Was it the killer or did Master Aeid move it before he died?"

"Wait," Skril said. "What notebook? What pattern in the dust?"

"I think I know what the missing notes looked like," Evon continued without acknowledging Skril's question. "I couldn't find it in the room, so I assume the murderer took it. Or someone else."

"What were the notes for?" Marla asked. "What was he working on?"

Evon ran his fingers through his hair. "I don't know. I just know I saw it on his desk—in different places—for the last few weeks. I never asked what his current project was."

"Pity."

Marla was flipping through the pages of Master Nasir's notes while they spoke. She reached one that made her eyes pop.

"Look at this," she said, holding the open notebook up so the other two could see. It was a detailed drawing of Master Aeid's body. Very detailed.

"That's amazing," Skril said. "It looks so real. They must have gotten an artist to draw it for us."

Marla compared the copy she had been holding with the original notebook. "The original is even better. Look at this. I knew Master Nasir was talented at sketching, but I had no idea he was this good."

"Flip to the next few pages," Evon said. "There are other drawings of the scene with the body's position included."

"This will be helpful, right?" Skril asked.

Marla nodded. "Definitely." She closed the book. "Sorry. We can look at the notes later. What else did we find?"

"He was stabbed twice," Skril said. "It looked like they missed the heart the first time."

"I don't think so," Marla said. "Those wounds were made by two different blades. The larger went into the lung, preventing the master from crying out effectively. The other went directly into the heart.

"There were also no wounds on his hands or arms...or

really on any other part of the body. That means he didn't fight back. He was surprised."

"But how?" Evon said. "How could someone enter the room, cross it, and stab Master Aeid without him seeing them or defending himself?"

"He knew the killer," Skril said.

"Exactly," Marla agreed. "The master knew the killer was there, but wasn't alarmed because he knew the person. They could get close without alarming him."

Evon rubbed his chin. "Maybe the killer used magic to freeze the master and then they got close that way."

"Nope," Marla said. "I checked for residual magic. The only ones who had used magic in the room before I inspected it were Master Aeid and Master Nasir. Master Nasir would have checked for residue like I did—and he cast some sort of preservation spell on the blood—and of course Master Aeid would use magic in his own office. The killer didn't use magic."

"Fine," Evon said. "So, the master was familiar with the killer."

Marla lifted a finger in the air. "But the knives weren't all of the plot. Someone tried to poison Master Aeid first. It may have been the person with the knives or it may have been someone else."

"What?" Skril asked.

"I took samples of the food and wine. I also took some skin samples from the master's tongue. I tested them at the alchemy lab and found Shu's Bite in all three. I don't think the killer realized how Master Aeid gets when he is in the middle of his research. Sometimes he forgets to eat all day, or at least prioritizing meals low on the list. He had very little poison in his body."

"Shu's Bite?" Skril said. "Isn't that pretty rare?"

"It's made from shu root, from Shinyan," Marla said. "The

export of the root is controlled strictly and it's very expensive. It takes a skilled alchemist to produce the poison from the root."

"Oh, right," Skril said, as if she'd reminded him of something he already knew.

Evon rolled his eyes at his friend. "So, they tried to poison him and then stabbed him when that didn't work?"

"Yes."

"All of that is interesting," Evon said, "but what can we do with the information? It doesn't point us to a killer."

"No," Marla agreed. "It doesn't. It's a start, though. Maybe there are other clues in Master Nasir's notes. I don't know about you two, but I plan on spending the rest of the night reading them over and over, and writing down my own observations. Maybe something will make sense."

"I can't do that," Evon said. "I have to go and meet the masters again soon to help them with the selection of the new Master of Prophecy. Or at least to give them the information so they can make a good selection." His frown was deep enough that Marla thought it might permanently line his face.

"Marla," Skril said, "will you work with me on this? We'll be able to do a better job if we do it together."

"Uh," Marla said. "I would, Skril, but you know me. I'm a loner. I like to work by myself. That way I don't get in anyone else's way and I don't mess things up for others."

"I'm not afraid of you messing things up for me. Even if you did make a mistake, I wouldn't ever hold it against you. Sometimes it's nice to be able to bounce ideas off someone else."

"We can still do that, Skril, but I'd rather go and do my own thing," she said. "We will probably have to go outside of the Academy for this investigation, and I travel better alone. You understand, right?"

Skril looked like his favorite pet weasel had just died. "Yeah. I guess."

"You'll do fine. You don't need me trying to take control of our investigation. It'll be good for you to carry out the task according to the way *you* want to do it."

Evon had watched the exchange silently, but he didn't remain silent. "So, you're saying it's for Skril's own good that he's forced to do it all on his own?"

Marla gave him a level look. "That's not what I'm saying. Not precisely, anyway. You're right, though. It is a good learning exercise for him."

"Don't try to spin it like you're doing him a favor, Marla. You didn't make the decision for his benefit. You made it for you."

She sighed. "Yes. I'm a loner, guys. You know that. Socializing isn't my thing, even with my friends. I want to be able to focus on the investigation without having to consider what my actions might do to a partner. I don't want to put anyone else in danger because of a decision I make." She took Skril's hand. "You understand that, right? I'm not rejecting you. I just want to concentrate on what I need to be doing, without worrying how it'll affect someone else."

Skril still didn't look any happier. "I understand."

"It's why most heroes are loners," Marla said.

"Who says?" Evon asked.

"No one has to say it. It's evident. Everyone knows it."

"Everyone? I certainly don't know it. How about you, Skril? Do you know that most heroes are loners?"

Skril shook his head.

"Hm," Evon said. "Fully two-thirds of those queried don't know that most heroes are loners. An interesting fact, isn't it, Marla?"

"Please. You two are just ganging up on me because you don't like my decision."

"No," Evon said. "That's not it. You can't make a statement like that without giving us evidence, or at the very least, examples."

"Really? You need me to cite examples?"

"Need? No. Want? Definitely."

"Fine. Forden the Risen, Brenain Kanda, and Moroshi Katai. There."

Skril worked his mouth for a moment. He finally managed, "Okay, but the most famous hero in recent times, Erent Caahs, traveled with his friends."

Marla smirked. "Hmm. Fully three-fourths of heroes discussed were loners. That's interesting, isn't it?"

Skril blew out a breath. "All right, fine. *Some* heroes are loners, but that doesn't mean you need to be."

"I know, Skril. I'm not saying I'm a hero or anything like that. I'm just being honest with you. I do much better alone. I'm sorry. I hope you understand."

"Yeah, I guess. Will you still discuss the investigation with me when you're here?"

She smiled and patted his shoulder. "Of course. I'm sure there will be lots of the investigation that happens here at the Academy. We can compare notes and keep Evon up to speed for when the masters finally let him take part."

Her two friends seemed satisfied with that, though Skril still wouldn't meet her eyes. She had hurt his feelings, despite him knowing her well. They'd get past it. More quickly than if they worked together and she barked commands at him during the whole thing. They'd be fine when it was all over and done.

"I better go to the masters," Evon said. "I'll see you guys...well, whenever I get a chance. Good luck with your hunt and be careful. Whoever we're looking for has already killed one person, and it was a master. Don't underestimate the danger."

"Yes, sir." Marla snapped a fist to her chest in a mock salute.

"I'm serious, Marla. Be careful."

"We will. I'm just trying to lighten the mood. Enjoy your time with the masters. It's actually a really good opportunity to work closely with them. You can learn a lot."

Evon headed toward the administration building, leaving Skril and Marla looking around awkwardly.

"I don't know about you," she said, just to have something to say, "but I think I'm going to go to my room and study Master Nasir's notes. Maybe there's enough there to figure out what to do next."

Skril gave her a forced smile. "That's a good idea. Good luck."

"Yeah, you too. We can talk tomorrow, after we've had a chance to look through the notes and think."

He brightened a little at that. "I'd like that. Thanks, Marla. Have a good night."

"Same to you," she said. She stood in front of him for a moment, not quite knowing what to say. In the end, she left it at that, turned, and walked out of his room to go to her own. She remembered her promise and stopped by the Medica to let Tan look at the notes before finally getting to her room.

Skril would get over this little hang-up, she was sure. For now, she had to turn her mind to the task at hand. There was a murderer out there and she needed to put an end to him or her. She sat at her desk with the notebook, anticipating the capture of the criminal soon.

𒀭 9 𒀭

The girl sat in a room with twelve other children, all younger than her. At seven, she was thin and almost indistinguishable from the other waifs grouped around her, whether boy or girl.

"You have been accepted into the Academy at Sitor-Kanda," the man said. "Some of you petitioned for acceptance and some of you were discovered." His eyes met the girl's, held them for a moment, and then moved on to scan the room. "But you all have one thing in common. You all have the potential to harness the arcane energy that suffuses the world. In short, you all have the potential to be heroes. We will teach you the skills to do great things.

"The Academy has many schools. Forty-nine, to be exact. As you may be aware, seven is a perfect number, whether physically, spiritually, or magically. Seven times seven is forty-nine, and so as you master the different schools, you will move closer to perfection. Of course, none have ever mastered all of the schools. Even though the ability to harness arcane power often brings with it an enhancement to learn more quickly than common folk, a lifetime is not enough time."

Marla's eyes were wide with excitement. She had finally been officially accepted into the Academy, a dream come true. She looked at the other children. They were big and small, skinny and plump, dark and light. She wondered which would be her friends during her studies.

"The curriculum here is very hard," the master said. "Many of you will not be here long. Some of you will quit," he scanned their faces, pausing on one or two and staring for a brief moment, "and others will be dismissed." He continued to swivel his gaze amongst the children, stopping on Marla for a good two seconds. She swallowed hard. What did it mean?

"We will give you every opportunity to succeed, but the nature of the school and of those who will train here is specific. We have an obligation to train the heroes of this world, an obligation we take very seriously. Perilous times are ahead and we must be prepared."

The master paused to allow his last statement to settle into their minds. Marla wondered what the others were thinking. As for her, she wondered what exciting types of magic she would be learning and when she could get started.

"You will all start at the School of Preparation. In that school, you will learn all the basic things you must understand for the other colleges. Bodily training, thinking critically, reading, writing, and other basic skills will be taught there.

"There is no set schedule, no time limit for any of the schools, save this first one. If you have not mastered the curriculum for the School of Preparation within two years of when you enter, you will be dismissed, never allowed to return. On the other hand, if you master what is required before the allotted time, you will be allowed to move on to another school immediately. There are five schools you must attend before you may go on to other colleges. They are Preparation, History and Literature, Scholarship, Fundamental Magic, and Language. You are not required to master any of these, other than the School of Preparation. Once you have been evaluated and judged to have adequate skills and knowledge, you may begin to study at the other schools of your choice. Is that clear to everyone?"

All of the children nodded or made weak statements of affirmation. Marla saw that some of them wore confused looks, though. The master didn't speak to them as if they were children. She was used to such adult language, but she wondered how much the other new students understood.

"I said," the master growled, startling more than half the inductees, "is that clear to everyone?"

"Yes, Master," all of the children shouted in unison. Some of the confused looks turned to expressions of fear. One small boy trembled.

"Very well," he said, smiling. There was no sign of his former anger, if it was really anger at all. Marla thought that maybe he acted angry to prove a point. As she thought this, the master met her eyes, nodded, and his smile turned friendly, like they were sharing a secret. Could he read minds, as the stories said?

"Now then," he continued, "are there any questions?"

A small hand raised in the back of the group. The master pointed toward the boy, a skinny, small, dark-haired lad with a thin face and dark holes for eyes. "Yes, you," the master said. "State your name first and then ask your question."

"My name is Kayin Melech," he said in a weak, squeaky voice. "What about the prophecy of the chosen warrior?"

The master frowned at the child. "Are we to speak about mythology now, about legends? Perhaps you would ask me of the Godan Chul or the Spirtu? Would you like to hear of them?"

The child's eyes lit up and he smiled, missing the master's mood completely. His mouth started to form an affirmative, but as his eyes crossed Marla's, she shook her head discreetly and he stopped. He took a more careful look at the master, finally registering his displeasure, and shook his head.

"No, Master," he said. He opened his mouth to speak again, but then apparently decided against it and closed it with a click.

The master glared at him for a moment before scanning the others. His face softened and he sighed.

"Oh, very well. There is a prophecy, received and written by the Great Prophet, Tsosin Ruus, about the 'Chosen Warrior,' or Malatirsay. You will learn more of the prophecy. It is, in fact, the purpose of this school, to train the Malatirsay in all he or she needs to know to save the world from the coming darkness. It is metaphorical. You will learn of the prophecy, but you don't need to worry about it now. You should be more concerned about proving yourself worthy to stay here rather than dream of being the hero of prophecy."

The children were shown to their bunks. The room held only twelve, arranged barracks style, but as the master spoke, two older boys brought in a thirteenth bunk and set it in the corner.

"We will temporarily put this extra bunk in the room, though it affects the energy flow through the room. Soon, at least one of you will leave us and then the extra bunk will be removed. As I call off your names, stand in front of the bunk I designate."

The master began to call out names...

MARLA JERKED HER HEAD UP, LOOKING AROUND confusedly.

She had fallen asleep while reading Master Nasir's notes and dreamed of her first days enrolled at the Academy. What a strange thing to be thinking about. She'd almost forgotten about that, about the master who seemed altogether too doubting of the Academy's true purpose. Some felt that Sitor-Kanda was to train groups of heroes rather than the Malatirsay, for whom the Academy was built.

She shook her head, stepped over to the basin, and splashed water on her face. She hadn't quite finished the notes before she had dozed off, so the first order of business was to complete that task. Another two hours and she turned the last written page in the little notebook. Now she was ready for sleep.

She had mastered the technique of seeding thoughts into her brain before sleep and allowing her unconscious mind to work on problems while she slumbered. Master Jusha would be pleased. The Master of Mental Magic had taught her the technique at the beginning of her mental training in his school.

After a few hours of sleep, Marla got up while it was still dark. She had read all of Master Nasir's notes, and though they were specific and concise, he hadn't listed anything significant she hadn't found herself. She was slightly disappointed, but also proud that she had matched what the master had found.

As she rose, she knew what she had to do. She dressed and jotted a short note to Skril, who would be stopping by to discuss the investigation.

SKRIL,

. . .

THERE IS SOMETHING I HAD TO CHECK ON. I SHOULD BE BACK LATER TODAY. WE CAN DISCUSS IT THEN. THANKS FOR UNDERSTANDING.

MARLA

IT WASN'T A COMPLETE EXPLANATION, BUT THEN AGAIN, SHE wasn't about to leave a detailed note lying around where others could read it. As a precaution, she sealed the envelope with a bit of magic, attuning it to Skril's aura, which she knew almost as well as her own. She had known him and worked closely with him for several years, so she knew his magical signature inside out. She slipped the note between the door and the frame where he'd see it when he came calling.

Then she headed to the administration office.

Each day, the logs for entry and exit to the Academy were kept at the main gatehouse, but at the end of the day, they were brought to the administration building for retention. She flashed the writ of permission the masters had given her, and the bleary-eyed clerk who looked to have just gotten to her desk waved her through.

She searched for a moment, and then found the records for the days surrounding Master Aeid's murder, which occurred on the twenty-ninth day of Fordenaytun.

She hummed as she scanned the records. Not only did the log contain visitors to the Academy—and their entry and exit dates and times—but also the exits and entries of Academy students.

Those who studied at Sitor-Kanda were not allowed to leave the campus except for special circumstances. At least, not until they attained graduate status. Even then, travel was strictly controlled any farther than thirty miles away until the graduate officially left their studies. A student could have mastered ten schools, but was still subject to the school's rules until they filed the appropriate Letters of Final Graduation.

First, the list of visitors. There were five who left within a day of Master Aeid's death. Two of them were from Shinyan: Zeng Bao and Zou Mei. They arrived at different times—three days apart—but that didn't necessarily mean they didn't know each other. She was interested in them because of the poison she had found in the master's food and drink.

The other three didn't seem related at all. There was Kaspar Wittich from Rhaltzheim, Yulia Kovs from Artuyeska, and Simon Bruer from Satta Sarak. The visitor log only required the nation or kingdom from which a visitor came, not the city.

Marla copied the information into her notebook.

There were also five students who left the Academy the day of the master's murder. Viktoria Fomenko went to Drusca, in Sutania, on an errand for the Master of Firearms, Liluth Olaxidor. Quentin Duzen traveled to Ebenrau in Rhaltzheim to visit family. Adamar Zyljor took leave for a research trip to Drugancairn. Ren Kenata departed on an errand for Master Nasir Kelqen. Mellarue Effrir went to Birie in Yteron to visit family. Marla made notations for those five in her notes as well.

She tapped the pen on her bottom lip, thinking. Was there a pattern here, some kernel of an idea of where to go? The poison lead seemed to be the strongest with the two visitors from Shinyan. It didn't feel right to her, though. Maybe it was a little too strong. Too obvious.

Marla wasn't sure if anyone else had discovered the poison. Master Nasir's notes did not include a reference to it. Did he miss that clue? Her suspicious mind found that to be unlikely. But if he did find the clue, why didn't he record it in his notes?

She didn't like how this was turning out. Why did she always have to second-guess herself like this? She carried out her investigation as she should have, so she should be happy things seemed to be working out.

But she wasn't.

Marla was already on her way toward the docks on the western side of the island when she abruptly stopped and turned her horse around. She wasn't sure why yet, but she felt that her destination should be to the east. She shrugged her shoulders as she rode toward the bridge to the mainland and told herself she'd figure it out before she got to where she was going.

She was going to do some good, old-fashioned interviews to see if she could shake loose any more clues.

❧ 10 ❧

There were two settlements within a day's ride of the Academy's northern bridge. The closest, Dartford, was familiar to Marla. She went there fairly frequently to sit in the inn's common room and listen to the tales of travelers. The other, Hamrath, was on the shore almost thirty miles north of the bridge. She had only been there once, so it was largely unknown to her. That was her first stop.

It took her the entire day to get to the town of Hamrath. It was essentially a fishing town, as could easily be seen by the boats out in their bay, sheltered by the island of Munsahtiz itself. Marla could see men working nets from those small boats, some casting them and others bringing them in with the captive fish inside.

As expected, the entire place smelled of fish and damp, with a strong salt tang. Marla wrinkled her nose as her horse clopped its way down the main street toward the inn she remembered from her previous visit. She'd stay the night. No reason to rush and try to get to her next stop when it was more than half a day's ride away.

A young boy sat outside the inn throwing rocks at a wooden target in the shape of a human. He ran up to her as she dismounted.

"Good afternoon, my lady," he said woodenly, as if he was reciting it from a lesson. "Welcome to Shenny's. Will you be taking a room or just enjoying a refreshing mug of ale?"

Marla chuckled at his performance. The boy was twisting his hands in one another and kicking at the ground as he went through the litany. "I'll be taking a room, if there is one available."

"Yes, my lady," he said. "There is space still. May I take your horse to the stables?"

"That would be fantastic." She flipped a two-copper coin to the boy. His eyes widened and he lost his previous disinterest in the situation.

"Thank you. I'll be sure to give her our best stall. I'll rub her down good, too."

"I appreciate that," she said, taking her saddlebags from the mare and throwing them over her shoulder. "Her name is Surefoot." The boy led the horse toward the stables as she entered the main doors of the inn.

Marla stepped through the doors to the common room of the inn, maneuvering the sword at her waist without thinking. Students were allowed to carry their weapons at the Academy. It was, after all, meant to train the students to be heroes. Warriors. She couldn't remember the last time she'd gone a whole day without her weapons at her side.

As she scanned the room, she realized that she'd been so anxious to get started on her investigation, she hadn't thought much about what she'd do when she got to Hamrath, let alone Dartford. Well, she'd figure it out. She was smart.

An older woman, tall and skinny, stood behind a long bar at one end of the room. A few more than a dozen people sat at the tables scattered around the room, most too engrossed in their meals or their conversations with others to look up when she entered.

She headed for the woman.

"Good evening," Marla said. "The boy out front said you had rooms still?"

"Evening," the woman said. Her voice was thick, like she'd been breathing the smoke of a fire. "Yep, we have a few. Want one?"

"I do, thank you. Just for one night."

"That'll be three silver. Evening meal and breakfast are included."

Marla handed the coins over. She didn't have a lot of experience with innkeepers—she hadn't traveled much—but the one in front of her was too reserved. Almost as if she didn't like people at all. Weren't innkeepers supposed to be friendly and gregarious?

"Uh," Marla said. "Any news? I'm a bit behind. I heard there was some kind of trouble over at the Academy."

The woman—who, Marla realized, hadn't even given her name—shook her head as she fished out a key to Marla's room. "Can't say I know much of that. I don't keep track of them Academy folks."

"Oh. Anything else interesting happen? Anyone strange passing through?"

The woman stared at Marla for a moment. Was that surprise in her eyes, or disbelief? Then she shook her head and pushed the key toward Marla.

"Strange like a slip of a girl asking questions, fishing for information?"

Marla gulped and took the key. She didn't know how to answer the woman.

"Dinner is in two hours. Breakfast starts at dawn. Your room is number three, down the hall to the right."

"Thank you." Marla headed down the hall to her room.

She closed the door behind her and slumped against the wall. *You, Marla, are an idiot.* She knew intellectually what she needed to do to gather information, but she'd never actually had to try to get information from someone. That innkeeper saw right through what she was trying to do. *Damn.*

Marla put her saddle bags on a chair and splashed her face with water in the basin. She'd have to think a little more before trying to find clues. Talking to people was harder than she'd thought it would be. Oh well, live and learn.

After lying on the bed for almost two hours, trying to work through in her head what she would need to do, she left her room and sat down in the common room. It was starting to get busier, some of the locals coming around for the evening meal and to relax with their friends. Marla stayed at the edge of the crowd, her back to a wall, and watched. Every time her eyes crossed to the bar, she saw the skinny woman staring at her. She had to suppress a shiver.

Despite the weight of the innkeeper's eyes on her back, Marla tried to chat up one of the toughs the inn kept around to break up fights. The man was large with a glare that could fry an egg. He stood at the edge of the room, surveying the area like a hawk hunting for its next meal. As Marla approached him, nothing in his stance changed. His beefy arms were still crossed over his chest, his feet were planted firmly in a wide stance, and his head was erect and unmoving. His eyes, though, locked onto her and followed her.

"Hi," Marla said.

The man grunted.

"You probably see and hear a lot of what goes on here." She paused to allow him to speak, but he remained silent. *Well*, she thought, *what do I expect? That wasn't a question. Master Nasir always said when interviewing people, you needed to ask questions that require specific answers.*

"Uh, have you seen anyone acting strange around lately? Or heard someone talking about a job at the Academy?"

The mammoth man in front of her didn't even move his eyes this time, but she got the definite sense of them rolling at her clumsy questions.

She waited another few seconds and, when it was clear the man wasn't going to talk to her, she skulked back to her table. Someone had already taken her seat, though.

After her disastrous attempts at trying to tease out information from the innkeeper and the tough, Marla didn't even have the heart to oust the newcomer from her place. She found another seat and sat silently, wondering if she should have made an issue out of losing her table. It was probably better not to cause any trouble. Instead, she ate her meal and nursed an ale, feeling more uncomfortable than she had ever felt at the Academy. It was a totally new experience for her.

She scanned the room, watching and listening for anything that might be useful, but she had to be honest with herself: she wasn't good at this information gathering stuff. It seemed so easy during her studies, but the reality was much harder than she would have thought. It was a painful lesson that though she was competent, even masterful, within the confines of the school, she didn't know much about the way things happened in the world outside. What other things she understood as truth were not accurate?

She could only sit for so long without looking like she was spying, she realized. During the two hours she remained in the common room, she heard snippets of stories and bits of news, but nothing related to the Academy except one man who was on his way there to try to sell them a new design for a crossbow he had invented.

All in all, Marla had to admit that it was a wasted trip. She sighed as she drained the last bit of liquid from her mug, set it down on the table, and got up to leave. On her way back to her room, she glanced at the bar and saw the innkeeper still staring at her. Horrible woman.

Once she was back in her room, Marla sat on her bed and pulled out the investigation notebook. What was she even doing here? She had fancied herself a sleuth, dreaming of stumbling onto a clue that would solve the whole murder. She was the star student at the Academy, able to learn more completely and more quickly than any of the other students. Why wouldn't she be able to follow a hunch and uncover the evidence she needed?

She was a fool.

Several masters had told her that the outside world wasn't like the Academy. She had always taken that with a wry smile. They must have been trying to keep her humble. Well, she now had proof that things weren't as easy as she had believed. People outside the Academy, they didn't have all the knowledge and skills she did, but they certainly weren't stupid. Not all of them. She still had a feeling that the innkeeper had won, even if she didn't know what the contest had been.

She slammed the notebook closed, unable to concentrate. It wasn't late, but Marla felt like her motivation had been stolen, her energy leached out of her. The best thing to do was go to sleep, get up early, and head to Dartford. At least she knew people there. It was familiar, and maybe she wouldn't stumble over her own feet like she had in Hamrath.

She didn't bother undressing, only removing the hidden knives strapped to different parts of her body and taking off her boots. She lay down on her bed and was soon fast asleep.

A scratching sound brought Marla out of her sleep. It wasn't something to cause immediate panic, but a gradual awareness of something being out of place.

Marla opened her eyes to the outline of the ceiling in the dim moonlight coming through gaps in the shutters covering the window. What had woken her?

Skritch. Skritch.

She narrowed her eyes and scanned the room, still not quite able to place the sound. Maybe it was a rat in the floor or scratching at the walls?

"Don't rush me," a voice whispered. It sounded like it had come from just outside her door. "I'll get it. Give me a minute."

Marla pulled her blanket off and reached for her sword.

"Too long," another voice whispered. "I'm kicking the door in. Remember, grab her and leave. The boss wants her alive unless we *have* to kill her."

Marla crossed the room in an instant, putting her back against the wall next to the door. She readjusted her grip on her sword, wishing now she had grabbed her dueling knife as well. She fought better with both blades in tandem. Well, the sword would have to do.

The door burst open with a crack and slammed against the wall on the other side of the doorway. Four men rushed in. Lantern light from the hall glinted off the blades they held in front of them. Marla had to squint to see in the brightness.

The men stopped, their heads swinging back and forth in confusion. The one closest to her looked back toward the door.

"Agh," he shouted. "She's—"

Marla kicked him in the mouth, muffling whatever he was going to say with her foot. These men were obviously amateurs, and she wouldn't kill them unless she had to. She had trained her entire life for combat, but that didn't mean she was comfortable with taking someone's life. If she could incapacitate the men without killing them, that would be preferable to cutting them to ribbons with her sword.

As the man she kicked careened off a wall and fell to his knees, the other three tried to get at her with their weapons.

Two had knives and one had a sword. It seemed they had forgotten they were not to try to kill her.

She sighed. No matter. She could tell they would prove no match for her Academy-trained skills.

The sword-bearer lunged at her, attempting to skewer her to the wall. In the confined space, Marla raised the elbow of her sword arm and turned her wrist so her blade, pointing down, deflected the attack harmlessly. The man's sword stuck into the wooden wall as his momentum brought him directly toward Marla. She brought her elbow down again, smashing it into the attacker's nose. Blood exploded outward as he staggered.

The other two men looked at their knives, the sword she had in her hand, and the half of their little group that had been stopped so effectively and with such speed. A quick glance at each other was all it took for them to reach an agreement. They both shot past Marla, through the door, and into the hall. A quick right turn and they were running for all they were worth toward the back entrance of the inn.

Marla watched them go, blinking at the unexpected response.

Though she should have known better, the distraction worked in the intruders' favor. The man she had kicked slammed into her, knocking her against the wall. Her head bounced from the solid beam and her vision blurred. By the time she shook her head to clear her sight, the remaining two had followed their friends, sprinting down the hall like the gods themselves were after them.

Heavy pounding came down the hall from the other end and Marla brought her sword back up.

"More of them?" she hissed. "What is going on?"

A huge shape cast a shadow in the hall as she swung toward the doorway, sword at the ready.

It was the tough she had tried to talk to earlier. She stopped her blade in midswing.

"What happened?" he asked.

She pointed her sword down the hall, toward where the men had escaped. "Four men kicked my door in and attacked me. They ran off that way when I convinced them it was a bad move."

He cocked his head at her, but then apparently decided to go check it out himself. He pounded down the hall and disappeared down the stairs.

"What did you do?" a voice said from behind Marla.

She whirled, sword ready to strike. It was the innkeeper, her bony body wrapped in a robe and her hair disheveled.

"I didn't do anything," Marla answered, "unless sleeping while four men kicked my door in to attack me qualifies as doing something."

The old woman sniffed and examined the damage to the door latch. "This wouldn't have happened if you had kept your fool mouth shut."

"What? You're blaming me for this?"

"Learn some sense, girl. I don't know who you are, but you're obviously looking for something that's too big for you. Now you've tipped 'em off, you better grow eyes in the back of your head. Tch."

The big man plodded back up the stairs into the hallway. "They're gone. Quick ones, those were." He looked at the sword still stuck in the wall. "Uh, you want that?"

Marla waved toward it. "Go ahead and take it. Maybe you can stick it in the man who put it there sometime."

The innkeeper watched her man pull the sword out and inspect it. "Good job, Ham. You, at least, scared them off. I don't like it that they came up the back way like that. Don't like this kind of trouble." She swiveled her head to look at

Marla again. "In the morning, I want you gone after breakfast."

"I understand," Marla said. "I'll go ahead and leave now. I won't be getting any sleep in this room anyway. I'm sorry for the trouble, but regardless of what you think, I didn't try to bring it here."

The woman turned her head as if to spit, but then seemed to realize she was in the hallway of her own inn. She swallowed with a grimace. "Learn to have a more delicate touch when you're trying to get information or you won't last long, no matter how good you are with those weapons you carry."

With that, she glided down the hall, Ham following on her heels testing the balance of his new sword.

At least she didn't ask me to pay for damages, Marla thought. *I better get out of here before she thinks of it.*

Marla put on her boots and strapped her weapons on in minutes, and then headed for the stables. The boy wasn't around—most likely sleeping like all reasonable people were at that time of night—but another of the inn's toughs was sitting in a chair leaned up against the wall inside. He was whittling something.

"I need to get my horse," she told him. "The chestnut mare."

"'Kay." He continued to work his knife on the wooden piece in his hand.

It didn't look like he was going to help, so she saddled the horse herself and led her from the stable. The man's eyes followed her, but he didn't say anything else. This was definitely a strange place. Was this normal for the world outside the Academy? The only other place she'd ever gone was to Dartford, and it wasn't like Hamrath at all. Marla started to worry that all the things she'd learned while at the Academy wouldn't mean a thing out in the wider world.

She shrugged the idea off. No use thinking about it now. She had a ride ahead of her, and several hours until it was light out. She directed her horse southeast and began the journey to Dartford at a walk.

By the time she made it to Wolfen's Rest in Dartford, Marla was tired, hungry, and grumpy. She'd been in the saddle for hours traveling generally east. Right into the morning sun.

The waifish girl who tended the horses at the inn waved at Marla as she dismounted.

"Hi, Marla," she said.

"Hello, Bissa."

"Want me to take care of her?"

"Yes, please. Thanks." She flipped her a coin and stomped inside. The girl would take her saddle bags and bring them inside for her.

Hours of frustration and anger had been building up in Marla, so the first thing she did was to tramp up to Josef, the innkeeper, in the corner of the room.

The man was unassuming and sociable, which is what Marla thought all innkeepers should be. Not like that horrid woman from the night before. He nodded to her, showing more of the skin revealed by his receding hair, and smiled. It slipped a little and he winced as if she'd struck him when she met it with a glare.

"Josef," she said.

"Good morning, Marla."

She growled at him.

"...or maybe just a hello for you, then. Not in the best of moods?"

Marla gritted her teeth, but wrangled her anger under control.

"You or anyone else in here know anything about things happening at the Academy? Things like murder and theft?"

Okay, so maybe she wasn't controlling it quite so well as she had thought.

"Uh, no," Josef said. "You want an ale or some wine? How about you sit down and have some breakfast?"

The six other patrons in the common room were looking at her. They seemed to be waiting for something to happen. Like she might rip a chair apart with her teeth.

"Yeah," she said. "I could use some food. And some ale." She sat down and, once her breakfast came, ate in silence. When she was finished, she waved at Josef, who came over to her table. "You got a room?"

"I do. You wanna take a nap? You look like hell."

She chuckled. The food had improved her mood considerably. "I feel like it. Let me rest for a few hours and then maybe we can try this whole conversation thing again."

"Works for me. Go ahead and take number five. Here's the key. We'll settle up when you're in a better mood."

She took the key and her saddlebags, which Bissa had brought in as Marla was eating, and went to her room. She propped her sword up next to her head, put a knife under her pillow, and went right to sleep.

Four hours later, she woke and stretched, groaning at the little aches she always felt when she hadn't slept enough. It would have to do, though. She couldn't lie around all day.

After a sorely needed bath, she headed down to the common room of the inn. Josef was there, of course, along with a couple of serving girls. Only half the tables held people, but that would change soon, as the evening crowd started trickling in.

She took a table against a wall and waited for someone to come and ask what she needed. Josef himself stepped up to her table.

"Feel better?"

"Yes," she said. "Thanks. Sleep and food can do wonders for a bad mood."

"You don't have to tell me. You gonna be staying long?"

"Nope. I just wanted to check up on some information and then I'll head back to the Academy."

He rubbed his chin. "Yeah, about that. I didn't get a chance to answer you earlier, but I haven't heard anything out of the Academy. Something happen there?"

"You could say that. One of the masters was murdered."

"What? Really?" He sat down across from her. "That's not good. Did they find who did it?"

"Nope. That's why I'm asking questions. I was hoping to shake a few clues loose."

"Hmm. Well, you made enough of a scene earlier. If someone knows something, maybe they'll come see you." He got up. "Food? We have some nice roast mutton and some beef stew."

"The stew sounds good. Thanks."

The innkeeper went to the kitchen and spoke to one of the serving girls. She came back with a mug and a small loaf of bread.

"Here's to get you started, Marla," she said. "I'll be back in a minute with the stew."

"Thanks, Daphne."

"No problem." She hurried toward a full table where a man was waving her down. She deftly dodged the grasping hand of a man at another table.

Marla had half a mind to go and break his fingers, but she didn't want to cause any trouble when nothing really happened. If he actually touched Daphne, she'd do something. The serving girl was much too sweet a person to be subjected to that.

When her food arrived, she ate slowly, watching the other patrons as they ate, drank, and chatted. A few times, she felt eyes on her, but when she searched for the source, the person had averted their gaze.

She finished her food and sipped her ale, trying to figure

out how she could ask more questions without repeating what happened in Hamrath. As it turned out, she didn't need to do anything to make something happen.

AND THAT'S HOW SHE CAME TO BE SITTING AT THE TABLE while Yarl and Benny dragged the men who had attacked her out of the room.

Two sips in, Marla decided she wasn't going to sit and wait for the boys to get information for her. She walked up to Josef.

"Where did the boys take those men?"

"They took them to the private dining room at the end of the hall on this floor. Why?"

"I'm thinking I want to ask them some questions myself."

"I thought you might. Go on. Try not to break anything else, will you?"

She flashed a smile at him. "Sure thing."

All seven men—the five attackers bound with ropes, Yarl, and Benny—were in the dining room Josef directed her toward, all of them glaring at each other. At least, all but one of the attackers who was still slumped in his bonds.

"Hey, guys." She walked in and closed the door behind her. "Mind if I ask some questions?"

Yarl nodded to Marla, but never took his eyes from his captives.

Marla chose the largest of the attackers. It just so happened he was also the one who had tried to get grabby with Daphne earlier. The same one whose fingers she had broken when he reached for the knife that had been on the floor. She smiled at his half-closed left eye, fat lip, and cuts around his face, and how he had been repaid for trying to grab at the serving girl after all.

"Who hired you?" she asked.

The man glared at her.

Marla looked toward the bouncers, then back at the man. She reached out, took his swollen lip between her fingers, and pinched hard.

The man shook his head vigorously, trying to pull free from her grip, while groaning in pain through clenched teeth.

Marla stared into his eyes and released his lip.

"So, who hired you?"

The man tried to glare again, but his eyes were slightly glazed from the pain.

Marla reached out again, more slowly.

"Okay, okay. It was Alaric Permaris." He muttered something under his breath that sounded a lot like "bitch," but Marla ignored it.

"Good. Where can I find him?"

"You can't. He always deals with us through a messenger. I don't know who hired him, either. We work on orders, a job now and then. We were only told your description and that we needed to rough you up. We weren't gonna kill you or anything."

She sniffed. "You weren't going to rough me up, either, tough guy." She turned to Benny. "Were they carrying anything?"

"Only the stuff on the table."

Marla scanned the items. Some coins, mostly silver, a few tinder sets, a smooth stone, and some knives that were scratched and pitted.

"You guys can take what you want of that. We'll just call it a fee for letting them live."

Both of the bouncers gave her smiles. Each was missing at least two teeth.

Marla tried to think of something else she needed to ask, but could only come up with one more thing.

"Were your instructions specifically for me or did they cover several people?"

The man stared into her eyes for a moment, but then looked down. "Anyone from the Academy who was asking questions, but also you specifically. Red hair, young, beautiful. We figured that was you."

Interesting. Somehow she'd already caught the attention of someone. Was it because of Hamrath? She doubted word could have gotten from there to Dartford so quickly. There had to be something else to it.

"Thanks, guys," she said to the bouncers. "I don't know if Josef wants anything more from these, but I'm done. Do whatever you want with them."

"Should we kill them?" Yarl said with a grimace. He'd do it, but he obviously didn't like the idea.

"No," she said. "I don't think so. They weren't out to kill anyone, only to beat them. They got that back already."

"Okay. We'll check with Josef."

Marla went back to the common room.

"Alaric Permaris," she said to Josef. "Know him?"

Josef had been mid-swallow from the mug in his hand. He finished and wiped his mouth. "I've heard the name. He's a mid-level thug, mainly someone who gets stuff done by hiring other thugs. He deals in information, stolen goods, and occasionally a killing, but not too much of the last. Did he send them?"

"Yeah. Any idea how I could find him?"

"None. He usually doesn't deal directly with the ones he hires, and he doesn't bother with Dartford normally; too small for him. He sends a messenger with instructions and payments. I've heard of him being seen around Drugancairn, but also around Ebenrau. I think he moves around."

"Great. I'll have to think about it. Maybe there's a way to locate him."

"Are you done with them?" Josef asked.

"Yeah. I told the boys they could take the coin the men had. I also told them I didn't think they needed to be killed. They got their beating. I figured letting them go was the best thing."

"I agree, though I may take some of the money for the damage they did."

Marla felt her face flush. "Um, yeah. Sorry about that again."

The innkeeper laughed. "It's no worse than any other tavern fight. You ended it quickly, so there wasn't too much damage."

Marla thought about staying the night at the inn, but it was only a few hours ride back to the Academy and she wanted to sleep in her own bed. She settled up with Josef, then gathered her things and headed back to Sitor-Kanda.

She hadn't found any valuable clues, but she had discovered that there was more to it than a simple murder. Evon and Skril would probably want to hear what she'd found. Maybe telling them would help her to figure out what to do next.

❧ 12 ❧

On the way back to the Academy from Dartford, Marla let her thoughts wander as Surefoot settled into her own pace on the familiar road. Memories of her early years at Sitor-Kanda, after she had been accepted as a student, flooded her mind.

She had been so excited and her parents so proud that she would be able to learn. The greatest concentration of knowledge in the world was centered at the Academy at Sitor-Kanda. Everything she could ever want to know.

"Make sure that you act correctly," her father told her. "Be polite to the other students and especially to the masters. Apply yourself and put all your efforts into everything you do."

"I will, Papa."

Her first few days were rough. Word had gotten around that she hadn't come in through the normal recruiting or recommendations. Worse, her confrontation with Barda Sirusel was well known and his family was important and rich.

That made things awkward. Some of the other students shunned her, not wanting to take sides for or against Barda.

99

Others were actively rude, showing their loyalty to the child of a noble house.

For the first two weeks, she cried herself to sleep at night. Her mother tried to help.

"It's not so bad, Marla. You don't have to please them. If the other children want to be small-minded, you can show them how wrong they are. Instead of thinking about them, think of your studies. Focus on those and take pleasure in doing a good job. It won't make it all hurt any less, but soon it won't bother you as much. You'll see."

She did as her mother said, developing a loner mentality. In her first year, she outshone all the other children her age. By the time she was nine years old, she could reasonably be referred to as the star of the Hero Academy.

That only made the other children resent her more. Which caused her to draw away even more from others and rely solely on herself.

"There's Marla," they'd say. "The masters' pet. Their little toadie. What a good girl, doing everything they say and begging for the best grades. Little pet Marla."

She never responded to their laughter and their jibes. Her father had told her that would only make them taunt her more. He'd learned that from his own experiences as a boy. Instead, she doubled down on what she was learning.

She mastered her first school—the School of Preparation —in just four months. It was faster than any student in recent history, but it wasn't seen as too extraordinary.

Marla mastered her second school by the time she reached the day her parents estimated was her ninth birthday —they didn't truly know when she had been born. The school was also in the Preparatory and Administration Lycad, but it was a prestigious one.

The School of Fundamental Magic taught the basics of most of the magical fields of study the Academy specialized in. Her mastery surprised and shocked many of the students, and some of the masters.

But she was just getting started.

As Marla worked her way through many of the schools, the direct teasing eased up. Perhaps because she was becoming more obviously the best student in the Academy, or because all the children were getting older and setting aside childish teasing. It didn't really matter to her. What did matter was that there were forty-nine schools full of information within her reach and she planned on mastering them all.

Though the taunts had slowed for pre-teen Marla, she still wasn't accepted socially. Whereas before, the other students treated her poorly because of loyalty to Barda Sirusel—or from plain meanness—she started to hear whispers the others thought she couldn't hear.

"She thinks she's too good for the rest of us."

"That one always looks down on everyone."

"Marla is too busy sucking up to the masters to pay attention to lowly students."

None of it was true, of course, but the words hurt all the same. She had grown older, had gained more knowledge and skills, maybe had even acquired a bit of wisdom, at least relative to other children her age, but that didn't stop her from noticing how all the other students had friends and she had no one. Not that she needed them. She was self-sufficient.

Maybe that wasn't true. She did have her parents, but that was little consolation to a girl in the throes of adolescence.

Then she had met Skril Tossin. He was older than her by three years, more mature than most of those she had regularly seen in her classes. With only a little more than three hundred students in the Academy, it seemed strange that she had not seen him before. All she knew was that when she witnessed someone she did know—Barda, the boy who had started all her problems—trying to bully him, she needed to do something.

It didn't take much.

Marla hadn't seen Barda actually knock the other teen down, but the bully was standing over the smaller boy, who was crouched on the ground, trying to cover up as much of his body as he could by curling into a ball.

She walked up to Barda, raising her hand, palm up. A pale, flickering flame appeared in it, dancing a fraction of an inch above the skin.

"I know my eyes must be fooling me," she said, rolling her wrist and making the flame turn circles as it pulsed. "You can't be trying your same old tricks after all these years. It's too hard to believe that you might be trying to bully someone else. Someone smaller than you."

In the years since their first encounter, both she and Barda had grown, but she did it faster. She had no doubt he would be taller than her in a few years, but for now, she could stand flat on her feet and look him in the eye.

But that wasn't what made him hesitate. She could see the reflection of her flame in his eyes. He knew she had mastered a school of magic—everyone did. Would he believe she would use it against him?

"Stay out of my way," he said to the boy he was accosting. Then he turned and walked away, his friends swarming around him like flies around carrion.

Marla extinguished her flame and reached down to help the boy up. He took her hand with a grin and got to his feet.

"You okay?" she asked.

"You're Marla. Marla Shrike." He was smiling too hugely for someone who just barely escaped being pounded by a bully.

"Yeah." She wasn't sure what he was getting at.

"You've already mastered two schools. Two!" His brown

eyes sparkled when he said it, like he was more excited about it than she was.

"Uh huh."

He put his hand out toward her so quickly, she almost parried it and struck him in reflex. But he only wanted to shake her hand. She offered hers to him.

"I'm Skril Tossin. Thanks for helping me."

"Don't let that idiot think you're afraid of him or he'll never stop."

"Oh. Um, but I am afraid of him. I can't fight, and I definitely can't use magic as well as you can."

"You should learn," she said. "To fight, I mean. Don't do magic against another student. The masters won't allow it. I was hoping he wouldn't think of that when I made him think I was threatening him."

Skril shook his shaggy head. The brown mop looked like it had never been formally introduced to a brush. "I haven't had time to take any combat classes. I kind of have a full schedule."

"You should make time. Studies are fine, but everyone needs to know how to defend themselves. This is the *Hero* Academy after all."

"You're right. Oh, I better get going. I'll be late for my history class. Master Aubron hates it when students are late. Thanks again. Maybe I'll see you later."

"Sure."

She didn't think much of it. People were supposed to say stuff like that when someone helped them with a bully. Marla put it out of her mind and went on about her day.

But that wasn't the end of it.

Skril found her a few days later as she was eating lunch. As was her habit, she had taken her tray out to sit under one of the trees on the lawn near the dining hall.

"Hi Marla," the young man said, bouncing up to her excitedly. The plate of food on his tray hopped, but he managed not to spill it. Another boy about the same age was with him. He was taller than Skril, and opposite in appearance from the other boy. Whereas Skril was shorter, with dark hair and eyes, and his hair a shaggy mess, the newcomer was blond-haired, blue-eyed, thin but fit, and neat and tidy with his hair combed stylishly.

"Oh," she said. "Hi, Skril."

"This is my friend Evon Desconse. Can we eat lunch with you?"

"Um," she said, "yeah, I guess. Hi, Evon."

"It's nice to finally meet you, Marla," Evon said.

"Finally?"

Evon's fair complexion was very effective at showing the boy's blush. "Yes. I mean, I know who you are and everything, but we've never met."

Marla squinted at him. Come to think of it, maybe she did recognize him. She'd probably seen him around the Academy, but she hadn't ever met him or heard his name.

"You're kind of famous," Skril said while he happily sat and arranged his tray in front of him. "Which is saying something because you're so young."

Evon shot his friend a look that communicated the thought clearly: *you're being insulting*.

"I'm not much younger than you are," she said, taking a drink from her cup of water.

"Three years," Skril said. "For me, anyway. Two years for Evon."

"What?"

"I know how old you are, and what you've studied, and all the school records you've broken. So far."

Marla raised an eyebrow and looked to Evon, who had smacked his palm to his forehead.

"Skril," he said. "Do you remember how we talked about

just saying whatever comes to mind and how it can be creepy to some people?"

"Yeah," the darker-haired boy said, his ever-present smile not slipping the slightest bit.

"Well, you're doing it again." Evon turned to Marla. "He's a researcher at heart. He likes to know about...well, everything. He devours any news he hears about you and your accomplishments. Along with basically any other information he hears about anything. Don't make too much of it. He sometimes reminds me of the names of some of *my* cousins that I can't recall at the moment."

Marla shook her head and tore a piece of bread from a larger chunk to pop it in her mouth.

"So?" Skril said, swinging his head back and forth from Marla to Evon, smile widening, if anything.

"So what?" she asked.

"Can we eat lunch with you?"

Marla traded a look with Evon, who had also seated himself already. "Uh. Sure. Take a seat."

Skril swiveled his head, first to Evon and then back to Marla, and finally down to himself in a seated posture. His eyes widened a bit, but he only smiled at Marla again.

That first lunch was a little awkward, with Skril chattering the entire time, Evon commenting only when directly addressed by the other two, and Marla doing her best to tolerate the entire thing.

"...and that's why I think people don't come up and talk to you much," Skril nattered on. "They're intimidated. I mean, who wouldn't be? You're the youngest person to ever master a school, let alone two. And you're so good at combat. Boys three or four years older than you are afraid to fight you, and—"

Evon put a hand up. "We get it, Skril. Breathe. Maybe eat something. Sorry, Marla, he's excited."

"I picked up on that," she said. "Do you really think people are too intimidated to talk to me? I mean, I always thought it was just that no one liked me."

Evon pointed to Skril, who had opened his mouth to say something. The dark-haired boy's shoulders slumped and he shoveled a bite of food into his mouth. "There are students who resent you, for one reason or another, but there are also a lot who feel uncomfortable approaching you. We know the feeling."

"You?"

"Skril and I have talked about saying something to you before. He's fascinated by your accomplishments, and I always thought you'd have an interesting outlook on things. But you're Marla Shrike, master of two schools and counting. Who are we to walk up and start chatting with you?"

"You're students, too," she said. "We're all here to learn. So what, I mastered the School of Preparation. It's no big deal."

"School of Fundamental Magic," Skril said around a mouthful.

"Okay, that one too," she conceded. "Still, it's no reason for people to avoid me."

Evon smiled at that.

"What now?" she asked.

"It's exactly what I told Skril. I said you don't think you're better than anyone else. It's that everyone *thinks* you think you're better than anyone else."

"Yeah," she said. "That's exactly right. Do I come off as having a superior attitude like that?"

"Not right now, no," Evon said. "I think maybe it's your confidence. Some people feel intimidated by that."

"But not you?"

"Nah, not really. I mean, what you've accomplished and

what you can do is impressive, but everyone has their own strengths."

"Yeah," she said. "My father always says that."

That was the first of many lunches. Soon, the three were spending more time together and before she could think about it, Marla had two friends. Real friends. It was a first for her, and it made all the difference in the world.

But still, she'd never admit that she needed them.

❧ 13 ❧

Marla stopped by Skril's room when she got back to the Academy, but he wasn't there, so she headed over to Evon's. It was evening, so she expected he'd be there studying. She wasn't disappointed.

Her blond friend answered the door, holding a book.

"Oh, hi, Marla. Come on in." He went back to his chair as she came in the room.

"I thought Skril would be here with you," she said.

"No. He's out following up on a lead."

"A lead? What kind of lead?"

He set his book aside. "Just after you left, Master Nasir released another page of his notes. He was waiting for some results back from the alchemy school. His notes explained there was poison in Master Aeid's food and wine."

"Yeah. I already knew that. I told you and Skril."

"I know. Well, Skril went to the visitor logs and found that two people from Shinyan had visited and left around the time of the murder. He wanted to check up on it, search around on the west docks, but he waited for a day so he could take you with him. He finally gave up waiting for you and went over there himself."

"Oh. He didn't want to take you with him?"

"I couldn't go. I'm still working with the masters on choosing a new Master of Prophecy. They released me for today only a little while ago. I need to be back at it early tomorrow morning, but I might be done soon."

Marla didn't like the sound of that. "I was searching for clues and was attacked. Twice. They were serious, too."

Evon's head snapped up. "Are you okay?"

"I'm fine, but Skril can't fight as well as me. I'm concerned for him. When's he supposed to be back?"

"He didn't say. It should be safe at the docks. I mean, it's still on Munsahtiz. The Academy runs the docks. There's not high crime in the area or anything."

"You're right," Marla said. "But then again, the Academy is supposed to be safe, but someone killed a master."

She stayed with Evon for another hour, describing what had happened to her. Skril didn't show up and she was having trouble keeping her eyes open.

"Listen," she said. "I'm going to grab something to eat and then get some sleep. If Skril hasn't checked in by the morning, I'll go looking for him. If you see him, either send him to me or let me know, okay?"

"You bet," he said. "I'll be meeting with the masters at dawn, and I probably will be with them all day, so you won't be able to contact me. Hopefully all three of us can update each other tomorrow evening."

She gave him a tired smile. "He'll probably have a story about how he extended his search when he found a rare bird and followed it for hours. I'll see you tomorrow."

As she headed toward her own room, the smile slipped from her face. It *was* like Skril to get caught up in something like a rare bird, but she had a bad feeling it wasn't the case this time. The thought of him encountering a group of men like the ones who had attacked her shot worried feelings through her. They quickly turned to anger. If any two-bit thug dared to harm her friend, there wasn't enough magic in Dizhelim to save them.

❦

QUENTIN DUZEN STARED AT THE ENCHANTED PIECE OF glass in front of him. At first, he only saw his own reflection, his short-cropped blond hair and blue eyes. His tunic was wrinkled and his fair skin had circles under the eyes. It had been a busy few days.

The image in front of him melted and was replaced by a view of a room in which three others sat.

The communication prism was a marvel, even to an Academy graduate such as himself. To create the device took high level spells in light magic, transmission magic, sound magic, and a very skilled craftsperson in the artificing of items of power.

They were prohibitively expensive.

"Where are you, Quentin?" the dark-skinned man said.

Quentin didn't like his demanding tone and was going to call him down for it, but realized as he opened his mouth that Ayize Fudu probably didn't mean anything by it. He, like all of them, was probably anxious. It was only Quentin's fatigue that had made him immediately take offense. He closed his eyes for a moment to regain his composure.

"That's not important. What is important is that I have contacted some of our associates and things are going as I have directed."

Ren Kenata leaned his black-haired head nearer to his half of the glass. "As you have directed? A master has been killed. How can you be so calm?" A slight Teroshimi accent tinged his voice, a sign that he too was nervous. Ren was normally very precise and nearly perfect in his enunciation in the common tongue of Ruthrin.

"Sit back, Ren," said Inna Moroz, the only woman among them. She sat with perfect posture, pretty face framed by dark brown hair. The prism's image in the mirror was clear enough that he could see her brown eyes considering him. "Quentin is well aware of what has happened. So, Quen, where are things right now?"

Quentin wanted to smile. Inna always had a way of cutting through everyone else's agenda in a manner that made them want to thank her. Part of that was her natural beauty, of course, but part was also the particular training she had chosen to pursue at the Academy. One had to watch themselves carefully around her or find themself doing something reckless at her mere suggestion.

"As we discussed before, the masters are occupied with choosing the new Master of Prophecy. Tradition dictates that they consider *every* option. It will be several more days yet until they are free to investigate the murder."

"What about the adepts the masters are letting investigate?" Ren Kenata asked.

"I have seen to that. They are not Master Nasir. A few of them have taken to the false trails I have laid. They will be occupied long enough that they won't figure anything out."

"Are you sure?" Ayize said.

"Ayize," Quentin said, "what are you worried about? You have left the Academy. Did you plan on returning? Whether you leave permanently now or later, it's much the same. Do you really think with what we are doing, there will ever be a place for you there again?"

"I...no, but—"

Ren ran his fingers through his hair. "When will you join us?"

"It won't be long. I need to make sure no one has found anything pointing toward us or where we've gone. Once I join you, we can continue with our plans."

"Ayize," Inna said, "tell Quentin what you found out today."

Ayize's face scrunched up like he could taste the words he was about to say. "Izhrod decided to go off on his own, do his own thing."

"Izhrod Benzal," Quentin said. "He always was just short of being a dappled snuffler, rummaging around for treasure in a waste pile, thinking he will become rich. Does he feel that he knows better than us what to do? Is that it? Or does he see some reward that only he can claim?"

"Yes, to both questions. He said, and I quote, 'I'll not wait around for a commoner like Quentin to finally determine the best plan. That could take years. No, I'll take matters into my own capable hands.'" Ayize even managed the whiny, condescending noble's voice Izhrod spoke with.

Quentin shook his head. "No matter. I assume he took Ulfaris with him as well?"

"Of course."

"Well, good riddance to the both of them. We'll continue as planned. Jumping ahead will do nothing but cause mistakes. We'll not work against him, but we will not spend any resources to help him, either. He's made his choice."

"We already told him that," Ren said. "He had nothing but kind words for you and your family."

Quentin smiled at that. "I'm sure he did. If there is nothing else? I could use some sleep before I check up on how things are going with the investigators. Contact me if anything happens outside of the plan. I'll be there soon."

The others said their farewells. The last thing he saw before the glass turned back to a normal mirror was Inna's smirking face.

Quentin understood their anxiety. He, too, had spent most of his life at Sitor-Kanda. He had learned, trained, shaped himself into someone who could act when the days of prophecy came.

Well, those days were here, though things wouldn't happen exactly according to the popular belief.

He and his cohorts were doing what they could to mitigate a bad situation. He wasn't a fool like Benzal, believing he was the savior everyone expected to appear. Quentin was much more pragmatic than that.

The simple fact was that the entire world could not be saved. Instead, a select group would survive. A group he would choose. Others might think him a fiend for what he was going to do, but he recognized it as something else.

It was always better to save a few than to lose all.

❧ 14 ❧

Marla dreamed of flying. She wasn't sure how she was flying, but in the manner of dreams, the how wasn't nearly as important as the act itself.

The land opened up beneath her as she passed north from the Artuyeska region. Trees, mountains, and rivers rushed past her gaze. Then she was into the Cridheargla, the Croagh highlands with its small lakes and bogs and rugged landscape. Villages nestled in the hardy trees, the smoke of cooking fires winding their way up into the air only to be scattered as she flew through them.

A quick turn toward the west showed her the vast expanse of the Grundenwald Forest and beyond it, the great city of Ebenrau. She angled toward the southwest, the continent of Ascesh on her right with its glistening peaks draped with never-melting snow.

Below her, she could see the island of Munsahtiz, the home of the Academy, where she had started her journey. She zipped past the massive complex of buildings and fields, flying south over the Verlisaru Forest, crossing over the Kanton Sea toward Arcusheim, jewel of Sutania.

Ahead of her were the massive mountains called the Shadowed Pinnacles, and beyond that, the Sittingham Desert, but she wasn't going that way. Instead, she looked toward her right where she could somehow see The Great Enclave, Arania, and even Shinyan, with just a tip of Teroshi at the edge of her vision across the Cattilan Sea.

She turned left, toward the east, skimming along the foothills of Ianthra's Breasts until the land opened up in front of her. She picked out the Mellanor Forest and, seemingly carved out of the middle of the trees, the grand city of Satta Sarak. In seconds, she had flown over the city and circled back north toward the Heaven's Teeth. She looked down at the mighty Alvaspirtu River and headed over the small strip of Kanton Sea, back to Sitor-Kanda.

Slowing her flight speed, she skimmed the lawns of the administration area of the Academy. In seconds, she was floating through her window, settling into her bed, and sinking into blissful slumber.

Light between the shutters on that window pierced the room and made Marla's face itch. She wrinkled her nose and rubbed at her cheek, but the warmth remained. Cracking an eyelid only rewarded her with spots that danced before her eyes.

"Ugh," she said.

She guessed she needed to get up, though she didn't want to. Why couldn't she go back to that dream, the one where she was flying over all the world? Oh well. It was well and truly gone now.

Marla was pretty sure what the dream meant, or at least why she had it. The investigation, trying to find out what happened to Master Aeid, was a unique opportunity to go out and see things in the world. She could follow the clues to wherever they led, to a reasonable extent. The thought of it excited her.

She reluctantly tore her blanket off and stood up. First off, some breakfast, then a bath. After that she'd check on Skril. He was probably sleeping in. If there was one person who liked sleep more than her, it was him.

She got dressed and strapped on her weapons. Sure, she wouldn't need them on Academy grounds, but she was accustomed to wearing them all the time, which was at least tolerated, if not encouraged. She felt naked without them.

She hadn't gotten a message from Evon, so he must not have had any contact with Skril. That concerned her a little, but she didn't let it weigh too heavily. Skril had gone off on short leaves before, searching for one kind of knowledge or another. He lost track of time when he was learning. She chuckled at that as she finished her breakfast and headed for the bath.

A half-hour later—she was very efficient with time when it came to bathing—she was knocking on Skril's door. She knocked several times, but there was no answer. She tried the door, but it was locked. As she contemplated picking the lock, a door on the other side of the hall opened.

"Oh," the young man said. "Marla."

She visited Skril often, so she recognized his neighbor. Nawin Culster wasn't particularly friendly toward her, but he wasn't rude, either.

"Good morning. Have you seen Skril?"

"Not in the last day or two, no. I figured he was working with you investigating the master's murder."

"No," she said. The masters hadn't done anything to try to hide the fact that students were investigating, knowing the news would leak out anyway. Not a chance they could keep something like that secret when there were so many people involved, especially since the offer was made to all of those eligible at once. "I was away for a couple of days myself. I just got back."

"Hm. Well, I haven't seen him. If I do, I'll tell him you're looking for him."

"Thanks. I appreciate it."

"Sure."

He closed his door, leaving her to decide if she'd pick the lock on Skril's door. She shook her head. It wouldn't do her any good. It wasn't as if he was trapped in there or anything.

She spent the rest of the day checking up on the other investigators. The ones that were still at the Academy, anyway. Half of them were gone, according to the travel log. No one filled the thing out like they were supposed to. When someone returned, they were supposed to edit the book and indicate they had come back, but no one ever did. If you believed the log book, most of the students went off and had never returned to the Academy at all.

She made a point of signing herself back in since she was there, suppressing a pang of guilt at doing exactly what she had just mentally chastised others for doing. It hadn't seemed important enough to do it right away when she returned the night before.

Marla did find Ailuin, though. The woman had been working on the investigation, but she'd also been going to some of her classes, something Marla hadn't been doing.

"Ailuin," Marla said as she caught her leaving the School of Alchemy.

"Hey, Marla. How are you?"

"Um, I'm fine. How are you?"

"Pretty wonderful. Why wouldn't I be? I'm a student here."

From anyone else, Marla would have taken that for fake optimism and would have become suspicious, but not with Ailuin. She was like that all the time. How could anyone be so downright cheerful, even in the midst of a murder investigation?

"Have you seen Skril?"

"I'm afraid not," Ailuin said. "At least, not for a couple of days. He's been working hard on the investigation. He's not even going to his classes. Why? Do you need anything? Maybe I could help."

"No. It's not a big deal. I was gone for a couple of days and I haven't been able to find him since I came back."

"Ooh. Were you out investigating? Did you find anything? I haven't gone off the Academy grounds. I want to keep up with my studies."

"I had a couple of clues, but they led to dead ends."

"I see. Well, at least now you have fewer clues to follow up on, so that's good."

Marla barely refrained from rolling her eyes. "Yeah. I suppose. Anyway, I better get back to looking for Skril. Have a good afternoon."

The girl smiled, radiating warmth despite the unfortunate pinched look that remained on her face. It was amazing how she barely saw Ailuin's features when they talked. There was such a contrast between how she appeared—like a bitter old woman, but young—and what her true personality was.

"Thank you, Marla. You too. Good luck finding your friend. Oh, and with the investigation. Let me know if you need help with anything."

"I will. Thanks."

Marla went straight to Evon's room from there. He didn't answer his door, either.

"Damn it," she muttered. "What is going on?"

"Are you talking to yourself again?" Evon asked, walking up the hallway. "I've told you about that. People will think you're crazy."

She frowned at him. "People will *know* I'm crazy, you mean."

"Yeah, or that." He nudged her out of the way and put his key into the lock, turning it with a click. "Come on in."

She followed him into the room. "I still can't find Skril. Do you know anything?"

"I know a few things, but nothing about him. At least, not any more than I did last night. Did you check the travel log?"

"Yeah. He signed out to go to the docks, even though he really didn't have to since it's still on the island. Nothing since then."

"He probably did it because he used a horse. It's a long walk. Did you go to the west dock to try to find him?"

"No. He couldn't be there for more than a day. It's not that big. Now that I know you haven't heard anything, I'll probably head over there, though, ask around to see if anyone remembers him being there."

Evon hoisted his pack onto the table. "That's a good idea. I'd go with you, but I need to go back to the masters in less than an hour. They only let me out so I could eat and take a break. We're almost finished. Soon, I'll be able to help you and Skril with the investigation."

"That'll be nice."

"You're not even going to ask me about the selection process for the new master?"

"No."

"Really?"

"Really."

"Why not?"

"Because, Evon, I'm sure they told you not to say anything to anyone. I won't give you the satisfaction of telling me you would love to tell me but that you can't."

He brought his eyes up to meet hers, a hurt expression on his face. He only held it for a moment before it disintegrated into a smile, then a laugh.

"You know me too well. You're absolutely correct, of

course. Damn you and your big brain. You ruin all my best jokes."

She winked at him, but couldn't quite manage a smile. "I'm hoping my brain can figure out what's going on with Skril. I'm starting to worry."

"Me, too. Why don't you head to the docks and see what you can find? When I get finished with the masters—hopefully it's only a couple of hours more tonight—I'll be completely at your disposal to help find him. If you haven't found him already by then."

"Sounds good. Thanks, Evon. I'll talk to you later."

She left his room and went back to her own. The docks were less than a score of miles outside of campus, but she picked up her pack—already stuffed with her typical supplies for almost any occasion or emergency—and pulled on her cloak before heading to the stables.

It was still early evening, but the ride to the docks would take her nearly five hours. Accounting for a few hours of searching—she hoped it wouldn't take longer than that—she wouldn't be getting back to the Academy until morning. Another sleepless night.

She mostly had her horse walk, but brought her to a trot or a canter for short periods of time to make the trip quicker. Surefoot was in good shape, but Marla didn't want to stress her, so she accepted the time traveling as an opportunity to think.

When she finally made it to the docks, she brought her horse to a stable at the edge of town and started checking the inns and taverns to see if anyone remembered Skril being there.

It was the fifth place she went to, a tavern called Kanton Krab, before someone could help her. The tavern keeper, a tall, thin man with a scar all the way down the left side of his face, rubbed his stubble and made a humming noise.

"A short young man with shaggy dark hair, dressed in a blue tunic and brown pants? I seem to recall that he was in here a day or so ago."

Marla had taken a chance that he was wearing those clothes. They were his favorites and she put the chance at better than half that he'd been wearing them.

"Was he asking for information on anything?" she asked.

"Sure was. Smiling and laughing, he was joking with some of the patrons. Nice young man, seemed like."

"Yes, that's him."

"Left with two fellas. One was Shinyin, a little taller than your friend. The other had hair the same color as the boy's, but shorter, about your height, but wider than you. Not fat, mind you, but a bit bulkier than you. Course, you're a dainty thing, compared to the dock workers that come 'round here."

"Do you know where they went?" she asked.

"Nope. I don't pay attention to everyone that comes in the door. I listen real hard when they order drinks or food. The rest of it ain't my business, if you know what I mean."

"I do. Thank you."

She stopped at three more places near the tavern, but got no further information. Before leaving, she checked with the harbor master's office. The Harbor Master wasn't there, of course, not that late at night, but one of his assistants was there, on duty to make sure any vessel coming or going had filled out the proper paperwork and paid their fees.

He seemed to be happy to have someone to talk to. He hadn't seen Skril, but he was able to confirm that the only two vessels to have left in the last day were both barges heading south to Sutania.

With that done, Marla walked back to the stables, got her horse, and made the trip back to the Academy. On the way, she let her mind drift.

She had always found that the best way to solve problems

was *not* to focus on them and will herself to find a solution. Instead, she had learned to frame the situation in a way that presented the available facts, as well as the desired outcome, then let her mind gradually come up with something viable in the background while she tried her best not to think of anything at all. The hours-long horse ride was perfect for that.

Skril was missing. He had been searching for clues, ostensibly about the poison that was native to Shinyan. He had gone to the docks because he had seen in the visitor log that two people from that nation had come to the Academy before the master's murder and then left shortly after. He had apparently found something significant enough to cause him to leave the tavern with two men, one of whom was Shinyin. He had not returned to his room, as far as she knew.

As for the solution she was looking for, that was obvious. She wanted to find her friend. There was no way of tracing him or the two men he had met, not from a busy dock. It wasn't like she could follow a trail in a town.

That was about it. She pondered it for a moment, then purposely emptied her mind and let it drift. With the slow clop-clop of the horse's hooves, she felt herself relax, almost to the point of drowsing. She shook her head to make herself more alert and kicked the mare into a trot for a little while. The cool air brushing back her hair and rushing across her face helped her fight the drowsiness.

She soon slowed her horse to a walk again and tried to enjoy the solitude.

A memory of Skril formed in her mind. It was when he and Evon had joined her for some classes in the Craft Lycad. Specifically, it was in the School of Artifice, an introductory set of classes on how to make items of power. Of course, being a beginner class, it focused more on making the items themselves. At that level, they only learned the most basic of enchanting spells. Adding more powerful magical characteristics came later.

They had thought it would be fun to take the classes together, since they rarely had a chance to be in the same learning environment at the same time. It was a good memory, one that brought a smile to her face.

They didn't forge items for that particular class, but they did cast some. The project they chose was to make pendants for each of them, alike except the stones set in them. Marla's contained a ruby chip, a nod to her red hair. Skril's contained sapphire—just because he liked the color—and Evon's a bit of yellow diamond, on account of his blond hair.

They'd worked on the design for several days. They wanted it simple—they were beginners, after all—but still distinctive. It had to be something unobtrusive, not gaudy, and without edges that could cause problems as it moved around when they were training in other schools.

They settled on a simple teardrop, but with an etched sword crossed with a quill.

It was brilliant, the perfect balance between a warrior's symbol and a scholar's. As they worked on it, the design changed, becoming a bit more complex with the sword and quill transforming from etchings to reliefs and the gemstones being moved to the center, right where the two implements crossed.

They worked for several weeks on them, casting them from the same ingot of gold alloy and then shaping them. They had all become proficient at basic magic by then—though Marla was the only one of the three who had mastered that school—and they took turns casting—in the magical sense, not metallurgical, this time—over each of the three gems.

Skril put a bit of light magic into them so that they glowed softly. That was convenient in all sorts of ways. It let them find the jewelry in the dark, as well as being bright enough to see by, if barely.

Evon refined Skril's spell by giving the pendants the ability to vary the amount of light, from a very soft glow to being bright enough to comfortably read by. Of course, the light was of the color of the gems, so Marla and Skril would have a hard time reading too much by the red and blue glow of theirs, but Evon could use his almost like a small mirrored lantern.

Marla added the functionality of warmth, transforming them into heat sources. She also made it variable, so that at the lowest setting, they would merely feel comfortable when slipped over the head, even if they'd been sitting in a cold room. With a mental prod—infused with a nudge of magical impetus—they could heat enough to warm the hands if the jewelry was cupped in the palms.

They received top marks for the works, which they all appreciated, but that wasn't the most important thing. She wasn't sure how the others felt, but to her, the pendants were a symbol of their friendship. She magically prodded the pendant around her neck, causing it to flare with heat and light. On the dark road, she could see the glow leaking out through the cloth of her shirt. She smiled and allowed the pendant to go back to its base setting.

And just like that, she knew what she was going to do.

It was another two hours before she arrived back at the Academy. She brought the mare back to her home stable, went to her own room, and caught a few hours of sleep. She woke soon after dawn and hurried over to Evon's room, after swinging by Skril's to check one more time if he was there.

He wasn't.

Evon was already up, of course, studying something or another.

"Hey," she said.

"Good morning. Any news?"

"Skril's still not back in his room. I found a tavern keeper who remembered him. Said he left with a couple of guys, one of them Shinyin."

"Oh," he said. "Is that good or bad?"

"I'm not sure it's either." She shook her head. "Anyway, that's not the important part."

"Okay, what's the important part?"

She pulled her pendant out of her top and held it in front of him. "This is."

"Um," he said. He pulled his own pendant out and held it up to her. "Yeah, I've got one, too, remember?"

"Yep, I do." She raised her eyebrows.

He blinked at her. "And?"

"And, Skril has one, too."

"Yes..." His eyes widened. "Yes! He does. We made those together."

"Right."

"And we each put magic in them. Together."

"Yes."

"So...what are you getting at?" he said, tilting his head to the left.

She smacked his shoulder. "You know damn well what I'm getting at, Mister almost-officially-a-master-of-prophecy-and-scrying."

He laughed. "Well, not a master, but at least someone who has mastered the school."

"Still."

"But I get your meaning. That's a great idea. I can work up something to try to locate him with his pendant."

She smiled. Things were finally going her way. "That's what I thought."

"It'll take me a couple of days, though."

"What?"

"You know how hard this stuff is. I'll have to put together a scrying apparatus and the alchemical mixture to fill it with. Then I'll have to attune it using our pendants and maybe another belonging or two from Skril's room. I'm sure you can get in to swipe a couple of things. All that will take some time and a lot of work. The most time-consuming is making the solutions and the device itself."

"Damn," she said. "I was hoping since you had mastered the field of knowledge and everything, you would be able to just, you know..." She waved her hand around in front of her.

"Uh, no. You know better than that, Marla. You've mastered how many schools? You know nothing is easy like that. It may have been in the Age of Magic, but now? Nope. Get me some things from his room, ones with a powerful attachment to him, and I'll get the materials together. The masters have released me, so I can start working on it right away."

She sighed. "Fine. I'll go do that right now. The sooner we can find him, the better. So help me, if he's looking at butter-flies somewhere, I'll strangle him with his own pendant."

Evon gave her a crooked smile and pulled his cloak on. They headed out of the room together.

❦ 15 ❦

The River Road was one of the major thoroughfares in the eastern part of Dizhelim's main continent of Promistala. Named for the mighty Alvaspirtu River and its offspring the Gwenore River, it wound through foothills and stands of trees, tracking the waterways for almost two hundred of their more than five-hundred-mile length. It began its journey at the great city of Ebenrau, in Rhaltzheim, and ended when it split into the Genta Highway going west and the Trail of Sarak continuing on south.

Skril Tossin stood on the River Road, looking southward and wondering what he was doing there. He absentmindedly fiddled with a small, round trinket he always carried. As his fingers slid over the object, little slides and buttons clicked, jingled, and whirred. His horse aimed a big eye at him, watching his hands.

The young Academy adept had gone on a few research trips in his time at Sitor-Kanda, but those had all been controlled and organized affairs.

Not at all like this one.

It was still a shock to him that he was on the road at all.

Sure, he'd traveled the River Road before, but not to where he now stood, somewhere between the Mellafond Swamp and the Heaven's Teeth, the high mountains to the east of the Academy.

The trip began when he tried to follow up on the poison Master Nasir had found in Master Aeid's food and drink, a poison that was made using the Shu root. There was only one place the Shu root grew, and that was in Shinyan.

He remembered that Marla had actually told him about the poison before Master Nasir added it to his notes. Of course she did. Still, with the confirmation of the master, he decided to do something about the information.

One thing led to another and then he had met Lang Zhen and Nazar Menaurum at the docks. They gave him information about a merchant who dealt with imported items, which led him to the lead he was following now.

The thing was, this type of thing wasn't what he did. It was more like something Marla would tackle, charging after the bad guys, ready to beat them up until they told her everything she needed to know.

He wished she was there with him now. He was no fighter, no hero. He was scared just standing there on the road, a road that was patrolled by at least two kingdoms and probably as safe as his room back at the Academy.

Skril looked longingly northward, back toward where the road branched off to the west, toward the Academy. He couldn't see the intersection, of course—there were twists and rising terrain and trees in the way—but he could picture that narrow road toward Dartford and then back over the bridge to the Academy. His home.

He shook his head, angry at his feelings. Was he some child, homesick after only a day or two? No. He was an adept of the Academy at Sitor-Kanda. He had mastered three schools there, had learned and done fantastic things. He'd be fine.

Marla and Evon would be proud of him when he returned, after solving the mystery of Master Aeid's murder. They would see that he could achieve great things, too.

Still, he did wish Marla could have come with him. He hoped she was all right. Maybe he should have waited for her, asked her again to work with him? But that might have risked the trail growing cold. It was already several days old.

No. He'd see this through, solve the murder, and return to his friends triumphant. Skril adjusted his pack as he surveyed the road ahead of him. There were clues to be found yet, questions to be answered. The mystery wouldn't solve itself.

He clicked his tongue and headed his horse south. The merchant he was looking for was named Leul Abrete, a traveling purveyor of exotic items. According to the people Skril had met, he was the only one east of Shinyan itself who might be selling the Shu root. That meant that unless the killer traveled to Shinyan to get the poison or its ingredients, he or she would have had to have gotten it from Leul.

As a traveling merchant, Leul made his way from city to city selling his wares according to a rough schedule. Skril was reasonably certain of where the man would be. Generally speaking, of course. He had just left Munsahtiz and was supposed to be heading south. Skril, traveling light, should be able to catch the slower man towing a wagon with his wares. The Academy adept figured it would take just a handful of days to catch up, maybe a bit more or less depending on exactly when the merchant had left and the condition of the road.

So far, he'd made good time. The road was in excellent condition. It was mostly unpaved this far south of Ebenrau, but it was flat, with few ruts. That meant Leul's wagon would have been rolling along at a rapid pace as well.

There was nothing for it but to keep on the road until he encountered the merchant, so Skril set his mind to wandering and settled in for a journey of a few days.

As luck would have it, he chanced upon a merchant wagon in the middle of the afternoon two days later. It was a boxy thing, about as big as a Gypta wagon, but square instead of rounded on top. And without all the colorful paint. Thinking of the traveling people immediately made Skril think of Evon, who was fascinated by their entire culture, and especially their history.

He felt a pang of regret he wasn't back at the Academy now. It was about time for the midday meal and he'd be sitting in the grass, under a tree, eating with Evon and Marla. He missed them. It was pathetic he was so homesick after such a short time, but he couldn't help how he felt.

He turned his mind back to the wagon. It had packs and items strapped to the sides, which he figured was the reason it was squarer than the Gypta homes. There was a door that made up half of one of the sides that would be opened upward and propped open to double as an awning for when the merchant made it to a city and was ready to trade. Two barrels were secured to the back, no doubt full of water. Between them, a set of steps were folded and strapped tight, leading to a smaller door.

It was a familiar sight. There were many traveling merchants who made the Academy part of their rounds. It was not only because they sold a great quantity of items to the students and masters, but they also bought things made at the schools of artifice, things that couldn't be obtained anywhere else. It could be a lucrative trade, dealing in magical items, and the Academy was one of the few sources for such things.

Skril was in luck. The wagon was pulling off the road, to a clearing that looked to have been regularly used as a stopping place for travelers. It was a hollow in the trees, bordered by a jumble of rocks to the northeast to block the wind, a small stream beyond them. The sun was low in the sky off to Skril's right, afternoon turning to evening. The merchant must have wanted to stop early to get a good place in case others stopped as well.

The man jumped down from the seat of the wagon and walked up to the horses to free them from the traces. He looked to be of average height, with an impressive build. Most of the merchants Skril had seen were a bit overweight. This man looked to be fit. He couldn't tell under the shade of the hat, but Skril thought he was young too, though not as young as Skril was.

The man's clothes didn't reveal much. They were the typical dark pants, white shirt, and dark high-collared coat of a traveling tradesman.

Skril slowed his horse to a walk, wanting to give Leul the opportunity to unhitch his horses and start preparing his campsite. He didn't want to bother the man any more than he had to. A few minutes, and then he'd approach and offer to help Leul start a fire. Then he could ask him about his wares, and especially about selling Shu root on Munsahtiz. The next step of his investigation would be complete.

As planned, Skril dismounted and walked his horse into the clearing just as the merchant finished hobbling his horses.

"Hello there," Skril called out. He hoped he wasn't bothering the man.

The merchant snapped his head toward Skril. "Ho, traveler. Good evening."

"Good evening," Skril said. "Stopping for the night?"

"Yes. There's not another good spot for at least ten more miles. Figured it would be good to stop early rather than to have to pick out the next place in the dark."

"You're a merchant?" Skril asked, mentally kicking himself a moment later for the stupid question.

The merchant didn't seem to notice. He smiled under the dark mustache and swept his arm out toward the wagon. "Yes, sir. Leul Abrete, at your service. Do you need anything?" He looked around. "There doesn't seem to be much of a crowd. It's a perfect opportunity for you."

Skril smiled. "Nice to meet you. I'm Skril Tossin. I can't think of anything right now, but let me ponder and I might come up with something. Can I help you make a fire and share it with you?"

"Surely, lad, surely. Thank you, indeed."

Skril tied his horse off on the branch of a tree at the edge of the clearing and set out to gather any deadwood he could find. It didn't take long. It seemed there had been a storm, or at least some winds, lately. Broken branches were plentiful and he soon had more than enough fuel for a fire.

Once the fire was started, Skril sat on one of the stools Leul had taken out of one of the wagon's compartments. He sat fiddling with his toy as the merchant went about gathering a cooking pot and a triangle to hang it from. It irritated Marla and Evon when Skril fiddled with the object, creating the strange noises, but it helped him when he felt nervous.

"Would you like an ale?" Leul asked.

"Thank you, but no. I have my waterskin."

"Oh, come now. How are we to relax and tell tales if you're drinking water?"

"It's fine. Really."

"Nonsense." He brought a wooden cup to Skril. "I appreciate you being polite, but there's no need. I have a whole barrel of the stuff. Save your water. This will go better with food."

Skril took the cup. "Thank you. That's very kind of you."

"Pfaw," the merchant said, putting water from another barrel into the pot. "Just common decency, is all."

Skril sipped on the ale. "Can I help you with any of that?"

"No. You've done the hard work. Relax and I'll join you in a bit. In the meantime, tell me about yourself. Where are you headed?"

Skril took another sip. "Actually, I was hoping to find you."

"Me?" The merchant turned toward him, then he nodded. "Ah, so you do want to see my wares. You're playing sly, trying to get me to lower my prices."

"Oh, no, that's not it at all. I just...I wanted to ask you some questions."

"Questions, eh? Well, answers are free. Mostly." He chuckled to himself. "What kind of questions?"

Skril gulped down some more ale. His throat was dry all of a sudden.

"It's about Munsahtiz."

"You're from up there at the Academy, I take it?"

"Yes, sir. I'm a student there."

"I see. Shouldn't you be one who answers peoples' questions, then, and not asks them?"

Skril's thoughts came with difficulty. What was he talking about? He took another drink of his ale. "I guess so, normally. These questions are things that you know and that I don't, though."

Skril had lost track of where the merchant was in relation to him. He felt so tired all of a sudden.

"Oh, is that so?" the merchant said. "Then, by all means, go ahead. Ask."

Skril licked his lips. They were dry now, too. He finished the ale in his cup. "Okay. Thank you. I wanted to ask about Shu root. Have you sold any recently?"

"Shu root?" Why did Leul's voice suddenly echo, like he was down a well?

"Yes," Skril said. "Did you sell any at the Academy, maybe at the docks?"

There was no response. Skril turned his head toward where the merchant had been the last time he saw him, but all he saw was the wagon. Where did the man go?

"I'm very sorry about this," the merchant said from right behind Skril. His voice sounded different. Almost familiar. "I really am."

The ground turned sideways, slipping out from under Skril, and he felt himself falling.

❦ 16 ❧

Marla had no trouble picking the lock on Skril's door and letting herself inside. She smirked at the bed, blankets pulled tightly across with no wrinkles, pillow exactly in the center at the headboard. As always, everything was in its place and the room was spotless. She had never seen it anything less than perfect.

She only needed to search for a moment. She grabbed two of his things, scanned the desk in case there was anything that might indicate where he went—there wasn't—and left. She took one step, turned around, and quickly inserted her picks into the lock to relock the door. It wouldn't do for someone else to wander into his room because she left it open.

Evon was already back in his room when she got there.

"Did you get something we could use?" he asked her.

"Yep. I got one of his favorite hats and his pen. Those are two of his most cherished possessions. Other than that silly toy he carries around."

"Great. I got the materials for the locator. I just need to assemble it and put in the fluid."

Marla set the items down and looked over Evon's shoulder as he worked. She was familiar with the concept of a scrying pool and a locator, of course, but she hadn't ever made either one.

The concept was fairly simple. To scry—that is, actually see the subject you were looking for, required a small basin or pool filled with a special alchemical fluid called, appropriately, Scryer's Tears. The magic itself was more advanced than a locator, since it involved not only prophecy—or technically, scrying—magic but also light magic. If the caster wanted to hear, then sound magic was also required.

Evon was not advanced enough in light or sound magic to scry effectively.

The locator required a device, a small, flat dish filled with Scryer's Tears and several drops of another compound called Identification Fluid. Used in conjunction with a map that had already been enchanted, it was possible to get the general location of someone.

"Here," Evon said. "I got enough materials for making two of the locators. There's enough of the reagents to activate both of them. You never know when it might be handy to have one available. I'll show you how to build one. They're fairly simple."

She sat down next to him and they built the locators. It took a little over an hour. The most time-consuming part of building a locator was preparing the fluids and creating the actual components of the locator, but the School of Alchemy and the School of Artifice sometimes had some already prepared. They hadn't, so it had taken almost two days for Evon to get them.

When they were done, Evon wrapped the one he built in a cloth and put it inside a little wooden box just slightly bigger than the locator. The container was built specifically for the dish to fit inside snugly to keep the device from being broken.

He took Marla's locator and added the Scryer's Tears, whispering an incantation over it as he gestured with his right hand. The liquid glowed slightly white. While speaking another spell, he dripped four drops of the Identification Fluid into the dish.

"Hand me that hat, will you," he said. She did so, and he pulled a bit of string from it and dropped it into the liquid in the locator. "Now the pen." She handed that to him as well. He swirled the bottom end of it in the fluid, then shook the liquid off back into the locator's dish. Finally, he took off his pendant and dipped it into the liquid as well, saying something else under his breath Marla couldn't quite make out. It sounded like Alaqotim, the language of most words of power, but she wasn't sure.

The light coming from the liquid changed to a yellow color and Evon removed the pendant, wiped it with a cloth, and returned it to its place around his neck.

"Okay," he said. "Here we go."

He pulled the map closer to him. It had been created to magically depict Dizhelim, tied to the physical manifestation of the land. It was a fascinating thing, and it had taken Evon three months to complete it. She'd helped with some of the spells required since she was better with stone magic. Unlike many spell components, it could be used over and over again.

Evon moved the locator to where the Academy was on the map. The liquid continued to glow pale yellow. He moved it toward the docks, around the northern edges of Munsahtiz, then over toward the northern bridge to the mainland. It still glowed yellow.

As he moved it over the area of the bridge and nearer Dartford, the liquid changed color to more of an orange.

"Ah," he said, and he continued to slide the dish along the map.

When he moved it north, toward Ebenrau, the color went back to yellow.

"Nope." He moved it back toward Dartford, then continued south past the town. As he did, the orange returned and then intensified. When the dish got down past the Mellafond and the Cleft of Surus, the orange deepened.

"Do you think he went to Arcusheim?" Marla asked, watching the dish intently.

Evon slid it farther south on the map, but after a point, it began to lighten toward yellow again as he went toward Arcusheim. He shifted it back up until it was dark orange again, then moved it eastward.

It turned to red.

"Right there," Evon said. "It looks like he's east of the River Road near the southern part of the Heaven's Teeth."

"That's kind of wild territory," Marla said. "What's he doing down there?"

"I don't know, but it's probably not a good place for him."

"I agree," she said. "I'm going to find him."

"Not without me, you're not. Here, let me seal this up. The fluid will be good for another couple of days or so yet before it loses potency, so we can check it again to make sure we're on track."

He slipped the lid over the reservoir on the dish and snapped it in place, then he wrapped it up like the other locator and put it in another little wooden box.

"Let me go grab my stuff and we can leave." She took off running toward her room.

"I'll meet you at the stables," he said after her. "I'll sign us out in the logbook."

Marla and Evon passed through Dartford in the still and

darkness of the night. They didn't stop; it was a long way to where the locator had indicated Skril was.

Evon swayed slightly on his horse and Marla worried her friend had used up too much of his energy creating the locator. It was pretty advanced magic, and she knew as well as anyone the toll casting could take on the body.

"Stop staring at me like I'll drop dead at any moment," he mumbled. "I'll be fine. I'm just really, really tired."

"Do you want to stop and rest?"

"No. Let's go on another hour or two, then we can sleep for a few hours and get started again. Skril's probably moving, too, so we need to go faster, or at least travel for longer each day."

"Okay," she said, "but don't push yourself too hard. After you rest, we can always go harder later on."

"Mmm-kay."

He continued to sway, but didn't fall off, so Marla let it be.

They did stop and sleep for a few hours, getting up as the sun rose to start again. Evon looked to be in better shape after his brief rest.

"I told you," he said.

"Yeah."

They had the horses canter for a while, but fell back to walking. Evon narrowed his eyes at her.

"You okay?"

Marla's eyes flared, then dropped toward the ground. "I can't help feeling like it's my fault. If Skril gets into any kind of danger, I'll feel responsible for telling him I wanted to work alone."

"First of all, don't underestimate Skril. He's not the most expert fighter, but he can defend himself. Plus, he has a few magical tricks up his sleeve, too, you know."

"I know."

"Second, it's not your fault he went haring off after some

clue without taking anyone else with him. If he'd waited until you got back, you would have gone with him, right?"

"Yeah."

"So quit acting like he's a toddler. He's older than you, for Surus's sake. He's capable of making his own decisions."

Marla's mouth turned up into a crooked smile. "Really? Is that why you left in the middle of the night, foregoing sleep, rushing to see if you can pluck him out of any danger he might find himself in?"

"Oh, shut up. It's Skril we're talking about. He'd walk off a cliff while watching an interestingly shaped cloud. Seriously, though, don't be too hard on yourself. Your explanation was reasonable and Skril understood. He certainly doesn't hold it against you. We're all friends, and any of the three of us would do anything for the others. Thus our leaving in the middle of the night."

"I suppose. You seem to be shaking off the spell fatigue."

"I feel much better. I'll be back to my normal, robust self after we get a little more rest tonight."

"That's good," she said. "Do you want to try to use the locator again tonight? Will it drain your energy like that every time, or just the first because you were setting the apparatus up?"

"It won't be quite as bad, but it'll still take a heavy toll. That's complex magic. I think it would be best to wait until we're closer to where he was the first time I cast. That'll give me a chance to recuperate and will also be a more efficient use of the locator."

"Sounds good." It didn't, of course. Marla was anxious to get to her friend. They joked about it, but Skril was outclassed any time he was in physical danger. He could fight acceptably, compared to an average person, but his talents lay in scholarship and thinking. It didn't take much to put him in danger. A wild animal or two could easily do that. She needed to get to him quickly.

Evon was right, though. It would be a better use of their resources to wait to use the locator. She wished she could lend him some of her strength, or that she could cast the necessary spells herself, but she couldn't. She may be one of the most accomplished students at the Academy, but she couldn't do everything. Not yet.

She only hoped she could do what she needed to bring her friend back home.

❧ 17 ❧

Darkness. The world consisted only of darkness, with a few pinpricks of light. Were those stars?

Skril moaned and tried to rub his eyes, but his arms wouldn't move where he commanded them to. A soft flash next to him caused him to jump, or at least try to. All he managed to do was to vibrate his entire body.

His arms and legs were tied and he was lying on what felt like smooth wood. He wasn't sure what the flash was, but he also wasn't sure he wanted to know.

Careless of his desires, the wall at his feet lurched and moved away from him. Oh, not a wall. A door. It opened, flooding the small room with sunlight. He had to clamp his eyelids down tight to prevent it from burning out his eyes.

"You're awake," a voice said. It was familiar, but he couldn't place it. The glare through his eyelids was still too severe for him to see. He wasn't about to open them wide.

The light dimmed considerably as the door creaked closed. The agony the light had played on his orbs lessened. It was still too bright to open his eyes, but he would become accustomed to it in a few minutes.

"Take your time. You've been in the dark for a while."

He refused to take part in conversation until he could see where he was, who he was talking to. The mysterious voice seemed to accept his silence.

After a few minutes, Skril tentatively opened his eyes, blinking rapidly as he tried to focus, squinting to restrict the glare of some type of lamp. Not long after that, his surroundings emerged from the murk.

He was in a small room, essentially a windowless box. There were personal items strewn about the room: paper, writing materials, clothing, drapes and other cloth attached to the wooden walls. And in front of him, looking down at Skril, was a man sitting on what looked to be a bed from his vantage point on the floor.

A man he recognized.

"Quentin?" Skril asked.

"Ah," the man said. "You recognize me. That is either fortunate or unfortunate, depending."

"Depending on what?"

"On you, of course."

Skril closed his eyes for a moment and let his head drop back to the floor, his neck tired from craning to look up. "You think I might be able to sit up?"

"I think not," Quentin said. "Not just yet. The herb I put in your ale will keep you drowsy for a little while yet. I wouldn't want you to fall over and hurt yourself."

"Ale?" Skril said. "Oh, ale. You..." he focused on what Quentin was wearing. That tunic and pants. The coat with the high collar. His mustache was gone, though, as was the hat that had covered his hair. "You were Leul? Why?"

"You would have recognized me had I not disguised myself. Things would have been more difficult had you seen who I was when you first encountered me. All my careful planning would have been for nothing."

"Quentin, I don't understand. What planning? Why did you need to hide from me? Are you searching for Master Aeid's murderer, too?"

Quentin laughed at him. "No. Why don't you rest some more, Skril? We'll talk a little later. I'm afraid it will get a bit bumpy back here in a few minutes. I need to move the wagon."

He opened the door, flooding the back of the wagon with light. Skril squinted against it, but his eyes had become accustomed to the lamp, so it didn't burn as much as earlier.

"Wait. Quentin, why am I here? What are you doing?"

His answer was the door closing in front of him, plunging the tiny room back into blackness. Quentin had taken his lamp with him.

Skril tried to move his arms and legs to stimulate his circulation, but the ropes were too tight. He let his head settle back onto the floor and wondered what was happening.

Quentin Duzen was an Academy adept, like Skril. He had five schools mastered and he was more than a decade older than Skril, but they knew each other. They'd never been friends, but they hadn't been enemies, either. Why had the man tricked him with a disguise and drugged him? He tried to come up with possible reasons, but always kept coming back to one thought.

Skril was in a lot of trouble.

The Academy student dozed and lost track of time. He didn't think it was more than a few hours before he was next thrust from sleep by the sound of a latch clicking loudly in his little prison. When the door creaked open again, it was dark outside, past the pale globe of the lamp Quentin carried. It was set so the light wasn't too bright, which Skril appreciated.

"Are you thirsty?" Quentin asked.

"Yes."

Skril's captor filled a cup from a small barrel strapped to

the back wall, but then seemed to realize Skril couldn't drink from a prone position. Quentin set the cup down and hoisted Skril up onto the bench seat behind him. Once there, the man tipped the cup toward his prisoner's lips.

Skril started to sip, but then turned his head.

"It's not drugged, Skril," Quentin said. "There's no need. You're tied up and locked in the back of a wagon. What reason could I possibly have to give you more of the sleep herb?"

"You could be trying to poison me."

"If I wanted to do that, I could easily inject you with something. I wouldn't even need to do that if I wanted you dead. I could wait a couple of days until you died of thirst or I could slit your throat. There's really no reason not to drink, but if you don't want it..." He started to take the cup away.

"No. I'll drink."

Quentin put the cup up to Skril's lips and the younger man tried to gulp the water down. He hadn't realized how thirsty he was.

After he'd moistened his mouth and finished the water in the cup, he spoke. "Why have you captured me and what are you going to do with me?"

"Well, that's a bit of an involved tale. You see, the clues you're following, the Shu root and all that? It's all a deception. If it means anything, I am sorry it's you instead of someone else. I've always found you to be a tolerable fellow."

"Deception?"

"Yes. I had to lay down several false trails to keep anyone investigating things from figuring out it was me before I was ready for them. The poison and the Shu root, those were false information trails I placed to distract the students investigating the killing."

"You...planted poisoned food and drink at the murder scene?"

"Not exactly. I figured there was half a chance Aeid would succumb to them. It would have made it easier. If he disappeared, the response would have taken much longer, giving me and my associates sufficient time to flee. When those didn't work, however, I decided to use what was already in place to distract, even to sabotage, those investigating what I'd done."

Skril worked through what Quentin had said. He decided it wasn't a ploy. The man was actually confessing.

"You killed Master Aeid?"

"I'm afraid so, Skril. It was unfortunate it came to that, but he was about to do something that would have affected the plans I have worked so hard to implement."

"What plans are worth killing a master for?"

"You see, now we get to the meat of the issue. You are aware, I'm sure, that we are approaching the time of darkness prophesied by the founder of our glorious Academy. It will be a time of testing, of tribulation, perhaps of magic? I don't accept that the only path is for us to hope the Malatirsay shows up to fight the darkness. In fact, I think there is a more...diplomatic solution."

Skril shook his head. "You killed a master of the Academy so you could play politics during what might be the end of humankind?"

"Please," Quentin said. "You surely don't believe all you hear about dark creatures and only one person being able to fight them. It's all symbolic, Skril. Metaphorical.

"Now, I'm sure the danger is real; perhaps it's even as some of the scholars believe, that there will be one person coordinating all the efforts to stem the darkness. Still, that can't be the only solution. What if there was another way?"

"What other way?"

"What if it could be negotiated, if some could be saved without a long, drawn out war?"

"Negotiated? The prophecy says that the animaru will destroy all life on Dizhelim. How do you negotiate with mindless monsters?"

"Come, Skril. How often have you read or heard accounts of this nation or that nation being described as monsters in the histories of different conflicts. Do you really think a force capable of the destruction of all life would not be able to think enough to discuss terms?"

"Terms?"

"Yes. If you believe the part of the prophecy that says the forces attacking Dizhelim cannot be defeated, then it would stand to reason that an agreement to save some would be a better strategy than to fight, and die, in a war with such monsters."

"Quentin," Skril said. "You can't negotiate with monsters. You probably can't even speak to them."

"Ah, but you can. And I have."

"You *what*?"

"I have spoken to some of the animaru leaders and have struck a deal. If we help them to efficiently take control of most of Dizhelim, they will extend their protection to a core group of humans."

Skril looked at Quentin, wondering if the man had lost his mind, or if Skril himself had lost *his*. The older man couldn't have said what Skril thought he did.

"Quentin, please," Skril said.

"No. Don't say any more right now. Just think, Skril. You're smart. Think about what I've said. Ponder what it'll mean if we fight a protracted war that we can't possibly win. Decide if it's better for all to die or for some to live. Just think. I'll bring you some food and we can talk about this later."

Skril opened his mouth to say something, but Quentin put his finger in front of Skril's mouth.

"Just think about it."

Quentin got up and stepped out of the wagon. He left the lamp for Skril to see by, but it didn't matter. The younger man was busy replaying all that Quentin had said, from admitting he killed a master to confessing he was selling out the entire human race.

Quentin came in a half hour later with food. He carefully fed Skril some bread and stew, tipping his cup of water so the younger man could drink. Skril was too busy eating to speak and Quentin seemed content with the silence. When the meal was done, Skril's captor eased him onto the floor again, turned down the lamp, and exited the wagon. Skril took it to mean it was time to sleep.

By morning, Skril's bladder felt like it would burst. It would serve Quentin right if Skril urinated all over himself and the floor of the wagon, but he didn't.

The hour he had to wait for the wagon to open was excruciating. Skril tensed his muscles and tried to get into a position that eased some of the tension, but by the minute, he was aching more and more.

When Quentin did open up the back, Skril didn't wait for the other man to talk.

"I need to pee!" he said. "Fast."

Quentin blinked at Skril, but then seemed to realize he was serious. He helped the captive outside the wagon and then aided him in completing his business. If it wasn't for the pain mixed with relief as he finished, Skril would have been embarrassed. As it was, he figured it served Quentin right.

With that chore done, Skril was helped back into the wagon to await whatever Quentin had in store for him. It turned out that the plan included a cold breakfast and then another conversation.

"I've given you a night to think about it," Quentin said. "I want to know what you think, Skril. Do you think you could be convinced to join us?"

"Join?" Skril asked. He should have known that was what Quentin was getting at the night before, but his mind didn't seem to be working correctly. "You want me to join you?"

"I didn't say that. I'm asking if you think you could. You reacted pretty strongly when I told you about our plan last night."

"I..." Skril started, "was surprised. It was a lot to take in all at once, you know?"

Quentin sat silently, looking into Skril's eyes.

"It's not a choice you get presented with every day," Skril continued. "I mean, saving some people does seem like a better proposition than no one surviving. I'm not good at killing people, though."

"That's not a prerequisite. All I want to know right now is if you would be open to considering being on our side. Before much longer, everyone will have to choose a side. Which will you be on?"

"It does sound reasonable. I could see joining you."

Quentin continued staring at him. "Good to know. I have some things to do for now. We'll talk about it more later." He left Skril sitting up this time as he went through the wagon door and closed it tight behind him.

It was at least three hours before Quentin came back to him. The blond-haired man wore a frown. That didn't bode well for Skril.

The younger man started to say something, but Quentin swiveled his eyes to meet Skril's and the words died on his lips. There was a cold resolve in Quentin's eyes that caused Skril's palms to sweat.

"It's time to make a decision," Quentin said. "There are things that need to be done and I can't waste any more time here. I need you to tell me if you will join us."

All informality was gone. The next thing the prisoner said would likely change the rest of his life.

"I will join you."

Quentin's left eye twitched slightly, but otherwise his expression didn't change one bit. "Why?"

"It's like at the Medica. If someone has an infected limb, it's cut off to prevent the entire person from dying. It's always better to save something rather than nothing."

Quentin stared deeply into Skril's eyes, the blue seeming to flash with light. His shoulders slumped slightly. "I don't believe you."

Skril moved his mouth as if he was chewing on the next words he would say.

"You are simply saying what you want me to hear," Quentin said. "You are trying to prevent any...unpleasantness. You're afraid. As you should be." Quentin shook his head sadly, running his fingers through his short, blond hair. "I'm sorry, Skril, I really am. I wish it could be different."

Quentin reached out and grabbed Skril by the arms. Even if Skril weren't bound, he would not have been able to fight. The other man was larger and stronger than him, with a warrior's build. He nearly lifted the smaller man off his feet as he dragged him out of the wagon.

Skril stretched with his hands, trying to grasp anything he could. He heard a sound like cloth ripping and vaguely felt something in one of his hands, but they were numb from lack of circulation and he could do little more than squirm in Quentin's grasp.

It was twilight, the dim light giving the scene an eerie, gloomy look. The wagon was parked in a clear area about five times the size of the vehicle and surrounded by rocks. Tracks from the wagon's wheels wound out across the loose gravel and sand between two huge boulders and off toward some trees in the distance.

Skril couldn't see the road they had been on.

"I'll make this as quick as possible," Quentin said, removing his coat. "I'm going to immobilize you first, so there are no slip-ups. Don't panic. It'll be over in a moment. I really am sorry it worked out this way. Your moral sense is just too ingrained for me to ever trust you completely in what needs to be done. I hope you understand."

Skril knew he was in his last moments. "Quentin, don't do this. There are other ways. I don't know much. I won't say anything about what I do know. Please, don't—" Skril's mouth stopped in the middle of his plea. In fact, his entire body was locked rigidly in place.

It was a simple spell, one that Skril probably could have defeated if he'd been paying attention. Instead of speaking, he should have been casting his own defensive magic. He only had a few options with his hands bound—spells with verbal or mental components only—but he might have been able to resist the magic Quentin had just cast on him.

But it wouldn't matter. Quentin had mastered five schools at the Academy, including the School of Poisons and the School of Long Weapons Combat. Resisting this spell—a kindness if he really thought about it—wouldn't save him.

It was done. There was nothing Skril could do but to wait for Quentin to finish what he had started.

As the blond man picked up the spear leaning against the wagon, Skril thought of Evon and Marla, the best friends anyone could ask for. He wished he could see them once again before...

A sharp pain in his chest interrupted Skril's thoughts. He saw in his frozen vision the shaft of the spear sticking from his torso, angled in such a way that it had to have gone directly into his heart.

He barely had time to register the fact before his sight faded.

❧ 18 ❧

Marla examined the area around her. She and Evon had stopped south of the Mellafond and the main bulk of the mountains making up the Heaven's Teeth.

It was about where the locator had placed Skril on the map when they had checked in Evon's room.

The vegetation was thick around the road, but noticeably more lush on the western part of the landscape. With both the Mellafond and the Kanton Sea on that side, plants thrived. Not that they didn't do well to the east, at least for a little while. They were still near the Alvaspirtu River, but as a traveler went eastward, the trees got smaller and sparser until they gave way to the rugged terrain of the Tarshuk area and finally to the badlands where the land was cracked and dry, near Broken Reach.

Look around as she might, though, she couldn't see a trace of Skril. Of course, she wouldn't see any tracks, even if he had passed through a few minutes before. The hard-packed dirt of the River Road resisted such things.

"What do you think?" she asked.

"I think this is where he was, or pretty close," Evon answered. That was several days ago, though. Who knows where he could have gotten to since then?"

"Is it time?"

He cocked his head at her. "To use the locator?" She nodded. "Yeah, I think so. We could wander around here for days without finding any sign he had even been here."

"Okay. What do you want me to do?"

Evon shook his head. "We can't very well do it here in the middle of the road. Let's find a place to stop and then I can cast the spell. It isn't something I can do while sitting on a horse."

"Are you...feeling up to it?" she asked.

"Oh, sure. I'm over the effects of the first spell. I'm tired of riding and am a bit saddle sore, but it won't be a problem."

"Good. All right, let's go. Keep an eye out for a good place to stop. I'll do the same."

They found a perfect spot an hour later. It looked to be one that was used for a campsite frequently. There was even a ring of stones set up to use as a firepit. Piles of boulders at the edges of the clear area made it ideal, blocking the wind so the fire ring could be used without too much smoke. There was a small stream nearby, too.

They hobbled their horses, took their saddles off, and brushed them down. Then Evon began unpacking what he would need to use the locator while Marla gathered wood for a fire. It was close enough to sundown that they would stay the night. She looked forward to being warm. The nights had been chilly, especially with the wind whistling past them as they rode.

By the time she got the fire built and started, Evon had everything in place.

"It'll take me a little while to activate the locator again," he said. "You can eat if you'd like."

"No. I'll watch you. We can both eat afterward."

"Suit yourself."

He repeated the spell he had cast at the beginning of their trip. When he had activated the locator, he slid it across the map until it was over their general location, and then he moved it around to get an idea of which direction to go.

South and west both kept the color closer to its baseline yellow. He didn't bother with north since that was where they had come from. When he moved it east on the map, however, the liquid in the locator's dish began to tinge orange.

"We have a direction," he said, and slid it farther toward the west.

A few minutes of fiddling resulted in the locator glowing a deep, burnt orange, almost red. The area was southeast of them, not too far from where they were. At least, it didn't look too far on the map.

"There he is," Marla said. "He hasn't quite made it to the badlands or Broken Reach. Why on earth would he be going out that way?"

"No telling. We can ask him when we catch up to him tomorrow."

Marla smiled at the thought of surprising Skril with their presence. "Should we go now? If we go straight through the night, we could catch up to him before midday tomorrow."

Evon bit his lip as he thought about it. "I don't think we should. I won't be able to cast the spell again for at least a day or two, and it's possible we could get so turned around in the dark that we'd miss him altogether. Then we'll have to back-track after I set up the other locator. I'm not sure if the fluid in the first one will even last long enough for another use."

"I see your point. I'd really like to find him, though."

"Me too."

"But I guess you're right. If we overshoot him or he changes direction, we'd never know at night. At least in the daytime, we might see his tracks. There's no road in that area, so there's probably a trail to follow."

Evon looked at the map again. He narrowed his eyes like he was trying to memorize exactly where the locator showed Skril was. "We'll start an hour before dawn. By the time we need to go off the road, it'll be light enough to see any trail." He turned his head toward where they would be going. "Hang on, buddy. We'll see you soon."

"That sounds like a reasonable plan," she said. "Why don't you rest up a bit while I make us some dinner? You look tired."

"Thanks. The spell takes a lot out of me."

"I'll let you know when it's time to eat."

When dinner was ready, they ate a quick meal and went to sleep. Evon needed the rest, and Marla wasn't going to argue with a little extra sleep to balance out the deficit from the preceding two days. There was no need to stay up to keep watch. The road was safe enough and Marla counted on her awareness to wake her if any animals came near.

In the morning, they headed out on time. They witnessed a gorgeous sunrise, reds and oranges streaking across the sky slightly to their left. Marla wished they were with Skril already. He had a special fondness for sunrises.

The two Academy students left the road at the approximate place they had decided would be most efficient. The River Road continued south as the two headed southeast through the bushy vegetation there.

There was a trail of sorts, of matted down vegetation. From the many hoofprints and wheel tracks, it was clear that a wagon had gone through recently. The trees were spread out enough for the wagon to have made it between them.

The trail headed in the same direction they were going, so they simply followed it. Marla wasn't sure if that was a good thing or not. It did make their rate of travel better, but she wondered what a wagon had to do with Skril. Did it follow him or did he follow it? Or maybe he was with the wagon. But if so, why?

"I don't like this," Evon said.

"I don't either, but I'm not sure what to make of it."

As they traveled, the plant life grew more sparse and the trees got smaller in size. They were getting to the edge of the Tarshuk region, full of scrub and stunted, twisted trees like juniper, chaparral, wirebrush, and chokeberry bushes. Marla imagined Skril stopping to inspect one of the Codaghan's Spike trees, with its prickly exterior and twisted trunks.

"Smoke," Evon said, interrupting Marla's thoughts.

A dark plume rose ahead of them, behind some rock formations. It wasn't from a cooking fire, not unless someone was burning their lunch, along with a tent soaked in pitch. The thick, black smoke was too heavy for any ordinary campfire.

Marla kicked her horse into a gallop, racing toward the dark column spiraling up into the sky. She considered for a moment that it could be a trap, bandits waiting to ambush her, but then tossed the sentiment from her mind. The gods help anyone stupid enough to ambush her and Evon.

The two barreled around some boulders and passed in between two of the largest. Ahead of them in a clearing were the burning remains of a wagon. Worse, there was something in front of the destroyed vehicle.

A lump of familiar cloth. A yipper—the nickname for a prairie shrieker—was approaching it, sniffing the air. The dog-like scavenger would call its brethren if it found anything edible. After sampling the fare itself first.

Marla slowed her horse just enough so she could jump from the saddle. She nearly fell on her face as she slid to a stop in the loose dirt, frightening the animal away.

"Get out of here, you filthy beast," she said, drawing her

sword. It disappeared behind a rock.

Evon dismounted conventionally, after he had stopped his own horse. They both stood for a brief moment, looking down at what they could now see clearly was a body.

Skril's body.

Marla dropped to her knees and turned him so she could see his face. His arms and legs were bound with ropes. As she settled him to lie on his back, she spotted the spill of blood down the front of him.

So much blood.

It had dyed the entire front of his shirt red, soaked into his pants, and made a red blotch on the soil.

She felt for a pulse in his neck. Nothing.

Evon was next to her. She didn't even remember him coming close. She tried to clear her mind to cast a simple life magic spell. One to detect life. She flubbed the simple casting twice before finally being able to do it correctly.

The spell revealed no spark within the body in front of her.

"No!" she shouted. "No. Why? How? We were so close. How could this happen?"

She swept a stray lock of Skril's shaggy hair out of his face and stared at her friend. He was gone. Just like that.

Marla pulled Skril's head to her chest and let her tears flow. Skril. Poor, perpetually smiling Skril. Someone had tied him up and stabbed him in the heart. And the whole time, she and Evon were only hours away.

She vaguely registered Evon's hand on her shoulder. She didn't react. A little time. That's what she needed. Some time to process, to...what? To accept her friend was gone? To come to terms with being so close but still not getting there in time? That would never happen.

Marla continued to hug Skril's head to her as she wept. It was some time until she regained awareness of her surroundings. Evon sat a few feet away, his head hanging and his eyes red and puffy.

She set Skril down and opened her arms toward her friend. He moved over to her and they held each other, crying anew.

Her rapid breathing had slowed and she seemed to be able to think again. She squeezed Evon one more time, then patted his back and released him. She shook her head sadly as she looked at Skril once more.

The body was cold. He hadn't just been killed. Looking around more carefully, she saw that the wagon had been burning for a while, too. Some kind of merchant wagon, by the few pieces that remained.

"Someone killed him and just left his body here," she said. "Why burn the wagon? Was he traveling in it? Where did he get it, and where is his horse?"

"I don't know," Evon said. "I don't know why someone would burn the wagon but not Skril's body. It's almost as if they wanted someone to find him."

Marla's head snapped up. "That's right. That's exactly it. They wanted us to find him, to warn us. Whoever he was following out here must be mixed up in Master Aeid's murder. It might even be the murderer herself."

"Or himself."

"Quick, let's check what remains of the wagon. See if there are any clues there."

Evon started toward the wagon.

"Wait," she said and her friend stopped. "Don't move yet. I want to look at something."

Marla got to her feet and walked slowly around the area. She completed a circuit as Evon stood there and watched.

"There are tracks from the wagon coming in here," she said. "But look, over here, there are horse tracks going back out. It looks like...uh, three sets? That would be two horses that pulled the wagon and one more. Skril's horse. Okay, let's check out the wagon. I didn't want us to walk through the tracks before I got a chance to look them over."

They inspected the smoldering remains of the wagon, but found only a few bits of metal and glass.

"What are we going to do, Marla?" Evon asked. "We should take Skril back with us so he can have a proper funeral."

Marla looked to the body and then back to Evon. "I don't know. If we go back to the Academy now, we won't be able to follow his killer. If we don't, we might be able to catch up to the bastard and not only get justice for Skril, but probably solve the master's murder, too."

"Are we going to take Skril with us?"

"We only have two horses. Carrying his body could get messy in a day or two. What would he want us to do?"

Evon looked uncomfortably at the corpse of their friend. "He didn't really think there was anything special about a dead body. Remember when old Master Sinone died and he told us how he believed that once someone was dead, whatever power or magic they had moved on and the body was like any other natural thing, something to return to the dirt in one way or another?"

"I remember. He did tell me one time that he wanted things to be simple when he died. 'Just put me on a simple pyre and be done with it,' he joked. Do you think he really meant it?"

Evon sighed. "I think he probably did."

"Let's do it, then."

It only took a few minutes to find wood for a pyre. Despite there being fewer trees than where they had last camped, the area was not frequented as often, so no one had collected the dead branches that had fallen. They also didn't need to cut the fuel into smaller pieces.

Marla helped Evon place Skril's body on top of the wood they had stacked. They had already cut off the ropes and now they arranged their friend as if he were simply sleeping, arms crossed over his chest, covering the wound that had killed him.

Welts and scrapes circled Skril's wrists, made by the ropes rubbing his skin until it had bled. She pulled the sleeves of his coat down to cover them, gritting her teeth to keep herself from shouting profanities to the sky.

"You were the best of friends," she said to him. "I didn't tell you enough how much I appreciated you, how much it meant to me that you took time to talk to me all those years ago. You were always selfless and caring, and I repaid that by rejecting you when you asked for help in the investigation. My..." Her voice broke and she cleared her throat, blinking rapidly to clear the tears. "My choice killed you, and I'll have to live the rest of my life knowing that.

"I'm so sorry, Skril, that I didn't live up to the friendship you blessed me with. It's too late to make amends, but I promise that I will find who did this and I will kill him or her. It's all I can do now."

She looked to Evon, no words left for her to say. He closed his eyes and shook his head, his whole body quivering. It was fine. He could say what he needed in his own mind.

"May you find that there is more to the world than this simple life," she said. "May you be happy wherever you have gone."

With that, she cast the basic fire spell Flame Wash. Jets of fire shot out of her hands, catching the wood beneath Skril aflame. Soon, it grew to a raging inferno, so powerful the two had to step back several feet from the heat.

They stood silently, watching their friend disappear in the flames.

❧ 19 ❦

arla and Evon watched the conflagration, each lost in their own thoughts, until there was little left but ash and smoldering remains. The slight breeze was constant, but even standing upwind, the sickly-sweet scent of burning flesh and clothing scourged Marla's nose. She wrinkled it, but remained in place. It was a sign of respect, something she wished she had shown when Skril was alive.

After what felt like a dozen hours, she turned to Evon. They had both shed all the tears their bodies could provide. She imagined she looked much as he did, with red, puffy skin and dark circles surrounding her eyes. Their gazes met and they both nodded stiffly.

"Are you ready to find who did this?" she asked.

His upper lip on the left side curled up in a snarl and he growled softly under his breath. "Definitely."

Marla took one more look around the area, at the ashes of the pyre, the ashes of the wagon, and the rocks standing as silent sentinels, witnesses to the tragedy. She mounted, located the trail she had found earlier, and started her horse walking.

It didn't turn out to be as easy as Marla would have thought. She'd had some training at the Academy on how to track, but she wasn't even close to mastering that school in the Applied Knowledge Lycad.

When they had started, there was only one trail going back, but they soon ran into others. Who were these people, roaming about in the wilderness and leaving tracks everywhere?

"I'm not exactly sure we're still following the same trail," she admitted to Evon. "One of those offshoots we passed could be the real one. Hell, we even crossed over the original wagon trail we followed before."

"Just do your best. I'm no good at tracking, so it's all you."

Marla spat as the wind blew something into her mouth. She wasn't sure if it was a bug, a seed pod, or something else. It was usually better not to find out. "This one is going back toward the road, I think. If it gets there, we may lose it altogether."

Evon didn't have time to respond. His head snapped to the other side of Marla and his mouth dropped open.

"What—?" she started, turning in her saddle to follow his gaze.

Seven—no, eight—dark shapes burst out of the foliage. Coming straight for them.

"What the hell are those things?" she finished.

She almost turned to gallop away, but the creatures were moving too fast. The horse might be able to beat them over a distance, but it took time for one to build up speed. They'd reach her and tear her out of the saddle before her mare reached a fast enough pace.

No, she'd rather meet them face-to-face, with weapons out.

"Go," she yelled at Evon as she jumped from her saddle and drew her blades.

Movement in the corner of her eye told her Evon didn't do what she told him. Instead, he dismounted and drew his own sword as he swung a shield onto his arm from where it hung on his saddle bag.

"Stubborn, willful, son of a..." she said as the monsters approached.

They were humanoid, even though they loped fluidly on all fours as they ran, almost as if they were half—or more—animal. They ranged in color from dark grey to a deep black. Their heads, larger than a human's in proportion to their bodies, had oversized eyes and mouths with pointy, glistening teeth protruding from the latter. Sharp-looking claws tipped their fingers and toes.

None of them carried weapons. At least she and Evon were lucky for that.

The first of the creatures reached her and didn't slow a bit; it only lunged and swiped at her with its claws. She stepped to the side and deflected the limb with her dueling dagger, and then slashed with her sword.

It scored a hit. The monsters were fast, but weren't particularly skilled in combat. She and Evon would carve through them in moments.

Her encounter with the first creature positioned her so that none of the others could reach her, her attacker's body blocking them. Four of them slid to a stop and twisted their bodies to reach around to her. Three more slowed and headed for Evon.

Marla wheeled to engage with the five that had chosen to attack her and her eyes went wide.

The one she had slashed didn't seem any the worse for wear. A line of mud-colored blood adorned its chest, but that didn't affect its movement at all.

"What the—?"

She barely evaded the claws of two of the creatures attacking at once. A third set scored a shallow slash on her left shoulder. It was mostly mitigated by her heavy leather armor and cloak, but she felt the contact.

Gritting her teeth, she whirled into action, spinning and lashing out with both of her blades. She managed to cut three fingers off one of the creature's claws and to gash another's arms, but the monsters didn't seem to feel pain. They continued to attack with no indication that they'd been struck.

Another one landed a solid slash on her arm, tearing the skin through the flexible leather where the vambrace and rerebrace met. She hissed in pain and ran her sword through the offending monster, then kicked its body off her blade.

Only, it wasn't a *body*. The creature didn't slump or fall; it simply came at her again.

"I can't seem to hurt them," she called out to Evon. He was evading and striking at his own foes, already breathing loudly.

"Me...either," he panted.

Marla ducked a swiping claw and jumped out of the way of another attacker. They were closing in on her, nearly climbing over each other to get to her. Snapping teeth appeared right next to her face and she slammed her elbow into the thing's jaw, forcing its mouth closed. She couldn't keep this up much longer. There were too many of them, and if she couldn't kill them, what was she going to do?

Two of her aggressors seemed to think Evon was a better target. They headed toward her friend, leaving only three to attack her.

"Oh, no you don't," she said. That many would definitely overwhelm Evon.

She brought a spell to mind and cast it. Fire missile was a

relatively low-level magic, but because of its simplicity, it needed no gestures or verbal components. Marla simply willed the magic into being and directed the attack.

The pellet of condensed fire punched through the shoulder of one of the creatures heading toward Evon. It screeched and stumbled, then turned back to her. It bared its teeth and mindlessly charged her, apparently forgetting all about Evon.

"Evon, use fire. Fire Missile hurt it."

She immediately cast the spell again, this time maintaining the casting for two seconds. Four of the pellets flew out, each one doing damage.

That was more like it.

Her dagger went back into its sheath while she slashed and parried with her sword. More importantly, she continued to cast fire magic at the creatures. One of them disappeared after she had hit it several times. She half expected it to pop back into being right beside her, but it never did.

With the success of Fire Missile, she tried Flame Wash, spraying flame over two of the monsters at a time. One caught fire, while the other received serious burns. Both screamed.

Weakened as they were by the magical fire, she was able to cut into them more effectively with her sword as well. Wounds that would be deadly to normal enemies still didn't kill them, but a lost arm affected how one of them could fight.

She took several appendages for that very reason.

The battle was long and bloody. She and Evon ended the final creature, each of them spraying it with fire at the same time, and they both slumped with fatigue. She was bleeding from several cuts on different parts of her body and Evon was even worse off.

In all, two of the eight disappeared when they apparently

received enough damage. The other six lay dead at their feet. She didn't know what was with the disappearing ones, but as long as they didn't reappear, she wouldn't worry about it.

Marla shuffled over to Evon. "Are you okay?"

He looked askance at her. Blood dripped down the left side of his face from a gash on his forehead and his right arm hung limp. With slashes all over him, he definitely didn't look okay.

"I'm alive, which seemed beyond my abilities until you figured out the fire thing. Good job on that, by the way."

"Pure accident." She moved slowly over to her horse, which had the good sense—or lack thereof—to stay in the area. She pulled out a bag of bandages from her saddle bag. "Let's get these cuts bandaged up so we don't die slowly of blood loss. Those damn things better not have given me a disease."

"Come here," he said. "I can cast a healing spell. It's not that powerful, but it can close up some of your cuts."

"Use it on yourself. Yours are worse than mine."

"No, I'm not—"

"Evon, don't argue with me. Look at your cuts and look at mine. Heal yourself. If you want to, and if you still have the strength left after you've finished, you can heal me. Okay?"

Evon grumbled but reluctantly agreed.

"I really need to learn some magical healing," she said. "I've mastered mundane healing—mainly for the anatomical knowledge—but magical healing would be so much better. It never seemed to be worth the trouble. I figured I'd always have the Medica, at least until I leave the Academy. I expected that day to be a long way off."

Evon nodded as she spoke, casting healing magic over the worst of his cuts. His eyes were already closing. He'd need sleep after this.

Marla limped over to where a few of the dark creatures'

bodies were. "What are you?" she asked, pushing on one with her boot.

Her inspection didn't last long. She shuffled back to Evon. A long cut on her left thigh made it painful to walk normally. It would be days before she walked right.

"We should rest," she said, "but I don't want to do it here. These things give me the creeps. How about we ride for a way and then stop to sleep?"

"I'm with you," Evon said. He swayed like he was going to fall asleep and tumble over right there. "I don't want to be here if more of those things find these."

Marla hadn't thought of that, but it was a good point. "Can you ride?"

"I will."

"Good enough. Let's go."

The main road was only a few hours away. When they got to it, they traveled north on it until they found a suitable camp site. They found themselves at the spot they used as a campsite the day before.

They dismounted near the fire ring they had used before. Once they settled in, they could have some dinner, clean their wounds more thoroughly—there was a stream no more than a hundred yards away—and then they could get some rest. Maybe what they needed to do would be clearer after a little sleep.

Marla had just taken her horse's saddle off when the crunch of horse hoofs on the dirt path indicated that someone else had joined them.

"Marla? Marla Shrike. Is that you?"

✵ 20 ✾

Marla spun toward the sound. She knew that voice.
"Ailuin?" she asked, incredulous. "What are *you* doing here?"

The slender, pinch-faced woman smirked. "I would guess the same thing you're doing here. Looking for murderers."

Marla must have grimaced because the other woman flinched as if Marla had raised a hand to attack her.

"Marla? Are you all right?" As Ailuin's eyes scanned Marla, they widened. "Oh, my. You're hurt. What happened?"

"Did someone attack you?" another voice, this one male, said.

She hadn't even noticed Erlan Brymis on his horse, off to the side of Ailuin. He was tall and could be described as hefty, with a warrior's physique. Sitting on his horse, in his heavy tunic, he almost looked like a knight.

Two Academy adepts, and both of them investigators of Master Aeid's murder. It occurred to Marla—too late—that Ailuin had been talking about the investigation. She couldn't know about Skril. Could she?

"You might as well come join us," Marla said. "It'll take a while to tell it all."

The pair dismounted and joined her and Evon.

"First of all," Marla said, "why are you here?"

"No," Ailuin said in a tone that indicated that it was not a discussion. "First thing is to get your wounds all healed up."

That's right. Marla had almost forgotten. One of the four schools Ailuin had mastered was the School of Magical Healing. Hers and Evon's wounds would be nothing to a healer of Ailuin's caliber.

"Thanks, Ailuin," Marla said. "That would be great. Take care of Evon first, please. His are worse than mine."

Ailuin smiled at Marla and then turned and smiled even more at Evon. "Hi Evon."

"Hi, Ailuin. Erlan."

It only took a moment for the healer to finish with Evon. Then she turned her attention to Marla. A cooling wave of healing magic washed over Marla, and the aches and pains that she'd believed would be with her for the next several days were gone. She took in a deep breath.

"Oh, that feels fantastic. Thank you."

"You're welcome. Now, as to why we're here, it should be obvious. We're searching for Master Aeid's killer. Isn't that why you two are here?"

"No," Evon said. "Not really."

"Oh," Ailuin said. "Well, once Master Nasir gave us the alchemical report that the Shu's Bite was found in Master Aeid's food and wine, we started looking. Everyone knows the poison is made from Shu root, which only grows in Shinyan.

"Well, we checked with the west dock for visitors from Shinyan. One thing led to another, and we found out about a merchant that frequents the Academy who carries Shu root when he can get his hands on it. His name is Leul Abrete.

Anyway, he's a traveling merchant and his normal route takes him from the Academy down toward Arcusheim, so we came looking for him. We had hoped he'd be able to tell us about anyone he sold the root to."

"We haven't found him yet," Erlan said.

Things had started to make sense to Marla. "Nor will you."

"What?" Erlan said.

"Let me tell you why *we're* here."

Marla explained how they had worried for Skril and how they had made the locator, figuring out their friend was essentially where the four adepts were sitting now. She detailed how they had tracked him, with the locator and good old-fashioned trail-following, to the area surrounded by rocks.

She and Evon took turns telling the story, but when it came to the part where they had found Skril, Marla took over. Evon could barely get a sentence out. The hurt was too fresh. Marla focused on speaking and tried to distance herself enough to get through the tale.

"And we burned him in a pyre and started searching for who I think is your merchant. It was all a ploy to trap any of the investigators."

"But why?" Ailuin asked, hand still in front of her mouth from the shock of what she'd heard.

"They wanted to get rid of any who might solve the mystery and find them," Erlan said.

Marla nodded. "Yes, but there's more. I think they deliberately set out several different strings of clues. I tried to get information in Hamrath and Dartford and was attacked in both places. I still don't know which was the true trail to follow, but it doesn't matter now."

Ailuin's thin eyebrows shot up. "Doesn't matter? Why do you say that?"

"Because at this point, I couldn't care less about the investigation of Master Aeid's murder. I want to find the bastard who killed Skril, and then to practice some of the techniques Master Iryna taught me to see if there's anyone else I can kill for it."

Ailuin stared at Marla as if she had suddenly grown wings. Bat wings. Marla met her eyes calmly. Master Iryna was the Master of the School of Interrogation and Coercion, commonly referred to by some students as the Torture School.

"I'm with her," Evon said. It was Marla's turn to widen her eyes. "Luring Skril to this place, tying him up, then killing him deserves nothing less. I don't know any of Master Iryna's techniques, but I'm willing to learn them for this."

Erlan cleared his throat, obviously uncomfortable. "You still haven't told us how you got all cut up."

Marla was still having a staring contest with Ailuin. She blinked at Erlan's question and looked toward him, tilting her head slightly.

"Oh, yeah," she said. "Well, as we were following what we thought might be the right trail, these creatures attacked us."

"Creatures?" Erlan asked.

"Yep. They were human-shaped, but their skin was dark—different shades from light grey to charcoal colored—and they had sharp claws and teeth."

"They were also basically immune to normal weapon attacks," Evon said. "We could cut them, but it didn't seem to do anything. We finally figured out they were weak to fire."

"To fire," Ailuin repeated.

"Flame Wash, Fire Missile," Marla said. "We haven't mastered the School of Fire Magic like Erlan here has, but we can cast some of the basic spells."

Erlan sat up straighter at that. "The fire magic killed them?"

"Yes," Marla said.

"Can we go see the bodies?" He sounded a little too excited about the whole thing.

"How about in the morning?" Marla said. "It's about to get dark. I'd rather do it in the daylight. I don't think there will be a problem with scavengers. Those creatures smelled foul. Unnatural."

Erlan nodded, though he didn't look too pleased.

Marla looked at Ailuin again. "What about you two? After you look at the bodies, what are you going to do now that you know the merchant was a trap?"

"I don't know," she said. "I suppose we can decide in the morning, after we've looked at your monsters. Someone should probably go and tell the masters about unidentified creatures roaming around and attacking people. It sounds like you two aren't going back for a while."

"Not until we've found the one who killed Skril," Marla said. "You know, there's more than a fair chance that once we catch up to the killer, we'll be able to find out more about Master Aeid's murder. It may be the same murderer. You could come with us."

"We'll think about it," Ailuin said. "There's really no reason to rush into a decision. Let us take care of our horses and then we can eat something. Tomorrow is soon enough to make plans."

Marla gave the other woman a crooked smile. "Fair enough." Ailuin always was one to keep her composure and keep her keen mind on track, no matter what the circumstances. She and Evon could use her skills in their hunt. Erlan's would come in handy, too, for that matter. It wasn't every day four Academy adepts with mastery of more than twenty schools between them had the chance to combine their talents toward one goal.

"Here, let me help with that," Evon said, walking over to

Ailuin's horse and patting it on the cheek before loosening up the girth strap so he could take the saddle off.

Marla's grin grew toward a proper full-mouthed smile that crinkled her eyes when Ailuin patted her hair and straightened her robes before moving over to Evon.

"Thank you, Evon," she said sweetly. "That's so very kind of you."

Marla shared a look with Erlan and he chuckled.

"Oh, hells," Marla said. "I might as well help you, too. Just don't get any ideas."

"Perish the thought," the man said.

I n the morning, the four got up, ate a quick breakfast, and were on the way to the corpses of the dark crea- tures before the sun had even shown itself fully in front of them.

Marla felt great. After their battle the day before, she had expected to have several long days of pain as she healed, but Ailuin's healing erased it all, and she woke refreshed and ready to continue with her hunt. After showing the other two adepts the bodies of her attackers. She really needed to get some healing magic in her repertoire.

It was difficult to see too far ahead because they rode straight into the sun, but Marla led the others slowly toward their destination by focusing on the ground a few feet ahead of them. When they finally got to the spot, she swung her eyes up to gaze upon the whole of their previous day's battlefield.

There was nothing there.

She twisted in her saddle, looking at the area around them. It was the same place. She recognized the rock forma- tion to the north and the crushed foliage where the creatures had come charging toward them. There was even a little bit of the creatures' blood, though it was more black than brown after sitting for so long.

"What?" Evon said behind her. "Where are they?"

Ailuin and Erlan sat in their saddles, looking around with confusion on their faces.

"I don't know," Marla said. "They're gone. This is the place, but the bodies aren't here."

"Were they dragged off by animals?" Ailuin asked. Marla felt affection for the older woman that she didn't disbelieve their story immediately.

Erlan dismounted and searched the ground. One of the schools he mastered was the School of Woodcraft. Though tracking was its own school, the two overlapped. He was much better at reading trail signs than she was.

"No," he said. "There aren't any drag marks. There are prints, though, going that way." He pointed toward the south. "They look like these others that came from over there. They're nothing I recognize, sort of a cross between a person, a hunting cat, and a wolf."

"But how?" Marla asked. "We killed them. How did they get up and walk away?"

"Regeneration, maybe?" Ailuin said. "Some of the legendary magical creatures could do that. You did say that only magic harmed them. That's another trait some monsters in the stories had."

"You believe in legendary creatures?" Evon asked. "Like spirtu, ilyu, or finchoi?"

Ailuin raised her chin. "After studying at the Academy for so long, there are few things I would disbelieve on their face. Whether something exists or not must be proven—or disproven—to me before I will make a firm decision about them."

"Oh," he said. "Yeah. I guess you're right. Who are we to

not believe in something when we do things the rest of the world wouldn't believe possible?"

"Exactly," she said, forming her pinched face into a smile.

"That's great and all," Marla said, "but we're talking about half a dozen monsters that woke from the dead and continued on whatever rampage they were on when they found us. We have to follow them."

Ailuin shook her head. "And what would we do when we found them?" she asked. "If they don't stay dead, what are we to do, kill them over and over again until we get tired and they kill us for good?"

"I don't know, but we can't just let them run loose. Most people don't have magic. Can you imagine what even a handful of them can do to normal people? Besides, two of them disappeared when we did enough damage to them. Maybe if we continue to attack them after they're dead, they'll all disappear for good as well."

"It's worth a try," Evon said. "If you two don't want to come with us, we'll understand, but Marla and I are going to follow them. I couldn't live with myself if they attacked some travelers and killed them. Sitor-Kanda is called the *Hero* Academy for a reason, and it's not just that the Malatirsay is the prophesied hero of humankind."

Evon swung back into his saddle and turned his horse toward the south.

"Hold on there, Mr. Impatient," Erlan said. "Give me a chance to get back on my horse. I'll lead you. Don't go stomping through the trail and making it difficult."

Evon smiled at the bigger man. "Thanks, Erlan."

"I'm coming, too," Ailuin said. "As you say, it's our responsibility. Maybe we can figure out how to kill them permanently."

Erlan took the lead, leaning forward in his saddle and walking his horse to study the trail as they went. Marla could see the tracks but didn't try to rush him. He was obviously checking to see if any smaller trails peeled off the main one. She didn't like the thought of stumbling into the middle of an ambush.

"Huh," Erlan said soon after they started.

"What?" Marla asked.

"Oh, there are some other tracks that pass through this area, heading back toward the main road. It looks like three sets of horse prints. It probably doesn't mean anything. Those creatures didn't ride horses, did they?"

"No."

Erlan shrugged and they continued on. A few hours later, they were all surprised to see the smaller set of the creatures' tracks join up with a larger trail.

"It's a large group moving together," Erlan said. "The same type of creatures, it looks like. They all have the malproportioned, clawed limbs. Some of them seem to walk with their hands as well as their feet."

"Yeah," Marla said. "We saw that. When they charged us, they got down on all fours. They're fast. How many do you think there are?"

"Don't know. A lot. It's tough with all the overlapping tracks. It could be a couple dozen or it could be several hundred keeping in relatively tight formation with a consistent width."

"Wait," Evon said. "It sounds like you're saying they might be traveling in ranks. Do you think they're smart enough to do that? Like, actual troops in an army?"

Erlan continued to scrutinize the tracks. "I'm not sure. I was just saying that the number of them could vary. A group ten wide could be a few rows deep or it could be thirty rows deep. After a point, it's hard to tell. I think we're dealing with at least two or three dozen, maybe as much as three or four hundred. Sorry I can't be more exact."

Ailuin shaded her eyes from the sun, which had climbed toward its apex. "You can't simply put your ear to the ground or taste the dirt to figure it out?"

Evon started and looked at her just in time to catch the wink she threw at him.

"You can't—" Erlan began and then chuckled when he saw her smiling. "Okay, Master Alchemist, very funny. Can you whip up a potion that'll do the same thing?"

"Perhaps," she said, "but there's really no time. How far ahead are they, do you think?"

"Based on how dried out the broken branches on the bushes are, I'd say a few hours. Not much more. We can probably catch them if we try. We won't have to search for the trail with it this blatant."

"I'm going," Marla said.

"Me too," Evon agreed.

"I suppose we should all go," Ailuin said. "Someone will need to heal you two when you stumble into hundreds of indestructible monsters. Ianthra save me from the bravery of fools."

They followed the trail for three more hours before they heard their quarry ahead of them. The sounds were not what Marla would expect from an organized military group. There was no jingling or clanking, and no commands barked out as they would be with a human host. Instead, there was the thumping of feet and an occasional noise that could have been speech, but it was too far for her to recognize as such.

She and Erlan left the horses and the other two humans at the bottom of a small hill and sneaked up to the top to peek over at the monsters.

"Be careful not to skyline," Erlan said.

"Psht," Marla scoffed. She knew enough about tracking not to make that stupid mistake.

She scanned the landscape ahead of them. There were still

trees and scattered bushes in the area, though they were becoming thinner as they headed to the southeast, transitioning from the Tarshuk region to the barren area that used to be called Lusnauqua. Weaving through those trees was a force of dark figures.

"Two hundred?" she asked.

"Yeah," Erlan said. "Maybe a little less. Still, that's a lot. Eight of them cut you and Evon to ribbons."

"That was before we knew about the magic," she said. "And with you being a Master of the School of Fire Magic, it shouldn't be a problem. You soften them up and I'll cut them to pieces."

"Hmph," he said. "It looks like they're heading for that open area. I think they'll turn east in ten miles or so. They'll probably pick up speed once they get out of the trees, too."

"Looks like it. We're going to need to hit them before then."

"Hit them?"

"Come on," she said. "Let's go and tell the others."

They slid down the hill until there was no chance of being seen from the other side, then stood up and jogged back to the horses.

"A couple hundred," Marla started as soon as they were all together. "They're going to change directions and probably pick up speed soon. The trees are going to thin out quite a bit."

"Two hundred," Evon said. "That's kind of a lot."

"We can handle them. We know their weakness now."

Ailuin and Erlan faced each other. Marla was afraid they were going to quit right then.

"Do you have a plan?" Ailuin asked. Bless that woman.

"I do. There's a place, five or six miles away, that looked to be good for an ambush. We can go off here to the left and easily make it around them. We'll be waiting for them as they come through. It's the last area where the trees are as close together as they are now, but there's a clearing. If we do it right, we can catch them as the clearing widens out, right after they have to narrow their formation to get through."

"You're sure they'll go that way?" Evon asked.

"Um, no," she said. "But I'm fairly confident they will. If they veer off to one side or the other, we'll still be ahead of them and be able to attack before they know what's happening. With how much noise they'll make charging through the foliage, we won't be surprised. But they will. I'm willing to listen to anything you have to say, but we'll need to make a decision fast or we'll lose the opportunity. I can't tell, but it's possible the murderer is with them. It's way too much of a coincidence that they're here at the same time."

The others remained silent for longer than Marla was comfortable with. If she had to go and try to do it herself, she would. There was no way she'd let the opportunity pass her by to possibly grab hold of Skril's killer. She knew it wasn't one of the creatures because they didn't use weapons, but that didn't mean they weren't working with—or for—the one who did the deed.

"Fine," Evon said. "I'm in. If there's a chance of getting Skril's killer, I'll take the risk."

Ailuin sighed loudly. "I'll go."

"Me too," Erlan said. "You'll need my fire magic."

"Great," Marla said. "Let's get going. We have some hard riding ahead of us. For a few miles anyway."

❧ 22 ❧

They reached the clearing before the first of the monsters did. The horses they left far enough away that they wouldn't be at risk, and then they moved quickly to their selected ambush spot.

Marla closed her eyes, listening. The steady thump, thump, thump of dozens of feet reverberated in the air and thrummed through the ground. There were more of the verbal noises—it sounded even more like speech to her now —but she still couldn't make it out. It was probably some kind of grunting language. Nothing to concern her at the moment.

"They're almost here," she whispered, drawing her sword but leaving her other hand empty so she could more easily cast spells. Though she knew fire spells that didn't need gestures, using somatic movements could make them stronger or shorten the casting time, not to mention aiding her in aiming and directing the magic. She wanted every advantage she could muster.

The others got ready in their own way. Evon drew his

short sword, Erlan his long sword, and Ailuin readied the staff she had pulled from where it was strapped on her horse.

The first of the dark bodies crashed through the brush into the relatively clear space between trees. The humans stood still, waiting for more to appear.

When there were thirty or more of the monsters in front of them in the clearing, Marla gave a sign to Erlan. He stabbed his sword into the ground so he could use two hands and began to softly speak words of power as he gestured with both hands.

As he did, Marla observed their enemies flooding the ambush spot. It hadn't registered before, but it occurred to her that something was missing. Dozens of forms crashing through the low bushes at speeds that would make a horse tire and not one was breathing heavy. Looking closer, she was sure that they were not breathing at all. What did it mean?

Her musings were interrupted by a flash of red-orange light shooting from Erlan's outstretched arms to the monsters in front of them. Fire magic struck the first one with such force, it lifted the body up and threw it back into those behind it. Then the magic flowed into another, then another, then another of the dark creatures, burning at their skin as it did.

The place erupted in screeches and shrieks. Marla wasn't sure if it was their language or if they cried out in pain, but it didn't matter. She cast Fire Missile at several of her foes on the side of the group and charged in, slashing with her sword.

This encounter was going much better than the one the day before. For one thing, there were four of them now, but probably more importantly, she had learned their weakness.

She used that knowledge to the fullest.

The creatures that had been burned were more suscep-tible to her sword, as if it softened up their natural protec-tion. They still shrugged off most cuts, but her blade went deeper and caused more damage. She waded into the mass of dark monsters, carving her way through.

Erlan alternated between casting and swinging his blade, doing nearly as much damage as Marla. Evon was making a good accounting of himself as well, casting spells similar to Marla's and using his sword on the injured foes. Ailuin had enchanted her staff so that when she struck with it, fire blasted out of it and crushed parts of the creatures' bodies on contact.

Ailuin had mastered the School of Long Weapons Combat and it showed. The woman was a blur of graceful movement, strikes and defensive maneuvers melting together so beautifully, Marla paused to watch it.

Until a sharp set of claws tore into her shoulder and reminded her where she was.

The wound was superficial, but it did manage to call her anger forth. She blasted the offending monster with Flame Wash, cut its hand off at the wrist, then rammed her sword into its eye.

She whirled, cutting down creatures around her, her red hair flying loose from its clasp. In seconds, the area around her was clear.

When she looked back toward where her enemies had come from, she saw something that made her blink. There was a young woman, a human woman, with long, dark hair. She was on her knees in the middle of the monsters as they rushed forward to attack. What the hells?

Was this the murderer they were looking for, a human traveling with those beasts?

Oh. No. The girl looked to be tied up. A prisoner, then? She rolled out of the way of one of the creatures clawing at her as it came toward the other humans, then came back up to her knees. Their eyes met for a brief moment. Well, once her captors were taken care of, Marla would see to the prisoner. Hopefully she wouldn't be trampled. For now, there was more fighting to do.

She set to it with fervor.

❧

WHEN EVON WITNESSED THE NUMBERS OF THE DARK creatures pouring out of the trees and into the open area in front of him, he thought his heart might explode in his chest. He looked down at the sword in his hand. It was vibrating.

No, it was trembling. Just like the hand that was holding it.

He didn't consider himself cowardly, but he also didn't believe he was all that brave. The way his body betrayed him now—the trembling, the weakness, the inability to move—made him revise his perception.

He was scared near to death.

A whoosh off to his right drew his eyes and he watched, eyes wide, as a lance of fire shot out from Erlan's hand and struck one of the first monsters. It passed through the hapless creature and kept going, blasting through the next and moving on. He'd never actually seen the spell cast, but he knew it was Traveling Flame, an intermediate fire magic spell. If it could do that much damage, what could an advanced or master level spell do?

Off on the other side of Erlan, Marla charged into the clearing, fire missiles shooting out from her left hand as she cut into her foes with the sword in her right. Based on the damage he saw his friend doing, Evon believed Marla's assumption that fire not only harmed the creatures, but made them more susceptible to damage from the steel weapon.

Erlan continued to cast and Ailuin, having apparently enchanted the staff she carried, launched herself into the battle. She had mastered the weapon and was devastating in its use. The creatures fell before her, a combination of the severe blunt force from the weapon and the magic wreathing it.

Evon shook his head. It was no time to freeze. His friends were fighting for their lives. He would *not* be a liability.

With a growl, he threw off the paralyzing fear and prepared to cast Fire Missile himself. He didn't need to charge in; several of the dark forms had swung out toward his side of the open area to avoid the fire from the others.

Wouldn't they be surprised?

While he was not as accomplished as the others in combat magic—his forte was scrying and prophecy—he could cast basic spells in most of the types of magic. The pellets of condensed flame he conjured into being zipped forward and punched into three of the creatures in front of him.

He followed up with his sword, just as Marla was doing. It seemed easier than it had the day before, most likely because he now knew to use the magic instead of incessantly hacking at the nearly indestructible creatures with his sword.

That and the three dynamos of devastation alongside him.

Evon settled into a rhythm of casting fire, then cutting. There were challenges, of course. He was an accomplished swordsman, but he hadn't mastered a school of combat like his three friends had. He received some slashes and was knocked off balance several times but managed to stay upright and alive.

It seemed like hours—though it was probably only minutes—of fighting. His arm felt like lead and the spells were coming more slowly, his ability to channel the magic of the world fatiguing. It didn't help that he was also bleeding in several places, though not nearly to the extent of the day before. He thought of taking the shield slung on his back and defending while casting with his right hand, but couldn't find a convenient pause to do so.

Finally, their foes appeared to be lessening. Instead of three or four of the mindless monsters swarming him at a time, only one or two confronted him. The humans just might finish this thing without dying.

Erlan alternated between casting and swinging that long sword of his, doing considerable damage to the creatures. Ailuin had slowed down; obviously tired, but still effective. Marla, of course, was casting and hacking at a rate that made Evon shake his head. She was *so* strong, magically and physically.

But the red-haired woman was looking at something. More creatures to reinforce those they'd already dispatched? He glanced in the direction of his friend's stare and was shocked to see another human. A woman, curled up into a ball in the tamped down vegetation, trying to keep from being trampled. Right in the middle of what had been the main mass of the monsters they were fighting.

Her arms and legs were bound with ropes. A prisoner, not a person traveling with the creatures. Evon dodged a claw swiping at him and looked back in time to see her roll backward, out of the way of monster charging past her, and into the ferns and long grass between trees.

The woman raised up on her knees in the foliage, long dark brown hair a tangled mess around her head. Hers and Marla's eyes met briefly, but Evon's friend still had foes to fight, so she didn't hold the gaze long. He saw little more than half a face through the unknown woman's mane, but what he glimpsed told him this woman was stunning, even in her obviously abused state. Evon stared at her for a moment, as much as he could spare in between attacks.

When he was able to look again, there was no sign of the prisoner. He continued to search as he fought, but didn't see her again.

❦ 23 ❦

Shortly after seeing the woman, Marla encountered one of the creatures that was larger—and hairier—than the others she'd fought. It seemed faster and stronger, too, though that may have been because she was tired after fighting for who knew how long. Regardless, she made short work of it, blasting it in the face with Flame Wash and cutting it down while it screeched in pain from the fire.

The battle wound down after that, the four humans finishing the dark monsters that were left. Even seeing the damage the humans caused, none of the attackers ran away. They simply charged and were destroyed.

When the last one fell—Erlan had the honor of ending that one—Marla slumped and sat down on one of the creatures' corpses. She was exhausted and injured. Looking around, she noticed she was not the only one. She and Evon ended up worse—by the look of his wounds—than they had the day before. Ailuin swayed, leaning on her staff while blood leaked from her in several places. Erlan's clothes were torn, but Marla glimpsed chain mail underneath, so he wasn't bleeding quite as much as the other three.

Evon limped up to Marla. His head was turned in the direction the creatures came from, searching for something.

"You saw the girl?" Marla asked.

"Yes."

"She disappeared a while ago."

"I'm going to look for her, Marla. She looked like she was a prisoner."

"Leave off, Evon," she said. "She obviously doesn't want us to find her, and we don't have time to search."

"She looked injured, all trussed up like that," he said.

"She's not tied up anymore," Marla said, pointing toward the ground near where she had last seen the woman. "Her ropes are right here. I don't like it any more than you do, but we have to let her make her own way. We spent enough time dealing with these—" She spat on the ground. "And we have important work to do. You know that."

"I know, but—"

"Let's go. She'll be fine. She got the ropes off. That's the important part. The area is full of roots, vegetables, and fruit. It's all anyone can ask. Come on. We have work to do."

Evon scanned the foliage. "Fine." He walked a few steps toward where the girl had been and looked more carefully. He sighed, then came back to Marla.

The four headed back toward their horses.

"I guess I was wrong about Skril's killer being with those creatures," Marla said. "Which means he or she is still loose."

"That's all you have to say about what just happened?" Erlan said. "Those things, I've never seen anything like them. What are they? Shouldn't we take one of their corpses back to the Academy? If there are more of them, they could be a big problem to anyone without magic."

"Speaking of which," Ailuin said. "They are apparently susceptible to more than just fire magic. I imbued my staff with light magic and it hurt them just like the fire did. I'm under the assumption that it's not the type of magic, but the fact that it *is* magic, that makes a difference."

"That's all great and academic," Erlan said, "but aren't we missing the important thing?"

Marla turned toward the man. It was irritating that she had to tilt her head up to meet his eyes. "The important thing is that we find the one who killed Skril. We'll follow the trail you mentioned earlier. It occurred to me during the battle that you said you saw the tracks of three horses earlier. It's too much of a coincidence not to be the trail we're looking for."

"Uh," Ailuin said. "We won't be going with you to follow anymore trails. We came here because of the murder investigation, but these creatures are a higher priority right now. The masters need to know about them. I'm sorry. Erlan and I talked about it when you two were arguing earlier."

Marla looked to Evon. Her friend nodded. At least he was with her. "That's probably a good idea. Thanks for the help with this part of it, though."

Ailuin gave Marla a sad smile. "You're welcome. Why don't we ride off for a distance, away from the smell and sight of all this, and then I can heal everyone."

"Are you sure?" Evon said. "You look pretty tired." Marla smirked. He had made a big mistake telling a woman she looked tired, but he covered it nicely. "Umm, like we all do."

"It'll be fine. I have enough power left for that. Erlan and I will be taking it easy for the next couple of days, resting while we travel."

"Are you sure we can't bring one of the bodies?" Erlan said.

"Those creatures smell foul enough alive, thank you very much," Ailuin said. "If you would like to travel with one of them, then be my guest, but don't expect me to join you."

The big man rubbed the back of his neck and cast his eyes sheepishly at the ground, but didn't push the issue.

Once Ailuin healed them yet again, moving was less painful. Marla was still dead tired, both from the fighting and from being healed, but it was manageable. They found the other trail soon enough.

"Okay," Erlan said. "Here it is. Are you sure you don't want to come back with us to the Academy?"

Marla shook her head. "We need to follow this. I won't be kicking myself for going back home and letting the trail get cold. Those monsters put us far enough behind. Thank you two for all your help. Be careful going back. I doubt those creatures are wandering the roads, but you never know. Please tell the masters what we told you, and what we're doing."

"We will," Ailuin said, "but don't expect it to keep you from having to answer some hard questions when you get back."

Marla nodded. She knew well that what Ailuin said was true. They bade each other goodbye, and Marla and Evon headed southwest, following the three sets of horse tracks, while the other two followed the trail northwest toward the River Road.

At first, it looked like the trail Marla and Evon were on was going to join the main road, most likely destroying any chance they had to track the three horses. Before it reached the River Road, though, the trail turned south, traveling parallel with the road, though Marla estimated it was at least a half mile away.

"Why?" Evon asked. "Why don't they use the road? It would be much faster that way."

"Maybe they don't want to be seen. After all, Skril already found them, and Ailuin and Erlan were on their way to finding them. Maybe there are others in the mix."

"Yeah, I guess," he said. "I don't know if it's good or bad. I mean, it's good that we can follow the trail, but this huffing through the wilderness leaves something to be desired."

In the first two days, the terrain had transitioned from the sparse trees and bushes to a more desert-like landscape of dirt and spiky plants, then started to become more verdant as they traveled south. It still wasn't forest, but it was better than being exposed to the sun the entire day and clomping through sand and loose gravel. Between the difficulty of the terrain and having to constantly keep the trail in focus, they were only traveling twenty or twenty-five miles a day.

After the first couple of days, they ran out of food and their water was getting low. Towns dotted the River Road at various distances from each other. It was easy to see the lights at night and often even the buildings themselves during the daytime, especially if they crested a hill and could see portions of the road. They left their tracking long enough to get supplies, then they resumed following the trails.

Several miles above where the River Road intersected with the Genta Highway heading west, the tracks finally merged with the well-worn roadway. At first, Marla panicked at the difficulty—call it what it was: impossibility—of tracking three specific horse tracks on an often-used road. On a hunch, though, she crossed the road, searched the land on the other side, and found the tracks continuing. The horses had merely crossed the road, not joined it.

It happened again a few miles later, as the River Road split into the Genta Highway going west toward Arcusheim and the Trail of Sarak going southeast toward Satta Sarak. Marla and Evon followed the horse tracks to the south.

Crossing the road, Marla shifted her sight to the mountains named Ianthra's Breasts—nicknamed the Teats—looming to her left. On the other side of those mountains was the great Mellanor Forest, all but surrounding Satta Sarak. She had seen many maps of the area, even seen it in her flying dream, but this was the first time she had visited it in person. She thought of how she'd like to see Satta Sarak, one of the great cities, one day.

Not today, though. She still had work to do.

The trail continued south, skirting the foothills of the Teats and angling slightly southeast. It had been more than ten days already since Ailuin and Erlan had left them.

"Where do you think the killer is heading?" Evon asked. It was a silly question, but Marla figured he was bored and needed conversation.

"Dunno for sure. I hope it doesn't continue to the southeast, though. That's rough territory. Fewer towns that way, so we better stock up at the next one we reach. Our supplies may have to last a while."

"Do you think we're catching up at all?" he asked her. "We've been at it for more than a week and a half, with no clue as to how far they are ahead."

"Yeah. I wish I was better at tracking. I think Erlan could have told us how far ahead they are. All we can do is keep following. Eventually, they'll either go someplace we can't track them, or we'll corner them. If they take us all the way to the Aesculun Ocean, they'd better be able to make those horses swim if they want to get away."

Evon chuckled, but it sounded forced.

They did find another town, a few miles off the trail they were following. As they discussed, they got supplies for at least another week. Not that they needed the water; there were abundant streams in the area. Still, now they could focus on catching their prey.

Another two days, and it was clear the horses they were following were heading where they least wanted to go.

Marla cursed and muttered under her breath, "They're going to Fyrefall."

❧ 24 ❧

Fyrefall.

The name evoked many emotions. It was a label laden with history and saturated with the power of mythology.

It also happened to be on the list of places the students were forbidden to go.

Marla thought back to a lecture she'd attended several years before. Aubron Benevise, the Master of History and Literature, stood tall at the podium on the stage of one of the larger lecture halls in the Preparatory and Administration Lycad.

His lectures were always well-attended, and not only because all students were required to show a competency in the schools in the Prep and Admin Lycad. Preparatory Studies, History and Literature, Scholarship, Fundamental Magic, and Language were the schools comprising that group, and all were required by every Academy student.

Master Aubron's speaking ability really drove the high attendance, though. He was dynamic and passionate. He spoke and gestured so articulately that his listeners could see what he was describing. Marla had always enjoyed listening to him.

"Fyrefall," he said, nearly shouting the word. "An insignificant speck on the face of Promistala, let alone Dizhelim itself." He scanned the audience, making eye contact with several students, pinning them to their seats with his eyes.

"Yet..." he continued, "...is it truly? Many know of the hot pools, the volcanic vents, the steam geysers in the area. The heat, they say, is the reason for the name. The ancients couldn't spell words correctly, they surmise, and so it is named Fyrefall, with a Y.

"But I am here to tell you that it is not an insignificant thing, not a mere spelling error, that gives this dubious place its name. No!" He shouted it so suddenly, at least three people in front of Marla hopped nearly out of their seats.

"No," he said more softly. The words following became softer still, tapering off in their volume to become almost a whisper by the time he finished. "As with much in history, there is more to this than meets the eye. I would like to share this information with you, if you are inclined to receive it."

It was always amazing to Marla how riveted everyone was during one of Master Aubron's lectures. Including herself. She found herself leaning forward in her seat, not wanting to miss a word. The entire hall was silent as a tomb, save for the master's voice.

"Many thousands of years ago—for those historians among us, it was five thousand, five hundred, forty-four to be exact—there lived and ruled a king. His name was Tazi Ermengo, and he ruled over a fair-sized land near the eastern edges of the Shadowed Pinnacles.

"This was a time before the great nations and empires were formed, and much of Dizhelim was divided into small kingdoms. The particular area of King Tazi's kingdom of

Awresea would one day be assimilated into the great nation of Gentason, but that would happen much later.

"King Tazi was a proud man. Some would say arrogant. Others would perhaps use different words. Suffice it to say that the king thought very much of himself and his kingdom.

"'Awresea is the wonder of all Dizhelim,' the king pronounced. 'Soon, it will be known far and wide. All people of reasonable intelligence will submit themselves to my rule, and all will prosper.'

"The king commissioned a great castle to be built for his home. It was made completely of stone, and the streets within and around it were also fashioned of stone blocks. Such was the craftsmanship—and historians agree there was more than a bit of magic involved—that the magnificent structure was erected of only the hardest materials. A bastion to represent the rule of the haughty king.

"'Can you not see,' the king said upon the dedication of the castle when construction was completed, 'that I have made a structure impervious to harm, a great fortress to withstand any assault. Even Fyorio cannot do me harm, such is the wondrous craftsmanship of my home and seat.'

"Now, Fyorio, the God of Fire, was not a tolerant god. He heard the king's boasting from his seat in the Srantorna, the abode of all the gods. A mortal, boasting and challenging a god? Such things were not done.

"In a fit of rage, as the God of Fire was wont to have, he traveled to the surface of Dizhelim in an instant and stood there looking down from Darkeye Peak—the high peak farthest east in the range that would come to be called the Wall of Salamus, and later the Shadowed Pinnacles—onto the lands of Awresea.

"It was a fertile land, with fields surrounding the king's castle and fine forests surrounding those. Several waterways crisscrossed the area, making it green and beautiful. And in the center of it all was the dull grey of the king's new stone castle and all the sterile areas immediately surrounding it.

"As the god stood there, observing the scene, King Tazi's voice echoed over the stone.

"'So great is my kingdom and the heart of my lands that no force—water, nor air, nor ice, nor the fire from Fyorio's heart—can cause my people to tremble.'

"The god had had enough. He spoke, and with his magic, he magnified his voice so that all assembled in front of the king could hear. 'So sure are you, King Tazi Ermengo, of the tiny speck of a kingdom Awresea. So confident in the works of human hands are you that you would mock a god?'

"The people shivered in fear, afraid that the king had made a grave mistake in taunting the god. But the king was not afraid. He scoffed, saying, 'You have no power over me here, master of fire. Can you not see my magnificent home, constructed entirely of stone and stronger even than the heat of your ire? Bluster if you must. You cannot harm Awresea.'

"Fyorio's rage intensified and his eyes glowed red with the heat of his anger. His magnified voice blasted out once more. 'So be it, worm. Now you shall see the power of a god.'

"Fyorio called forth his magic and cast it toward the land before him. With his left hand, he threw the fires of a volcano across the fields surrounding the castle, burning them to ash in a moment. With his right hand, he cast raw flame, the heart of a great blaze, and burned the forest for miles around the castle, leaving the ground desolate and dark.

"King Tazi stood proudly in the courtyard of his castle, ash floating over and settling on the people and the stone. 'Is that all your power, God of Fire?' he asked. 'Behold that you have not made a single scratch on my home. It is beyond you. Go back to Srantorna and admit to your fellows that you have been bested.'

"Fyorio, for his part, simply chuckled at the king's words.

Then, it became laughter and the sound boomed out throughout the land. 'So sure are you still,' the god said. 'I, in my mercy, have used the smallest part of my power. Mercy, but not for you. I will allow your subjects to flee. I will not destroy them if they hurry and leave what was once your kingdom. Any that remain two hours from now will be destroyed utterly, along with the flimsy abode of which you are so proud. Two hours and I will transform these lands into an example of the fallacy of human hubris.'

"The king continued to scoff, explaining to his people that it was a ploy by the god to cause them to leave the safety of the stone so he could kill them. Most of the people believed in the king, but not all. A meager percentage of them fled, riding and running ahead of the king's threatening words.

"'You have made your choice,' the king told them as they fled. 'Henceforth, if you are found within my kingdom, you will be slaughtered for the cowardly traitors you are.'

"When two hours had elapsed, those who had fled continued, trying desperately to outrun the horror they imagined an angry God of Fire could inflict. Fyorio watched them go, the very few who had been smart enough to partake of his mercy. Then he turned his gaze back to the arrogant king.

"'And so,' the god said, 'you have chosen your own fate. Witness now, little king, the consequences of taunting the Voordim.'

"This time, Fyorio did not concern himself with grand gestures or fantastic displays of light and fire. He simply closed his eyes, gathered his power, then brought it forth as he opened them again.

"The land opened up beneath the king and his gathered subjects. Great rents, wide as wagons, grew as the entire world shook around the hapless humans. Fire and lava from beneath shot up, spraying in a great wave over the people.

Bodies burst into flame and turned to ash in an instant, too fast for most of them to even scream, let alone try to run.

"King Tazi alone was kept from the flaming death, so precise was Fyorio's control. The ruler watched as his subjects turned to ash before him.

"But the God of Fire was not yet done. He caused more lava and flame, superheated from the bowels of Dizhelim, to fly up into the late morning sky, a great mass of red-orange fluid that crested like a wave and crashed down onto the highest towers of the castle. In its wake, the hard stone of the castle—of which the king was so proud—melted away like ice under boiling water.

"Too late did the king realize that stone could melt, proving ineffective in protecting against Fyorio's wrath.

"After the great structures had been melted to slag in front of him, only then did the God of Fire turn his wrath to the man himself.

"'So you see,' Fyorio said, 'the folly of your words.'

"'Please,' King Tazi begged. 'Please, great lord, show me mercy as you did my subjects not two hours past. I will proclaim your superiority to all I meet. I will build temples in your honor. I have learned my lesson. Please, allow me to live.'

"Fyorio shook his head, though the king could not see him from so great a distance. 'No. You are a despicable man and a petty, vengeful despot. You promised to kill those who were smart enough to flee. Should you not be rewarded in like fashion?'

"The king dropped to his knees, weeping, but the god paid him no heed. With another swipe of his hand, the largest wave of molten stone yet crashed over the king and the remaining bit of stone where he knelt. When it settled, there was not a trace of the man except a few gems that had been set in his crown. They, too, disappeared as they sank beneath the molten lake.

"The former site of the kingdom of Awresea and the great castle of stone that was the pride of its former king was now a flat, rapidly cooling mass of stone. But that was not enough for Fyorio's purpose. He called his magic once more and the land shifted, rippling and rolling like the waves of the sea. Deeper, there were other changes. When the god finally finished, the stone had receded, leaving a mix of rock and soil, dotted with vents and hot pools and holes out of which occasionally blew steam and foul air.

"Fyorio looked over the dozens of square miles of newly transformed land and decided it was good. 'Fyrefall.' His voice boomed out so that even those fleeing, now miles away, could hear him. 'I name this land Fyrefall. May its existence never fail to impart the lesson King Tazi learned this day: human hubris is a deadly thing.' The god transmitted the tale to his faithful priests, so that they would write it down as a lesson to all. In their writings, the name of the place was spelled in the ancient way, with the word that came into existence in reflection of the God of *fyre*.

"And with that, Fyorio went back to Srantorna. Never again since has Fyrefall been inhabited by humans."

❧ 2 5 ❧

Marla looked out across the landscape. The trees and bushes were squat and rugged. She figured they had to be to survive in this most inhospitable area. A mist hung over much of the land, steam pouring out of several cracks in the ground and hanging over pools so hot that vapor and air shimmered above them.

She tried to imagine fields and a castle and people living and working in the area, but she couldn't. As Master Aubron's story said, no one ever settled in the region since Awresea had been destroyed.

"Uh, Marla," Evon said. "That's Fyrefall."

"I know, Evon."

"It's on the list of forbidden places. We're not allowed to go in there."

Marla followed the tracks with her eyes. The three horses they'd been following for two weeks and over two hundred miles went straight into the forbidden area.

"I'm going," she said. "I'm not about to come all this way and then turn around now. We're close to finding Skril's killer. I can feel it. You can go back. I'm going on."

He frowned at her, his eyes darting from her face to the tracks and back to her. "Damn it." He sighed. "I'll go with you. Gods know that you need someone to keep you from getting into trouble."

"Good enough. Let's make camp. Sundown is less than two hours away, and I'd rather not make camp in there if we don't have to."

"You know it's more than twenty-five miles across, right?" he asked. "We might still have to camp in there, depending on how long it takes us to get through. That's if the trail doesn't stop inside Fyrefall."

"We may have to, but that distance is doable in a day. We'll start early tomorrow morning and see what happens."

Evon grumbled as he saw to his horse. Marla sympathized. She didn't like going into a forbidden area either. The masters would definitely punish them for it, but they had to keep going. One way or another, she was going to catch Skril's killer, and no forbidden place was going to stop her.

Marla's nose wrinkled the next morning as they walked their horses through the start of the cracks that spewed steam. The two hot pools they passed between were smoking, giving off not only steam, but an acrid cloud of...something.

"That is a horrible smell," Evon said.

"Yeah," she agreed. "There's obviously sulphur in there. It's probably corrosive, too." She hadn't mastered the School of Alchemy, but she did study there and was already a competent alchemist. "Let's try to stay out of them so we don't get cooked or dissolved."

"That's a suggestion I'll follow gladly," he said.

As they followed the trail, they came close to geysers, which occasionally spat streams of water and steam into the air, rather than leaking or oozing it like some of the crevices did. The mist felt good, drizzling down on them after it had cooled in the air. It was the only thing resembling a pleasant experience she'd had since her horse set hoof in the gods-forsaken place.

There was very little animal life to be seen, but whether that was fear of the humans or because there were few animals suited to the environment, Marla didn't know. But she wasn't here to hunt or watch birds, lizards, or rodents. They had plenty of rations left and the important thing was the trail. They had to be getting closer to the killer. Didn't they?

By early evening, Marla was tired of being in the saddle for yet another day, tired of relentlessly following the hoof prints they'd been chasing for so long. Because of it, part of her actually appreciated when a group of riders suddenly appeared behind them and to the south.

She and Evon had been traveling due west, and the flicker of movement at the edge of her peripheral vision barely registered enough for her to turn her head. When she did, though, she saw a mass of horses with riders, a few of them drawing back short bows nocked with arrows.

"Down!" she shouted to Evon. To his credit, he flattened himself to his horse's neck even as she did. Two arrows passed within a foot of her. "Let's go. We won't survive if they all start shooting at us."

She jerked the reins to the right and kicked her horse into motion. It wouldn't be long until the attackers figured out that not only was the horse a bigger target, but that one or two arrows into Marla's mount would effectively leave her helpless to run.

She glanced back over her left shoulder as she raced forward, making sure Evon was following. He was doing better than that; he was gaining on her right side, steadily moving up to pass her.

They swept around a large rock and through some trees. Their short, twisted branches didn't provide much cover, but they were full of jagged leaves, so they at least obscured the archers' vision of the two fleeing from them. Marla had a sad thought that they might not be able to find the trail again after fleeing so blindly, but it was more important to survive than to remember where they were at, so she continued on, riding as if her life depended on it.

A mile away, she realized her mistake as they galloped between two large rock formations into a narrow space that ended at a cliff rising upward like a fortress wall. Marla whirled her horse around, looking for another way out, and found only one, a narrow opening between the cliff and some boulders that didn't look big enough for their horses to enter.

"Bastards," she said. "It's either stop and try to fight here or ditch the horses, Evon."

He looked around frantically. The expression on his face told her he understood what she was saying. They had been maneuvered into this place. She wouldn't be surprised if there were more men waiting through the narrow opening.

Already, they could hear their pursuers stomping toward the entrance of the box canyon. There was no more time.

"Come on," she said. "I'm not dying here just to keep my horse." She dismounted, snatched her pack from the saddle bags, and sprinted toward the crack of space that seemed their only salvation.

"Wait, Marla," Evon said. "Over here, quick."

Marla was surprised when her body changed direction without any conscious effort on her part and she headed for her friend. She hoped he knew what he was doing; otherwise he had just killed both of them. When she got there, she smiled.

He had found another small corridor through the rocks, one that was invisible unless you were basically within it. How had he seen it?

She slapped her horse on the rump, mentally sending an

apology to her, and shuffled into the corridor. Evon did the same thing, sending his horse running after Marla's toward the entrance to the trap. Hopefully their pursuers wouldn't realize what they did until they had escaped completely. She also hoped they wouldn't shoot the poor equines before realizing their saddles were empty.

It was a tight fit through the space, her pack dragging along the sides and her shoulders scraping the jagged rock. Thoughts of it narrowing and trapping them invaded her mind and she expelled them violently, not wanting to think about it.

Behind them, she heard the pursuers enter the space where their horses still were. Shouts of "they're on foot" and "they went into the tunnel" reached Marla's ears, and she hoped they weren't talking about the corridor she was in. She could do nothing more than keep pushing forward, Evon right behind her.

After what seemed an eternity, Marla pulled herself out into a wider space. It opened up rapidly, from a hall of rock where she could touch both sides at the same time to an opening two wagons could fit into. Then, it opened up even more to a field of hot pools, some of them of several bright colors—greens, yellows, and oranges—and more vents and geysers than she'd seen at one time since they entered Fyrefall.

She stopped and scanned the area around her, looking for an ambush. Her heavy breathing from the run, mixed with Evon's panting, accompanied the hissing and splashing around them. There were no other sounds. Most importantly, there were no other *human* sounds.

"I don't think they knew of that way," she said. "Good job finding it. You just saved our lives."

"Not yet I haven't," Evon told her. "We need to get out of here. They'll eventually find it and come."

He was right, but what should they do? They didn't have horses any longer and they were severely outnumbered.

"Let me think," she said. "We can try finding a way out that way while we come up with something." She pointed toward another jumble of rocks. They found a patch of dirt that climbed steadily upward, out of the bowl they were in.

The climbing was difficult, with loose soil that slipped underfoot and the acrid gas floating in the area stinging their eyes. Once through the rocks, the terrain flattened out before tipping up again. It was a small mesa, with several large pools scattered around, some at the same level and others that sat in depressions like craters.

As Marla passed too close to the lip of one of the craters, the soil gave way and she started to slip down the slope. Evon caught her with one hand, grasping a nearby bush with his other, and kept her from going down.

A stick Marla had kicked while scrambling back up bounced down the slope and landed in the pool with a hiss. Steam and a cloud of gas wafted up from it as the liquid in the pool attacked it.

Marla swallowed hard. If she'd landed in that pool, her skin would have started dissolving off her bones and there would be no way she could have gotten free. She plopped down on the flat part of the trail and tried to catch her breath.

"Thanks," she said. "That was too close."

Evon was panting from the exertion of helping her back up. "Yeah. Don't do that again."

They started off again, picking their way between pools and vents. Rocks thrust up from the soil ahead of them, dark grey and glistening with moisture. Marla squinted at one large formation.

"Is that a cave?"

Evon narrowed his eyes at the place Marla was pointing

to. "I think it might be. Do you think we can hide in it until they give up looking for us?"

"I doubt they'll give up. It's obvious they were searching for us. Who knows, though. Maybe the cave system goes somewhere else and we can get out of the area."

"It's worth a shot," he said.

When they came close, she found the cave was a jagged rift in the stone. It looked as if someone struck the rock right in the center with a gigantic pickaxe and fractured a large, triangular piece from it, then took the piece away. The word ominous popped into Marla's head. With the wisps of steam roiling out from the space, it looked like nothing so much as the opening to a dragon's lair. If dragons existed, or ever had.

"Stay here for a moment," she told Evon. "I don't like that steam coming out. There may be a vent or something inside."

He nodded to her and she stepped forward to the mouth of the cave. It was more than six feet high and wide enough for her to easily enter it, but she was still wary.

A wave of putrid air wafted toward her and she gagged, backing up.

"Ew, now that is foul." She rubbed her nose and spat, hoping it would get rid of the taste in her mouth. "It's not the normal sulphur smell. It smells like..." She moved her right hand in a simple gesture and called forth magical light dancing above her palm, one of the simplest of the light magic spells. Holding her breath, she moved the light toward the cave opening and saw what she expected.

Three carcasses lay on the floor just inside the cave's opening. They looked to be some kind of deer. She could see no obvious wounds on them.

She backed up, rejoining Evon.

"Three animals. Dead. There must not be enough air in the cave, or there is something else that's poisonous to breathe. We're not going through that passage, not unless we can hold our breath for an hour or two."

The disappointment on Evon's face was plain.

"Let's get going. We'll find another way. We should hurry. Those men are going to figure out where we went pretty soon."

He followed after Marla. "It's too bad we can't make them believe we're dead."

She stopped so quickly he almost ran into her back. "What did you say?"

"Uh, I was just joking."

"What did you say?"

"I said it's too bad we can't make them believe we're already dead. Then they'd stop looking for us."

She tilted her head at him. "Evon, you're a genius. That's exactly what we'll do."

"What, die? It was a joke, Marla. A *joke*."

"Yeah, yeah. Do you have rope in your pack or is it in the saddlebags still on the horse?"

"I have maybe twenty feet of it," he said. "Why?"

"Because we're going to make them believe we're dead. Then we can walk out of here without worrying about them following."

Evon stared at her, his mouth open.

"Come on," she said. "We have work to do."

He followed her as she headed back to the cave, pulling the rope out of his pack.

When they got to the cave, she had him stay back again.

"Here, tie this to my waist, just in case. If I misjudge and pass out, drag me out of there."

"I'm not so sure that's a good idea, Marla."

"It'll be fine. Watch me to make sure I don't lose consciousness."

She took an exaggerated breath, then darted toward the

cave opening. Just inside it, she reached down to grab what she was after, then backed out more slowly. When she was a few steps from Evon, she released her breath and started breathing normally as she dragged the carcass of one of the animals toward her friend.

Evon stood there, holding the rope, as if she was some kind of strange creature.

She took a breath and went in again, snatching and dragging another carcass over to the first.

"Now," she said, "take off your coat and put it on this one." She indicated one of the dead animals."

"My coat?"

"Yes, your coat. You have another one, but more importantly, the men saw you wearing that one."

Evon's eyes widened, telling Marla that he had finally caught on. He was a brilliant student, but creativity wasn't one of his strong points. Her friend quickly took his coat off and struggled to get it over the forelimbs of the carcass. Even as he did it, Marla did likewise, dressing the other animal in her coat.

Once they'd done that, she began dragging the animal back toward the pool she had almost fallen into. Evon pulled the carcass with his coat behind her.

"Tie the end of the rope to that tree," she said. "Make sure it'll hold the weight. I'm going to tie the other end to my carcass and lower it down. We'll do yours after that."

Between the two of them, they were able to get both of the animal carcasses into the pool. Like the stick before, the foreign objects made the pool hiss and smoke, even bubble a little. Marla used the rope, hanging on it to kick at the dirt on the slope to make it look like someone had slipped down the hill and into the pool.

"Won't they be able to tell those are deer and not people?" Evon asked.

"I don't think so. By the time they get here, the carcasses won't be more than melted meat. I just hope enough of the coats are left for them to really buy the act. I'm also hoping they get here soon enough so that everything doesn't completely dissolve."

"I liked that coat," Evon said, looking at his coat wrapped around a carcass and slowly melting away.

"It's not worth more than your life," she said. "Come on, we need to make it look like we slipped and fell into the pool, which means we need to erase our trail from here on out and go hide somewhere."

"How are we going to do that? Tree branches and leaves, using them as a broom?"

Marla showed all her teeth. "Nope. There are advantages to having mastered the School of Air Magic."

This time, she let Evon lead, after he'd untied and stored his rope. She followed behind him, casting simple air spells to whisk away the tracks they made as they progressed.

No sooner had they moved beyond another grouping of rocks than they heard men shout.

"They must have found the other exit," Marla said. "Hurry it up. I want to be far enough away that they won't be able to see us."

The path they took not only wound around rocks that obscured them from view, but it also angled upward. Marla was satisfied that they could not be detected.

Though they couldn't see, they heard the men rushing up to where the trail slipped into the pool. Marla and Evon stayed low, their backs against a boulder, and listened.

"They came this way," a man shouted. "Come on. They couldn't have gotten far."

"Wait," another said. "The trail ends here. It..."

There was some other conversation with those behind the front men, but it was too low to hear.

"They fell into the damn pool!" one of them shouted. "Look, there they are, floating and—" Retching noises cut off what the man was saying. Marla smiled.

"Damn, there goes the bonus for bringing them in alive. Do you think we can fish their bodies out of there to bring them to the boss?"

"You go right ahead and try to get down there and back up while carrying whatever's left. I'm not getting dissolved for no bonus. Those are the clothes they were wearing. That's good enough for me."

There was more discussion, but eventually, the men went back the way they had come.

"I think they're leaving," Marla said.

"We better give it some time, though. I don't want to come out of hiding to find that they posted sentries or anything."

And so they did give it some time. Several hours, in fact. From their hiding place, they couldn't be sure, but it seemed a safe bet the men had gone.

"Just to be safe, let's make ourselves comfortable. It'll be dark soon and if the sky isn't cloudy, we should have enough moonlight to get out of here."

Evon frowned at her.

"What?" she asked.

"You do realize we don't have horses anymore, right? We're going to be walking from now on, until we can get new mounts."

"You could always jump in the pool and not have to worry about it anymore."

❧ 26 ❧

Marla and Evon traveled half the night, coming down the other side of the plateau they had been hiding on and moving onto the flatter part of Fyrefall. The full moon lit up the terrain so brightly, they had no trouble traveling. They saw no fires or any other indication that their pursuers were still around. In fact they discovered something that argued the contrary.

"These horse tracks are fresh," Marla said, picking up a handful of turned up soil. "Those droppings aren't even a day old, either. I'd say that's pretty clear evidence that they fell for it. That's one problem solved. Let's see if we can find a nice, sheltered area where we can get some rest."

Within a few hours, they found a patch of thorny bushes butted up against several decent sized manzanita trees, their glossy red wood reflecting the moonlight. They chanced upon an opening to a hollow within the briars where they couldn't be seen unless someone was inside the actual opening. If someone got that close, they would have already been discovered.

They settled down to rest. Both of them were tired, and Marla didn't see a need to keep watch because anyone finding them would literally step on them coming into the hollow.

They slept until the sun had already risen above the horizon. Not that they knew that from within their little bush cave. Only when they emerged did they see that they were on the edge of Fyrefall. The landscape in the direction opposite the rising sun was less barren than the land they had been traveling through, and the foothills of the Shadowed Pinnacles were closer and clearer than they'd seen before.

"Oh, thank Surus," Evon said. "I've had about enough of the land of heat and death."

"Oh, come on," Marla said. "It really wasn't that bad, other than the men trying to kill us, and the flesh-dissolving pools, and the deadly air in that cave. We didn't even run into any dangerous creatures. The only animals we saw saved our lives. I think the masters highly exaggerate its danger. On the forbidden list. Pshaw."

"We got lucky. Count yourself fortunate and let's get moving. There's no telling if those horsemen will still be around, wishing they had a second chance at us."

"You're such an old woman," Marla said. She smiled in anticipation for how he would react. He hated it when she called him that. When he didn't, she looked over at him questioningly. "No response?"

He was inspecting the ground, his head tilted at an odd angle. Marla went to stand next to him, trying to see what he was looking at.

"Talk about lucky," she said. "That's...those are..."

"Yes. It's the tracks of three horses traveling together. The same three horses we were following before, I'm pretty sure."

"I agree," she said. "Who would have thought?"

"Let's not overthink it. It's a gift from the gods."

"Are you getting all religious on me now?" she asked. "Are you going to drop to your knees and start chanting to Vanda next?"

"Oh, shut up. Come on. We've been given another chance. Let's catch the bastard this time."

Marla shouldered her pack, loosened her sword in its scabbard, and started walking. "You coming?" she asked as she followed the tracks in front of her.

It was another day and a half until anything significant happened. They had been following the tracks while constantly scanning the landscape. Lusher vegetation finally started to appear, confirming that they were truly out of Fyre-fall for good. They didn't see signs of the horsemen, or any other human for that matter. That suited them just fine.

They finally came to a stopping point.

"The trail splits here," Evon said.

"Yep."

"How? All this time I thought we were chasing one person with three horses. Unless the person set one of the horses free—which doesn't fit because the single track trail doesn't wander, but continues on straight—that means there were at least two people. There could have just as easily been three."

"Yep."

"Is that all you're going to say?" Evon snapped. The long days of travel seemed to be fraying his nerves. Unlike Marla, who was as even-tempered as she normally was.

"How about this? I think we should split up."

"What? Are you mad? Why would you even think that?"

"Well," she said, "we may finally be catching up to them. If we choose one fork, it could be the wrong one, and then we'd have to backtrack. If we each take one and go for a set distance—I don't know, maybe five miles or so—it might become clear which one we should follow, so then we can meet back here and follow the one that most likely has the murderer."

He let out an explosive breath. "Does that really make sense to you?"

She nodded. "Yeah. Why, it doesn't to you?"

"I...uh, no. No, it does not. What if we split up and then run into those horsemen again?"

"Then it'll be the same as if both of us run into the horsemen again. We'll die. We can't take that many men whether it's one or both of us."

Evon shook his head. "Well, okay. I have to agree about that. Still, splitting up is a bad idea. We should definitely *not* be splitting up."

❧

EVON NEVERTHELESS FOUND HIMSELF FOLLOWING THE single horse track by himself while Marla was following the trail with two tracks.

"How does she always do this to me?" he said aloud. "I mean, I'm a smart guy, right? Even if I do talk to myself. Ugh!"

Maybe she was right. There had been times when he couldn't quite follow her strange, twisted logic and things always seemed to turn out all right. Of course, they'd never been fighting for their lives during any of those times, either.

At least the trail was easy to follow. There didn't seem to be a lot of people in this area. It was a true wilderness. He would occasionally spot animal runs off to the side of the trail he was following, but it was obvious the creatures who made those paths were not as large as a horse. He found some tracks in the soft ground he thought were from a deer's cloven hooves, but the trail he was following was clearly made by a horse, with the indentation of a horseshoe embedded within them.

So, on he tramped. They had agreed to going five miles and then meeting back at the fork. It seemed a waste of time to him, but he'd found long ago that it was better to let Marla have her way. She was a force of nature. You didn't argue with a storm, and if you were smart—or at least sane—you didn't argue with Marla Shrike.

Evon smiled. Whenever he and Marla and Skril got together, they...

The smile dropped off his face when he remembered that Skril was gone. His friend had been killed. He would never sit and joke around with him and Marla again. Evon gritted his teeth. He would kill that son of a—

The trail he was following suddenly stopped.

Evon looked back, thinking maybe he had missed it, veering off while he was thinking. He hadn't. It came up to where he was standing and then it just disappeared. As if some great flying thing snatched the horse and rider up off the ground and carried it away.

He searched, looking for any marks that the trail had been erased. Thinking more creatively, he even inspected the trail closely to see if he could detect the horse walking backward in its own prints to confuse anyone tracking it. Unless the horse was smarter and more skilled than most of the students in the Academy, that hadn't happened.

A sick feeling bubbled up in Evon's belly. How would someone lay down a trail that went nowhere? Forget how they did it, *why* had they done it? Only one reason made sense.

Evon turned around and started running back toward the fork. It was nearly four miles away, but he needed to get there as soon as he could. There, and beyond, to where Marla had followed the other trail.

They had been split up, and it had been done for a purpose.

❧ 27 ❧

Marla watched Evon stomp off down the fork in the trail they had been following. He was muttering to himself, something he tended to do when he got aggravated. She would have liked to have discussed their plan further and tried to genuinely convince him, but he was stubborn and that would take time. They didn't have any of that to spare.

As it was, the solution they chose may waste time by making at least one of them backtrack. It was a gamble that they would figure out which trail was the correct one within five miles, but it was the best she could think of.

Anyway, it was too late now. Evon had already started on his five-mile trek, so she'd better begin hers as well. She glanced back at her friend, disappearing around a bend.

"Be safe, Evon," she whispered. She wouldn't be able to handle the guilt of him being injured on top of what she already felt about Skril. She shook her head and got started. The sooner they met back at the fork, the better.

The trail she followed was clear enough that she didn't have to concentrate on it. The horses walked one behind the other, though not exactly in line. Did they do that because of the foliage they passed through or because the second horse was riderless and being guided by a rope tied to the first? She imagined the rear horse was Skril's, but she couldn't count on it. Her friend's killer could have had companions, so she might face two foes instead of just one.

The path wound around trees—there were more now that they had left Fyrefall—and other obstacles, but generally headed northwest. That was to be expected. Arcusheim was north by northwest, but there were other towns and villages scattered between the Shadowed Pinnacles and the shore of the Kanton Sea. As far as she knew, there weren't many settlements directly to her west, at the base of the foothills. Who knew, though? She'd never actually been to this part of Dizhelim before.

It was fortunate that the trail with the two horses happened to go this way, while the other paralleled the mountains. That told her this one was more likely to be the important trail. Wouldn't the killer be heading toward civilization? Maybe it was a leap in supposition, but she wanted to do everything possible to make sure she faced the danger, not Evon.

Her musing cut off as she crested a hill and got a view of what was beyond. It was a proper forest, though one with terrain that jerked upwards in fits and starts and included ragged crags scattered between the trees.

She immediately developed a fondness for the look of it. Rugged but beautiful. This was what nature should look like. A large area of soft and beautiful trees could be so...boring. She smiled as she continued after the horse tracks that led down the hill and into the trees.

In the transition from more open land to the collection of trees, right where the sunlight transformed into dappled shadow, she heard a subtle snap. Her heart dropped and she dove at the ground, hoping to avoid whatever trap she had set off.

A puff of orange cloud surrounded her head, causing the world to spin crazily.

Then even the dim light went out.

MARLA ROLLED ONTO HER SIDE WHEN HER AWARENESS returned. At least, she tried to. Her body didn't seem to be cooperating. She wriggled but couldn't move the way she wanted to. Instead, she stopped moving, breathing in and out slowly, trying to give her brain the time to punch through the fuzz surrounding it. Honestly, it felt like her brain had been wrapped in the softest lamb's wool and cradled in a box that was a little too small for it, creating pressure just short of pain, but irritating as hell.

Where had she been? Oh, that's right, the trail. There was the trap and the cloud...

Damn! She had fallen for a gas trap. Like a dummy, she had jumped to the ground to avoid unpleasant physical obstacles, but put herself right in the field of effect of the gas.

Her mind worked on that thought. She tried to move again, but was unable. But she was thinking more clearly now. Ropes. She could feel rough fibers around her arms. That could only mean one thing.

"Marla Shrike," a voice said.

Her lids fluttered and finally opened. She was in a bed, or at least a pallet, and there were walls around her. The light was good enough to see by, but dim enough that it wasn't too bright for her sensitive eyes. Sitting directly in front of her was a man with short blond hair. She recognized him, she thought.

"Quentin? Quentin Duzen."

The man ducked his head in a little seated bow.

"What are you doing? What am I doing here?"

"Come now, Marla. With your mind, your abilities, you should be shaking off the effects of the dreampuff by now. Don't play ignorant with me. *You* tell me what I'm doing here, and why you are here."

Her thinking was becoming clearer, as he said. She ran through what she knew about the man. Though she didn't know him well, she did know some things. He was an adept like she was, a student who had mastered more than three schools at the Academy, but continued to study there. If he had left the Academy for good, he would be called a viro. She had a feeling that was now the correct term for him.

He had mastered five schools: Preparatory Studies, Fundamental Magic, Long Weapon Combat, Explosives, and Poisons. That would explain how he had set the trap for her, though it didn't make her feel any better that she had fallen for it. Of course, mastery was not everything. He had a deep cross-section of studies in the other schools as well, as most students had. As she had. Racking her brain, though, she couldn't remember what other things he excelled at. It probably didn't matter at this point.

"You," she said, letting iron into her voice. "You killed Skril."

"And?"

She gritted her teeth. "And Master Aeid. Why, Quentin?"

"It's all very regrettable, Marla. Especially young Skril. I didn't know him well, but he seemed a good person. I enjoyed interacting with him when we were at the Academy."

"Did you enjoy *interacting* with him when you stabbed him through the heart?" she spat, straining against her ropes to get to him. As before, though, she couldn't move. He had tied both her arms and legs tightly. She was helpless.

Quentin looked at her calmly, his eyes revealing nothing about what he was thinking. After a long pause, he let out a breath. "No, Marla. I did *not* like having to do that to him. If it's any consolation, I did bind him with a spell so I could end him quickly, and without pain."

"That's very kind of you to *kill* him quickly."

The fuzz around Marla's brain was receding. She ran through her options. She couldn't do anything physical because of the ropes. Even if she still had all her weapons, she didn't think she could cut the bindings. Many of the spells she knew required somatic components, and since she couldn't gesture, those were out. A few of her spells could be cast with only vocal components, and even fewer could be cast without even speaking, only channeling the magic mentally. Those were beyond her at the moment because her mind wasn't completely clear, but soon...

"As for why you're here, Marla, that should be obvious. Like Skril, you have followed me and pose a threat to my plans. What shall I do about that?"

"Plans?" she said, more to stall him than anything else. Wasn't that how it worked in stories? Get the bad guy talking so you could have time to figure out an escape? "What plans? Why are you doing what you're doing, Quentin? Did Master Aeid do something to you?"

"Oh, that? No, no. Master Aeid was going to announce something that is the subject of rumor already, but which would hold more weight with a master of his standing behind it. His announcement may have affected the plans I have in place, uniting the Academy and others. I couldn't allow that. I did try to talk to him about it, but you know how stubborn he was. So unfortunate. I rather liked Master Aeid."

Marla stared at Quentin. "You...killed him over something he *might* say?"

Quentin stood from his chair and paced in front of her bed. "I'm afraid so."

"What? What could he have said that would merit such a thing?"

He stopped pacing and turned to face her. "Haven't you figured it out yet, Marla? You always did have a blind spot for this particular subject. He was about to proclaim that you are the Malatirsay. Unquestionably and undoubtedly."

"I'm what, now?"

"Don't pretend you haven't heard the whisperings, Marla. You have already—at your young age—mastered more schools than anyone in history. Your skills and ability to assimilate the Academy's education are beyond question. With Master Aeid's support, you would formally be recognized. He was the Master of Prophecy, after all. I'm afraid I couldn't let him make that announcement."

"But I still don't understand why. What difference does it make to you?"

"Let's just say that I can't allow a united defense at this time. It would interrupt my plans in the most terrible of ways."

Marla stared at Quentin. He did seem sincere in his regret, but that didn't mean he wouldn't kill again. Being sorry was not the same thing as resolving not to do something again. He'd killed Skril, too.

It was easy to see where this was going. He would eliminate her like he did the others. If her being called some name could interrupt his plans, then her existence could definitely do so. But why hadn't he killed her yet? There was only really one reason.

She blurted it out. "Let me join you. If me being recognized is so important, let me lend my recognition to what you're doing. It will work out for both of us."

He stepped over to the bed and squatted down so his eyes were level with hers. "Are you saying that you would join forces with the one who not only killed a master of the Academy, but also your friend?"

Marla ran through what she remembered from her classes in the School of Psychology about lying and how to detect it. She had to make him believe her. It was the only way to escape.

"Yes," she said calmly, looking him right in the eyes. "I regret that happened, but honestly, if you have to kill me, none of that will matter. If I can be useful, though, I can help make it so you won't have to kill anyone else."

"Hmm. That's intriguing." He stood. "I'll think about it. It's evening now. I'll return in the morning and we can discuss it. At that time, I'll make a decision. Sweet dreams."

Quentin left, closing the door softly behind him.

Once her captor was gone, Marla's breathing rate increased and her heart thumped more and more quickly in her chest. Did he believe her? Could she convince him that she was worth more to him alive than dead? She wasn't sure how convincing her performance was. It would have fooled many, either inside or out of the Academy, but what of Quentin? He had almost a decade more instruction at the Academy and she wasn't sure what he'd learned. He had most likely had the same classes in the School of Psychology and the same training in the School of Acting and Disguise.

She dropped all thoughts of that and focused on her breathing, which was becoming more rapid. She was starting to panic. It was exactly the wrong thing to do. Her body tightened against the ropes and soon her restrictions would feed that panic. She couldn't let that happen. If she didn't control herself, she would hyperventilate.

Stop! she screamed in her mind. *You are an adept at the Hero Academy. Act like it, or you'll die like Skril.*

She forced her body to go limp, concentrating only on her

breaths. Slow. Inhale. One...two...three. Exhale. One...two... three. Repeat. She clamped down on her thoughts, pictured her brain in a vice on a work bench in the School of Artifice. Steady.

She lay motionless for several minutes, breathing slowly in and out. Gradually, her racing heart settled and she didn't need to focus as strongly to keep her breathing even. Drops of perspiration slithered down her face, her neck and chest, and her back, like she had been fighting hard physically for an entire day. Now that she was calm, she only wanted to sleep.

But no, she couldn't. Quentin would come back and when he did, he would decide what to do with her. He was looking for an excuse not to kill her. She believed he had wanted to spare Skril, too. But would that be enough?

It hadn't been for her friend.

She couldn't leave her fate to the decision of someone who was obviously pressing on the edges of sanity. It would be a sad thing to leave the decision of her life or death to how effective she was at convincing him she would be a good ally. He'd never believe she'd let him get away with killing Skril.

It was settled, then. She had to do something, to escape somehow. If she was still in this room when he returned in a few hours, she would be murdered and there wasn't a thing she could do about it. If she had any hope, she needed to act now.

But how? Marla scanned the room. Quentin had kindly left a wall lantern lit so she would have light. It was too high up for her to use to try to burn the ropes off. It was over her head. There was the chair he had been sitting in, but not much else. The bed under her didn't have any sharp edges she could use. There were no windows and only the one door. It had a normal doorknob, not a latch or lever, with a keyhole. She had heard something click when he left, so it was probably locked.

Her spells. She was a master of the School of Air Magic

and had training in several of the other magic schools. Now was the time to go through them, spell by spell, to see if any of them would be helpful.

The useful fire spells she knew required somatic components, gestures of some kind, or at least a visual path to aim them. With her hands bound behind her, those were out. Water spells? She could maybe soak the ropes, but she wasn't sure if that would help or not. It was a shame she didn't know more voice magic. So many things seemed more important out in the world than they had at the Academy. If she ever got out of this mess, she would definitely revise her priorities.

When. *When* she got out of this mess.

What about Evon? Had Quentin captured him? Was he here, too, or even better, had he followed to rescue her? That would be fantastic, but she wasn't going to count on it. It just didn't seem like a mistake Quentin would make.

There had to be something. She just needed—

It suddenly felt like someone had grabbed Marla by her mind and shook her back and forth. Not her physical brain, her mind. Like some of the spells she had been subjected to in the Academy, psionic spells that captured one's senses and rung them like a bell. She felt it travel through her, making her ache and soothing her at the same time.

What the hells? It was...it was like all the magic of the world had been turned on its head, and her along for the ride. She closed her eyes and shook her head. When that didn't help, she laid back on the bed and kept her eyes closed, hoping it would all pass.

It did, slowly.

She heard footsteps, then a click and the door flew open. Quentin stood in the doorway, looking at her.

"What did you do?" he demanded.

"Nothing. I thought you did something."

He looked around the small room, relaxing when he didn't

seem to notice anything out of sorts. "Something significant just happened. Magic just...shifted." His eyebrows raised and a smile crept onto his face. "Ah, the portals. Maybe he's getting a toehold in this world."

His head snapped toward Marla, looking surprised he had said it aloud. Without another word, he turned, stepped out of the room, closed the door, and locked it.

Strange, Marla said to herself. *He's definitely losing it. More reason not to count on being able to convince him to spare me.*

Quentin said something about magic shifting. She thought he was right. But what did the shift mean? The world felt different, a little, but she couldn't put her finger on *what* was different. Whatever it was, hopefully it would help her. The gods knew she could use it.

She went back to her mental list of the spells she might use and finally settled on a novice air magic spell called Knife of Air. It required gestures as well as a verbal component, but the movements were simple. If she focused, she might be able to cast the spell and aim it well enough to cut her ropes. She might also cut herself with it, but it was worth a try.

She tried for more than a half hour. Her first attempts did nothing but to produce a slight breeze, but she kept at it. She found an angle at which she could move her bound wrists so that she could mostly perform the necessary gestures. Several more minutes allowed her to aim her palms while doing the movements to shoot the magic upward, between her arms.

Sweat poured down her forehead as she taxed her mind, putting everything she had into the spell. If Master Esiyae had seen her, Marla would have died from embarrassment to be working so hard on such a simple spell. Still, she continued. Finally, she was able to produce a legitimate air knife that shot from her palm and cut into the ropes.

Unfortunately, it also cut into her arm. She bit down hard to keep from cursing. It hurt more than a regular knife would because as it cut, the air pushed the flaps of skin aside, causing excruciating pain, like a strong stream of water used to clean a paper cut. Also unfortunately, it didn't cut the ropes enough for her to break them or squeeze out of them. Blinking away tears, she prepared to cast the spell again, hoping her aim would be a little better next time.

By the time she cut the ropes enough to break them and free her hands, she had several cuts in her arms, and blood had mixed with sweat and slicked her palms. The gashes felt like most of the blood in her body had leaked through them and like they had been dipped in salt to boot. When she peeled the ropes off and inspected the wounds, they didn't appear nearly as bad as they felt. That was at least one good thing.

With her arms free, she cast the spell again easily and cut the ropes from her legs—with no loss of skin or blood from those appendages.

She was free of her bonds, but still a prisoner. There was more to do before she could escape in truth.

She was running out of time.

❧ 28 ❧

Marla considered her options. She was passably skilled in stealth, but there were no windows in the room. She could pick locks, but she didn't have tools and there wasn't anything in the room she could use as such. She could fight—both with weapons and without—and she was pretty sure she could beat Quentin, but the situation was unclear. Did he have a weapon available, and were there others there with him? She was confident she could beat him even if he had his spear and she was unarmed—well, fairly confident—but with him armed and another person or two to help him? She wasn't sure. She was tired, hungry, and not in the best condition at the moment.

To be sure, she would have to do something else, something that left no chance of failure. She had to use magic.

There was only one spell that would fit the bill. The problem was that she had never been able to cast it effectively, though she had tried many times. It was one of the most advanced air magic spells she had been taught, one that she had only ever seen the Master of Air Magic at the Academy cast.

Master Esiyae had said on many occasions that Marla should be able to cast the spell, but that something was holding her back. Whether it was some type of mental block or simply the inability to metabolize the magic necessary, Marla didn't know. This particular spell had three components: verbal words of power, gestures, and infusion of the surrounding magical power, called *qozhel*.

There were few spells that were powered from ambient qozhel. Most spells took their power from the caster or elemental forces for the particular spell. Could she put all her learning together and cast it effectively where she had failed before? She could see no other way to escape without fighting her way out. For all she knew, those horsemen from Fyrefall could be in the next room.

That would be bad.

She decided to try the spell. It was called, aptly enough, Hurricane.

Marla spent a few minutes preparing her mind for using the magic around her, feeling it, pushing at it, moving it around. When it seemed to her to be a physical thing, something she could inspect and manipulate, she took a relaxed stance, legs shoulder-width apart and arms loose at her sides. Then she began the complex, scripted movements of the spell, all the while drawing in power from around her, transforming it to magic usable for the air spell.

She chanted the words to bring forth the power, speeding up the movements until she was a whirlwind herself, arms flailing as she continued to channel the energy.

When it seemed the magic would explode out of her of its own volition, Marla threw her arms out, sweeping toward the door of the room, and yelled the last word of power. If any had been standing near her, they wouldn't have heard it, though. The wind that had sprung up carried the sound away as quickly as it was spoken.

The space around her went silent for half a breath.

Then air exploded outward with a whistling scream capable of shattering glass with its own sound. But the wind of the spell was more powerful than that. It slammed into the walls, tearing them to pieces and scattering them. On all sides of Marla, there was whistling and tearing and devastation. For less than a minute, she had unleashed the raging fury of nature in that small area.

And then, suddenly, it stopped.

Marla collapsed to the ground and immediately lost consciousness. As she faded into unknowing, she wondered if she had just killed herself, and possibly Evon.

For the second time in a day, Marla came suddenly awake. She gasped, pulling in air, reminiscent of the spell she had cast. The spell she had *successfully* cast. How long had she been unconscious?

She looked around and her mouth dropped open. She was surrounded by pieces of wood, most of them barely bigger than her outstretched hand. They radiated out from the center—from where she lay—like there had been an explosion. She guessed there had been, in a way.

She got to her knees, barely able to do even that. She felt so weak, and her entire body was trembling.

The sun was up, and had been for at least two hours, so she could clearly see the wreckage around her. At most, the building she had been in had three rooms, just a small cabin. Trees surrounded it, some of them twisted and broken and others uprooted by the fury of her spell.

There were no other people around.

She slowly got to her feet, stumbled, righted herself, and turned in a circle. There was some shape off to the side, in between two trees. She stumbled over to it and found what was left of an iron-bound wooden chest. Mixed in with the remains of the container were her sword and knife, still on her belt. She raised her head and thanked whatever god or power or trickster had made it possible, then she dropped to her knees again and began to laugh herself silly.

Evon found her like that, head in her hands, laughing and crying at the same time.

⚬⚬⚬

EVON HAD QUICKLY CALMED HIS FRIEND DOWN AND GIVEN her some water.

"I went back to the fork and you weren't there," he told her. "I followed the trail until both tracks stopped. I've been searching the area ever since. It's been almost two days."

Marla stared at him. She couldn't think of what to say. To be honest, she couldn't think at all. Every thought seemed to echo as if she was screaming at the top of her lungs in a mammoth cave. It gave her a headache, so she simply stopped thinking.

"Marla," Evon said. "What happened?"

She blinked at him. "Quentin."

"Quentin? Quentin Duzen, from the Academy?"

"Quentin Duzen. Killed Master Aeid. Killed Skril. Kill me."

"Marla? Are you all right?"

She mechanically took another drink and a piece of cheese he offered her, then lay down. Maybe a little rest would make things right.

When she woke again, Evon was sitting next to her. She could think well enough to notice his red eyes and tired expression. He must have stayed awake to watch over her.

They stayed right where they were, in the middle of the debris, until she was able to carry on intelligent conversation. Once she could, there was only one thing on her mind.

"Did you find bodies? Did I kill Quentin?"

"No," Evon said. "I'm afraid not. I searched the area. There's no one else here." He looked uncomfortable and swallowed hard. "I did see two horse tracks, though. They went north."

Marla shook her head, the only thing she really had the energy for. "He got away. Again."

"Yes, but maybe you injured him. I don't really see how he could have survived all this." He gestured to the debris all around them.

"I don't know," she said, almost a whine. "Maybe he cast a shield or was behind a tree or something. Damn lucky. I finally was able to cast Hurricane and he somehow eluded it."

They remained in place for two more days. Evon fetched water from a nearby stream and foraged for wild vegetables. It didn't seem likely Quentin would be coming back, so they risked staying put while Marla recuperated.

She wasn't exactly sure how she'd managed to cast the spell, but she was more concerned about what it had done to her. It was almost as if it had taken some of her health away and converted it to magic. Or that the wind had actually come from her, and it tore through her body tissue to escape. She didn't like it. She felt off, like something had been broken inside her.

"I'll have to ask Master Esiyae about it," she said. "I don't think it's supposed to do that. If it is, it's no wonder no one else wants to cast the spell."

Evon nodded, but she could tell he was worried about her.

"Don't worry about me," she said. "I found my sword and knife. I'm just tired. It'll pass. Once I put both my blades through Quentin's eyes, I'll be fine."

He looked doubtful, but didn't say anything further. She appreciated it.

"Where are we, anyway?" she asked.

"A few miles from where your trail ended, maybe six or so from the fork in the road. I never would have found you if not for the explosion that tore this cabin apart."

She looked toward her feet. "I'm...sorry for insisting we split up."

"It's all right," he said. "If we had been together, we probably both would have been caught. He might have killed one or both of us right away to make things simpler. I'm glad you're alive, and I'm overjoyed that *I'm* alive." He winked at her and she felt better about things. A little. His expression grew serious. "Marla, what did you do? How did you destroy everything around you like that?"

"It was Hurricane."

"The spell you've been wrestling with?"

"Yeah. Master level air spell. I've never been able to cast it, but...did you feel the shift?"

Evon blinked at the change in subject. "Shift?"

"The shift! Did you feel magic lurch, like it was turning inside out or something. Maybe an hour or two before I cast Hurricane?"

"I did feel something," he said. "It actually made me fall down and I thought I might throw up."

"I think that's why I was able to cast the spell. It was like magic got stronger. Or at least different. Quentin said something about portals and 'him getting a toehold in this world.' Something has changed, Evon. It helped me to escape, but I don't know if it's a good thing overall. I've never heard about something like this. I've never read anything either, and I've spent an awful lot of time in the libraries at the Academy."

"Yeah, but all those libraries are new. The books were obtained and spread around the Academy libraries after the great fire destroyed all the precious books from the Age of Magic."

"Yeah. I wonder what was in all those books and scrolls that were lost. I know the masters scoured Dizhelim to rebuild the greatest collection of books in the world, but some of those destroyed were one of a kind, written or annotated by Tsosin Ruus himself. Where can we get information on what happened with that shift?"

"We'll have to deal with that later," he said. "Right now we need to figure out what to do. You're in no condition to travel long distances, and we still don't have horses."

"I've been thinking about that," she said. "We can't very well stay around here. There's a small chance he'll come back with reinforcements, but there is a chance. The way I figure it, we're fifty miles or so from Arcusheim. I think we should head there."

"Fifty miles! Marla, with how weak you are, we won't make it more than ten miles or so a day, especially going north. The vegetation gets thicker going that way, and I don't think there are any roads this close to Fyrefall."

"Then what do you suggest?"

Evon's eyebrows shot up. He probably wasn't expecting to have to come up with a plan himself. "I...don't know. I only know it's not going to be easy to make it all that way."

Marla grabbed her friend's hand and met his eyes. "Evon, we can't stay here. Not only is it dangerous, but it would serve no purpose. We need to get to a town or village, or to Arcusheim. Somewhere. We'll eventually need to get back to the Academy so we can tell the masters what happened. We'll take it slow, stopping when we need to, foraging or hunting. Between the two of us, we have more knowledge and skill than a dozen people who have not studied at the Academy. We'll be fine. We have to do this."

He sighed and squeezed her hand. "Yeah, I guess. I just

don't...I mean, you're so weak from the magic and we don't know if it'll get worse or if something else will happen or—"

"Relax." She chuckled. "You sound like my mother. We'll go slow. I'll get stronger as we go along, you'll see. I don't feel injured, just very tired. Drained. I won't push my limits. A few miles a day at first, until I get my strength back. Okay?"

"Sure. Why not? I shouldn't expect anything to go our way, right? Isn't that how things always go?"

"From what I've seen? Yes. Definitely. I miss Skril and his optimism."

"Me, too."

They had already searched the area and found no trace of Marla's pack and supplies. She figured Quentin had taken them or that they were still tied to one of his horses from when he captured her. In any case, they had only Evon's pack and what it contained, which was precious little in the way of food.

"We have your water skins, and there are plenty of streams and rivers in the area," she told him. "We'll have to set snares when we stop for the day, and eat whatever fruit and vegetables we find. It'll be fun, like a camping adventure."

He gave her a side eye and shook his head. Her attempted positive spin didn't budge his sour mood.

They headed due north, knowing they'd eventually get to Arcusheim, the Genta Highway, or the shore of the Kanton Sea. There was no way they could get lost if they kept moving northward. With the rising sun at their right shoulder, they started off.

A mile into their trek, everything changed.

"Is that what I think it is?" she asked, pointing at some bushes a few paces away from them.

"I don't believe it." Evon stepped over and squatted to get a better look. "Yep, horse tracks. Two of them, to be exact, traveling one behind the other, the back horse slightly to the left of the front one."

Marla's face cracked with a wide smile. "Yes! There are still gods of luck in the world."

"Luck?" Evon said. "Bad luck, maybe. You aren't seriously considering following after him again. Didn't you learn your lesson?"

"Oh, come on, Evon. He obviously thinks I'm dead, that I killed myself by wielding magic I didn't know how to use. He's not half wrong. It was dark, so he wouldn't have seen me lying there. With that type of damage to everything, how could he think I had survived? Even if he did, he was probably running for his life. If I had lived through that, then I obviously had more power than he could deal with. He won't be expecting us."

"He won't be expecting us because we would have to be crazy to go after him. He almost killed you. He *did* kill Skril. I don't relish the thought of him getting another chance with you and having me there as a bonus."

"We don't have to try to get him right away," she said. "We'll use his trail to get to whatever city he's going to and then we'll decide what to do. It'll make our travel easier if we don't have to blaze our own trail."

"You're trying to get me killed. That's what this is. There can be no other explanation. For some reason, you want me dead, but you don't want to do it the easy way by sticking your sword through me. Instead, you want to make me suffer first."

"Nah," she said, laughing. "I'm just trying to add some excitement to your life. And trying to keep track of the murderer who killed both Master Aeid and Skril. We'll be so far behind him, he'll never know we're here. We now have a path to follow instead of bashing our way through trees and undergrowth." She looked at the faint path, not much more than an animal trail. "At least we won't have to bash through as much."

"Let's just keep going," Evon said. "We both know I won't win this argument. We might as well bicker while we're moving."

❦ 29 ❧

They followed the trail—slowly. Marla didn't speak for a while, not wanting to aggravate her friend more than she had already. She didn't want to argue about their path forward, but it was logical for them to follow the horses' trails. They would get to a road or civilization sooner and they may get the bonus of catching Quentin eventually as well. He had to know where he was going, right? Why not follow his tracks and take advantage of it?

It took six days to get to the city of Arcusheim. Neither of them had ever been there before.

"What now?" Evon asked.

The trail had gone right onto the Genta Highway near Arcusheim and they both assumed Quentin had entered the city. There was no way they could track him now. The trail was lost forever in the shuffle of one of Dizhelim's main roadways. Probably hundreds of feet, hooves, and wheels had been over the horse tracks since Quentin had passed.

"We could try to search for him," she said, watching Evon carefully for the reaction she expected. He simply sighed and stared at her, the edges of his mouth turned down.

"Why don't we have a real meal and get a room at an inn so we can sleep in a bed for a change," he said. "After that, we can discuss how looking for him in a city this size is a stupid thing to do."

Marla was smart enough to recognize that Evon was at the edge of his tolerance. She agreed and they found an inn to do what he had suggested. Luckily, Quentin hadn't taken her purse off her sword belt, so along with her weapons, they both had a moderate amount of money. Most of their trip hadn't presented them with opportunities to spend any of it.

"We can get some supplies tomorrow," she said.

Evon bounced his coin purse in his hand, judging its weight. His frown deepened.

"There's not much left. I wish we had enough to buy even one horse to share, but at this point, we'll have to be careful if it's going to stretch long enough to get us supplies to go home. We won't be spending every night in an inn. We're going to need to forage or hunt."

Against Evon's wishes, they spent eight days in Arcusheim, scouring the streets for any sign of Quentin Duzen. The first thing they did was to buy cloaks to cover themselves so they wouldn't be recognized.

There was no real method to their search. The pair asked questions at apothecary shops, weapon vendors, and taverns. Quentin was a striking man, muscular and handsome, with his blond hair cropped short. It wasn't a common hairstyle. Still, all the questions in the world didn't seem to do any good.

"Are you satisfied?" Evon asked her on the seventh day. "I don't think he ever actually made it into Arcusheim, or if he did, he's got a house here and is hiding out. We really need to get back to the Academy. The masters must think we've abandoned the investigation, as well as our studies. Hells, for all we know, the other investigators will already have solved it."

"*We* have already solved it," she snapped. "Quentin admitted as much." She took a breath. "But yes, you're right. I think we wasted all this time on an impossible task. We'll get one more good night's sleep and leave tomorrow to go home."

Evon put his hand on her shoulder. "Thank you."

"Yeah, sure."

The days in the city had done wonders for their appearance. They weren't as haggard as they had been when they limped into Arcusheim, and Marla had recovered completely, feeling like her old self. She wasn't happy to slink back home in defeat, but what else could they do?

With a last look at the city, they stepped onto the Genta Highway, heading east toward where it met with the River Road.

It took them six days to reach the intersection and to begin traveling north. Making the trip without their horses seemed an endless slog. Taking time to forage or hunt for food ate up valuable traveling time as well.

"I hope Surefoot is okay," Marla said as they headed toward their home so many miles away. "She doesn't deserve to be abused or harmed. I guess I'll never see her again or know what happened to her. That's another thing I owe Quentin for. I'll kill him twice for that."

Evon plodded beside her, face toward the north, not even bothering to look at Marla. "I'd settle for once."

They spoke little, both of them tired of the endless journey. At least for Marla, part of her frustration was also that she'd be returning to the Academy—however long that would take—in defeat. They had valuable information for the masters about the investigation, Quentin, Skril, and those dark monsters they had fought, but it still felt like she had lost in every contest that mattered.

The River Road was frequently traveled, and they passed

people on the road, or were passed. Some were going south, but others going north on horses or in wagons or carriages. Every time someone traveling faster than them went by, Marla spat the dust from their passing from her mouth, adding a curse or two to expel the indignity. As far as she'd seen, she and Evon were the only ones stupid enough to travel the road on foot.

"Why don't these people stay home instead of kicking up dust as they pass the poor, weary travelers who have to rely on only their feet?"

Evon chuckled, a dry, pathetic sound. "We'll get to the section where there are more villages soon, then you can curse at the people who are sitting comfortably in their homes, too. In no time, we'll..." he trailed off as they rounded a bend in the road and saw someone up ahead.

A man sat at the side of the road. He looked to be conversing with his horse, which was standing nearby, packs strapped about it like it was a mule.

"I told you," the man said to his companion, "we have a few more miles to go before we stop for the day. Why must you always be so lazy?"

He noticed Marla and Evon and swept his hat from his head and bowed. "Good afternoon, travelers."

"Good afternoon to you," Evon said, a slight tinkle of laughter in his voice. It made Marla think of Skril.

The man looked young, maybe a decade older than Marla. His clothes hung on him, ill-fitting over his scrawny frame. His head, covered with light brown hair, barely came up to Marla's chin, but still, there was something about him. His brown eyes seemed to hold more wisdom than his youth would account for, and in the depths, she just made out some sort of mystery. Overall, his features made a strange sight.

"How are your travels?" Evon asked, always the polite young man.

"I suppose they are what all travels should be. They are both wondrous and wearying, educational and energy-sapping, both what I would choose above all else and that which I abhor the most." That last part was said with a frown cast at his horse.

"Are you a poet, then?" Marla asked.

"Oh no. I am a simple scholar and historian. Pofel Dessin is the name. It is my pleasure to meet you."

"A scholar?" Evon asked. "Well met, Pofel Dessin. I am Evon Desconse and this is my friend Marla Shrike. What is it you study?"

"Unfortunately, I have many interests. I cannot seem to keep myself to one, or even a few, subjects. When something strikes my fancy, I pursue it with all my strength. At the present moment, I am studying some of the ancient sites that were key in the War of Magic. I have recently left Broken Reach and am heading to the Sittingham Desert. Fascinating places. But I don't have to tell you that, do I, my *adept* friends."

Marla caught the slight inflection when the man said adept. "Do we know you?" She narrowed her eyes at him.

"You do now, my friends, though we have just met. It is obvious, however, from your bearing and your movements, that you have training in physical arts. The way you hold yourselves also indicates that you are confident, not haughty like many your age, but sure of your competence. I also sense power in you. Those things together tell me one thing: you have studied at Sitor-Kanda, and my guess is that you still do." He bowed to them again.

Evon looked back and forth from Marla to Pofel, eyes alight. "That's very good. You obviously have more experience than your age would account for as well."

"I have learned some things in my travels," Pofel said. "For example, did you know that in the investigation of a crime scene, inspectors will often miss vital clues if they are distraught or in some other way emotionally affected by what has happened?"

Marla's eyes narrowed even further and her hand strayed to her sword hilt. "What are you getting at?"

Pofel put his hands up, noticing Marla's posture change. "Nothing, nothing. I have simply learned from interviewing some brilliant investigators that it is often advantageous to go back over a crime scene with a calmer, more rational mind that is detached from emotional anchors. It can often make the difference between finding the clue that leads to solving the mystery and making foot-weary circles looking for answers."

Pofel's horse took the opportunity to push the man with its head.

"Ah, my friend here seems ready to continue our journey. It was a pleasure meeting you, Evon, Marla. Good luck with your quest. Remember, it is sometimes advantageous to back-track to be sure one has been thorough."

Without another word, Pofel picked up his horse's reins and led it back into the center of the road, heading south. In a few minutes, he turned around the bend and was lost from sight.

"Strange man," Marla said.

Evon nodded, but she could almost see his mind churning.

"I'm only saying that he had a point," Evon said as the pair continued on their trek north.

"He's a crazy man," Marla answered. "Don't you think it was kind of creepy the way he said that out of the blue? I mean, who says those kinds of things to people they just met?"

"Forget all that. Think about what he said. He's obviously pretty smart, the way he picked out right away that we were from the Academy. What he said sounds like it has some merit."

Marla pulled up short, grabbing Evon's arm and spinning him to face her. "You're talking about going back *there*, Evon. The only reason I'm not falling apart over what happened is that I'm trying to keep busy, to focus on other things, so I don't have to think about it. About him."

"I know. I feel the same way, but like you always tell me, you have to push everything else away and focus on what you need to do. I think we need to go back, look for anything we missed. We were in no condition to do a good job of it when we were there."

"It won't matter. It's been too long. There won't be anything left that can help us. All we'll do is dredge up those feelings, those images, again. I'm not going."

Evon sighed as she released his arm, straightened her back, and turned back toward the north, stepping like she was marching to a gallows.

"I'll do it without you," he said, following a few steps behind.

"What?"

"You do what you want. I'm going back to where we found the wagon. Where we found Skril. I'm going to look over the area with fresh eyes and see if there's any other clue we might have missed."

Marla stopped and stared at him, her mouth open.

"You can either wait for me on the road or you can continue on. Either way, I'm going to do it."

The two were silent for the better part of two days, up to where Evon planned to leave the road, go east, and head back to the scene of Skril's murder. As he stepped toward the trail the wagon had made—mostly erased by the growth of the vegetation—he didn't bother to say anything to Marla.

Marla watched him take a few steps before turning and following. She caught up and walked beside him for a while, neither of them looking at the other.

"Thank you," he whispered as they trudged toward their friend's final resting place.

"Sure."

When they arrived, the scene looked much as it did when they had left it. There was no smoke, of course, and the remnants of the wagon had deteriorated more, but nothing had disturbed the site.

The pair poked around in the wagon, kicking the charred pieces of wood to scatter them. They found the remnants of a lantern, a spoon, and a few coins, but nothing important.

The place where Skril had fallen showed no sign that it had been soaked with the blood of their friend, and the ashes of the pyre they had made for him sat in a circle where they had fallen.

"Nothing," Marla said disgustedly.

"Well, it was worth a try." Evon kicked at the ground. A puff of dust went into the air as he scattered the dirt near where Skril's body had been. He looked down like he was going to spit, but stopped and knelt instead. He reached down and scratched at the dirt.

He wasn't facing Marla, so his back was blocking her view. She moved around him to see what he was doing as he stood up.

He had a piece of cloth in his hands.

"What is it?" she asked.

"A bit of ripped clothing. It looks like a piece of a grey tunic."

"Skril doesn't wear grey. He doesn't like it. Didn't...like it. Too bland, he always said."

"I know."

"Then whose is that?"

Evon brought it closer to his face, turning it in his hands. "It's pretty fine cloth, like what a prosperous trader would wear. Or what someone wearing a trader disguise would wear."

"Do you think?"

"I don't know, but there's one way to find out. I still have the other locator kit."

"Let's do it," Marla said.

They set up the other locator in the clearing.

"It works better with at least two or three items, particularly something closely related to an item owned by the person, like the necklace with Skril. It may not work at all."

"And it may not even be Quentin's clothing," Marla said.

"I know. Just try it and see. Maybe we'll get lucky, even though I feel like I've had my quota of luck already."

Evon activated the locator and moved it along the map. When it got near the northern part of the Teats, it flashed orange.

"Feel like backtracking one more time?" Evon asked Marla.

"Feel like it? No. Do I think we should do it? Hells yes. If there's any chance we can find Quentin this way, I'm all for it."

They packed up the locator and map and headed back to the River Road. This time, Evon was the weak one and Marla had to slow her pace to his. There was a chance, though, and that made all the difference in the world.

They traveled another three days to where the locator had shown them the orange color. It was just north of the foothills of Sinis Mountain, at the edge of Ianthra's Breasts. They searched, but it was a large area with difficult terrain, so they decided to use the locator again to narrow in on their prey.

Evon had shaken off the weariness from using the locator before, and cast his magic again without hesitation. When he placed the device on the map where they currently were, it glowed yellow.

"Damn," he said.

"Is it broken? Doesn't it work anymore?"

He moved the locator slowly in an ever-widening spiral from where it had indicated their target was a few days before. By the time it turned a pale orange, it was close to Arcusheim.

"What does that mean?" Marla asked. "Is he on the move, going back to Arcusheim?"

"No. I think it means we can't get it to lock onto a true location with only that small scrap of cloth. We can go chasing Quentin where the map shows, but I think when we get there, it'll show us another place, maybe even point back to here. It was a good try, but I think we need something with a stronger connection than what we have. I'm sorry, Marla."

"You don't have to be sorry. It was a good try. It's not your fault. Let's head back home. Maybe we'll think of something on the way. The gods know we'll have enough time, traveling on foot."

"Back to foraging and camping on the side of the road," he said with a sigh. "We might have enough money for one or two nights at an inn, and to get some supplies, but that's it."

"So be it," she said.

Marla pushed her anger down to a slow simmer. She was so tired, and rage wouldn't help her right now. They had a long trip ahead of them, longer now that they'd chased the thin thread of a lead farther south. There was nothing else they could do, though. It was time to go back home.

❧ 3 1 ❧

Six more days of traveling, foraging, trying to stay alive, and they were camped off the River Road a half mile or so, just south of the Mellafond. They had made a fire, chancing it because they were in a sheltered hollow near a cliff. Doing without was miserable. Hot food always tasted better.

As they finished their evening meal and were preparing for bed, the sound of horses reached their campsite. Marla reached for her sword, but did not draw it. It could be other travelers only wanting to share their fire.

Six men on horseback rode up to their fire and dismounted.

"Evening," one of them said in a dry, gravelly voice. "Can we share your fire? Been a long day on the road."

"Sure," Marla said. "We're done with it anyway. We were just about to leave. Help yourself." She got up and stepped closer to Evon, who was hitching up his pack.

"Not so fast," one of the other men said, moving to the side to block their path. "We didn't say you could go."

"You don't want to do this," Marla told the man. "You really don't."

"We don't, huh?" the first man said. "You're wrong there, woman. We do want to do this, and you'll cooperate if you know what's good for you. All we want is whatever you have, and what's under those tight pants of yours. We haven't had a woman in weeks. We'll be gentle. Be nice and we won't even kill your man."

"Oh," Marla said. "That's all? Well, you should have said so to begin with. Who's first?"

The man handed his reins to one of his companions and stepped into the firelight. "That would be me."

"Good," she said. "I was going to suggest that." She turned toward Evon and whispered "Ready?" He nodded and she sprang into action.

Spinning while drawing her sword, she lashed out, a quick horizontal slash in the same direction she was rotating. There was a wet slurp and the man's eyes doubled in size. Then, both hands went to his throat and he made a gurgling noise and fell forward onto his face.

All hell broke loose, the other five men rushing to draw their own weapons. Three of them fell dead before their blades even left scabbard or sheath. Two remained, one near Evon and one near Marla.

"Every time I try to help someone, tell them that they don't want to do something, they always try to prove me wrong. Do you know how frustrating that is?"

Evon flicked some of the blood from his sword. "I know, but what are you going to do? People are generally stupid. Attacking us with only six men. How ridiculous." He stalked toward the man near him while Marla shuffled closer to the other.

"Now, don't do anything hasty," one of the men said.

"Here, I'll even throw down my sword. No reason we can't discuss this."

Marla put an exaggerated look on her face like she was seriously thinking of the man's offer. Then she shook her head. "No, I don't really think so. My delicate sensibilities have been damaged. Your friend there, the one with no throat, not the one with the leaky heart, he said you were going to take advantage of me. Me, a poor, innocent maiden nearly alone and completely scared on the road. How can we let that pass?"

The confusion on the man's face disgusted Marla. "I'm telling you that you're going to die like your friends. By all means, take it personally."

He jumped at her, swinging his sword downward like he wanted to cut her head down the middle. It was one of the most pathetic attacks Marla had ever had the misfortune to witness. She calmly side-stepped, slapping the sword away with her dueling dagger, and punched her sword through his eye. His body twitched, then fell to the ground as she slid her sword from him.

The other man actually threw his sword down and ran away screaming.

Evon jerked his head in the direction the man had gone.

"No," she said. "There's no reason to kill him. He won't come back and bother us."

"Good." Evon wiped his blade on the man he had killed earlier. "Killing someone in combat is one thing, but in cold blood? I don't like that. Gods, I can't believe I'm saying killing another human is okay to begin with."

"Having your friend murdered and almost dying several times yourself will do that to a person," she said. "I agree with you, though. If this one"—she kicked the last man she'd killed —"had been really planning to disarm himself, he'd be alive right now, too. But more importantly, we now have horses. It won't take anything close to as much time to get back to the Academy as we expected."

They searched the men and found objects that clearly pointed to them being bandits. A few loose gems, several purses with assorted coins, a locket with a woman's picture in one of their pockets, several different knives, and fine clothing stuffed into one of the saddle bags all indicated these ruffians were not simple travelers.

After they had taken everything of value, Marla and Evon mounted two of the horses, tied the others with a rope to keep them close, and headed north on the road. They stopped again in a few hours to get a night's sleep. They were far enough from where they had left the lone man, but alternated watches just in case.

EVON WAS HAPPY THEY FINALLY HAD HORSES. AT THE FIRST small town they came to, they sold the extra four horses. They now had more than enough money to stay at inns each night if they wanted. After two months on the road, that was a luxury they couldn't pass up.

Marla didn't seem content about anything, and happiness did not even come into the picture.

"Of course we'd finally get horses when we're so close to home," she grumped. "It couldn't have been two or three weeks ago. No, that would be too easy. Surely don't let them find horses when she is weak and can't travel quickly. Of all the stupid luck..."

Evon stopped listening. He nodded his head occasionally over the next several days, but that was all. His friend had been in a foul mood since they started riding. Sure, she hadn't been happy before, when they were making their way on foot, but her anger had taken an exponential jump as they neared their home.

"You're afraid of dealing with the masters," he said as it finally struck him. She didn't look pleased at being interrupted during a particularly salty rant about the world and all those in it. "That's why you're acting like a bear with a sore tooth."

"Oh, shut up," she said.

"No. You've been talking nonstop all day long. Saying nothing of importance, but talking anyway. I want to hear what you think about what I said. You're worried about going back and facing punishment for breaking the rules."

She glowered at him. Then her shoulders slumped and she sighed. "Nothing went how I thought it would. First Skril, then going into Fyrefall, losing track of Quentin, then getting caught by him, then losing him again...it's all too much. At least if we had come back with Quentin, or his body, the masters might be more forgiving, but I failed in everything I set out to do and I dragged you along for the ride. They're going to flay me and feed me to the wolves. Then they'll prohibit me from leaving the Academy grounds again until I'm ninety years old."

"Don't be so hyperbolic. They'll probably just kill you. They wouldn't want the wolves to get indigestion, and they won't want you to be hanging around to pester them." He smiled when he said it, but she was having none of it.

"Leave me alone so I can think. We'll be there tomorrow and I'll have to explain what I did." She shook her head, then spat. "I'm really sorry for pulling you into this, Evon. I know how much you hate breaking rules or getting in trouble."

"I went with you into Fyrefall of my own free will. I don't remember you tying me up and dragging me along physically."

"Yeah, well, that hardly means I didn't coerce you. Thank you for helping me, though."

"Skril was my friend, too. We did what we had to. We'll face whatever the masters concoct for us and we'll learn from it. Maybe we'll get a bit of wisdom out of the whole thing."

Marla growled under her breath but didn't say anything else. Evon decided it was best to let her stew for a while. Her anger would eventually drain out; it always did. He truly hoped it did so before they had to meet with the masters. If she let it make her flippant or disrespectful, it would go worse for them.

The remainder of the trip was fairly pleasant as long as he ignored the mutterings and colorful curses of his companion. As time passed, they stopped to camp early each night— there were no towns between the Mellafond and Dartford— and got up well after the sun was up. Marla still wore her frown, but she wasn't actively trying to argue with him, so it wasn't as bad as it could have been.

The terrain became familiar, and Evon recognized that they could make it to the Academy within a day if they pushed the pace. They could have gotten rooms in Dartford —they still had the money from the bandits, after all—but Marla didn't want to deal with people. He agreed that it would be a bad mix with her current mood. So camping it was. No matter what the masters did, though, he swore that the next day would not end without him taking a bath. It was patently ridiculous to be so excited about that, but that's how he felt. Dipping his body in a cold river could never compare to soaking in hot water.

While Evon felt relief flood into him to be in territory they knew well, Marla grew more aggravated. She muttered under her breath and cursed out loud at things they encountered along the road. Things like birds making too much noise, pollen that puffed from some of the flowers occasionally, dust covering her boots, and the road itself. The road especially made her as touchy as a wet cat.

Soon, he kept reminding himself. *We'll be back home soon.*

For better or worse.

❦ 32 ❧

Evon suffered through it all in silence, counting down the miles until they reached the bridge and then got to the Academy proper. As they reached a narrowing of the road, Marla rushed out in front as if no longer able to tolerate him being even a few feet ahead of her.

It was a place they both knew well, only a few miles from the bridge between the mainland and Munsahtiz. Trees crowded the roadway, leaving barely enough room for two horses to pass each other. The restriction only went on for a few hundred yards, but it gave the sensation of being in a tunnel. Evon had always liked the section of the road. It felt like the kind of path he'd seen pictures of, manicured trees flanking some lord's estate. He found a smile coming to his lips.

"Move, move," Marla said ahead of him, breaking up his pleasant thoughts. Ahead, several people were coming the other way on foot. Marla was waving them over, obviously believing she had the right of the entire roadway.

Evon shook his head. She could be a real trial when she was in a black mood.

"Get out of the way, boy!" she shouted, and Evon leaned to the side to see who she was screaming at now. "You're lucky I didn't run you down."

A young man with red-brown hair hanging loose down below his shoulders started, obviously surprised to find a horse jostling him to the side.

"Sorry," he said. "I guess I was caught up in my own thoughts."

"That's no excuse," Marla hissed. "Watch where you're going."

Evon could see where this was going. The last thing they needed was conflict so close to home. "Marla," he said. "It's fine. No harm done. Let's go."

She didn't even turn to acknowledge Evon. She pulled her reins and stopped her horse, glaring at the man in front and to the side of her.

"Well?" she said.

"Well what?" the man answered.

"You have nothing to say for yourself, *boy?*"

Evon sighed and shrugged his shoulders while he met the eyes of one of the man's companions, a dark-haired beauty who looked vaguely familiar.

"I said all I need to say, *girl*. I was preoccupied. I apologized. Go on your way."

"Girl?"

"You're not much older than me," the man said. "Maybe younger. If I'm a boy, then you're a girl. I can explain the words, if you like. If you don't understand them."

Well, that was it. Nothing Evon could say at this point would stop her.

Marla bared her teeth at the man. "Don't give me lip, *boy*, or this *girl* will kick your ass."

And then it happened, probably the worst thing that could have occurred. Evon's eyes grew wide when the man started laughing. Laughing! If only he knew how dangerous the woman he was laughing at was.

"You find that funny?" Marla asked, her fair skin going scarlet with anger.

Evon put his hands up. "Marla, please. Let's just go. He apologized."

"No, Evon. I've had it. These past days have rubbed me raw. I could use a little exercise to blow off steam."

Evon met the young man's eyes and put his hands up in front of him while shrugging. He scanned the man's companions while he was making his apologetic gesture.

Marla leaped out of the saddle and landed right in front of the man. "So, how about it, boy? You want a duel?"

"A...did you say a duel?"

"I did."

"We're not in Arania. I don't duel."

"Then I guess I'll just whomp you for a little while, trying to build up a sweat."

The man looked at Evon. "Is she serious?"

Evon sighed. "I'm afraid so. She's a little...intense sometimes."

The man laughed again. He was brave. At least that much could be said. Brave or stupid.

A flash of motion, and it registered to Evon that Marla had thrown a punch at the man's face, her action a blur.

And he had sidestepped it as quickly. He looked as if he stopped himself from counterattacking automatically, like if he had let his body do what it wanted, he would have struck back. Maybe he did have some skill.

"Is that your idea of a duel?" he asked Marla calmly, as if she hadn't just tried to knock his head off his body.

"No," she said. "That was my idea of the start of a brawl. Duels involve weapons."

"You're mad," he said.

"I am. Mad that you won't duel me like a man. I guess you *are* just a boy."

This was getting serious. "Marla," Evon said.

"Oh, shut it, Evon. I won't injure him permanently, just knock him around a little until he learns some manners."

The older man, one of the young man's companions, fuzzed and there was suddenly an arrow nocked on his bowstring and drawn to his cheek. The man's white eyes seemed fixed on Marla, his body unmoving as a statue. Who *were* these people?

"No, Tere," the young man said. "It's fine. I could use some exercise, too. Besides, someone needs to show this *girl* why she shouldn't be so rude. I just hope she can sit her saddle when I'm done bruising her arse." He had the audacity to smile at Marla. "It is a nice arse, though. I'll give you that."

Evon shook his head. Despite her penchant for snug clothing, Marla never responded well to compliments like that.

Marla gritted her teeth and drew her sword and her dueling knife.

The man held his hands up. "Hold on, hold on. Let's move down the road a bit. I don't want my friends to get hurt when you swing those blades around wildly trying to hit me."

"I won't cut anyone but you," she said in a voice so cold, Evon wondered if he could tackle her to stop this without getting gutted himself. "I hit what I aim for."

"Fine," the man said. "Then let's move away a bit so that when I throw you to the ground, you won't trip any of them as you roll across the dirt."

She tensed up, ready to charge, but Evon risked putting his hand on her shoulder. "Marla, if you insist on doing this, at least be respectful to those who moved out of the way without you screaming at them."

Marla grunted and pushed past the man and her horse to where the trees opened up and the road widened out.

The man, much too calmly for Evon's liking, followed her.

Without warning, Marla charged, slashing at him with her sword.

The man simply twisted at the waist, letting her weapon whiz past him. He pushed her shoulder with his left hand, causing Marla to break her form a tiny bit. Just enough time for him to draw one of the swords from his back.

Marla, of course, didn't lose her balance. She was much too experienced for that. She moved like a snake, delivering a backhand blow.

Which the man deflected with his own sword. Her knife moved in, a fraction of a second later, and a second clang echoed out as his other sword, somehow out of its scabbard and in his hand, parried the follow-up attack. Without any noticeable shift in his stance, he kicked out at Marla, almost as if he had been planning the move from the start.

Marla hopped back, out of the range of the strike, glaring at her opponent.

The man, for his part, had a slight smile on his face. He was enjoying the confrontation!

Marla charged in again, her weapons a blur. Evon couldn't even tell which glitter in the sunlight was which blade.

But apparently the man could. She struck at him at least half a dozen times, and he parried each of them. Surprisingly, he was in such control of himself, he was able to sweep at Marla's lead leg. Which she raised out of the way.

At the same time, the man trapped her blades with his own and shouldered her, ramming into her chest and causing her to back up, off balance and spitting mad.

"Not bad, boy," she said as they circled.

The man nodded, but remained silent. Marla tensed

further, obviously insulted that he didn't return the compliment in kind.

Marla lunged, attacking several times in succession with straight line attacks, short movements that were too quick for most swordsmen to deal with.

Again, though, the man did deal with them. He began to whirl, using soft, flowing movements with his blades, so graceful it nearly brought a tear to Evon's eyes. It was simply beautiful, a perfect example of classical Shinyin techniques. How had this man gotten so good?

He transformed his movements into something different than the classical forms. Evon had studied enough to recognize the graceful blend of master sword techniques from at least three nations, though he could never have the skill to perform them himself.

The man continued to press the attack, spinning and slashing, so fast Evon couldn't tell whose blade was whose. Only the symphony of clinks and clangs told him that the attacks were being turned aside. A worried, sinking feeling in his belly whispered that the man wasn't even at the limit of his skill.

Marla stepped to the side while parrying and then came at him with strong, hammering blows, like the ones the Clavian Knights used with their longer than average swords. Somehow, she was able to channel her power so the blows appeared to have more mass behind them.

The man seemed content to parry and evade the blows. Evon thought he might be trying to tire Marla out.

Almost in answer, Marla began to huff her breaths. She controlled them well, but what she was doing, at the speed she was doing it, was akin to sprinting for two miles. He wasn't sure how long she could continue. All the while, her opponent moved smoothly, using as little energy as possible, breathing easily.

Suddenly, Marla's leg flew out. It almost seemed like someone else's appendage, on the ground one moment and then lashing out at the man.

He took a half step back, pivoted, and slammed the pommel of his sword into her leg. It threw her into a spin and she rolled in the direction of the strike, coming to her feet several feet away, but favoring her other leg.

Evon gasped at the same time he heard a similar sound from one of the man's companions. He thought it was the tall, dark-haired woman.

Marla spit a few strands of hair out of her mouth and muttered a few words.

No, Evon thought. *She wouldn't.*

When he saw her gesturing, he knew she would. "Marla!" he shouted, but it was too late.

The force of her spell slammed into the man, throwing him back several feet. He twisted slightly in midair, touching the ground with rounded shoulders in a way that seemed almost soft, and rolled back onto his feet, his stance firm and swords held out in front of him.

Marla beckoned for him to attack.

He apparently decided he would take her invitation.

The man smoothly sheathed his swords, made a few motions like he was limbering up his wrists and arms, and charged, picking up speed until he was at a full sprint.

Evon was afraid to see the result. Marla was casting again. He wasn't sure, but it looked like an air spell. A powerful one.

The man kept running at her.

He had passed the halfway mark when Marla's spell shot from her hands toward her opponent. How was she going to explain that she had killed or maimed a random person she had met on the road? Evon wanted to close his eyes, but he couldn't. He stared, transfixed, at how it would play out.

The shimmer of Marla's spell slammed into the man.

No. No, it didn't. It reflected off something, pushing him slightly off-course, but not tearing into him as Evon had thought it would. As it glanced to the side, Marla's eyes went wide.

And then the man's foot slammed into her abdomen, a powerful and perfect flying sidekick landing in the most torturous of ways.

Marla's body bent over the kick and she left her feet, flying backward several feet while both her blades left her grip. Air rushed out of her in a grunt, and whatever was left came out in a soft whoosh when she landed. She was able to roll out of it and come to her feet, but she was unsteady on her legs.

The red-haired woman began to wheeze out more words of power, and Evon knew that this time nothing would stop her short of killing her opponent.

He jumped in between the two. "Enough Marla!" he screamed. "Enough. It's getting out of hand. If you two continue, someone is going to die. What are you going to tell the masters about that? You can't just go around trying to kill people." Evon looked back and forth between the two combatants. "Besides, I'm sorry to say it, but he beat you fair and square. You know magic isn't part of a weapons duel."

Marla glared at the man, then at Evon. She picked her weapons up and slammed them into their scabbards.

"Here." Evon offered a water skin to Marla and watched her for a moment. "Are you all right? That was some kick."

Marla snatched the skin from him and took a drink. "I'll be fine. Kicks like a damn horse, that one. Surefoot has kicked me and it didn't hurt that much."

The man turned and walked back toward his friends. One of them said something, a shocked exclamation of some kind, though Evon couldn't hear what she said. Whatever it was, he agreed. He had never seen *anyone* beat Marla like that.

Marla was watching the man. "Hey," she shouted. "What's your name?"

"Aeden," he said. "Aeden Tannoch." He didn't even sound winded.

"A Croagh?" Marla asked.

"Aye. What of it?"

"Nothing. Listen, I may have been a bit rude—"

"Gealich claidhimh d'araesh slaoch. A bit rude? You gave me the impression of trying your best to kill me."

"Only after I saw that you weren't so easily harmed. I'd never have attacked anyone else like that." She cocked her head like she typically did when something had occurred to her. "Damn, you know, that's actually true. I would never have attacked anyone else like that. Not anyone I didn't want to kill. But I knew you could take it. Where'd you learn to fight like that?"

"I was born Croagh aet Brech, of the Tannoch clan."

"I've fought Croagh before," she said. "Sparring, mind you. None of them could fight like that. And the Raibrech isn't strong enough to block the spell I used on you."

"I've been through a bit more than the average highlander. I've picked up a few things along the way." He turned and started walking toward Dartford.

"Wait." Marla tossed Evon the waterskin and jogged—slowly and carefully, and a bit lopsidedly—toward the man and his friends. "Maybe we can start over. I was a jackass. After the last few weeks, even Evon is lucky I didn't kill him."

"She came close," Evon said.

"Yeah," she continued. "It's been rough. My best friend was killed and I...anyway, I was wrong. I'm usually not such a bitch. Please, can we start over, be civil?

"*I* was civil," Aeden said.

"You were. I admit it. It's all my fault. That bad energy, that anger, it's gone now. Beat out of me, as it were. Plus, I'm exhausted and sore. Just a little bit of your time. We're near Dartford and you seem to be heading that way. How about I ride ahead, have a meal waiting for you all when you arrive. I'll pay for it. I'd just like to talk a bit."

Aeden looked at his friends. They didn't seem to have strong opinions one way or another. The one wearing a hood down low seemed to want only to hide somewhere. What was the deal with that?

"Fine," Aeden said. "We'll be there in a few hours."

"Great. It'll be closer to two, I think. I'll see you there."

A small boy stepped forward. Evon had almost missed him entirely. "Masters?"

Marla's brows drew down. "What?"

"That one. Evon? He said you wouldn't want to explain killing someone to the masters. Are you a hero, from the Academy?"

Marla slowly nodded. "Yeah, we both are."

"I knew it." He smiled like he had won a bet.

Marla shrugged. "We'll tell you all about it when we eat, okay?"

The boy nodded energetically.

As Evon got back on his horse and prepared to follow Marla back the way they had come, he looked toward the woman who was with Aeden. She looked even more beautiful close up. Why did she look so familiar? He only met her gaze for a brief moment before he tore his eyes from her and flicked the reins to start his horse moving.

For some strange reason, he was really looking forward to the upcoming meal.

33

Marla had Josef set them up in one of the private dining rooms. She sat near the fire, a barely touched mug of ale next to her, with her eyes closed. She was finally starting to relax, though she was sore and her bruises made even slouching in a chair uncomfortable. It served her right for being such a shrew earlier.

Evon paced the floor. Why did he seem so nervous? She had noticed his obvious interest in the tall, dark-haired woman with Aeden. She smiled at the thought. Had he been smitten so easily?

The door opened and Josef stepped in. He swept his arm out as he moved aside to let the others enter the room. "I will have Daphne come to you immediately. Bread and ale are on the table already. Let me know if you need anything else."

"Thank you," Aeden said as Josef left.

Marla stood up. Her aches protested, but she tried not to show the others how sore she was. "Welcome." She tried to sound as jovial and upbeat as Skril ever was. "Help yourself to what's here. We can order some food when Daphne gets here."

Aeden's friends piled into the room. She hadn't paid close attention to them before, too caught up in her rage and then the combat, but she looked at them now as they moved around the table and sat.

There was that old archer with the white eyes, the one who had drawn an arrow and pointed it at her. Next to him was a statuesque beauty with a massive mane of red hair and very little in the way of clothing. Two shorter women found seats next to each other, one with dark blue hair of all things. That one looked to have some northern blood in her. Teroshimi or Shinyin.

There was the young man in robes, his dark hair matching the wild scruff on his face. Next to him a young boy sat. She didn't remember seeing him at all until he had asked the questions about the masters. Easy to overlook, that one.

And there was the taller, dark-haired woman in Gypta clothing—like the boy and Aeden himself. She was stunning, so much so that Marla felt a little tinge of jealousy. It was obvious she had captured Evon's attention. Though he nodded to each of the others, his eyes always seemed to go back to her. Why did she look familiar?

The visitors took up mugs or broke into the bread, but didn't speak. An air of discomfort permeated the room.

"I really do have to apologize, Aeden," Marla said. "I'm difficult to get along with sometimes, but I'm rarely that rude."

Evon nodded, though he did so absently, studying the tall woman while trying to act like he wasn't.

"It's no excuse," Marla continued, "but it's been difficult, aggravating, and dangerous for me lately. I let it sour my mood and I'm sorry I took it out on you. In a way, I'm glad, though. If someone else had raised my ire, I would probably have given them some serious bruises. Instead, I have the bruises and have learned a lesson from it all."

"What lesson?" Aeden asked, still seeming hesitant to engage fully in the conversation.

"Don't judge a warrior by his appearance, maybe? You have armor, but you dress like a Gypta. Who'd have thought one of the People could fight like that, let alone use magic."

"What do you know of the Gypta?" the boy said, surprisingly firm.

"She wasn't clear," Evon said. "It's just that the Gypta are known for their craft, not their combat prowess. I've made something of a study of the People. I greatly admire your families." His eyes flashed toward the woman again, who dropped her eyes, which had been locked on Evon as he spoke.

"What I'd like to know," Marla said, "is how you took a simple spell from the Raibrech and made it that powerful."

Aeden looked at her suspiciously. "How do you know about the Raibrech? My people don't exactly make it a secret, but it's not openly talked about with outsiders, either."

She raised her mug to him. "Evon has his fascination with the Gypta, and I have done my fair share of research into the Croagh."

"Why?"

"Look at me, Aeden. I have red hair and green eyes. Can you tell me that you haven't suspected that I have some Croagh blood in me? For that matter, your barely clad companion there"—she gestured toward Lily—"looks to be at least part highlander as well."

"I had noticed," Aeden said.

"As had I, with myself," she continued. "I wanted to know what my possible ancestors were like, what their culture was, how they lived."

"Your *possible* ancestors?" Aeden said.

"Yes. I...I'm not sure what my ancestry is. I was found in

front of the gate at the Academy when I was an infant. I've no idea who my real parents were."

Aeden's eyes lost focus for a moment, almost as if something had occurred to him, but it passed quickly.

"That's terrible," the dark-haired beauty said. The sadness in her eyes and the little pout her lips made did the impossible and made the woman even more beautiful. "Someone just put you there where an animal could have eaten you?"

"I hardly think that was the case," Marla said, "though I can't know for sure. I would assume if they went to the trouble of bringing me to Sitor-Kanda, they probably watched until the groundskeeper found me and brought me inside."

"The groundskeeper?" the archer asked.

"Yes. The Academy has no use for infants. The groundskeeper took me into his home, adopted me, raised me as his own. At least until I was able to be accepted into the Academy. But none of that is important. The point is that I think I have highlander blood in my veins, so I learned what I could about the Croagh."

Daphne, the serving girl, came in and asked them their choices of the food the kitchen was making that evening. After everyone had made their selections, she left and the room got quiet. Aeden seemed to be lost in thought, looking at Marla like he wanted to ask her something.

The shorter dark-haired woman leaned in and whispered something in Aeden's ear. He jumped and blinked twice.

"Marla," he said, "do you remember anything? Anything at all from before you were left at the Academy?"

"Psht," the woman next to him said. "People don't remember things from when they were an infant. That's ridiculous."

Aeden shook his head. "I remember something. I used to dream it. It repeated often when I was a child and I still experience that dream occasionally."

"Yeah," Marla said. "I have a dream, too, like that. I've had it since I was little also."

Aeden leaned forward, his eyes growing more intense. "Will you tell me?"

Marla immediately felt she was saying too much. She had never told anyone about the dream, not even her parents. "It's nothing, just a silly dream."

"I'd like to hear it," he said.

"What about yours?" she asked. "Will you tell us?" She figured for sure that would make him drop the subject.

"I will."

Damn. "Then you first."

He sighed. "Fine. It was when I was just an infant myself. I was swaddled in a rough cloth. It was raining, but I wasn't cold. A giant man—he seemed that way to me, anyway—was holding me and we were near a fire. There were others around, all giants compared to me. They were making sounds, talking in a language I didn't understand yet.

"Then there was a flash of lightning and a boom that shook my entire body. A squealing cry rang out nearby, the screeching I understood better than the language of the adults. My head lolled and I blinked to focus, finally seeing another person, this one a woman, holding another bundle of cloth. That bundle was crying, scared by the thunder, no doubt, but probably cold, too. The rain fell on all of us, but the other bundle wasn't near the fire.

"The man holding me and the woman holding the bundle talked in soft, sad tones. The bundle cried again and the man spoke more harshly. The woman took the bundle away and I never heard from or saw it again.

"For much of my young life, I was quiet, rarely speaking unless absolutely necessary. The dream seemed to tell me that if I made noise, I would disappear, too. In my child's mind, I equated making noise with death.

"I often wondered what it all meant, what happened. The man, of course, was my father, our clan chieftain, and the woman was my mother. The other bundle, well—"

Marla's heart dropped from her chest and her vision got blurry. She found she was shaking her head.

"It can't be," she whispered. "It can't...I can't." She realized she was babbling and blinked tears away so she could see everyone around her. They were all staring at her.

She took a deep breath, trying to calm her racing heart. "My dream. I, too, was near a fire, but too far to feel its warmth. Something was going on, something that felt like doom, but I couldn't understand it. Why couldn't I tell the one holding me that I was scared? The shadows seemed to close in on me and I felt things falling from the sky on me. A loud boom shook me and I cried, trying to tell the giant person how scared I was. She brought her face close to mine, red hair framing it and blocking out everything else, and made comforting noises.

"Then I saw a face in the arms of another person. It looked at me and blinked. I tried to reach out, but my arms wouldn't work like they should have. For a moment, I met eyes with the other one like me, wrapped in cloth and being held, then harsh, guttural words made the one holding me respond with sadness. Soothing whispers reached my tiny ears and we were suddenly moving, farther from the fire. I continued to cry, but it did no good.

"I only felt the abandonment as I lay there on the stone step with huge doors in front of me. I knew somehow that time had passed, but didn't understand enough to judge how long it had been. The only other thing I knew was that I had been found lacking, unworthy of being loved."

Her last word seemed to hang on the air and then silence swept in, only broken by the popping of the log in the fire.

Aeden squeezed his head with his palms. "It's impossible."

He shook his head repeatedly. "I found, after suffering through the dream and my thoughts for many years, that there was an obscure law in my clan. If the clan chief birthed twins and one was female, that one would be sacrificed because she would leach power from her brother, who would eventually become clan chief. Though they tried to keep it secret, I found out that it had only happened once in the entire history of our clan.

"With my father. With my...sister."

Marla's world shattered, along with her composure. Tears flooded from her eyes and she began to breathe rapidly, becoming light-headed. She knew she was making a fool of herself in front of people she didn't even know, but she couldn't help it. Gods, could it be true?

Aeden stepped over to her, tears in his own eyes, and carefully put his arms around her, bringing her into a soothing embrace. She stood motionless, frozen, but then was able to wrap her own arms around him. She shuddered with racking sobs, unlike anything she had ever felt in her life.

Aeden squeezed her. "You look like her, you know. Our mother."

❦ 34 ❧

The door opened and Daphne came in with their food. She stopped in front of the two of them hugging, tears in their eyes, and almost dropped the platters she was carrying. She quickly set them down on the table. Then she turned and fled.

Marla held onto Aeden for a little while longer, then stepped back and wiped the tears from her eyes. For some reason she wasn't even embarrassed.

"I haven't cried like that since...no, I've never cried like that. Daphne will be going straight to Josef to tell him. You can expect him to poke his head in and check on us shortly." She laughed and the rest of the tension in her dissipated.

"Miera," Aeden said. "That was our mother's name."

"Fire beauty," Marla said. She knew enough Chorain, the language of the clans, to recognize it.

"And our father, our clan chief, was called Sartan Tannoch.

"Great strength," she said. "Clan chief, eh?"

"Aye. Oh, Marla, I wish you'd have known them. Father was the perfect image of a highland chieftain. Strong, wise, fair, and honorable. Mother was strong, but she was also kind and gentle. She could kill someone, but always tempered her judgment with her caring heart. They were the perfect complement to each other."

"Were?"

Aeden dropped his eyes and frowned. "Yes. I'm afraid they're both dead. I'll tell you about it later. It's a very involved story. For now, let me introduce you to my friends and family.

"Here is Fahtin Achaya, my adopted sister. She's the one who found me when I was nearly dead and nursed me back to health. Her father, the leader of our family, took me in as a son. Raki Sinde is like a little brother to me. He has been with me since we first left the caravan."

Marla nodded to them. An adopted sister, huh? Fahtin had been bouncing on her seat as Aeden introduced her and now she launched herself at Marla, wrapping her up in a hug. Marla, uncomfortable with the gesture, spoke to distract her from the situation. "I'm Marla Shrike, as you may have heard."

"I always wanted a sister," Fahtin said. "In addition to the bratty brother I already have." The woman actually stuck her tongue out at Aeden. He just smiled at her.

Raki was much more subdued. He waved at Marla and she returned the gesture. Then he looked at his feet as if the whole thing embarrassed him.

But she was being rude. "Oh, this is my friend, and increasingly my conscience, Evon Desconse."

Evon stood, bowing formally to Fahtin and Raki, and spoke. "*Mei sain avar, avar sai ik.*"

Fahtin clapped her hands and giggled, then settled down to bow back. "*Jai avar sai ik, ais bhi mei sain ik.*" Raki did the same, actually looking Evon in the eye.

Aeden tilted his head and considered Evon. "It's rare for outsiders to care enough to learn the greetings."

"I have a preoccupation with the People and have studied them a fair amount. I read a bit of Dantogyptain as well. Fascinating language." He met Fahtin's eyes. "I'm glad to see you escaped safely and appear to be unharmed."

"Escaped?" she asked, looking back and forth from Evon to Aeden.

"Yes. From those dark creatures who held you prisoner. I have to apologize for leaving but—"

"She's *that* girl?" Marla said. "I knew she looked familiar. Damn, I'm sorry Fahtin. Evon wanted to stay and find you, bring you to a safe place, but I told him we had to move on, that you had already crawled away and you could take care of yourself. It was true, but I regretted the decision after we had gotten a few hours away."

Fahtin's eyes lit up. "Oh! You. The red hair. Aeden, these are the ones who attacked the group of animaru who held me captive. These are the ones who saved me."

"No, no," Evon said. "We just provided a diversion. You had already slipped your bonds and were well on the way to freedom. I just wanted to apologize for not helping more."

"You saved my life, no matter what you say. Thank you. Both of you."

Aeden got a pensive look on his face. "Curious that we were so close to meeting, but didn't."

"Maybe it wasn't time yet," Evon said.

Conversation paused, as if everyone was thinking about what Evon had just said. Aeden cleared his throat a moment later and continued.

"The one here is Tere Chizzit. He's also—"

"The oldest one here by far," the old man said, giving Aeden a look that seemed to Marla to be some kind of sign. "It's an honor to meet you, Marla, Evon. Any family of Aeden's is a friend of mine." Under his breath, he added, "It's a good thing he stopped me or I'd have put a hole in your head."

The others were introduced as well.

The red-haired woman with more skin showing than clothing was Lily Fisher. The shorter woman with the dark brown hair was named Aila Ven. Jia Toun was the woman with the dark blue hair.

The young man in the robes seemed preoccupied, staring into space. Aila elbowed his arm as Aeden said the man's name: Urun Chinowa. He resumed his staring at nothing.

Aeden had just introduced the woman with her hood drawn down, Khrazhti—a strange name Marla had never heard before—when they were interrupted.

As expected, Josef entered the room with Daphne in tow. They were both carrying platters of food. The innkeeper looked at Marla and then each of his other guests as if searching for something. Marla waved his concern away.

"Josef is a friend. We go way back," Marla said. "Josef, I would like to introduce you to my twin brother, Aeden."

"Oh," he said. "Oh! Twin brother? Gods, I can see it, now that you mention it. Why didn't you tell me when you were here before? For Marla's kin, I'd give you a special rate on rooms."

Aeden laughed. "Thanks, I appreciate it."

The mood lifted, the food made it to the table, and Josef and Daphne left them to their meal.

After the excitement of the last few minutes, everyone dug in and ate with fervor.

Evon suddenly gasped and all eyes went to him. "I just figured it out, Marla. Oh, I wish Master Aeid had lived to see this."

Marla shook her head. "Evon gets excited by apparently trivial things. A lot. What are you going on about, Evon?"

"I realized the mistake we've been making with the Bhagant."

"The Bhavisyaganant?" Aeden asked. Marla stared at her brother.

"Yes," Evon said. "The...how do you know that name?"

"It's kind of a long story. I'll tell you about it later, if you want."

"Oh. Okay. Anyway, we've been wrong all this time. Marla, I've told you for years that you're the Malatirsay, but I was wrong."

Marla swallowed the food she was chewing. "I told you that you were. I can't accept I'm the one. It just doesn't feel right somehow."

"Yes, yes. I'm telling you, though. I figured out our error. The plurality, it's not meant to signify importance or honor, or not only that, anyway. It's plural. The Malatirsay isn't one person, it's two."

"Two?" Fahtin asked.

"Yes, two. Marla and Aeden are the Malatirsay. Together."

Aeden made choking sounds and Marla was on her feet, ready to help. He managed to wash the food down with a gulp of water. "No," he said. "The Master of Prophecy at the Academy told me yesterday I wasn't. He said he already knew who it was."

"Do you remember the name of the master you talked to?"

"Umm, it was Marn something."

"Marn Tiscomb?" Marla asked.

"Aye."

"He's a moron. Gods, he's barely a master. They should have pushed him out a third-story window years ago."

"Marla," Evon said, "be nice." He turned to Aeden. "She's partially right, though. I guess they did decide to make Marn the master. The previous master was murdered a short time ago. It started all the troubles Marla and I have been through. The pool of qualified candidates was a bit shallow."

"If it wasn't for a technicality, they would have chosen Evon. He was Master Aeid's First Student, *assector pruma*." Marla leaned in and cupped her hand to her mouth like she was telling them a secret. "Don't tell Evon, but our nickname for that title is First Ass."

Evon rolled his eyes at her, but ignored her last sentence. "I wouldn't have taken it," Evon said. "I'm too young to be a master."

"You'd be a better choice than any of the others, especially Marn."

"You're distracting us, Marla." Evon turned back to Aeden. "Aeden, if you read the Song, you'd see there are criteria upon which to recognize the Malatirsay."

"Oh," Aeden said. "You mean like the ninth and twelfth quatrains?

Golga ua rotta aun utta
> *Malatirsay mortiyu dutrota sain*
> *Deh morita sain ma tutta deh stirota sain*
> *Sunha jintoka deh apruta sain*

Malatirsay, sau deh katata sain
> *Ik do dah baneta sai, ma ik dah adata sai*
> *Alaga ma laya paru*
> *Dvara dabana agni deh joddita dara sain*

"Are those what you're talking about?"

Evon's mouth dropped open and Marla understood why.

As Aeden said the words, she felt magic flowing around the room.

"Uh, yes," Evon said. "Exactly those things. How did you know?"

"Aeden has the entire Song memorized, in Dantogyptain," Fahtin said. "You should hear him sing it. It's beautiful. That's how he does his magic, with the words of power from the Song..." She trailed off when she caught sight of him shaking his head at her.

"Oh, come on, Aeden," she said. "It's your sister. You can tell her."

"I'm sorry, Evon," Aeden said. "You were saying?"

Evon was having trouble keeping up with the conversation. "Do you know what those words mean?"

Aeden nodded. "Roughly, though my translation may not be completely accurate.

HERO FROM THE EAST AND NORTH
    Malatirsay faces death
    Dying but living still
    Learns the secret to prevail

MALATIRSAY, SPLIT ASUNDER
    One to two, but back to one
    Separated but brought whole
    Welded by the fire's touch

"That's about as close as I can get."

Evon sputtered, then cleared his throat. "That's...very good."

"Thank you," Aeden said. "I didn't mean to interrupt you. Please continue with what you were saying, Evon."

"I...oh! Well, there were phrases in there that didn't seem

right. I've always had problems with them, even when it was generally recognized that Marla was the Malatirsay. She's the most accomplished student the Academy has ever had and it was just thought that she was the one. Not by everyone, by any means, but a lot of people believed. But it didn't seem to fit completely. Now it does. You two, together, are the ones we've been waiting three thousand years for."

"Incidentally," Evon said, "why did you go to the Academy?"

"There were several reasons," Aeden answered, "but the main one was to tell them I was told I was the Malatirsay."

"Told by whom?"

Aeden ran his hand through his hair. "Uh, maybe it would be better if I just told you our whole story. Things are going to get complicated unless you know it all."

"That sounds good to me," Marla said. "After we get that out of the way, I can tell you what we've been up to. I think it would interest you."

❧ 35 ❧

"**I** think maybe it would be better to start from the beginning," Aeden said. "It'll make more sense if I do that."

"Yes," Marla said. "I'd like to know how you got involved in all this business with those dark creatures."

"Animaru," Fahtin said.

Marla eyed the Gypta girl. Animaru? The dark creatures in the Prophecy? She let it pass for now, sure it would be covered by Aeden's tale.

"I'll give you the short version of things," Aeden said. "I was raised by the clan until I was fourteen years old. I had passed my Trial of Combat and was completing my training by taking the Trial of Magic." He held up his left wrist, pulling his sleeve back so everyone could see the tattoo there. Marla knew it meant he had passed the Trial of Combat.

"I failed the Trial of Magic and was sentenced to be beaten to death by the clan. After the other warriors had brought me close to death, my father was to have struck the final, fatal blow. He hit me hard enough to knock me out, but not enough to kill me. Fahtin found me, out looking for firewood for the caravan. She brought me back, and the family nursed me back to health and adopted me. I traveled with them for five years.

"During that time, I continued to train every day, as well as learn new things."

"Like music," Fahtin said, smiling and obviously caught up in the tale.

"Yes, like music. I learned to sing and to play the fiddle passably. More importantly, I heard the Song of Prophecy, the Bhavisyaganant, for the first time. I felt some kind of power stirring in me when Jehira—Raki's grandmother—sang it during a celebration. I begged her to teach it to me. It took some work, but she finally agreed.

"From the beginning, it felt like I had always been waiting to learn it. It was...a part of me. When I sang it, power infused me, and I was finally able to successfully cast the spells of the Raibrech, spells I had learned years before but was never able to cast."

"You feel power when you sing the Song?" Evon asked.

"Aye."

"Can you show us?"

"Isn't that what I did when I fought with Marla?"

A twinge of pain in her abdomen reminded Marla that he had.

Evon nodded. "Yes, but I mean, could you show us with only the Song? Can you sing it for us? If it's not too embarrassing?"

Aeden opened his mouth, but Fahtin spoke first. "There isn't anything to be embarrassed about. He has a wonderful singing voice." '

"I didn't mean it that way," Evon said. "I just meant that singing in front of people can be embarrassing, or maybe nerve-racking is a better term."

Fahtin seemed satisfied with the response. She bulled on. "Sing it for them, Aeden. Please."

Aeden gave her a flat look. "If it would keep you from interrupting my story every other sentence, I'll do it."

"Oh," she said, flushing slightly. "Sorry. It's kind of exciting, hearing the story. Much better than living through it."

Aeden patted Fahtin's hand. "Yes, better. Okay, if you'd like, I'll sing the Song, but then we need to move on with the story or we'll be here all night."

He took a drink and cleared his throat. Then he launched right into the Song of Prophecy.

From the first words, Marla felt the pressure building. She knew it well. It was the sensation of magic accumulating, swirling around them, pressing in on all sides. Strangely, though, it was more concentrated around Aeden, as if magic from the surroundings was coalescing and stacking around him, like an aura.

She didn't know many words in Dantogyptain, but Evon did. Her friend sat there, transfixed, eyes wide and unblinking, mouth slightly open. His eyes got a watery look and Marla thought he might tear up. Even more telling was that not once during the Song did Evon look at Fahtin. He was completely focused on Aeden and the words gliding out of his mouth.

Fahtin was right. Aeden put out pure, beautiful tones, even without any music accompanying him. In fact, music might have diminished the pure power her brother was building with his notes.

A quick look around showed that the others were affected by the singing as well. She wasn't sure how many times his companions had heard him sing this Song, but half of them looked stricken with emotion and even Tere's blind eyes were fixed on Aeden, as if he were watching the magic itself.

And then the Song was done. Aeden slumped slightly. He

took another drink from his mug and Marla noticed that his hand was shaking. His eyes met hers and he put it under the table, where it couldn't be seen.

He explained, "It's hard to sing the entire Bhagant without using the magic in some way, releasing it, so to speak. It builds up in me and begs for me to set it free."

Everyone else sat silently, almost as if in a trance, until Evon spoke.

"That is the most magnificent thing I have ever heard. Gods! Master Aeid would have given his right arm to have the chance to hear that and study you."

"I can sing it for him, if he likes," Aeden said, fidgeting on his seat like he was uncomfortable with the attention.

"That's not possible," Marla said. "He's the one who was murdered, the reason Marn Tiscomb is now the Master of Prophecy."

"Oh," Aeden said. "That's right, you mentioned that before. I'm sorry."

"It's all right," Evon said. "Do you want to finish your story now, or do you need a few minutes to relax?"

"How about we wait a few minutes," Aeden said. "I'd like to get some air first, if you don't mind."

"That's perfectly fine," Marla said. Truth be told, she felt a little frazzled herself. Being that close to the power had her body vibrating like a taut rope in the wind. "Take your time. I'll put some more logs on the fire and ask Josef to bring more drinks."

Marla watched Aeden as he left the room to go outside. She almost went after him, but then decided to let him be. He was her twin brother, true—though it was still hard to believe it—but that didn't mean she could read him easily. She didn't know what his little mannerisms and expressions meant. She'd learn, but for now, better to take what he said at face value. Time enough later to read his real thoughts into what he said and did.

He didn't take long. By the time Josef and Daphne brought more drinks, Aeden was stepping back into the room, looking ready to continue.

"So I was telling you about learning the Song," he said, launching right into it. "Once I felt the stirrings of magic, I practiced singing it constantly, but I also practiced the Raibrech. For those who don't know, the Raibrech is the collective magic of the highland clans. It consists of words of power and specific motions to make the magic do things. I learned the gestures and words when training with the clan, but had never been able to do the magic, as I said.

"After I learned the Song, I found that the block within me had gone away and I was able to use the magic, though it was weak.

"Time went on, and I continued to practice as the family traveled. We finally came back around to the highlands, my homeland, five years after I had been left for dead. I was nervous, but with my adopted family around me, I was willing to face whatever came. That was good, because we were going to trade with the Croagh, with my village among others.

"But when we got there, something was terribly wrong. My village was burning and corpses lay everywhere. Humans and dark twisted creatures I'd never seen before, but many times the number of humans compared to the attackers.

"I found my mother, half her head torn off. It looked like it had been done with claws, like the claws I saw on the dead, dark forms on the ground. I found my father, too, the only one left alive in the village, and that just barely.

"He told me what he had done, all those years ago, breaking the tradition and striking me in such a way that I didn't die. He told me it was the only thing he could do. I told him what had happened to me, about the kindness of the family, and I told him that I had learned to use the Raibrech. He made me show him, and with the last of his strength, he pronounced that I had passed the Trial of Magic, and marked me accordingly."

Aeden pulled the sleeve up on his right arm. There was another tattoo there, but this one wasn't the product of ink and needles. It radiated magic to Marla's senses.

"Before he died, he told me they had found the secret to killing the creatures. Life magic. He—"

"What?" Marla asked. "Life magic?"

"Yes."

"What about fire magic?"

"That can work to harm them, but you can't kill them with fire magic, or any other kind of magic. Only life magic can destroy them. They are unalive, the opposite of life magic."

"Then what happens when you hit them with fire magic until they don't move anymore?"

"They stay dormant for a while until they can regenerate their power, then they get up and keep going where they left off." Aeden looked at Khrazhti for some reason when he said it, and she nodded her hooded head. Marla wondered why she hadn't taken her cloak off or lowered her hood. What did the woman look like? Josef had interrupted them before she could speak earlier.

"Damn it," Marla said. "That means we didn't kill any of the ones we fought."

"You fought animaru?" Aeden asked.

"Yes, including the ones that held Fahtin captive. I'll tell you our story after you finish yours."

"Oh, right," he said. "My mistake. Where was I? Oh, my father. He told me they had figured out life magic kills them, but too late to save the village. We gathered the corpses of the village and burned them on pyres. I wish I had known about you then, Marla. I would have told him."

"I wonder if he knew I wasn't dead," Marla said.

"I don't think so. He would have told me about you. I think my mother couldn't do what the tradition required and kept the secret all those years, even from him. I wish she could have seen you. I can't imagine what it must have done to her to give you away like that.

"But let me continue. The caravan tried to go to another Croagh village, in another clan's territory, but we found it had been destroyed, too. Fahtin's father decided it was time to leave. We headed back toward the west, but the creatures found us two weeks later and attacked.

"I still don't know how I did it, but I used one of the spells of the Raibrech in a very powerful way. I destroyed the small group of animaru that attacked us, though they killed several of my family members before I was able to do it.

"Jehira, Raki's grandmother, told me then that I was the Malatirsay and told us the creatures were animaru, like in the Song. She said the animaru had been searching for me, first in the highlands and then when they stumbled upon me in the caravan. They all came straight for me once they saw me, ignoring any other human unless they were in the way. I decided I needed to leave the caravan for the family's safety.

"Fahtin held me to a promise I made her, so I had to let her come. Raki followed us and we had to let him travel with us after that. Tere found us when we were traveling through the Grundenwald to avoid the animaru, but when Raki got attacked by a barb plant, Tere took us to Urun, who is a priest of Osulin. Once he healed Raki, he joined us as well and we headed for the Academy."

Aeden paused and looked from Evon to Marla. "Is that confusing? Do you follow so far?"

Marla nodded, though she wanted to ask questions. She

held them, though. There would be time later for more specific information.

"Okay, good. So, we ran into more Animaru at Drugancairn, where we also met Aila. We ended up plunging into the Alvaspirtu River separately to escape a large force of animaru, and we finally came back together near the Tarshuk region. When the animaru caught up to us there, we had to stand and fight. We survived, but Fahtin was captured, so we immediately started after the group that took her. By the time we found her, she was already heading back toward us with a tale of some heroes saving her and killing all the animaru." Aeden winked at Marla.

"Since we were already so far from our path to the Academy, and it seemed like the animaru had been heading toward Broken Reach, we decided to go there and try to take out their leader. We made it to the old fortress there, where the animaru had set up their headquarters, and cut through their forces to find their leader.

"The funny thing about it is that their leader, the high priestess of their god S'ru, didn't know about humans. She thought that when they were defeated in battle, they went dormant for a time and then regenerated, like the animaru did. The whole concept of life and death was unknown to her. Urun was able to suppress her magic while the rest of us battled her physically. When we told her how humans that have been killed are gone forever, she was shocked. Her god had never told her that, and even by his own rules, she and her troops should not have been dispensing final destruction.

"In the end, she gave a vow to help the humans and fight her kin. Well, half kin. She herself is half human."

"Wait," Marla said. "Their leader is half-human? How could someone do that to a whole race, the race one of her parents belonged to?"

"She was deceived by her god," Fahtin said. "When she

learned the truth, she made a decision and forsook him, pitting herself against S'ru. He even marked her in such a way that every animaru in Dizhelim chased after her to kill her."

Evon leaned forward. "Really? Did they get her? Is she gone now?"

Aeden was looking uncomfortable and his eyes kept darting to his cloaked companion. Marla had a suspicion why.

"Uh, no," Aeden said. He looked questioningly at Khrazhti and the hooded head nodded. "We fled from them until the mark expired."

"We?" Evon asked.

"Yeah. Khrazhti?"

The hood came down and Khrazhti removed the cloak covering her. Evon's sharp intake of breath sounded like thunder in the quiet room.

"I'd like you to meet Khrazhti," Aeden said. "My friend and companion. She's over three thousand years old, can fight as well as anyone I've ever seen, and is a master of magic on top of it. And she's a good friend."

Evon's eyes were wide as he stared into the woman's glowing blue eyes. Her skin was blue, and there was a lot of it visible. Marla noticed a pattern in Aeden's companions. Like Lily, Khrazhti had barely any clothing on. She was sure it was more than just showing off her fantastic physique. But none of that mattered.

"You...you're an animaru," Marla said.

"She's my friend," Aeden growled dangerously.

"No, that's not how I meant it. I mean that it's amazing. I've never formally met one, not one that wasn't trying to kill me. She's...well, she's beautiful. The ones I've seen were so ugly."

Marla noticed that Khrazhti's color changed slightly, darkening on her face. Blushing?

"I'm sorry," Marla continued. "I'm not speaking intelligibly. Khrazhti, it's a pleasure to meet you. Any friend of my brother is a friend of mine." She put out her hand and Khrazhti took it. Then the blue woman smiled. She smiled! An animaru. Marla was definitely going to need to talk more with Khrazhti. Three thousand years old! The knowledge she must have...

Marla couldn't take her eyes off Khrazhti. She hadn't been lying when she said the animaru was beautiful. Different, yes, but also with an exotic beauty she'd never seen. Her glowing blue eyes, pupilless, still somehow expressed emotion. She had only a tiny ruff of hair on the top of her head and had other things protruding from her scalp where most people would have hair. They were almost like tentacles, but smaller, maybe more like very thick hairs made of skin. Her blue tint was fascinating and it was clear that anatomically, she was very much like a human, though very tall. Her clothing—or lack of it—revealed a warrior's physique, toned muscles that twitched as she moved.

Marla blinked, but couldn't seem to tear her gaze from the former leader of the animaru.

Aeden cleared his throat and Khrazhti sat back down. "Anyway, like I said, she joined us and we had to flee because of S'ru's mark. We went to Satta Sarak to try to catch a boat north so we could finally get to the Academy, but masses of animaru chased us and we had to leave the city before they got there so they wouldn't attack all the innocent people there. The boat was to leave the next day.

"On our way out, we ran into another problem. A brace of Falxen had been sent to kill Khrazhti. That's when she remembered that Izhrod Benzal had told her he was going to open another portal to Aruzhelim to bring more animaru over. We had to stop him, but we needed to inform the Academy of the animaru, too, so we split up. Khrazhti, Fahtin, and Raki went with me to find Benzal, and the rest went with Tere to go to the Academy."

"Wait, did you say Izhrod Benzal?" Evon asked.

"Yes. He was the one who brought Khrazhti and her troops over from Aruzhelim. Apparently, portals can only be opened at specific times and he told her when the next one would be."

Evon threw a glance at Marla, worry on his face.

"What is it?" Aeden said.

"We know Izhrod," Marla said. "He's an adept at the Academy. That means he's mastered three or more schools and is still learning at Sitor-Kanda. At least, he was. I doubt he'll ever go back now."

Aeden nodded, silently pondering. "He also told her he was the Malatirsay. He told me the same thing."

Laughter burst out from Marla. She couldn't help it. "Don't worry about that. He always did think he was much more important than he actually was."

"Oh. Okay. So—"

"Falxen?" It occurred to her what he had said earlier. "You said a *brace* of Falxen were after you?"

"Yes. There were twelve of them altogether."

"That's at least two full braces, possibly four," Marla said.

"Yeah," Aeden said nonchalantly. "They were tough."

"*They were tough*. Falxen are the most skilled assassins in

Dizhelim. Even one is deadlier than a dozen trained fighters. What—?"

"Let him finish the story, Marla," Evon said. "He'll get to it."

Marla huffed, but motioned for Aeden to continue.

"Like I said, we split up. During our flight, we were taken to some kind of magical realm where there was a huge monster who spoke as eloquently as anyone I've ever heard. He said he was called the Epradotirum and that he was going to eat us."

"The Epradotirum?" Marla said. This was too much. She calmed herself as best she could. "Sorry. Go ahead."

"Yes, the Epradotirum, though he said we could call him the Epra. He was very polite, for someone who had plucked us from our own world for the sole purpose of eating us. We explained that we were on an important mission, which led to the Song, and we were able to convince him that I was the Malatirsay, something I still didn't believe. He said he didn't want to interfere in prophecy and so let us go.

"When we appeared back in Dizhelim, though, the assassins were there waiting for us. We fought and barely escaped. We continued toward where Khrazhti sensed the portal would open, but we ran into a human army who were on the side of the animaru. Once we got around them, we finally made it back to Broken Reach, where Benzal had set up to open the portal. The only thing was, he had already opened it and there were animaru everywhere. We fought through, met Khrazhti's father—an animaru lord—killed him, and went after Benzal.

"He was on top of the tower next to the one we were on, so we couldn't reach him. He had some kind of contraption that made a doorway to somewhere else, and they escaped through it.

"We tried to follow Khrazhti's senses to find him, but

something happened to the magic around us and she lost her ability to find him. We ended up coming back to Dartford, where we were supposed to meet Tere's group. They had been harried by the assassins and put in prison in Praesturi. They survived crossing through the Verlisaru Forest, but were attacked by the half dozen assassins that had followed them.

"They fought and defeated the Falxen. Well, most of them. Two of them defected and joined with Tere when they were spared. As it turns out, Lily here..." Aeden looked at Tere while he spoke, eyebrows raised. The archer let out a breath and nodded once. It seemed to Marla that he did it sadly.

"Lily," Aeden continued, "idolized Erent Caahs and had patterned her life after the hero. She was the first one to realize the truth. Tere is Erent Caahs."

"What?" Evon said. "But Erent Caahs is dead."

"You've seen his corpse, have you, boy?" Tere said. "I'll tell you what I've been telling these all along. That man *is* dead. Erent Caahs is no more. But truth be told, that was the name I was born with, the name I used until I decided I was better off without the world, and the world was probably better off without me. Now don't interrupt Aeden's story. This is taking too long as it is."

Evon sputtered, staring at the old man. Marla barely stopped herself from doing the same. Erent Caahs? She didn't belong in the company of all these people. Gods! Falxen, Epradotirum, surviving the Verlisaru, dead heroes alive again, it was too much. Next they'd tell her they had lunch with Surus and shared tea with the Great Prophet Tsosin Ruus, newly raised from the dead.

"Oh, I probably didn't mention it, but Lily and Jia were the Falxen that joined Tere. They were assassins, true, but when they found out the Falxen were working for someone who was bringing animaru to our world to destroy it, they knew where their priorities lay."

"To finish this quickly, we finally met Tere and the others in Dartford, went to the Academy to finally tell them about the animaru and the Malatirsay, and were rebuffed by Master Marn. Oh, and then we met an irritable woman on the way back who wanted to kill me painfully." Aeden smiled at Marla and she chuckled.

"Well," she said. "That was...amazing. We'll need to talk about all of this in more detail. In much more detail. For now, let me tell you a little about what we've been up to lately."

She started with the murder of Master Aeid, and then described their investigation, Skril's death, and their hunt for Quentin. She also mentioned that though she could introduce Aeden to the appropriate masters, she might be in a little trouble for going where she wasn't supposed to. On reflection, her journey had been mild compared to what Aeden and his friends had faced.

"By the way, Evon and I also felt magic acting strangely. I think now that the animaru coming over is somehow affecting the world's magic. We'll need to talk to the masters about that as well. Quentin said something about '*him* getting a toehold in the world' when we felt magic shift. After your story, I'm assuming now that *he* is S'ru."

After the tales had been told, the group separated into smaller collections of people so they could chat and get to know each other. Evon latched onto Fahtin and Raki to talk about the Gypta, and after a few short conversations with some of the others, Marla settled in to talk with her brother.

They stayed up late, trying to catch each other up on the lives they'd missed. Evon and some of Aeden's friends stayed up with them, seeming to enjoy the conversation. In the morning, they left the inn and headed toward the Academy.

Marla and Evon led their horses as they walked beside

those without. It was a longer trip than usual, but it seemed to take less time. It wasn't only because of the pleasant conversation, though. Marla wasn't forgetting that she'd have an accounting when she got back to the Academy. The masters would not be pleased about her and Evon going into forbidden territory. She'd have to tell them when reporting all they'd been through since they left more than two months before.

When they got to the Academy, it was dark. No one stopped them from entering the grounds. Everyone knew Marla and Evon, and there were few people out and about near the administration area at that time of night.

"Evon, take everyone to Meeting Room Two in the School of Prophecy. I'll take the horses to the stable and then fetch the masters."

Evon led the group away and Marla watched them go, swallowing hard. A quick trip to the stables and then she'd have to meet with the masters, at least the few she would try to find. She wasn't about to search the entire grounds looking for a large group of the masters. The ones she had in mind were the most appropriate for the explanation she had to give, but they were also the ones who would give her the most grief about her punishment.

There was no getting out of it. As Master Isegrith always said: if you had to do something unpleasant, better to do it sooner and get it over with.

Her luck was in, though whether it was bad or good was up for debate. She found Master Yxna Hagenai and Master Isegrith Palus in the headmaster's office. Headmaster Qydus glared at her as she knocked on his office door and stepped into the room. She wasn't fazed by it, though. She was used to his harsh looks. They were rarely an accurate gauge of his actual mood, though this time she wasn't so sure.

"Ah, so you have decided to return. To what do we owe the pleasure of this visit?"

"I'm sorry to interrupt, masters." Marla tried her hardest to look chastened. Being difficult would not serve her well right now. "There is something very important I must show you. Could you please accompany me?"

Master Isegrith raised her chin before she spoke. Marla almost flinched but stopped herself from doing so. "And what would make you think whatever you desire to show us is more important than what we're discussing?"

Marla's mind raced. How could she say what she needed to say without sounding argumentative?

"It's a matter of utmost importance, Master Isegrith. It... involves an invasion of monsters and the Song of Prophecy."

"Does it, now?" Master Isegrith said.

"Yes, Master."

As usual, Master Yxna came to Marla's defense.

"Does it involve Master Aeid's murder, Marla?"

"Yes, Master Yxna, and more. If you would please accompany me, we can explain it all."

"It is *we* now, is it?" Master Qydus asked.

"Yes, Master. Myself, and Evon, and a few visitors."

"Visitors?" Master Qydus asked, his sharp eyebrows reaching up his toward his bald scalp. "Do you not think you should explain first where you have been and what you have been doing? Ailuin and Erlan returned more than a month ago, but did not know exactly where you went."

Marla looked toward the ground. "Yes, Master. I know we will be having a long discussion about that. However, I ask you to allow us to postpone that for a short time to handle this other, more important matter. Please, come with me. I would explain it now, but it will be more effective after I show you what needs to be seen. I can give a short explanation on the way. Evon and the visitors are in one of the meeting rooms in the School of Prophecy."

"Oh, Qydus, let's go and see what she has to show us," Yxna said. "Isegrith, you too. No need to torment the girl. We can finish our current discussion anytime. I've found that when Marla says something is important, she does not exaggerate."

"Very well," the headmaster said. "I, too, know this about Marla. But we will have the other conversation, and soon."

"Yes, Master. Thank you."

Master Isegrith set the papers down she had been holding and followed the others as Marla led them to the meeting room. On the way, she gave them a few bits of information, just enough to prepare them. One thing she hadn't meant to tell them did slip, though.

Marla came into the room in a rush, rattling off the names of Aeden's group to the masters.

"...and you know Evon, of course. This," she gestured toward Aeden, "is Aeden Tannoch. Among other things, he is my long-lost twin brother."

Marla turned toward her guests. "For the masters, let me present to you Isegrith Palus, our Master of Fundamental Magic."

Master Isegrith swept her green robes aside and gave a half bow-half curtsy.

"Master Yxna Hagenai is the Master of Edged Weapons."

Master Yxna's expressionless face swung to take them all in. She nodded her grey-haired head politely. "It is a privilege to meet you, Aeden. All of you. Marla is at once the bane of my existence and the love of my life, the reason for my grey hair and my greatest triumph." She smiled at Marla, but the red-haired woman was too nervous to return the gesture.

Master Yxna stepped forward gracefully and clasped Aeden's wrist firmly in greeting. Marla's brother looked into her grey eyes and said, "It is an honor to meet you, Master Hagenai."

"And this," Marla said, "is our headmaster, Master Qydus Okvius."

Aeden's eyes met the headmaster's and the two seemed to be having a tug of war with their minds, each probing and analyzing the other. Master Qydus's face was stern, as always. Marla hoped Aeden didn't think the master was giving him mean looks.

The two clasped wrists, but there was no warmth in it. It didn't appear to be antagonistic, but neither did it look friendly.

"It is an honor to meet you as well, Headmaster." Master Qydus only nodded.

"So..." Marla began, but Master Qydus interrupted her.

"Where is the animaru?"

He was already looking at Khrazhti, shrinking in the corner with her cloak wrapped about her and her hood covering her face.

Marla pointed toward Khrazhti and squeaked out, "The cloaked one."

Master Qydus stepped up to the cloaked woman. He was a tall man and could loom with the best of them, especially with his face custom-made for scowling. "Please, remove the hood and cloak, child. I would see you with my own eyes." At least, that's what Marla thought he said. He was speaking Alaqotim, but no dialect she recognized.

Khrazhti's head swung toward Aeden. Marla's brother had tensed, the fingers on his left hand curling into a claw and the right hand inching toward the hilt on his shoulder. Master Yxna's eyes drilled into his, communicating danger. Aeden's mouth went to a straight line, but he nodded to Khrazhti.

She took the hood from her head and then stepped out of the cloak, revealing herself completely to the masters.

The tension was broken by the headmaster's next action. In the blink of an eye, his face transformed, a smile as large as Marla had ever seen straining his mustache. He stepped forward and took Khrazhti's hand.

"You are magnificent," he said to her, bringing her hand up so he could kiss it lightly. "And so beautiful. I had not imagined the dark creatures of the prophecy being so enjoyable to look upon."

Khrazhti's face went through several changes, from fear and tension to confusion and finally coloring slightly in embarrassment. She answered the master in the same language he had been speaking. "I thank you."

"Ah," the headmaster said in Ruthrin as he released her hand. "So it is as I deduced. You do speak classical Alaqotim. Marvelous. You understand Ruthrin as well, I am told?"

Khrazhti, finally smiling, nodded. "I do. Aeden has taught me much, as well as my other friends."

"Very good. Come, let us sit. There is much to discuss."

And with that simple exchange, all the tension was gone.

Aeden and the others spoke with the masters, telling their story and their plans. Marla was fascinated even though she had heard the stories the day before. It was still amazing to her. Also, she was able to mostly keep quiet and let the others talk. She knew her conversation with the masters was coming, but there was no reason to hurry it along.

By the time they were done, the masters had promised Aeden their support. They would speak with the other masters, but they seemed to think they would not need too much convincing. They also offered training for Aeden in whatever subject the Academy could provide. Master Qydus pointed out that the existence of Sitor-Kanda was dedicated to the Malatirsay. In the short term, he would also allow the group to use horses and other resources from the Academy to continue with their mission.

The first thing they needed to do was to prepare to leave the next day. They needed to get to Izhrod as quickly as possible and stop him from opening any more portals. The fewer animaru there were, the easier their job would be in stopping them from destroying all life in Dizhelim.

Rooms were provided for all of Aeden's friends, and they fell into bed and to sleep quickly. Before Marla knew it, it was time to go and rouse the travelers.

❧ 37 ❧

"So, are you ready to go?" Marla asked Evon.

Evon kept looking back to where Fahtin stood with the others. Aeden and Urun were seriously injured, and some of the others had wounds, too, but his eyes were only on the tall Gypta girl. "I'm ready."

"She'll be fine. They'll be fine. Better that you and I do this. It's fitting, in a way."

"Yeah," he said absently. "Fitting."

Marla and Evon had traveled with Aeden and his friends to find Izhrod Benzal. Khrazhti still couldn't sense him, but Marla had been fairly certain she knew where to find him. He had always bragged about a family holding, an ancient fortress not too far from his home in Artuyeska. That's where they headed.

At first, the travel had been uneventful. Then they chanced upon a man fleeing from his village, claiming it was being attacked by monsters. They knew what that meant and rushed to aid the village. The party killed a lot of animaru there, and they found Aeden's boyhood friend, Greimich.

Even more important to Marla, though, they met a

messenger who had found a very special item. He had a small toy that was as familiar to Marla and Evon as their own hands. It was the little egg-shaped object Skril used to fidget with constantly. Not a toy *like* the one Skril had. It was *the* toy Skril always carried around. It had the scratches Marla put on it when she knocked it of his hands once accidentally and it tumbled over the paving stones under their feet. She would have recognized it anywhere.

When Marla asked the messenger where he got it, he said he chanced upon it outside Arcusheim, near a small estate in the countryside. He even sketched a map for her. Marla took it to Evon a few minutes later, and her friend knew immediately what she was thinking. It was their final clue to where Quentin Duzen was.

"Are we going to go after him right now?" Evon had asked.

"No," she'd said. "We told Aeden we'd help him with Izhrod, and we're going to stick to our word. Besides, they don't know where the fortress is. We have to lead them. After, though, we're going to pay Quentin a little visit."

They kept their plans secret, not wanting to complicate Aeden's mission. They led the others to Izhrod's fortress, obviously now occupied, and then they ran the man to ground.

The fighting to get through the fortress was brutal and the party suffered some injuries, but none too serious. Then they found the man himself.

Izhrod Benzal had been with a large group of powerful animaru. The party of heroes had proved victorious, killing the man and all his companions.

Unfortunately, Aeden and Urun were both injured seriously in the fighting, and Evon's healing wasn't up to the task of making them sound enough to accompany Marla on her mission to find Quentin. Marla revealed the mission to Aeden, but left out some of the details so he'd be content to recuperate. The party agreed to split. Marla and Evon would go to find Quentin, and the rest of them would return to the Academy and heal. In their condition, it would take them longer to get back than it had taken to get to the fortress, but that was fine. Marla and Evon would meet them back at Sitor-Kanda when they were done with their task.

So off Marla and Evon went, heading west at a quick pace. Their plan was to use roads as much as they could. They were past hiding. They would be coming for Quentin, and they didn't care if he knew.

According to the messenger Marla had talked to, the old estate was in the foothills of Ianthra's Breasts, to the east of Arcusheim. They left the North Road and got onto the River Road again, heading south.

"Here we are again," she said to Evon.

"Yeah."

"It seems like so much has happened since we traveled this way before."

"Because it has," Evon said. "It was a lifetime ago."

Marla thought about that, the steady thump of the horses' hooves putting her into a contemplative mood. "I miss Aeden. I hope he's okay."

Evon laughed. "Already used to having a brother around, eh?"

She shrugged. "I guess. I've gone my whole life not knowing what I was missing and then he appears and we go on an important mission and...I don't know. I kind of got used to being around him. I'd know he was my brother, even if there wasn't all that evidence. He *feels* like my twin. It would be a great tragedy if something happened to him just when we finally found each other."

"Something happen to *him*? Marla, the man is a master of combat. Plus, he's surrounded by his friends, including, I might add, one of the greatest heroes who ever lived. I'm more concerned about something happening to *us*. Quentin's no slouch, and he probably has others with him. Maybe other Academy adepts. We don't know how deep this conspiracy goes. Him, Izhrod, and who knows who else is part of their group. We should probably focus on keeping ourselves alive so we can go back to Aeden and the others."

"Others?" Marla asked, smiling at her friend.

"Uh, yeah. You know, to all our new friends."

"All of them?"

"Yes." He sighed. "But especially Fahtin. Is it that obvious?"

"Oh no," she said. "Not to anyone who is blind and deaf. Or doesn't have a sense of smell, or isn't breathing."

"Okay, okay. Focus."

They made good time and found a little-used road exactly where the messenger's map showed it was. A strange rock formation that looked a bit like a badger, if one tilted their head and squinted at it, marked the opening.

There were tracks on the dirt road.

"These aren't that old," Marla said. "I think we found the place."

They took it slower after that. Marla's experience with the trap that allowed her to be caught by Quentin was at the front of her mind. She definitely didn't want to relive that experience. She hadn't tried Hurricane again since then, but even if she could get it to work again, best not to get caught at all.

Damn, she thought. *I should have asked Master Esiyae about the spell when I was back at the Academy.*

Before long they saw a structure nestled on a hill a few miles away. It wasn't a grand building, and it didn't have much of a wall, but it did look like some noble's home, or what had been a noble's home many decades ago.

The main building was squarish and three stories tall in

the middle. The wall, mainly decorative but probably suffi-cient to keep animals out, was serviceable, but built with blocks of stone and not even ten feet high. The rough profile told Marla that even should they have to climb it, it would pose no challenge.

When they first caught sight of it, the day was ending and shadow was running across the land.

"We have a choice to make," she said. "We can continue on in the dark, hoping no traps have been set on the road, or we can wait until morning and hope no one sees us. We're pretty exposed on parts of the road. Most of it goes near enough trees to hide us, but not all."

Evon hummed as he scanned the road ahead. "I don't know. I don't like it. Maybe we can wait until daylight and go through the trees, only using the road when it's screened from view."

"It'll be hard to do that with the horses," she said. "Not impossible, but tougher."

"You know how Quentin works. He's mastered the schools of explosives and poisons, and he has a fondness for traps. How did no one ever notice he'd be a villain with the mix of schools he's mastered?"

"Yeah, you're right," she said. "I'm fairly certain he wouldn't trap the roadway, but not enough that I'd risk trav-eling it at night. Fine, let's find a sheltered place, get some sleep, and start out at first light. It shouldn't take us more than a few hours to get to the hilltop."

It took almost four hours to arrive at the estate. They hadn't run into any traps, or even detected any, but better that than to have risked it in the dark.

The first thing Marla noticed was that the estate building was larger than it had seemed from several miles away. It would take them quite a while to search the entire thing. As they watched, eating some of their trail rations, they saw no sign of life. On the one hand, they could get over the wall without being spotted. Probably. Unfortunately, they also didn't know if they had the right place. Marla pictured in her mind bursting into a dining room and scaring the wits out of some poor family sitting down to eat their evening meal.

"There's nothing for it but to do it," she said. "We can leave the horses here and climb the wall toward the back, where it's close to the trees."

"This is it," Evon said, clenching and unclenching his fists. "For better or worse, we're finally here."

✥ 38 ✥

The wall proved to be no problem at all, as expected. The massive stone blocks used to build it were stacked and not mortared, leaving cracks big enough for them to fit their booted feet and their hands and climb up with little more effort than climbing a ladder. They topped the wall and dropped to the other side.

Even after so much neglect, the trees—grown wild and bushy—were in rows. The grasses and weeds in between would have been a manicured lawn. Marla could see it in her mind as she looked around for any sign of inhabitants.

She found none.

Using the trees and long grass as cover, they hurried to the closest outer wall of the main house. Though a good part of the yard and house was shaded, she could see no lights burning in the house. Had they guessed wrong? Was Quentin somewhere else? If so, they were out of tricks. She couldn't imagine how they would find him.

They found a side door, probably one for servants. It was plain and smaller than doors for guests or residents. Evon tried the lock while Marla continued to look for movement.

It was locked.

"Here, switch with me." She pulled out a few slender tools from her pack. It took her less than a minute to coax the lock open, and she opened the door slowly to minimize the squeaking of the hinges.

"That really comes in handy," Evon said.

"Just a little thing I picked up while studying at the School of Artifice. Locks are simple machines, after all, so the School of Mechanista Artificing is all kinds of useful."

They slipped into the darkened hallway on the other side of the door and closed it again, then waited for a few minutes so their eyes would adjust before starting off again.

Marla tapped her finger on the doorframe, impatient to get going, but she knew it was better to go in seeing the best she could. It paid off. They only took three steps before she noticed the first trap.

"Stop," she whispered to Evon. She bent down and inspected a slightly raised section of the wooden floor. It was a trigger, one meant to sink slightly when walked upon. No doubt it pressed on a mechanism to do something nasty to them. As she carefully lifted the piece of wood and traced it to a cleverly hidden depression in the wall, she wanted to whistle, but wisely didn't.

"Wow," she whispered. "This is definitely something Quentin would do. The mechanism moves this other mechanism over here. This one mixes the two chemicals separated by a thin glass plate. If I recognize them correctly, they're treated firebloom and fusehair, and if they mix, they immediately create an explosion. A powerful one. Big enough to turn most of this hallway into a crater. Let's not set it off, okay?"

Evon nervously licked his lips. Maybe he'd expected this mission to go better than the last one. The sentiment wasn't lost on Marla. She worked her mouth to moisten it. It was dry for some reason.

"This has Quentin's name all over it," she said. "What, did Izhrod and Quentin take the same Trap Setting for Villains class at the Academy? We'll take it slow. Keep your eyes open for anything that looks out of the ordinary. It'll only take one trap like this to end us for good."

Evon nodded. They moved on.

They found one more trap in the hallway and slipped by that one as well. By the time they had gone down two more halls, Marla was freely perspiring.

They finally reached an area that had lamps mounted to the walls in the shape of torches in sconces. There still had been no sign of anyone else, but it was obvious the two were not alone in the estate. The lamps used mundane flame and oil reservoirs.

The house was silent. Lamp flames sizzled and popped occasionally as Marla passed. The floor changed from the simple wood of the first few halls they had traveled to worn carpets, and then to slightly less worn carpets that had been cleaned somewhat. That indicated they were going in the right direction. When they reached polished floors made of hardwood, it only confirmed that suspicion.

She had found only one trap in the lit halls, another sign they were going where they were supposed to. Marla breathed a bit easier, believing they would soon be where Quentin wouldn't have set traps. She couldn't see him doing that for areas he—or whoever else he had here with him—frequented. There would be too great a chance of accident that way.

Just as she thought about there being fewer traps, she heard a click.

"Freeze!" Marla hissed, and thankfully, Evon did as she commanded. "Did you feel the floor give at all?"

"No. It did feel like I crushed something with my left foot, though."

"Stay there and don't move." Marla squatted, distributing her weight as evenly as possible so as not to change how her feet were pressing to the floor. She inspected around her feet and saw nothing that indicated she had stepped on any kind of trigger. She hadn't felt anything when she was walking, but she wasn't going to risk their lives on it.

When she was as sure as she could be, she stood upright again, looked Evon in the eyes, and took a step toward him.

Nothing happened.

She breathed a sigh of relief, but the ordeal wasn't over. She started searching around Evon's feet for any sign of a trap. She didn't find anything.

"Your left foot, you said?"

"Yeah," he answered. His voice sounded strained. "Am I going to die, Marla?"

"Not if I can help it. Just keep still while I figure out what's going on."

For the life of her, she couldn't figure out what that sound had been. She could find no evidence of any kind of trap or trigger. The walls didn't appear to contain any mechanisms, nor the ceiling. The only conclusion she could come to was that whatever it was, it was so small that it was completely covered by Evon's foot.

"I'm going to move your foot around, just a little bit," she said. "I need to see if I can find what made that noise. Once it's visible, we can figure out how to disarm it, if possible."

"Okay."

Marla got down on the floor, her face just a few inches from Evon's left foot. She pried the tip of his boot up.

"Oh," she said, slumping as her entire body relaxed.

"Oh?" Evon said nervously.

"Yeah. Go ahead and move your foot."

"You...you want me to move my foot?"

"Yep. Go ahead."

She heard him swallow, then he slowly lifted his foot and moved it a few inches away.

Marla picked up the pieces she had seen and held them up to Evon.

"Are those...walnut shells?"

"Sure are," she said. "You stepped on someone's shells."

The outrush of air from her friend made Marla want to laugh, but she restrained herself. They still had work to do.

"Let's keep an eye out not only for trap triggers, but for things on the ground. It would be better not to make any sound, if we can help it."

"Yeah," he said shakily. "Okay."

They soon reached a stairway going down.

"Of course there's a basement," Marla said. "Why would there not be?"

The stairs were stone, or maybe hardened earth. It was hard to tell with the layer of dust on them. Marla didn't care to inspect them. She did notice, however, that there were many footprints on them. Human shoes and boots, and claw marks that could only be animaru. They were nearly there.

Voices ahead tipped them off long before they saw anyone. Marla couldn't quite make out what was being said, but she hugged the right wall of the passage that swept in that direction. She motioned for Evon to stay put and she inched her way forward until she could peek around the corner.

The hallway widened into a large room, roughly square and carved from the ground itself. The finish was uneven, like it was in a cave, and it had an opening at the opposite side. Between her and that opening were several figures. She only had eyes for one.

Quentin Duzen, his short blond hair with its typical mixture of styling and messiness, stood with his side to her, talking with three other humans. Marla recognized them all.

39

Tildus Uworn was a large man, and muscular besides. He had mastered the School of Blunt Weapons Combat, and his war hammer lay on a table near him. He had other schools under his belt, too, but nothing that would present a challenge to her and Evon like that weapon would.

Ren Kenata was not so large as Tildus, but he was fit and fast. His black hair was cut short and he wore the distinctive clothing she always saw him in: a mix between the traditional Teroshimi battle robes and more utilitarian trousers and tunic. He had mastered the School of Edged Weapon Combat, as Marla had, and she was very familiar with him and his classical Teroshimi swords. She had sparred with him numerous times and beat him every time they squared off against each other, but of course, that was one-on-one. There were three of them to the two of Marla and Evon.

The third person with them made her heart ache. Inna Moroz was a pretty, brown-haired woman whom Marla knew well. She and Inna had spent a fair amount of time studying together as they were mastering the School of Air Magic. The woman was keenly intelligent and had a knack for magic, as well as for the ranged weapons she had also mastered: a pair of small crossbows with several modifications to make them deadlier than normal weapons. She was dressed in soft, flowing trousers and tunic that were tight enough in the right places to distract male students at the Academy, but still loose enough for her to move easily. They looked similar to Gypta clothing, though in subdued browns. It made Marla think of Fahtin, which made her feel even worse.

She and Evon were going to have to fight these three, in addition to Quentin.

Then there were the animaru. Four of them, ones that didn't look like the simple creatures she had fought when she had first encountered them. Two of them almost looked like completely hairless humans, except for the pointed ears, sharp teeth, and claws at the end of their hands and feet. One of the others appeared to have scales. Those three were like the ones she had fought when they took Izhrod down. The other one was roughly man-shaped, very large, and covered with dark hair.

Marla slipped back toward where Evon waited. She motioned for him to backtrack to where they could talk without being heard.

"Trouble," she said.

"What is it?"

"Quentin is there, of course. He was speaking to the animaru, which is why I couldn't seem to understand earlier. I thought it was just that it was too low to hear, but it was Alaqotim, that ancient dialect that Master Qydus spoke to Khrazhti. I was listening for Ruthrin.

"There were four of the animaru. I wish now we had questioned Khrazhti about the different types. None of them are the normal seren type she told us about. One looks like a snake, another looks kind of like a gorilla, and two are what I think she called semhominus. Those last two often use magic, according to her."

"So we have Quentin and four animaru, two of which may be able to use magic?" he asked.

"That's not the worst of it. Tildus Uworn, Ren Kenata, and Inna Moroz are also with him."

"Inna?" Evon said, nearly in a whine. He had a crush on her for years, but she hadn't seemed interested. In fact, though she used her charisma and her looks as many pretty women did, Marla couldn't remember her ever spending a lot of time with men. She figured the woman was just a solitary person, which was fine with her.

"Yeah, I know. It breaks my heart. I like Inna."

"Ren is a better swordsman than I am," Evon said, "and my blade isn't a match for Tildus's hammer, if he connects with it."

"I think we can take them, but with the animaru, too, it'll be tough. I'm not really sure what to do. We could have come all this way and end up being killed for it. I wish we had brought some of the others. I wish Aeden had been in a condition to join us."

"Yeah, well, if wishes were gold, we could own a kingdom," he said. Wow, he was really taking this Inna thing hard. "What are we going to do? There's no shame in leaving and coming back another time, maybe with backup."

Marla chewed on the idea. He was right. It might be better if they engaged in a strategic retreat and came back better prepared. It didn't look like Quentin would be leaving this place anytime soon.

She opened her mouth to agree, but stopped when she heard footsteps.

"Surus's shitty bunghole," she cursed. "Come on, we need to get out of here."

Which was a problem, since they were in a long hall with

no other side passages.

They turned and shuffled, trying to keep as silent as possible, back toward the stairs. Marla could still hear the footsteps and they didn't seem to be speeding up, so she took that as a good sign that they were being quiet enough.

As she set her foot on the bottom stair step, the sound she had been fearing rang behind her. The footsteps, clearly claws clicking on the hard floor, sped up. One look over her shoulder confirmed that all four of the animaru had seen her down the long hall and were charging. The only thing to be grateful for was that they hadn't shouted an alarm. Maybe Quentin and the others weren't with them.

Marla looked over at Evon and he met her eyes.

"Up," she said. "Fast. If we can fight them alone, we'll be much better off."

Together, they abandoned all attempts at stealth and ran full tilt up the stairs.

The humans made the upstairs landing, then turned to face their pursuers. One of the semhominus threw its hand forward and a bolt of power shot toward them. Evon dodged to the side and Marla flicked a burst of air magic to deflect the attack. In the same motion, she rotated her wrist and sent an air missile back toward the caster. It crashed into the animaru, making it stumble into the wall.

"Take that, you filthy beast," Marla said, drawing her sword and her dueling dagger. Having weapons in both hands would limit the spells she could use, but she was not interested in a mage duel. She could do more damage with her weapons, especially since Aeden had told her about the creatures' vulnerability to life magic. She had imbued her weapons, as well as Evon's, with life energies every day since they left Aeden's group.

These monsters were about to learn that they could indeed be destroyed.

The big, hairy animaru bounded up the stairs on all fours, outpacing its fellows. When it reached the top, it leaped toward Marla without slowing, apparently picking her out as the more powerful of the two humans.

She gritted her teeth and smiled at it as she rolled to the side, coming up to her feet and slashing as the beast flew by her.

The snake animaru charged Evon and their weapons clanged together. The hairy creature was the only one without weapons. The other three wielded swords and looked as if they knew how to use them.

One of the hairless humanoids rushed in, slashing at Marla, while the other began to gesture. She knew what was coming and sprinted toward the caster, slipping to the side to evade the sharp blade trying to get to her.

The space around them was wider than the hallway below, but it wasn't a room. With three animaru trying to get her, she needed to take them out quickly or she'd be overwhelmed.

She reached the casting animaru as it was finishing its spell. She tracked its hand, already glowing, as it swung toward her.

Dropping to her knees, she slid the last three feet and stabbed upward with her dagger. The animaru grunted as she pierced its arm, the globe of power rebounding off the wall and sputtering into the ceiling. Marla came to her feet, twisted her dagger to increase the damage, and kicked the caster in the midsection. It flew back and slammed into the wall.

But the other two enemies were upon her. As she spun, she barely avoided the blade the other armed animaru had thrust at her, but there wasn't room to avoid the claws of the hairy creature. Its nails dug into her leather armor, piercing it in two places, and tore the skin on her left side.

317

Not wanting to scream and notify the humans of her presence, Marla hissed as she turned to parry another sword slash, and sliced down to take two fingers off the unarmed creature's other claw as it came for her.

This wasn't going as well as she would have liked. Marla spun away from the two attackers and checked on the third. It was picking itself up and joining the other two.

So, make that three attackers.

The armed animaru were skilled and the hairy one was extremely fast and strong. She needed something, an edge. She wished she knew more life magic spells. The other schools of magic didn't hit them as hard.

The three came at her again, wildly attacking and apparently not concerned with whether or not they would strike their companions. The two swords came in horizontally, from opposite directions, and the hairy beast leaped straight at her. She did the only thing she could think of.

She lunged forward.

Marla thrust her sword into the belly of the sword-wielder on her right, punching her blade through it before its wider strike could land. At the same time, she leaned her body to that side, narrowly evading the airborne enemy. With her no longer where she had been, the slash from the other animaru cut into the unarmed monster's shoulder, affecting its trajectory just enough to keep it from bowling Marla over.

While the other two were recovering their balance, Marla drove her dagger into the injured semhominus's eye, spinning away before it even dropped its weapon. The remaining attackers pivoted and attacked her more quickly than she had anticipated, and she found herself backpedaling and madly slashing at them to keep from being sliced open.

The two attacked relentlessly, sword and claw, giving her no opening to counterattack. It was all she could do to keep their attacks from landing.

She was nearing the edge of the stairs. It would be disastrous to fall down with her enemies so close.

Desperately, she used a simple light spell, one that didn't require gestures, but was also not that powerful. She called it into being, taking magic from the surrounding air, and formed it into a bright flash, directing it into the sword-wielder's eyes.

It did the trick. The monster blinked, obviously losing track of the things in front of it. Marla took the opportunity to slam her sword into its own and tear out its throat with her dagger. Not knowing if that was a fatal wound for animaru, even with the life magic imbued in the weapon, she followed up with a powerful horizontal strike, separating its head from its shoulders.

That would probably do it, she told herself.

The hairy monster crashed into her, knocking her to the ground. Its claws scraped at her armor, but thankfully it was too close to generate the momentum to tear into it. A fetid wave of putrid breath washed over Marla as it snapped its teeth at her, trying to tear her throat out.

Her sword was too long to be of any use and her left arm was pinned by the thing's body, trapping her dagger. Damn, it was strong.

She rolled, trying to dislodge it, but unable to do so. Its face was getting closer and closer to her wide eyes. Her mind frantically searched for a way to get it off her, but she was light-headed from hitting her head on the floor and from the thing's smell.

It suddenly stopped pushing toward her and snapped its head to the side.

Evon stood there, sword dripping the muddy muck these things called blood. He backed up a step when he realized his attack hadn't killed the hairy monster. It seemed only to anger it.

The beast pushed down on Marla and, in a flash, leaped toward Evon.

As the pressure on her chest released, Marla slashed out with her sword, cutting into the animaru's leg. She didn't quite hamstring it, but she did ruin its leap. It flopped awkwardly onto one side, then rolled and, favoring the uninjured leg, lunged for Evon again.

It had lost its chance. Marla jumped to her feet and threw a flurry of strikes at the creature from both of her blades, delivering several small wounds that bled freely. When it turned its attention back to her, Evon darted in and cut at its back.

After a few more attacks from each side, distracting and injuring it, it apparently realized it couldn't win. It bunched its muscles to bound over Marla down the stairs.

She got to it first.

Whirling and cutting repeatedly at it with both blades, she finally got inside its massive arms and rammed her sword into its chest. With a twist of the hips, she punched her dagger through its forehead. It twitched and dropped to the ground.

"Damn," she said, breathless. "Thanks for that." For someone who preferred to work alone, it was a rare treat to be saved by a companion.

"No problem," Evon told her, just as breathless.

"You hurt?" she asked.

"A little. You?"

"Some, but not enough to stop me. Want more?"

"Not really," Evon said. "But I guess we don't have a choice, do we? Do you think they heard us?"

"No, we don't, and I don't know if they did. I would think if they did hear, they'd be here now."

"Good point."

"I don't see how they wouldn't have heard us, though," she said.

"Another good point."

Evon used the healing spell he knew to remove the slashes they had both received. Marla didn't like him doing it because she didn't want him to tire himself out, but he insisted.

"You killed the snake, huh?" she asked.

"Yeah. It was fast, too. Fast as...well, as a snake."

Marla looked at Evon, tilted her head, then chuckled. "I see you're eloquent as ever."

"Oh, shut up. Are we going after the others or not?"

"We are. You ready for this?"

Evon looked askance at Marla.

They retraced their steps down the stairs and to the turn where Marla had spied on the humans before. The room where they had been was empty now. There was only one way they could have gone. The other exit.

Skimming along the walls, they approached the other passage from the side. Marla peeked around the corner and saw that the passageway beyond went on for some distance, torches providing not quite enough light to see everything, but letting her see that it went on for at least fifty feet. She didn't like the many shadowed areas, but there wasn't really anything she could do about it.

With a shake of her head, she started down the hall.

Marla slid along the wall, keeping to patches of darkness, Evon a step behind. There was no sound to guide her like before, no voices to orient her. Where had the Academy graduates gone? Just how far did this below-ground warren stretch?

The tunnel twisted, changing direction twice. Every scrape of her boot on the rough floor made Marla wince. In the utter silence, the little noises as they traveled sounded like announcements in the dark. The red-haired warrior took solace that she would hear the others before they heard her. After all, she was focusing on finding them and they didn't know she was here.

Did they?

She stopped as the hall widened. It wasn't like before, where it intersected what seemed like a room with fairly straight walls. This time, it actually widened into a bigger hallway. Like a cave system. The floor and walls seemed more jagged, less carved by human hands.

More natural.

A quick look at Evon told her he'd noticed it, too. Was it significant in any way? She didn't know, but it was one more thing to throw off her equilibrium.

She continued on, hugging the wall. Light pooled at the other end of the chamber, some fifteen feet or so away, just bright enough that she could see the outline of her own feet, though she didn't think someone further into the light's circle could have seen her.

A spike of panic, or something else, echoed in her mind. There was something more here. Something was not right. It felt like—

The air around her suddenly compressed, like she had emerged from a building into a storm outside. It was calm before, but now it felt...stagnant. Oppressive. Marla threw her hand out and it struck something before she could fully extend her arm.

Damn.

Evon shuffled. Marla could feel an aggravated aura from his direction.

Light flared into being, flooding the entire chamber. She blinked against it, raising her hand to shield her eyes.

Four faces were looking right at her. Four familiar faces.

"And the light will reveal all," Quentin Duzen said, standing two dozen feet away, hand on his spear.

❧ 40 ❧

"**S**hit, shit, shit," Marla hissed. She stretched her arms and found the extent of her invisible prison. It was a large bubble, surrounding her completely. A shield. She'd been stupid enough to let them capture her.

Again.

It occurred to her, too late, that Ren Kenata had mastered the School of Illusion. She and Evon hadn't been sneaking through the dark at all. The room had been well lit the entire time and they had been moving along the wall like idiots, in plain view of the others.

They were in a lot of trouble.

"Oh, Marla," Quentin Duzen said, "I'm so disappointed in you. After our last encounter, I would have expected you to count yourself fortunate and stay away from me. If you had survived, that is. I wasn't sure about that. And now here you are, at my mercy again."

Marla looked around, searching for something that would help her out of the predicament she was in. At the moment, she couldn't do anything to attack Quentin and the others because of the shield around her. Then again, they also couldn't attack her. Not until they dropped the bubbles.

Ren Kenata, his handsome face framed by black hair, stood off to the side, near what looked like a portal device. Tildus Uworn, hammer in his hand, stood by Quentin, with Inna Moroz on the other side of the blond-haired leader. Marla met Inna's eyes, hoping to find at least some sympathy there, but though the woman had always seemed to like Marla, she didn't look friendly at the moment.

"Inna?" Marla said, but got no response.

"Let's get this over with," Tildus said, hefting his hammer and striding over toward Marla and Evon. "When I tell you, drop the shield on Marla."

Great, they were going to stand and watch as the big lummox crushed her skull with his hammer.

Marla needed something and she needed it quickly. She was familiar with the shields. They dampened magic so spells could not be cast through them, and they were durable enough that she'd never be able to cut through it with her swords. It was most likely strong enough to withstand a hammer blow from Tildus's massive arms and shoulders, but he would have them drop it just in time for him to strike.

Think, Marla. Think.

An idea came to her, something drawn from her studies. She wasn't sure it would work, Tildus and his hammer were only a few steps away.

Tapping her experience from several different schools, she began to cast. The spells she had in mind didn't require any gestures, material components, or spoken words. They were relatively simple, could be cast mentally through thought and absorption of the surrounding magic alone.

The first wasn't even so much a spell as a quality she was able to turn on with a slight magical nudge. It made her resistant to heat, a useful piece of magic from the School of Fire Magic.

The second was an uncommon spell, possibly unique, that she had come up with while experimenting with her fire magic, which she was fairly accomplished in, and her air magic, of which she had gained mastery. She had never bothered to name the spell. There was really no need. Cast with a thought and her ability to draw magical energy into herself, she didn't see that it needed a name.

Without moving, she focused on her hands and began to pour hot air out from them. The amount of magical energy detectable from outside her body was almost negligible, but the effect wasn't.

As she pumped more hot air into the space surrounding her, she felt the pressure build. It wasn't too uncomfortable yet, but it would get there soon.

Tildus took his time crossing the room. Quentin and Inna remained where they were, to Marla's right, and Ren was watching Marla from her left. He looked like he was trying to puzzle something out.

Tildus was only two steps away, already raising his hammer. Marla pushed harder, increasing the pressure in her little bubble. She could feel it; it only needed a little more force and it would blow the bubble apart. If she timed it perfectly, she could also incapacitate the hammer-wielding Academy graduate rapidly approaching.

"Ren," Tildus said. "Drop the—"

The pressure in the bubble had finally reached the bubble's limit. Before Ren Kenata could dismiss the shield around Marla, the entire thing exploded. Tildus's hammer happened to be rising up, almost directly in front of his face, when it did so.

The shock wave was powerful enough to throw Evon several feet into the wall, where he bounced and rocketed to the floor, sliding for a time before finally stopping. Marla hoped the shield had protected him from most of the force, but she couldn't concentrate on him now. She needed to take advantage of her freedom before the others attacked her at once.

As for Tildus, he wasn't as fortunate as Evon. Besides being blasted back from her—he had only been a step away when the bubble burst—his hammer had been thrown back at him, striking him squarely in the face. His body landed on the ground a dozen feet away, face and skull mangled by the equivalent of a hammer being wielded by a tornado. He wouldn't be getting back up.

Ren Kenata was the closest, so Marla lunged for him. He had somehow activated the portal next to him and was jumping toward it. He did always strike her as one who ran when the odds seemed against him. Leave it to the coward to try to escape.

Marla snatched at Ren's clothes, trying to haul him back to her. The slippery man shrugged his way out of his outer robes, leaving them in Marla's hands as he disappeared into the glowing doorway. She wasn't about to go through the portal, leaving Evon with the other two Academy graduates. Instead, she threw the clothing to the ground, drew her sword, and smashed the device next to the portal. The gateway immediately winked out. The other two would not be using it to escape. Even better, with Ren gone, Evon's bubble would have disappeared.

Marla sensed more than saw a projectile coming at her. She rolled to the side as a crossbow bolt pinged off the stone wall, passing through where she had been a moment before. She drew her dagger as she came to her feet and struck out at the bolt that followed the first one. She barely deflected it; Inna was using her mastery of air magic to boost its speed and to help aim the projectiles.

Quentin grasped his spear and charged.

Evon grunted from somewhere behind Marla.

"Get up, Evon. I could use a little help."

She wanted to rejoice when his sword rasped clear of the scabbard. Two on two. Those were much better odds than just a few minutes ago.

Inna was the dangerous one, at least for the next few seconds. With her modified crossbows and air magic, she wouldn't have to get within sword range to kill both Marla and Evon. Marla needed to do something to change that.

With a gesture and a few words, Marla threw balled lightning at Inna, then intercepted Quentin's sprint, slashing out at him with her sword. If she could give Evon a few more seconds, he could back her up. He'd taken a pretty good knock when her shield blew out and he was probably not recuperated fully yet.

Inna dove to the ground, dodging the lightning. When she regained her feet, she shot bolts from both of her crossbows and uttered familiar words of power. The bolts zipped toward Marla, changing their trajectory in midair to home in on her. The red-haired warrior blocked the counterattack from Quentin's spear, then cast a bit of air magic herself, upsetting the missiles coming at her enough so she could roll to the side and dodge them. Before they even struck the far wall, two more were airborne and Inna repeated her spells to give them a windy assist.

"Evon?" Marla said, casting again while parrying a spear thrust with her sword. Quentin swung the butt of the spear up and slammed it into Marla's lead leg. The best she could do was to shift her weight onto her other foot and try to let the leg move with the force of the blow. Even then, she almost tumbled as pain shot up her leg. She hoped the bone hadn't broken.

A figure flashed at the side of Marla's vision. It was Evon, sprinting toward Inna. It was a good choice. Quentin had mastered the spear and Evon wouldn't have stood a chance against him.

But there was another problem: Inna's expertise was in her ranged weapons and air magic. Evon was still a good twelve or fifteen feet from the woman and her crossbows still had at least three bolts queued in the firing mechanism. What Evon was doing was suicide.

Either that, or he had utmost confidence that Marla would help him out.

Damn him, but he was right.

Marla cast the strongest instant-cast spell she could, a ram of wind that could pick Inna up and throw her at least twenty feet. Doing so allowed Quentin to score a shallow gash on her other leg, but it wasn't serious enough to incapacitate her.

Inna crossed both hands in front of her and brought a wedge of air into being. It split the spell Marla had cast, pushing her back slightly, but mostly cutting and deflecting the oncoming spell. The woman brought her crossbows up to aim at Evon.

Marla parried a spear thrust, deflected a spinning strike, and jumped over a slash that would have cut deeply into her calf. Her angle was off and she couldn't throw a spell out in time to stop Inna from skewering Evon with quarrels.

She didn't need to. As he ran, Evon flicked his left hand toward Inna and several fiery missiles zipped toward her. She had to move her hands to form a shield of air, protecting herself and also ruining her chances to fire her own missiles.

Evon finally got within range and swung his sword at Inna. She blocked with the handle of one of her crossbows.

Another line of fire traced its way across Marla's body, this time on her left upper arm. She spun away, slapping at the spear that darted in to puncture her three times in rapid succession, like a snake striking. Evon would have to deal with his battle on his own. Marla needed to focus on Quentin. She couldn't allow him to strike her again.

The two wordlessly danced, one striking, then the other. They moved quickly as only two masters of their respective weapons could. Marla repaid his earlier attacks with a few gashes of her own, but neither did serious damage.

Though she wanted to check on Evon, the simple fact was that she couldn't spare the focus. She was better than Quentin, but she'd already been through so much this day. If she didn't do something soon, she'd be too fatigued to finish him.

After an attack, Quentin spun away, rotating his body and snugging the spear along his arm and back. As he rotated, he cast his left hand out and threw several objects toward Marla.

Not knowing what was coming at her, Marla pushed forth a wall of air magic, bouncing the objects up and away from her. They flew a few feet then exploded with red flares.

She had almost forgotten about the explosives. Quentin had mastered the School of Explosives. Why wouldn't he be using them in combat?

Marla had fallen into the dueling mindset. Training at the Academy did let one develop combat abilities, but by sparring too much, she had just naturally assumed they would be fighting by some kind of rules. The masters told her to keep her mind open, be creative, and use every advantage when fighting for life and death. She needed to remember that, or any trick Quentin used could end her.

She growled and attacked with a flurry of blows meant to press Quentin. He only had the one weapon, while she had two. If she attacked so fiercely that he couldn't counterattack, she could slip inside his guard and finish him.

The man was wickedly fast, his control of the long weapon extreme. She tried to attack his hands where they gripped the shaft of the spear, but he always had them in the correct position, one she couldn't reach with sword or dagger.

It was getting frustrating.

Twice more he tried to use his little explosives, but he could only do so when she was at spear range. If she was within sword range, he risked being caught in the explosions himself. Both times, she used air to push the devices away, letting them explode harmlessly. Everything was moving too fast for her to accurately throw them back at him.

It finally occurred to Marla that she wasn't utilizing all her talents. She had rarely met her match in combat, so she hadn't needed to stretch, to use everything at her disposal. She needed to now.

She whirled, sword point down to block aside a spear thrust. Her spin took her closer to Quentin, but not quite close enough to get to him with her dagger. She flicked it out anyway, hoping he'd flinch.

He didn't.

He also didn't see the motion she made with two of her fingers of her left hand. Or hear her whisper the two words of power to activate a spell.

Light flashed out, right in front of Quentin's face. He blinked, trying to clear his vision. While he couldn't see, Marla continued her spin, striking his lower legs with her calf, knocking him off balance. His stance was too strong for her to take him down completely, but it was a start.

Quentin stumbled, but then regained his balance more quickly than Marla would have liked. She was able to slip in a sword thrust, though, cutting into his side.

He grunted, snapping his spear rapidly from left to right in front of him, keeping her back while he blinked and finally seemed to focus on her.

She smiled at him.

Quentin sneered and threw his left hand out, spikes made

of fire shooting toward Marla. She swept her hand across her chest and deflected the missiles, then snapped her wrist as if batting his attack back at him. Jagged spears of ice shot toward him, which he deflected with a magical shield of his own.

The spear-wielder began to cast a more powerful spell, one Marla only half recognized. She didn't want to find out exactly what it was. With a strong mental push, she called up wind to buffet him. Surprisingly, it picked him up and knocked him off his feet.

Not wanting to analyze the sudden power of the spell, Marla charged in and was almost impaled by the spear Quentin thrust up at her. At the last moment, she managed to push it aside with her blade to keep it from going through her midsection.

Inside the spear's range, she slashed at him with her sword and cast her flash spell again. This time, he closed his eyes before the flare of light.

Allowing her to cut deeply into his right arm when he wasn't looking.

Marla rolled over Quentin and came to her feet. He jumped to his, but it was obvious he couldn't use his spear effectively. He could barely grip it with his right hand.

"There's no need for you to die here," she said. "Give up and I'll take you back to the masters."

He didn't bother answering, but instead started a spell.

She recognized the general forms if not the precise spell. It was a life spell. He was trying to heal himself.

"Sorry, then," Marla said. She charged, slammed her sword into the spear, knocking it from his hand, then punched her dagger through his right eye. His mouth widened into an O and then he fell back away from her, crashing to the ground.

Marla whirled, searching out Evon.

❧ 41 ❧

Evon was still fighting, thank the gods, but he didn't look to be in great shape.

Marla's friend moved sluggishly as he did his best to stay close to Inna Moroz. The woman, on the other hand, was using everything at her disposal to keep Evon away. As Marla stumbled toward the pair, the pain in the leg Quentin struck suddenly becoming more pronounced, Inna brought her one crossbow up to fire it at Evon. The weapon that had been in her other hand was nowhere to be seen.

How many bolts did she have left? It would only take one. Evon already had a shaft protruding from his left shoulder, the arm mostly hanging limp on that side. He lunged in with his sword, but he wasn't going to get to Inna fast enough to prevent him from being shot again. At that range, it was sure to go through his eye or throat.

Marla cast an air spell, the most comfortable magic for her to deal with when fatigued. A block of hardened air, barely visible as it flew across the room, slammed into Inna's hand, pushing the crossbow up and to her right. The bolt released and spun off away from the pair.

Right at Marla.

"Oh, for Surus's sake." She rolled under the missile and shakily came back onto her feet. She continued toward the combatants, Evon slashing with his sword and Inna blocking with a shield of air.

Evon slipped on some of the blood he had spilled on the floor, so tired he could hardly keep his feet. Luckily, it allowed him to dodge a sharp wedge of hardened air magic that Inna had cast at him. The woman cursed, wobbling on her own legs. It was amazing that they hadn't collapsed already. They looked more than ready to do so.

Marla finally reached the two as Evon looked to be preparing to lunge in and stick his blade into Inna's abdomen, and she looked ready to use the rest of her strength to impale him with a spike of air, the most economical use of deadly force at this point.

Marla had other ideas. She slid up to them, her foot slipping a little in Evon's blood as he had just done, but keeping her balance. She swung her fist and punched Inna square on the jaw. The woman's eyes rolled up in her head and she dropped to the ground.

Evon, barely able to pull back his sword thrust, dropped to his knees, exhausted.

"Thanks," he said, then leaned back and lay on the floor, panting.

Marla wasn't about to take chances. She pulled a section of rope from Evon's pack lying a few feet away and tied Inna's hands behind her back. Then she tore a long strip from the other woman's clothes and tied it in place as a gag on her mouth.

Only then did she turn her attention to Evon, who was still lying on his back, though his breathing had slowed to almost normal.

She inspected the bolt in his shoulder. "It's not barbed, but it's wedged in there pretty good. I should pull it out."

"Yeah," he said, his eyes still closed.

"It's going to hurt."

"I know. Just do it. I have enough strength to heal it a little so I won't bleed out. That'll have to do until I get some rest and some food."

She did as he said, getting a good grip and pulling it straight out with all her might. He screamed, but it was done. He cast a simple healing spell, and the blood flow slowed to a trickle and then stopped.

"Now let me sleep," he said. "For at least a little while. I feel like I'm dying."

She smiled tiredly. She felt much the same, but didn't bother telling him. He was already losing consciousness. After checking him for other serious wounds—and finding only masses of bruises—she let him be.

The leg that Quentin had struck wasn't broken, but it hurt like it was. She wished she could get a little of that healing herself. To get her mind off the pain, she explored the room.

First, she checked on Tildus. As she'd assumed, he was dead. When your head was so much pulped brain matter, there wasn't too much else you could be. She checked his pockets and his purse, but only found coins. She pocketed them.

Quentin was next. She checked him for a pulse, but didn't expect to find one. His pockets were empty, but his purse was full. She took that, too, wondering what he had done with the horse he took from Skril. Or her mare. She kicked his body as she thought about it, shooting pain up the leg he had injured.

Next, Marla inspected the device for the portal Ren Kenata went through. It was a standard design for magical transmission. They were expensive and had to be set up in advance. Further, they could only be used once, and only for a short time, before the magical power channeling through the device destroyed it. There were ways to figure out where the portal went, but she didn't know them. It probably didn't matter. He would have fled long since.

She got up to go check on Inna when she spotted Ren's robes, the ones she had torn off him and thrown aside. It couldn't hurt to search the pockets.

She was in luck. Ren's robes had several pockets sewn into the interior, and it appeared that the Academy graduate liked to keep things in those pockets.

Marla pulled out a number of folded papers and set them aside. There were no weapons, not even a small dagger, but he wouldn't need them with the swords he always carried. There was a curious stone with some kind of design etched into it, but what was more interesting was that it radiated a small amount of magic. She didn't recognize the symbol, but she would study it when she got back to the Academy.

In one of the pockets, she found some common spell components. Ash fly wing, common salt, and powdered crystal, among others. All in all, she was disappointed. She wasn't sure what she wanted to find, but this hadn't been it.

Grumbling to herself, she brought her findings back to where Evon and Inna were sleeping. Marla was going to have to stay awake for a while, just in case someone else was in Quentin's hideout and found them, so she unfolded the papers.

The first one she opened defied her attempt to read it. It wasn't magical, but the marks on the page didn't look like anything Marla had ever seen. It was either a language she had never seen a reference to—unlikely because she was nearly ready to be tested for mastery of the School of Language—or it was some kind of cipher.

The thought of that made her heart quicken a little. She

had mastered the School of Cryptology and enjoyed the challenge of breaking codes. She set the paper aside for when she could think more clearly.

Of the seven pieces of paper she had found in Ren's robes, only one was in a language she understood. It was in Ruthrin, the common tongue, and it was interesting in its own right. It seemed to be a letter—in fact, all the papers she found seemed to be letters—and appeared to be to Ren himself, though there was no greeting or ending signature.

MEET US AT THE ESTATE AS QUICKLY AS YOU ARE ABLE. WE ARE READY FOR THE NEXT PHASE OF THE PLAN AND WILL GO TO THE NEXT PORTAL POINT AS SOON AS WE ARE ALL TOGETHER.

THE MESSAGE WAS CLEARLY FROM QUENTIN, AND SHE WAS at the estate. But what was their plan, and where was the portal point the note spoke of?

The other six were all in the same scratching marks of the first one she had seen. What she would give to be well-rested and have the mental capabilities to work on it at that moment.

Contrary to her decision to leave the letters for later, she soon grew bored of sitting and watching Evon and Inna sleep. She chewed on trail rations and drank a little water, but needed something else to pass the time.

She picked up one of the pieces of paper. The marks on it didn't even look like characters in a written language. They seemed to be stray marks. There was no discernible pattern, at least not at first glance.

Softening her eyes and looking at it as a whole didn't reveal any secrets. Not that she expected it to. If Ren was keeping these communications secret, it wouldn't be a simple cipher. He was in with dangerous people, ones who didn't hesitate to murder former friends if they saw it as expedient.

What then? Marla tried simple substitution, a mark for a letter in Ruthrin. That got her nowhere. She hadn't thought it would, but she would start with the simplest and progress to more complex codes. It had been drilled into her head to do it that way.

She remembered several tests in the School of Cryptology where Master Asfrid gave the students a sheet of writing, challenging them to crack the code. Most of them went straight for the most complex system they had learned to that point, but not Marla. She found that the ciphers were almost insultingly easy, substitutions or offset systems that could be deciphered in her head. The other students were not happy when she turned her work in within minutes and they spent hours and hours until finally getting to the simpler methods.

But, no, this was not a simple code. It would use a key. Or maybe more than one key. It might also be a completely new language, one that had been made specifically for whoever was corresponding with Ren. If that was the case, it would be more difficult. If the writing represented words or sounds in some other language, the variations would increase in number exponentially.

She threw down the paper she held, glaring at it. It was something of a disappointment when it simply fluttered to the floor.

Honestly, she considered attacking it with fire magic.

"Paper cut?" Evon said, his throat rough from his snoring.

She tossed a water skin to him and he nodded to her, drinking a couple swallows of the water within.

"No," she said. "I'm just frustrated."

"You look like you wanted to kill that poor sheaf." He rubbed his eyes and blinked. "How long did I sleep?"

"Almost four hours. How do you feel?"

He glanced over at Inna, still unconscious, and frowned. "Like I was beat up, which is good, because that's exactly what happened."

"Yeah, kind of. Those air-assisted missiles are tough, though. You did a great job. And by that, I mean you survived."

"I did. I miss anything?"

Marla shook her head. "Nope, just me sitting here trying to break the code on these letters. I found them in Ren's robes."

"Oh. Do you want to get some sleep?"

"How about we go and find a room with a door before anyone else sleeps. I'd feel much better if there was a barrier to slow down anyone trying to finish the job these"—she swept her hand out toward the corpses on the floor before them—"started."

Evon agreed. They woke Inna, more roughly than was strictly necessary, and trudged up the stairs to the ground floor of the estate. They found a room down one of the halls and locked themselves in.

❧ 42 ☙

"**S**hould we search the rest of the building to see if anyone else is here?" Evon asked after collapsing from the chore of climbing the stairs and finding the room.

"Not yet. A little rest and some food and water and we'll be in better shape. Are you good for an hour or two so I can get some sleep?"

"Yeah." He looked over at Inna, still bound and gagged. His top lip raised on one side and he clenched his fist. "Rest. I'll keep an eye on things. If someone tries to come through the door, I'll wake you. I probably won't need to, though, with the noise it'll make."

Sleeping in shifts, they spent almost an entire day in their hideaway. When they were finally ready to move, Marla searched most of the building and didn't find anyone—or anything—else. Either the ones they encountered were the only enemies who used the place, or the others had already gone.

Evon had used his healing spells to finished mending his shoulder and then turned them on Marla to help her heal. They left any injuries Inna suffered alone, not wanting to waste the energy on her. She'd be fine, though not comfortable.

Four horses were roaming around in a fenced off area, one of them Skril's and, to Marla's relief, another of them Sure-foot. Marla's mount seemed in good condition, though she felt a little guilty that Evon's horse was nowhere to be found. Their saddles and tack were in the stable. The three rode the horses to where Marla and Evon left their own horses and then headed north, back toward the Academy.

They made good time going back, traveling on the River Road with their six horses. Though Marla would have preferred to stay the night in inns, trying to explain Inna, all bound up like she was, would have been difficult, so they camped instead. Either she or Evon went into a town or city for supplies every two days. With the money they took from Quentin's and Tildus's purses, they had plenty of funds.

Inna Moroz was quiet and didn't give them any problems until the last day of travel, at which time it seemed to occur to her what kind of trouble she was in. She grunted and gestured for them to take her gag off so she could speak, but neither of them had any sympathy for her. Evon had healed her of the chafing and her original injuries out of his own kindness, but that's where it ended. He wouldn't forget this woman tried to kill him or that she was in league to betray all of Dizhelim.

Finally, they arrived at the Academy. The first thing Marla did was to go to the headmaster—towing Inna behind her—to give him a report of everything that happened. After that, she set about finding her brother and her new friends.

They weren't hard to find, especially since Master Qydus told her exactly where they would be. They had only arrived the day before, and although they had availed themselves of the services of the Medica, they were apparently still tired from their ordeal.

After going first to Aeden—hugging him seemed to her like coming home after being gone for a long time—she arranged for dinner to be brought to a large meeting room where they could all catch up on things.

"...and then, after Ren Kenata fled through the portal and I destroyed the transmission device, we fought with Quentin and Inna and beat them. I tried to get Quentin to give himself up, but he left me no choice but to kill him. We didn't bother asking Inna."

"You killed her, too?" Fahtin asked, hand over her mouth.

Evon laughed. "No. Marla punched her in the jaw so hard it knocked her out. We tied her hands and gagged her and brought her back with us. Marla turned her over to the masters for judgment."

"I also found some letters in Ren's robes. Only one was in Ruthrin. The others were in some kind of code. I plan on cracking it within the next few days." She told them what the instructions from Quentin said.

"Then it's bigger even than Benzal and Quentin," Aeden said. "That's not good news."

"No," Marla said. "I'm afraid it's not. I expect once I figure out what the others say, we'll be even less happy." She took a drink of ale. "So, that's our story. What about you all? Did anything exciting happen on your way back here? Any trouble?"

Fahtin bit her lower lip and threw a nervous look at Aeden. Everyone was studiously *not* looking at the Gypta girl. Well, except for Evon. He couldn't seem to look at her enough.

"I had some visions on the way back," Fahtin finally blurted out.

"Visions?" Marla asked.

"Yes. They weren't just dreams. I...I don't really know how, but I believe they're true. Magical."

Marla looked at Aeden, who met her stare, apparently without discomfort.

"We're going to see if the masters can tell us anything," he said. "We wanted to hear what you have to say about them first."

"Okay. That sounds like a good idea. Fahtin, can you tell us about them?"

"Of course. They started with a view of Dizhelim, from up high. Very high. I could see the curve of the world, and as I looked, light flared in different areas. Not just in Promistala, but also in the other continents and islands of the world.

"Next, I viewed a darkened room where I couldn't see the walls. In the middle was a long, oval table. Seated around it were dark figures, cloaked and hooded, though I somehow felt they were human. A buzz surrounded them, as if they were talking but none of it made sense to me. There were thirteen of them.

"In the blink of an eye, I was in the heavens again, looking down on the continent of Promistala. A spot of darkness dripped onto the easternmost part of the continent and then spread as if it was ink. It grew, steadily but slowly, moving out from the original point and staining the land as it passed.

"Then I was suddenly in a large clearing in a wooded area. I don't know where, but I got the sense that it was a great forest. In the middle of the open space was a Gypta wagon. It lay on its side, one wheel spinning in a wind I could not feel. There were no people and nothing else but the grasses it lay on and the trees around it. The only sound was the raucous caw of a raven.

"Last, I was before an old man, sitting on a stone and overlooking the ocean. His appearance was that of someone ancient, but despite his appearance, he wasn't frail. He glowed with magical power and I was afraid he would turn his abilities against me. Then he smiled at me underneath his white beard and long hair, and I knew he wouldn't hurt me.

"But even as I smiled back at him, he began to rot. Before my eyes, his skin turned dark green, the disease spreading from his right hand, up his arm, and then to the rest of his body. He didn't react to it in any way, simply kept looking at me as the rot ate at his body. Soon, he was too weak to sit up straight and he began to slump. Thankfully, the vision stopped before I could witness his death.

"Those were my visions," Fahtin finished. "I don't know what they mean, if anything."

Marla looked to Evon. "What do you think?"

"I think her powers are trying to emerge," Evon said.

Fahtin's head snapped toward him. "What? Powers? I don't have any powers."

Evon's eyes softened from the wonder they held a moment before to sympathy. "I think you do, Fahtin. I've seen it before, and I believe your visions are simply disorganized attempts of your power trying to manifest. The Gypta have magic in their blood, more than most ethnic groups. With all the crazy things going on magically lately, it shouldn't be a surprise that you display some abilities."

Fahtin looked back and forth from Evon to Aeden. "But, I can't...I don't...I mean, what do I do?"

"I'll help you," Evon said. "First we'll record what you've seen, then we'll go from there. I can show you some exercises to try to connect more fully with your magic. I know it's scary, but it'll be fine."

"Listen to him," Marla said. "He's probably the best person at the Academy for this. The masters will help, too, but Evon will be a great resource."

"Okay." Fahtin slumped in her seat.

Marla patted the woman's arm consolingly. "Well, while all that is going on, I think I'm going to get started on trying to figure out these letters. It's obvious from the one we can read that there is more to this whole thing than Quentin and Izhrod. We're in the thick of it now. There are still animaru out there, as well as humans trying to help them destroy our world, and probably more enemies even on top of that.

"If ever there was a time for the Malatirsay, this is it. It's what the world has been holding its breath over for three thousand years. We can't let Dizhelim down."

EPILOGUE

Ren Kenata stood before the table instead of being seated in his normal place. He didn't like this position nearly as well as the other.

"What is the nature of this emergency? Were you discovered?" their leader asked. Her voice was firm, an edge of irritation in it.

"It's not exactly that," he said, "but I have news the Council needs to hear. There have been...complications."

"Tell us."

"The Council knows from my reports about the activities of Quentin Duzen and his associates. Animaru have been entering Dizhelim and the plan had been going along as well as can be expected.

"There were some issues with a few from the Academy getting too close to discovering what was happening. Quentin killed one adept and thought he had eliminated another, a very important other. The one that forced their hand and made it necessary to kill the Master of Prophecy when he was about to legitimize her as the Malatirsay."

"You speak of Marla Shrike," the leader said.

"Yes. She found us at the estate Quentin had been using to hide temporarily. She cut through the few animaru officers we had with us. I put shields around her and her companion, but she broke through them and began to attack the other three there."

"And you defeated her?"

"No. That is, while she was occupied, I fled through the portal we had set up. I thought it more important that the news be brought to you than for me to stay and battle. She is very strong."

The silence stretched far longer than Ren was comfortable with. He opened his mouth, but another Council member spoke first.

"That is an acceptable choice. Quentin and his associates had just about outgrown their usefulness. Is it possible that this Marla Shrike traced the location to which you traveled and then tracked you here?"

"No," Ren said. "She destroyed the transmission device as I went through the portal. She doesn't have the skills to trace where the other end was. Very few do. I was also careful to use several magical items and laid down multiple false trails in case somehow she managed to find someone who could."

"That is good," the leader said. "I see no reason why this emergency meeting is necessary, then."

Ren swallowed hard. This was the crux of the problem. "As I went through the portal, Marla tried to pull me back through. The only way for me to escape was to slip out of my robes. I left them at the estate, in her hands. There were... bits of correspondence in the pockets of the robes."

The leader leaned forward, a shadow ready to strike. "What kinds of correspondence?"

"A handful of responses from this Council to the reports I had sent, and one of instructions from Quentin to me, telling me to meet them at the estate."

"We have spoken to you about retaining items such as these, Ren Kenata. Your inclination to keep things when they should be destroyed has caused problems for you in the past."

"Yes."

"Correspondence from the Council would have been coded. She will not be able to read them."

"Probably," Ren said, "but not absolutely. She has mastered the School of Cryptology. She may be able to decipher them."

"And if she does? Is the information within of such magnitude that we need to eliminate the woman?"

"I believe the letters are vague enough so as not to give them all the information they need, nor would they allow her to identify the Council members, but they would serve to inform her that the Council does exist. Killing her has proved problematic. Trying to do so might well give them more information than the letters would provide."

"Very well. Is there any other bad news you wish to tell us?"

"No. That is all."

The leader paused, allowing time for any of the other Council members to speak. None did.

"We are not pleased with your actions, Ren Kenata. See that you do not make more mistakes. For now, we will do as we have always done. We will continue with our plans from the shadows. There is a world to win here, and we cannot afford to squander the opportunities presented. You will itemize the information contained in the letters you so foolishly gave into the hands of our enemies so we can prepare to counter any actions the Academy takes.

"Until you are called to meet once again, we are adjourned. Continue with your individual activities."

Ren Kenata ducked his head toward the leader, his mind already going through what the papers in his robe pockets had contained. It would take a while for him to shake the disapproved status he now held, but he was thankful he had not been punished. He'd complete his task quickly and then continue work on his own plans.

Things were moving quickly, the end coming. He needed to be ready when it did. He needed to make sure he was one of the few who would survive it.

PLEASE TAKE JUST A MOMENT TO LEAVE A REVIEW FOR the book. It will not only help me to see what you thought and to improve the next story, but it will help tremendously in indicating to other readers how you feel about the book. As an indie author, there are few things better than word of mouth to spread the news to other readers. Thank you in advance. For your convenience, **here's the link** directly to Amazon's review box (for the electronic copy of this book).

HERO DAWNING GLOSSARY

Following is a list of unfamiliar terms. Included are brief descriptions of the words as well as pronunciation. For the most part, pronunciation is depicted using common words or sounds in English, not IPA phonetic characters. Please note that the diphthong *ai* has the sound like the English word *Aye.* The *zh* sound, very common in the language Alaqotim, is listed as being equivalent to *sh,* but in reality, it is spoken with more of a buzz, such as *szh.* Other pronunciations should be intuitive.

Abyssum (*a·BIS·um*) – the world of the dead, Percipius's realm.

Acolyte – a current Hero Academy student who has mastered at least one school, but not three or more.

Adept – a Hero Academy student who has mastered at least three schools and continues to study at the Academy.

Aeden Tannoch (AY·*den TAN·ahkh*) – a man born to and trained by a highland clan, raised by the Gypta, and able to utilize the magic of the ancient Song of Prophecy.

Aeid Hesson (*AY·id*) – former Master of the School of

prophecy at the Hero Academy. He was murdered in his office at the Academy.

Aesculus (*AY·skyoo·lus*) – the god of water and the seas.

Agypten (*a·GIP·ten*) – an ancient nation, no longer in existence.

Ahred Chimlain (*AH·red CHIM·lane*) – noted scholar of the first century of the third age

Aila Ven (*AI·la ven*) – a woman of small stature who joins the party and lends her skills in stealth and combat to their cause.

Ailgid (*ILE·jid*) – one of the five highland clans of the Cridheargla, the clan Greimich Tannoch's wife came from.

Ailuin Lufina (*EYE·loo·in loo·FEEN·ah*) – one of the adepts at the Hero Academy who volunteered to aid in the investigation of Master Aeid's murder.

Alain (*a·LAYN*) – the god of language. The ancient language of magic, Alaqotim, is named after him.

Alaqotim (*ah·la·KOTE·eem*) – the ancient language of magic. It is not spoken currently by any but those who practice magic.

Alaric Permaris (*AL·are·ic per·MAHR·iss*) – the thug who hired the guys who attacked Marla in Dartford.

Aletris Meslar (*ah·LET·ris MES·lar*) – the personal clerk and assistant to Headmaster Qydus Okvius, of the Hero Academy.

Aliten (*AL·it·ten*) – a type of animaru that is humanoid but has wings and can fly.

Alvaspirtu (*al·vah·SPEER·too*) – a large river that runs from the Heaven's Teeth mountains to the Kanton Sea. The Gwenore River splits from it and travels al the way down to the Aesculun Ocean.

Animaru (*ah·nee·MAR·oo*) – dark creatures from the world Aruzhelim. The name means "dark creatures" or "dark animals."

Arania (*ah·RAH·nee·ah*) – a kingdom in the western part of the continent of Promistala, south and east of Shinyan.

Arcus (*ARK·us*) – the god of blacksmithing and devices.

Arcusheim (*AHR·coo·shime*) – a large city on the southern shore of the Kanton Sea, the capital of the nation of Sutania and the home of Erent Caahs before he left to travel the world.

Arto Deniselo (*AHR·toe day·NEE·say·low*) – a dueling master in the Aranian city of Vis Bena who taught Erent Caahs how to drastically improve his combat abilities.

Aruna (pl. Arunai) (*ah·ROON·ah; ah·roo·NIE*) – a citizen of the tribal nation of Campastra. Originally, the name was pejorative, referring to the color of their skin, but they embraced it and it became the legitimate name for the people in Campastra.

Asfrid Finndottir (ASS·*frid fin·DOT·teer*) – the Master of the School of Cryptology at the Hero Academy.

Aruzhelim (*ah·ROO·shel·eem*) – the world from which the animaru come. The name means "dark world," "dark universe," or "dark dimension." Aruzhelim is a planet physically removed from Dizhelim.

Atwyn Iaphor (*AT·win EE·ah·fore*) – a student at the Hero Academy, a companion of Quentin Duzen when he was still on campus.

Assector Pruma (*ah·SEC tor PROO·mah*) – roughly "first student" in Alaqotim. This is the student aid to a master in one of the schools at the Hero Academy. There can be only one per school and this person conducts research, helps to teach classes, and assists the master in any other necessary task.

Aubron Benevise (*AW·brun ben·uh·VEES*) – the Master of History and Literature at the Hero Academy.

Auxein (*awk·ZAY·in*) – an aide to the master and the First Student (Assector Pruma) at the Hero Academy. For larger schools, there may be more than one. In some schools there may not be any.

Awresea (*aw·reh·SAY·uh*) – a kingdom that no longer exists, the home of Tazi Ermenko who taunted the god Fyorio and was destroyed. The fiery, desolate location where the kingdom was is now known as Fyrefall.

Ayize Fudu (*aye·EEZ FOO·doo*) – a Hero Academy adept, one of Quentin Duzen's associates.

Barda Sirusel (*BAR·duh seer·oo·SELL*) – the boy who tried to bully Marla when she was a child.

Bhagant (*bog·AHNT*) – the shortened form of the name for the Song of Prophecy, in the language Dantogyptain.

Bhavisyaganant (*bah·VIS·ya·gahn·ahnt*) – The full name for the Song of Prophecy in Dantogyptain. It means "the song of foretelling of the end," loosely translated.

Biuri (*bee·OOR·ee*) – small, quick animaru that recall the appearance and movements of rodents. They are useful as spies because of their small size and quickness.

Boltshadow – one of the Falxen sent to kill Khrazhti and her companions. A former student at Sitor-Kanda, he is skilled at wielding lightning magic.

Brace – the term used by the Falxen for a group of assassins ("blades").

Braitharlan (*brah·EE·thar·lan*) – the buddy assigned in the clan training to become a warrior. It means "blade brother" in Chorain.

Brausprech (*BROW·sprekh*) – a small town on the northwest edge of the Grundenwald forest, in the nation of Rhaltzheim. It is the hometown of Urun Chinowa.

Brenain Kanda (*bren·AY·in KAHN·duh*) – a mythological heroine who stole magic from the god Migae.

Bridgeguard – the small community, barely more than a guardpost, on the mainland end of the northern bridge to Munsahtiz

Broken Reach – a rugged, unforgiving land to the southeast of the Grundenwald. There are ruins of old fortifications there.

Calarel Kelhorn (*CAL·ar·el KEL·horn*) – one of the adepts at the Hero Academy who volunteered to aid in the investigation of Master Aeid's murder.

Campastra (cam·PAHS·trah) – a tribal nation in the southwestern portion of the continent of Promistala

Catriona (Ailgid) Tannoch (CAT·ree·own·ah ILE·jid) – the wife of Greimich Tannoch. She is originally from the Ailgid clan, but now has taken the last name Tannoch.

Ceti *(SET·ee)* – a higher level animaru, appearing aquatic with small tentacles, even though there is no water in Aruzhelim. They are very intelligent and have magical aptitude. Some of them are accomplished with weapons as well.

Chorain (*KHAW·rin*) – the ancestral language of the highland clans of the Cridheargla.

Clavian Knights (*CLAY·vee·en*) – the fighting force of the Grand Enclave, the finest heavy cavalry in Dizhelim.

Codaghan (*COD·ah·ghan*) – the god of war.

Colechna *(co·LECK·nah)* – one of the higher levels of animaru. They appear to be at least part snake, typically highly intelligent as well as skilled with weapons. They are usually in the upper ranks of the command structure. Their agility and flexibility makes them dangerous enemies in combat. A few can use magic, but most are strictly melee fighters.

Cridheargla (*cree·ARG·la*) – the lands of the highland clans. The word is a contraction of Crionna Crodhearg Fiacla in Chorain.

Crionna Crodhearg Fiacla (*cree·OWN·na CROW·arg FEE·cla*)) – the land of the highland clans. It means "old blood-red teeth" in Chorain, referring to the hills and mountains that abound in the area and the warlike nature of its people. The term is typically shortened to Cridheargla.

Croagh Aet Brech (*CROWGH ET BREKH*) – the name of the highland clans in Chorain. It means, roughly, "blood warriors." The clans sometimes refer to themselves simply as Croagh, from which their nickname "crows" sprang, foreigners not pronouncing their language correctly.

Dannel Powfrey – a self-proclaimed scholar from the Hero Academy who meets Aeden on his journey.

Danta (*DAHN·ta*) – the goddess of music and song. The language Dantogyptain is named after her.

Dantogyptain (*DAHN·toe·gip·TAY·in*) – the ancestral language of the Gypta people.

Daodh Gnath (*DOWGH GHRAY*) – the Croagh Ritual of Death, the cutting off of someone from the clans. The name means simply "death ceremony."

Daphne – one of the tavern maids at the Wolfen's Rest inn in Dartford.

Dared Moran (*DAR·ed·mo·RAN*) – the "Mayor" of Praesturi. Essentially, he's a crime boss who controls the town.

Darkcaller – one of the Falxen sent to kill Khrazhti and her companions. A former student at Sitor-Kanda, her specialty is dark magic.

Dark Council – a mysterious group of thirteen people who are trying to manipulate events in Dizhelim.

Dartford – a small town on the mainland near the north bridge to the island of Munsahtiz.

Darun Achaya (*dah·ROON ah·CHAI·ah*) – father of Fahtin, head of the family of Gypta that adopts Aeden.

Denore Felas (*den·OR FEHL·ahss*) – a great mage in the Age of Magic, the best friend of Tsosin Ruus.

Desid (*DAY·sid*) – a type of animaru. They're nearly mindless, only able to follow simple commands, but they are fairly strong and tireless. They are about five feet tall with thick, clawed fingers useful for digging. They have the mentality of a young child.

Dizhelim (*DEESH·ay·leem*) – the world in which the story happens. The name means "center universe" in the ancient magical language Alaqotim.

Dmirgan – a town in Kruzekstan, where a young Erent Caahs killed a man he thought was a murderer

Dreigan (*DRAY·gun*) – a mythical beast, a reptile that resembles a monstrous snake with four legs attached to its sides like a lizard. The slightly smaller cousin to the mythical dragons.

Drugancairn (*DROO·gan·cayrn*) – a small town on the southwest edge of the Grundenwald Forest.

Ebenrau (*EBB·en·ra·oo*) – the capital city of Rhaltzheim, one of the seven great cities in Dizhelim

Edge – one of the Falxen sent to kill Khrazhti and her companions. A former assassin and bodyguard in Teroshi, he is skilled in the use of the Teroshi long sword and short sword.

Encalo (pl. encali) (*en·CAW·lo*) – four-armed, squat, powerful humanoids. There are few in Dizhelim, mostly in the western portion of the continent Promistala.

Erent Caahs (*AIR·ent CAWS*) – the most famous of the contemporary heroes. He disappeared twenty years before the story takes place, and is suspected to be dead, though his body was never found.

Erfinchen (*air·FEEN·chen*) – animaru that are shapeshifters. Though not intelligent and powerful enough to be leaders among the animaru, they are often at higher levels, though not in command of others. They typically perform special missions and are truly the closest thing to assassins the animaru have. A very few can use some magic.

Erlan Brymis (*ER·lan BRAI·miss*) – one of the adepts at the Hero Academy who volunteered to aid in the investigation of Master Aeid's murder.

Esiyae Yellynn (*ess·SEE·yay YELL·in*) – the Master of the School of Air Magic at the Hero Academy.

Espirion (*es·PEER·ee·on*) – the god of plans and schemes. From his name comes the terms espionage and spy.

Evon Desconse – a graduate of the famed Hero Academy and best friend to Marla Shrike

Fahtin Achaya (*FAH·teen ah·CHAI·ah*) – a young Gypta girl in the family that adopted Aeden. She and Aeden grew as close as brother and sister in the four years he spent with the family.

Falxen (*FAL·ksen*) – an assassin organization, twelve of whom go after Aeden and his friends. The members are commonly referred to as "Blades."

Featherblade – one of the Falxen sent to kill Khrazhti and her companions. He is the leader of the brace and his skill with a sword is supreme.

Fireshard – one of the Falxen sent to kill Khrazhti and her companions. She wields fire magic.

Forgren (*FORE·gren*) – a type of animaru that is tireless and single-minded. They are able to memorize long messages and repeat them exactly, so they make good messengers. They have no common sense and almost no problem-solving skills

Formivestu (*form·ee·VES·too*) – the insect creatures that attacked Tere's group when they were on their way to Sitor-Kanda. They look like giant ants with human faces and were thought to be extinct.

Fyorio (*fee·YORE·ee·oh*) – the god of fire and light, from whose name comes the word *fyre*, spelled *fire* in modern times.

Fyrefall – a desolate and dangerous land in the south central part of Promistala, full of hot pools, geysers, and other signs of volcanic activity.

Gentason (*jen·TAY·sun*) – an ancient nation, enemy of Salamus. It no longer exists.

Gneisprumay (*gNAYS·proo·may*) – first (or most important) enemy. The name for the Malatirsay in the animaru dialect of Alaqotim.

Godan Chul (*GO·dahn CHOOL*) – an ancient mythological race of spirit beings, created accidentally from the magic of the God of Magic, Migae. The name means, roughly "spirit's whisper."

Goren Adnan – the Master of the School of Military Strategy at the Hero Academy.

Graduate (at the Hero Academy) – a student of the Hero Academy who is either an adept or a viro/vira. That is, anyone who has mastered at least three schools at the Academy and is either still studying there or has left the school.

Great Enclave – a nation to the west of the Kanton Sea and the Hero Academy.

Greimich Tannoch (*GREY·mikh TAN·ahkh*) – Aeden's close friend, his braitharlan, during his training with the clans.

Grundenwald Forest (*GROON·den·vahld*) – the enormous forest in the northeastern part of the main continent of Promistala. It is said to be the home of magic and beasts beyond belief.

Gulra (pl. gulrae) (*GUL·rah; GUL·ray*) – an animaru that walks on four legs and resembles a large, twisted dog. These are used for tracking, using their keen sense of smell like a hound.

Gwenore River – a large river that splits off from the Alvaspirtu and travels south, through Satta Sarak and all the way to the Aesculun Ocean

Gypta (*GIP·tah*) – the traveling people, a nomadic group that lives in wagons, homes on wheels, and move about, never settling down into towns or villages.

Hamrath – a small town on the coast of the eastern part of the Kanton Sea, just north of the bridge from the mainland to Munsahtiz Island.

Heaven's Teeth – the range of mountains to the east of the Kanton sea, in between that body of water and the Grundenwald Forest.

Ianthra (*ee·ANTH·rah*) – the Goddess of Love and Beauty.

Ianthra's Breasts (*ee·ANTH·rah*) – a mountain range between Arcusheim in Sutania and Satta Sarak. Even though there are three peaks, the two that dominate were named for the physical attributes of the Goddess of Love and Beauty, Ianthra.

Inna Moroz (*EEN·ah MOE·roze*) – a Hero Academy adept, one of Quentin Duzen's associates.

Iowyn Selen (*EE·o·win SELL·en*) – a great mage in the Age of Magic, the love of Tsosin Ruus's life.

Iryna Vorona (*ee·REEN·ah voe·rone·ah*) – Master of the School of Interrogation and Coercion at the Hero Academy.

Iscopsuru (*ee·SCOP·soo·roo*) – the name of Benzal's fortress outside of Nanris in Kruzekstan; it's over eight hundred years old. The name means Rock of Surus in Alaqotim.

Isegrith Palas (*ISS·eh·grith PAL·us*) – the Master of Fundamental Magic at the Hero Academy.

Izhrod Benzal (*EESH·rod ben·ZAHL*) – a powerful magic-user, one who has learned to make portals between Aruzhelim and Dizhelim. The dark god S'ru has an agreement with him so he is second to none in authority over the animaru on Dizhelim.

Jehira Sinde (*jay·HEER·ah SINDH*) – Raki's grandmother (nani) and soothsayer for the family of Gypta that adopts Aeden.

Jhanda Dalavi (*JON·dah dah·LAHV·ee*) – the Head

Scrivener at the Hero Academy. He is in charge of the small army of scribes who make copies of books and who create many of the records necessary for the functioning of the school.

Jia Toun (*JEE·ah TOON*) – an expert thief and assassin who was formerly the Falxen named Shadeglide. She uses her real name now that she has joined Aeden's group of friends and allies.

Jintu Devexo (*JEEN·too day·VEX·oh*) – the high chieftain of the Arunai during the time of the false Malatirsay.

Josef – the owner of the Wolfen's Rest inn in Dartford, a friend of Marla Shrike.

Jusha Terlix (*JOO·shah TER·liks*) – the Master of the School of Mental Magic at the Hero Academy.

Kanton Sea (*KAN·tahn*) – an inland sea in which the island of Munsahtiz, home of the Hero Academy, sits.

Kebahn Faitar (Kebahn the Wise) (*kay·BAWN FYE·tahr*) – the advisor and friend to Thomasinus; the one who actually came up with the idea to gather all the scattered people and make a stand at the site of what is now the Great Enclave.

Keenseeker – one of the Falxen sent to kill Khrazhti and her companions. He is a huge, strong warrior who wields a massive battle axe.

Khrazhti (*KHRASH·tee*) – the former High Priestess to the dark god S'ru and former leader of the animaru forces on Dizhelim. At the discovery that her god was untrue, she has become an ally and friend to Aeden.

Kruzekstan (*KROO·zek·stahn*) – a small nation due south of the highland clan lands of Cridheargla.

Leafburrow – a village in Rhaltzheim, north of Arcusheim off the River Road, the location of a bandit ambush where Erent Caahs demonstrated his special spinning arrow technique.

Lela Ganeva (*LEE·lah·gahn·AY·vah*) – the woman Erent Caahs fell in love with.

Lesnum (*LESS·num*) – large, hairy, beastlike animaru. These sometimes walk around on two feet, but more commonly use all four limbs. They are strong and fast and intelligent enough to be used as sergeants, commanding groups of seren and other low-level animaru.

Leul Abrete (*LOOL ah·BREET*) – a traveling merchant for whom Skril Tossin searches to get information in the murder investigation of Master Aeid.

Lilianor (Lili) Caahs (*LI·lee·ah·nore CAWS*) – Erent Cahhs's little sister; she was murdered when she was eleven years old.

Liluth Olaxidor (*LIL·uth oh·LAX·ih·door*) – the Master of the School of Firearms at the Hero Academy.

Lily Fisher – an archer of supreme skill who was formerly the Falxen assassin named Phoenixarrow. She uses her real name now that she has joined Aeden's group of friends and allies.

Lis (*LEES*) – a minor deity who battled the sun, nearly killing it, and causing so much damage that to this day, it is weakened in the wintertime.

Lucas Steward – a young student at the Hero Academy. He's often used by the masters as a messenger because of his strong work ethic and reliability.

Lusnauqua (*loos·NOW·kwah*) – the rugged land surrounding Broken Reach, in the center of the eastern section of the continent of Promistala.

Malatirsay (*Mahl·ah·TEER·say*) – the hero who will defeat the animaru and save Dizhelim from the darkness, according to prophecy. The name means "chosen warrior" or "special warrior" in Alaqotim.

Manandantan (*mahn·ahn·DAHN·tahn*) – the festival to celebrate the goddess Danta, goddess of song.

Marla Shrike – a graduate of the famed Hero Academy, an experienced combatant in both martial and magical disciplines.

Marn Tiscomb – the new Master of Prophecy at the Hero Academy. He replaced Master Aeid, who was murdered.

Mellafond (*MEH·la·fond*) – a large swamp on the mainland to the east of Munsahtiz Island. The name *means pit of Mellaine.*

Mellaine (*meh·LAYN*) – goddess of nature and growing things.

Miera Tannoch (*MEERA TAN·ahkh*) – Aeden's mother, wife of Sartan.

Migae (*MEE·jay*) – the God of magic. The word "magic" comes from his name.

Moroshi Katai (*mor·ROE·shee kah·TAI*) – a mythological hero who battled the Dragon of Eternity to found the nation of Teroshi.

Moschephis (*mose·CHE·feess*) – the trickster god, from whose name comes the word mischief.

Mudertis (*moo·DARE·teez*) – the god of thievery and assassination.

Munsahtiz (*moon·SAW·teez*) – the island in the Kanton sea on which the Hero Academy Sitor-Kanda resides.

Nanris – the unofficial capital of Kruzekstan, more important than the actual capital of Kruzeks because most of the wealth of the nation is centered in Nanris.

Nasir Kelqen (*nah·SEER KEL·ken*) – the Master of the School of Research and Investigation at the Hero Academy.

Osulin (*AWE·soo·lin*) – goddess of nature. She is the daughter of Mellaine and the human hero Trikus Phen.

Pach (*PAHKH*) – in Dantogyptain, it means five. As a proper noun, it refers to the festival of Manandantan that occurs every fifth year, a special celebration in which the Song of Prophecy is sung in full.

Pedras Shrike – Marla Shrike's adoptive father, the groundskeeper for the administrative area of the Hero Academy.

Percipius (*pare·CHIP·ee·us*) – god of the dead and of the underworld.

Phoenixarrow – one of the Falxen sent to kill Khrazhti and her companions. A statuesque red-haired archer who had a penchant for using fire arrows.

Pilae (*PEEL·lay*) – a type of animaru that looks like a ball of shadow.

Pofel Dessin (*POE·fell DESS·in*) – a traveling scholar who meets Marla and Evon on their journeys.

Pouran (*PORE·an*) – roundish, heavy humanoids with piggish faces and tusks like a boar

Praesturi (*prayz·TURE·ee*) – the town and former military outpost on the southeastern tip of the island of Munsahtiz. The south bridge from the mainland to the island ends within Praesturi.

Preshim (*PRAY·sheem*) – title of the leader of a family of Gypta

Promistala (*prome·ees·TAHL·ah*) – the main continent in Dizhelim. In Alaqotim, the name means "first (or most important) land."

Qozhel (*KOE·shell*) – the energy that pervades the universe and that is usable as magic.

Quentin Duzen – a Hero Academy graduate, the antagonist against Marla and Evon.

Qydus Okvius (*KIE·duss OCK·vee·us*) – the headmaster of the Hero Academy, Sitor-Kanda.

Raibrech (*RAI·brekh*) – the clan magic of the highland clans. In Chorain, it means "bloodfire."

Raisor Tannoch (*RAI·sore TAN·ahkh*) – a famous warrior of Clan Tannoch, companion of the hero Erent Caahs.

Raki Sinde (*ROCK·ee SINDH*) – grandson of Jehira Sinde, friend and training partner of Aeden.

Ren Kenata (*REN ke·NAH·tah*) – a Hero Academy adept who was is not only one of Quentin Duzen's associates, but also a member of the Dark Council.

Rhaltzheim (*RALTZ·haim*) – the nation to the northeast of the Grundenwald Forest. The people of the land are called Rhaltzen or sometimes Rhaltza. The term Rhaltzheim is often used to refer to the rugged land within the national borders (e.g., "traverse the Rhaltzheim")

Ritma Achaya (*REET·mah ah·CHAI·ah*) – Fahtin's mother, wife of the Gypta family leader Darun.

Ruthrin (*ROOTH·rin*) – the common tongue of Dizhelim, the language virtually everyone in the world speaks in addition to their own national languages.

S'ru (*SROO*) – the dark god of the animaru, supreme power in Aruzhelim.

Saelihn Valdove (*SAY·lin VAHL·doe·vay*) – the Master of the School of Life Magic at the Hero Academy.

Salamus (*sah·lah·MOOS*) – an ancient nation in which the legendary hero Trikus Phen resided. It no longer exists. Things of Salamus were called Salaman.

Sartan Tannoch (*SAR·tan TAN·ahkh*) – Aeden's father, clan chief of the Tannoch clan of Craogh.

Satta Sarak (*SAH·tah SARE·ack*) – a city in the southeastern part of the continent of Promistala, part of the Saraki Principality.

Semhominus (*sem·HOM·in·us*) – one of the highest level of animaru. They are humanoid, larger than a typical human, and use weapons. Many of them can also use magic. Most animaru lords are of this type.

Senna Shrike – Marla Shrike's adoptive mother.

Seren (*SARE·en*) – the most common type of animaru,

with sharp teeth and claws. They are similar in shape and size to humans.

Shadeglide – one of the Falxen sent to kill Khrazhti and her companions. She is small of stature but extremely skilled as a thief and assassin.

Shadowed Pinnacles – the long mountain range essentially splitting the western part of Promistala into two parts. It was formerly known as the Wall of Salamus because it separated that kingdom from Gentason.

Shaku (*SHOCK·oo*) – a class of Teroshimi assassins.

Shanaera Eilren (*shah·NARE·ah ALE·ren*) – the Master of Unarmed Combat at the Hero Academy.

Shinyan (*SHEEN·yahn*) – a nation on the northern tip of the western part of Promistala, bordering the Kanton Sea and the Cattilan Sea. Things of Shinyan (such as people) are referred to as Shinyin.

Shu root/Shu's Bite (*SHOO*) – a root that only grows in Shinyan, the key ingredient to the poison Shu's Bite.

Sike (*SEEK·ay*) – a class of Shinyin assassins

Sintrovis (*seen·TROE·vees*) – an area of high magical power on which the Great Enclave was built. In Alaqotim, it means *center of strength*.

Sirak Isayu (*SEER·ack ee·SAI·yoo*) – a member of the Dark Council. He comes from the southern part of the continent of Promistala, near the Sittingham Desert.

Sitor-Kanda (*SEE·tor KAN·dah*) – the Hero Academy, the institution created by the great prophet Tsosin Ruus to train the Malatirsay. The name means roughly "home of magic" in Alaqotim.

Sittingham Desert – a large desert in the southwestern part of Promistala.

Skril Tossin – best friend of Marla Shrike and Evon Desconce, a Hero Academy adept.

Snowmane – the horse the Academy lent to Aeden, a chestnut stallion with a white mane

Solon (*SEW·lahn*) – one of the masters in Clan Tannoch, responsible for training young warriors how to use the clan magic, the Raibrech.

Srantorna (*sran·TORN·ah*) – the abode of the gods, a place where humans cannot go.

Surefoot – Marla Shrike's horse.

Surus (*SOO·roos*) – king of the gods.

Sutania (*soo·TAN·ee·ah*) – the nation south of the Kanton Sea, the capital of which is the city of Arcusheim.

Taron Gennelis (*TARE·un jeh·NELL·iss*) – one of the adepts at the Hero Academy who volunteered to aid in the investigation of Master Aeid's murder.

Tarshuk (*TAR·shuk*) – a semi-desert-like area to the southwest of the Heaven's Teeth range that has stunted trees and scrub.

Tazi Ermengo (*TAH·zee air·MANE·go*) – the king of the doomed kingdom of Awresea. He taunted the god Fyorio and was destroyed along with his entire kingdom, which was renamed Fyrefall.

Tere Chizzit (*TEER CHIZ·it*) – a blind archer and tracker with the ability to see despite having no working eyes. He is Aeden's companion in the story.

Teroshi (*tare·OH·shee*) – an island nation in the northern part of Dizhelim. Things of Teroshi, including people, are referred to as Teroshimi.

Thomasinus, son of Daven (*toe·mah·SINE·us*) – the hero who banded the remnants of the troops of Gentason together to create the Great Enclave. Once they elected him king, he changed his last name to Davenson.

Tildus Uworn (*TIL·duss YOO·worn*) – a Hero Academy adept, one of Quentin Duzen's associates.

Toan Broos (*TOE·aan*) – traveling companion of Erent Caahs and Raisor Tannoch

Trikus Phen (*TRY·kus FEN*) – a legendary hero who battled Codaghan, the god of war, himself, and sired Osulin by the goddess Mellaine.

Tsosin Ruus (*TSO·sin ROOS*) – the Prophet, the seer and archmage who penned the Song of Prophecy and founded Sitor-Kanda, the Hero Academy.

Tuach (*TOO·akh*) – one of the masters in Clan Tannoch, responsible for teaching the young warriors the art of physical combat.

Tufa Shao (*TOO·fah SHA·oh*) – the Master of the School of Body Mechanics and Movement at the Hero Academy.

Ulfaris Triban (*ool·FARE·iss TRY·ban*) – a Hero Academy graduate, companion to Izhrod Benzal

Urtumbrus (*oor·TOOM·brus*) – a type of animaru that are essentially living shadows.

Urun Chinowa (*OO·run CHIN·oh·wah*) – the High Priest of the goddess Osulin, a nature priest.

Vaeril Faequin (*VARE·ill FAY·kwin*) – the Master of the School of Mechanista Artifice at the Hero Academy.

Vanda (*VAHN·dah*) – a modern god, claimed by his followers to be the only true god. It is said he is many gods in one, having different manifestations. The Church of Vanda is very large and very powerful in Dizhelim.

Vatheca (*VATH·ay·kuh*) – the headquarters and training center of the Falxen. It is a mixture of two Alaqotim words, both meaning "sheath."

Vincus (pl. vinci) (*VEEN·cuss; VEEN·chee*) – Aila's chain blade weapons.

Viro/Vira (pl viri) (*VEER·oh / VEER·ah / VEER·ee*) – a former Hero Academy student who has graduated with a mastery in at least three schools and no longer lives at the Academy or participates in its function

Voordim (*VOOR·deem*) – the pantheon of gods in Dizhelim. It does not include the modern god Vanda.

Wolfen – large intelligent wolves that roam desolate areas in the Rhaltzheim.

Wolfen's Rest – the inn in Dartford, on the mainlaind not too far east from the bridge to the island of Munsahtiz.

Yxna Hagenai (*IX·nah HAG·en·eye*) – the Master of Edged Weapons at the Hero Academy.

LETTER TO THE READER

Dear Reader,

Thank you for reading the first book in the Hero Academy series. As you probably know, this isn't really the start of the story, nor is it the end, of course. The Song of Prophecy series is the logical place to start reading the story of the Malatirsay and of the adventures in Dizhelim. If you read this book first, you may have noticed that it references events that may leave you wanting more information.

I would suggest that if you liked this book, you go back and read the Song of Prophecy trilogy for a well-rounded understanding of how everything started. Then, by all means, continue on with the Hero Academy series. It'll still be here.

If you did enjoy the story, join my PEP Talk newsletter and you'll get some free books, one of which is the origin story of the hero Erent Caahs. It's a side story in the world of Dizhelim and it tells of how the hero came to be one of the most popular figures in the story world. The newsletter basically consists of information on book launches, things that might be of interest to fantasy readers, and the occasional recommendation for a book or series I've read. To join, you can go to my website at https://pepadilla.com.

Aside from those series, you might also enjoy some of my other series. You can check them out in the "Also By" section in the back of this book.

P.E. Padilla

AUTHOR NOTES

I've already written in author's notes for some of the other books in the Song of Prophecy series how Wanderer's Song was originally part of a multi-author boxed set, then how it became a trilogy, and finally how the story morphed into this Hero Academy series. What I haven't written about was how my plans changed in other ways for the story and what they currently are.

The Hero Academy series will be long. Very long. There are far too many things that happen on the way to the final event for them to be glossed over and covered in just a few books.

I have it all generally planned out, though, of course, the details are not all complete. The worldbuilding for the two series (Song of Prophecy and Hero Academy) is intense and expansive and I'm still learning about the world as I create more of the specific stories. So, though I have the general plan, each book is a discovery process as the details emerge.

I'm not sure exactly when I'll finish the series, but I am writing the books quickly. During July 2020 and January 2021, I'll be launching one book a month. Two of them are the remaining Song of Prophecy series books (already out as I write this), three of them are the first three books of the Hero Academy series (of which this book is the first), and two of them are companion novels set in the same world. Incidentally, those companion novels are freebies for my newsletter subscribers.

After this mad launch schedule, I plan on releasing books in this series fairly often (though probably not one per month), so there will be none of this waiting for several years for the next book (you know what I'm talking about).

For anyone familiar with the SoP series, this one is slightly different as to how it's written or set up. The stories consist of individuals or small groups of the familiar heroes and villains (and some new ones), and there are a lot of flashback type scenes. It makes me think of the old TV series Kung Fu where flashbacks were an integral part of the narrative. I hope that readers will enjoy this mechanism; I always have in reading and watching entertainment.

I'm pleased with the start of this series and am excited to explore Dizhelim and continue writing about the Hero Academy and all the fascinating characters populating the world. I can't wait to see all the specifics of how the world is saved...or not.

ABOUT THE AUTHOR

A chemical engineer by degree and at various times an air quality engineer, a process control engineer, and a regulatory specialist by vocation, USA Today bestselling author P.E. Padilla learned long ago that crunching numbers and designing solutions was not enough to satisfy his creative urges. Weaned on classic science fiction and fantasy stories from authors as diverse as Heinlein, Tolkien, and Jordan, and affected by his love of role playing games such as Dungeons and Dragons (analog) and Final Fantasy (digital), he sometimes has trouble distinguishing reality from fantasy. While not ideal for a person who needs to function in modern society, it's the perfect state of mind for a writer. He is a recent transplant from Southern California to Northern Washington, where he lives surrounded by trees.

pepadilla.com/
pep@pepadilla.com

Hero's Nature

Tales of Dizhelim (companion stories to the SoP and HA Series):

Arrow's Flight

Song's Prophet

Order of the Fire Series:

Call of Fire

Hero of Fire

Legacy of Fire

Order of the Fire Boxed Set

Made in the USA
Middletown, DE
09 August 2021

45721507R00227